Chris Bridges is an alumnus of the 2022 London Writers Award and was shortlisted for the 2025 McDermid Debut Award.

He previously wrote a weekly column for an LGBTQ+ lifestyle website and was a theatre reviewer for various sites.

As a former NHS nurse with a hidden disability, he likes to feature the untold stories of sick, dying, and disabled people in his work and smash the trope of the passive disabled character with a background role.

Chris lives in Hastings. He is fanatical about crime fiction. When not writing, he can be found reading compulsively or walking his uptight poodle, Frida Kahlo.

Also by Chris Bridges:

Sick to Death

Praise for *The Death Bed*

'Vivid, harrowing, and utterly compelling,
this is a bedside vigil I will never forget.'
Lesley Kara, *Sunday Times* bestselling author of *The Rumour*

'Filled with a sense of dread from first page to last,
this is a great read that builds to a chilling conclusion.'
Nikki Smith, author of *The Beach Party*

'Sinister and packed with twists, *The Death Bed* is impossible to put down. Chris Bridges delivers a masterclass in chilling suspense.'
D. S. Butler, author of *Bring Them Home*

'Darkly atmospheric and gripping . . .
a reading experience I won't soon forget!'
**Ashley Tate, international bestselling author of
*Twenty-Seven Minutes***

'No one can be trusted, and the twists keep coming.
I couldn't put it down.'
Jo Leevers, author of *Tell Me How This Ends*

'*The Death Bed* kept me intrigued and hooked until the shocking end.'
Marie Tierney, author of *Deadly Animals*

'As slick as it is sick, this compelling thriller drip-feeds
a sense of dread until the tension is unbearable.'
Jo Furniss, author of *Guilt Trip*

'Intriguing, atmospheric and unpredictably twisty'
**Catherine Kirwan, *Irish Times* bestselling author of
*The Seventh Body***

'Sick, twisted and impossible to put down!'
Naomi Williams, author of *The Woman in Ward 9*

'Dark, twisty and dripping with dread'
Carole Hailey, author of *The Silence Project*

'Fresh and distinctive storytelling'
Kingsley Pearson, author of *Flat 401*

'Simmers with tension and mystery'
Kathryn Sharman, author of *The Family at No 23*

'Intoxicating and riveting'
Bonnie Burke-Patel, author of *I Died at Fallow Hall*

'A brilliantly astute thriller'
Philippa East, author of *Little White Lies*

'An immersive page-turner'
Kate Kemp, author of *The Grapevine*

'The kind of book you lose sleep to keep reading'
Rebecca Hannigan, author of *Darkrooms*

'One of the most gripping novels I've read this year'
Sam Frances, author of *All Eyes on You*

'A novel injected with so much menace, you'll be left reeling'
Katie Huttlestone, author of *A Healthy Appetite*

'Compulsive, addictive and gripping'
Louise Swanson, author of *End of Story*

'A dark, tension-fuelled thriller that will have you
reading well into the night'
Ruth Irons, author of *The Perfect Guest*

'Another taut, chilling and propulsive thriller by Chris Bridges.
The Death Bed was jam-packed with plot twists and
a killer ending. Loved it!'
Natali Simmonds, author of *Good Girls Die Last*

'A taut, quiet and unnervingly atmospheric thriller that
will have you gripped'
Sean Watkin, author of *Black Water Rising*

Praise for *Sick to Death*

'A hugely gripping and enjoyable debut... Clever and witty.'
Abigail Dean, *Sunday Times* bestselling author of *Girl A*

'A gripping debut from a unique new voice in psychological thrillers.
Bridges writes with a stinging authenticity and tinder-dry humour.'
Erin Kelly, *Sunday Times* bestselling author of *The Skeleton Key*

'A slick and exciting debut that had me devouring each page...
A twist to rival *Gone Girl* left me gasping.'
Katy Brent, author of *How to Kill Men and Get Away With It*

'With the kinds of twists and turns that make you gasp,
and a protagonist to die for (excuse the pun!)
Sick to Death is hard to put down.'
**Jennie Godfrey, *Sunday Times* bestselling author of
*The List of Suspicious Things***

'A dazzling debut, skilfully crafted and full of surprises.
Beautifully written, utterly original and shockingly dark.'
Lesley Kara, *Sunday Times* bestselling author of *The Rumour*

'Thrilling, moving and thought-provoking, with a brilliant
central character. A skilful suspense novel.'
**B.P. Walter, *Sunday Times* bestselling author of
*The Dinner Guest***

'*Sick to Death* is an urgent and compelling thriller
from a much-needed new voice in crime fiction.'
Anna Bailey, *Sunday Times* bestselling author of *Tall Bones*

'More layers than a multi-storey car park, and
more twists than a roller coaster.'
**Carole Hailey, author of Kindle Number One bestseller
*The Silence Project***

'A stunning debut. . . the definition
of a propulsive and unforgettable psychological thriller.'
**Ashley Tate, international bestselling author of
*Twenty-Seven Minutes***

'It smoulders, until the very, very end. A tale of love, of betrayal,
of dead ends, of twists, of turns, of hope, of despair, assembled
in a way that is totally addictive.'
G. D. Wright, author of *After the Storm*

'Such a brilliant debut. So sharply written, with a frenetic pace
and nothing you expect. Clever and twisty with such a kick. . .
so refreshing.'
Louise Swanson, author of *End of Story*

'A unique and compelling debut that is impossible to put down. . .
slick and riveting.'
Ruth Irons, author of *The Perfect Guest*

'*Sick to Death* is a sizzling saucepot of a domestic thriller. A plot that begins with soft bubbles of tension, suddenly erupts into a glorious volcano of original twists and unexpected turns. I flew through it!'
Mira V Shah, author of *Her*

'Twisty, dark, and full of heart. A gripping psychological debut that had me completely hooked with no idea what to expect next. I didn't want it to end!'
Natali Simmonds, author of *Good Girls Die Last*

'*Sick to Death* is a taut slice of neo-noir that cleverly upturns tropes about disability, class and feminism!'
Rebecca DeWinter, author of *Best Friends*

'Crime fiction at its most intimate and honest as well as brutal in its execution of its final twist.'
Marie Tierney, author of *Deadly Animals*

'A twisty, sneaky little crime thriller. . . I found myself absolutely swept up into the life and mind of its disabled, furious and devious protagonist.'
Laura Elliott, author of *Guilty*

'I tore through this fresh and inventive debut that delivers a cracking plot, strong characters and a distinctive, witty voice.'
Jo Leevers, author of *Tell Me How This Ends*

'A super intense reading experience, much like reading a Daphne du Maurier and watching a Hitchcock film. . . at the same time. Like a thumbscrew, the tension never lets up until the inevitable yet surprising ending.'
Tania Tay, author of *The Other Woman*

'A powerful, original and compelling psychological thriller, propelled by dark wit and flashes of justified anger. The twists will keep you guessing. . . A superb debut.'
Antonia Hodgson, author of *The Silver Collar*

'A highly original, compelling thriller with three flawed, complex female leads. It had me turning pages into the early hours.'
Eleni Kyriacou, author of *The Unspeakable Acts of Zina Pavlou*

CHRIS BRIDGES

THE DEATH BED

avon.

Published by AVON
A division of HarperCollins*Publishers* Ltd
1 London Bridge Street
London SE1 9GF

www.harpercollins.co.uk

HarperCollins*Publishers*
Macken House, 39/40 Mayor Street Upper
Dublin 1, D01 C9W8, Ireland

A Paperback Original 2026
1

First published in Great Britain by HarperCollins*Publishers* 2026

Copyright © Chris Bridges 2026

Chris Bridges asserts the moral right to be identified as the author of this work.

A catalogue record for this book is available from the British Library.

ISBN: 978-0-00-869817-1

This novel is entirely a work of fiction. The names, characters and incidents portrayed in it are the work of the author's imagination. Any resemblance to actual persons, living or dead, events or localities is entirely coincidental.

Set in Sabon LT Std by HarperCollins*Publishers* India

Printed and bound in the UK using 100% Renewable Electricity at CPI Group (UK) Ltd

All rights reserved. No part of this publication may be reproduced, stored in a retrieval system, or transmitted, in any form or by any means, electronic, mechanical, photocopying, recording or otherwise, without the prior written permission of the publishers.

Without limiting the exclusive rights of any author, contributor or the publisher of this publication, any unauthorised use of this publication to train generative artificial intelligence (AI) technologies is expressly prohibited. HarperCollins also exercise their rights under Article 4(3) of the Digital Single Market Directive 2019/790 and expressly reserve this publication from the text and data mining exception.

*To all the nurses who I worked with during my career.
Thank you for not being like the people in this book.*

Content Warning:

The Death Bed, although fictional, tackles some events and issues that some may find distressing.

'People lose their health in a dark house, and if they get ill, they cannot get well again in it.'

Florence Nightingale

Prologue

THEN

It's not the first time that I've watched someone die. Death is a subject that I know too much about. Even if I were to stop being a nurse tomorrow the dying process would stay imprinted on my mind. Part of the roll call of disquieting things that I can't unlearn.

It plays out like it usually does. The breathing is slower and uneven, skin becoming sweaty and clammy, increasingly pallid. I wait, listening to each rattle and gasp, gauging the labour of changing respirations.

This death is different, of course. This isn't my usual routine. It's like nothing I've ever seen. The terrain is all wrong, to start with. The creaking of an old house instead of the moans and screams of a hospital and a cloying smell of potpourri instead of disinfectant. Soft light from the fringed lamp by the sofa rather than overhead strip lighting blanching my skin to a sickly hue.

Unlike in the hospital, I have no official role at this scene. No uniform to wear, no lists of urgent tasks or rules to obey. I don't do any of the things I'd normally do at this point.

There won't be any gentle moistening of dry mouths with damp sponges, no comforting of the soon to be bereaved. Not even any soothing physical contact from me.

Instead, I wait for the consequences of my actions to take effect.

This death is entirely different because I've caused it.

Part One

Chapter One

NOW

Sunday, 11 April 2010

The doors clamp shut as the hospital seals itself behind me. I walk towards the car park on aching feet, past the beds of hopeful plants that are choked with litter and cigarette ends, destined to die and rot under the lamppost that's been flickering for months.

Mrs North's husband is striding to his Ford Fiesta with more vigour than you'd expect from an octogenarian.

'Sister Laura. Can I just say again how much I appreciate everything that you do. I honestly can't express how much you've helped my Marian.'

'It's fine, Mr North. That's why I'm here. You drive safely, now.' I turn away and start stepping towards my car to signal the end of the conversation.

'You people are so good. You know that? You're angels.'

I smile weakly as I walk away.

His assessment is flawed. There's this mythology around nurses. A beatification. The lingering belief that we're somehow saintly. A few of my colleagues even think that about themselves, coasting around in clouds of self-satisfaction. But who is ever wholly virtuous? I might help people for a living but I'm a person with mundane human failings. The usual mix of impatience, irritation and resentment that we all have. A woman who happens to be well suited to doing this particular job.

If Mr North knew even a fragment of my past, then he'd recoil from me like I was an infected wound.

My legs move on autopilot, weak columns of flesh that feel close to useless after a Sunday afternoon and evening charging up and down a hospital ward. My hand is unlocking my car when I see her. She's running across the empty car park, her statuesque figure intermittently picked out as she passes through pools of lamplight, moving towards me. My fingers fumble with the handle. I clamber in, locking the door behind me, gasping for breath, my shaking hands missing the ignition as I try to ram in the key.

'Laura! Wait!' She's still running, impeded by heels, her unseasonal cotton dress fanning out around her legs. Her red hair piled up on her head, exactly as it always was, hennaed locks held in place by a complex arrangement of grips and slides. A couple of strands have come free and are attacking her face. She's close enough now for me to see that she's still painting on her signature cat-eye make-up. As she reaches the car we lock eyes. She stretches over and slaps her palms against the passenger window.

'I need to talk to you.' Her voice is unchanged. The high-pitched breathiness scrapes at me.

My ageing car rattles a warning as I pull away. When I dare to look in the mirror she's still standing there with her arms by her side, a vintage vanity case dropped down onto the tarmac.

My fingers reach for the radio, any noise to blast away my racing thoughts. A Nineties club classic is playing, one of Amy's favourites. The car swerves slightly as I stab at the button to turn it off, making the driver behind beep his horn.

The traffic thins as I approach the village. Hedgerows reach into the road, skimming the sides of my battered Metro, a pheasant skitters across in front of the car, wild eyed in the headlights. I start to breathe more normally, thoughts ricocheting around my skull.

Sadie Browne shouldn't be here. It's been over sixteen years since I saw her and there's only one reason that she'd come. Someone knows.

It's only when I get home and open the door of the empty cottage, that my thoughts start to form some kind of order.

After it all happened I was consumed by questions and puzzles. My brain filled with images of bloodstains, syringes and lifeless bodies. Faces contorted by hatred. That was when it looked like I was slipping downwards again. When missing Sadie was visceral, like a physical illness. Once I emerged from the fugue and mixed with society again I began to see her before me with alarming regularity. It was like when someone dies and you still spot them in the crowd. I'd see Sadies everywhere. Walking down the streets of Nottingham, striding across the fields with a backpack on, sitting at Peak District cafés. Only these Sadies would turn around and they were ordinary red-headed women, never as vivid or singular. Never my Sadie.

No prospect of answers or reconciliation.

I take off my coat and stand still, letting my thoughts

run wild. I learned early on that trauma can't be wilfully suppressed. The psychiatrists and well-meaning mental health nurses didn't tell me this. It's not like I could ever talk to them about what really happened. I learned this through experience. If I try to ignore the memories then they bounce back at me like a beachball in a swimming pool, resurfacing harder and faster. I have to allow them to inhabit me and exist. They're always with me. The only time I never think about what happened in London is when I'm working. The catharsis of nursing strips away all other thoughts. Something's wrong here, though. I see it now. The Sadie who approached me tonight looked exactly the same as when I last saw her in 1993. No middle-aged weight gain, no wrinkles, no greying hair. Which is impossible. She can't have been real. The corrosive thoughts that intrude my mind have finally become manifest. I'm losing it again, like I always knew that I would one day.

My hands are shaking as I spoon hot chocolate into a mug. The book I'm reading is on the kitchen table. Words sometimes calm my whizzing brain if I'm able to force myself to concentrate. My reading glasses aren't here. In my state of distraction, I've left them behind in the car. I step outside, key in hand. There's a handprint on the window where Sadie slapped her palms.

This is real.

It's starting again.

Chapter Two

NOW

Monday, 12 April 2010

The hospital is more welcoming in daylight. The corridors are littered with people, who nod and smile at me as I walk to the ward with gritty eyes and leaden limbs. A testament to a sleepless night where I failed to placate the cold fingers of worry crawling in my chest and stomach, finally giving in and letting anxiety have free rein. Walking round and round the cottage until morning came.

When something terrible happens to your mind it can leave a stain. It may not always be prominent but it's there, lurking. Echoing back at you like a child's shout into the mouth of a cave. In the beginning, after the first bad thing, I thought that recovery was impossible. As the fog lifted, I hoped for a total remission. That never came. I'm left with persistent memories. The doctors call it PTSD but that's too simplistic a label for the mess inside me. I think of it as scarring.

I initiated my emergency plans last night. I did what I've

done for many years and wrote things down to try to cling onto some stability. Scrawling in my journals to order my thoughts, then locking the notebooks away in a trunk, a leftover tuck box from boarding school. Part of the regime along with the pills and therapy that keeps me functioning.

The heat of the hospital starts to seep into me, along with the smells. Not the sweet tang of disinfectant that people associate with these places but the smell of unwashed people, of pus and excrement. Smells that seep into the plaster and bricks over decades.

No one greets me as I make my way to my office. The ward is ominously quiet apart from the perpetual ringing of call bells. As I round the corner I notice Briony, a newish staff nurse, waiting outside my office door. She's talking into her phone and doesn't notice me.

'I'll ask her but I'm not optimistic. You know what Sister Laura's like.' She pauses while whoever she's talking to answers. I'm frozen in a mix of embarrassment and indignation, unsure whether to front it out or to withdraw. 'I hear you. I mean, I know she's always good with the patients but she's such a—'

I step back and then walk round the corner again but this time with heel-clicking steps.

'Can I help?'

She mutters to whoever's on the phone, terminating the call and brushing her hand through her hair, which is cascading onto her collar. I'll need to remind her, yet again, to pin it up.

'I wondered if I could swap some shifts. I've got a thing I want to go to.'

I don't bother to hide my sigh.

'I can look at the rota. But it's doubtful.' She asked last

week and that time it was 'childcare'. I'm pretty sure that she doesn't even have children but I may be wrong. I try not to involve myself in the staff's personal lives.

Once I've refused most of her long list of requests she walks out of my office without looking at me. I hear a muttered aside of 'stuck-up bitch' as she walks out.

The half-filled folder on my desk with my interview preparation for the matron job reproaches me. The interview is still weeks away but I need to do more background reading. According to the departing matron it's a near certainty that I'll get this, but I don't want to go in and make myself look foolish in front of the senior nurses. The junior staff may think I'm distant and strict but at least I'm respected here. For the first time in my life I've achieved something solid and not messed it up.

I push the notes aside and walk out onto the ward, ready for this strange drama that I'm never the star of. Occasionally I'm featured: the salient nurse saving lives, the empathetic figure doling out advice and kindness in equal measures with a half-smile. Mostly I'm peripheral to the calamities of others. Not a bit part but more of a supporting role. Life as a secondary character, which is exactly how I like it.

The shift is neither pleasant nor unpleasant. New faces but with the typical ombre of pain and suffering written across them. I scurry around haunted by shouts of my name, yells of 'nurse' and the peal of the telephones, the shriek of the call bells. The usual things happen. Someone dies and I console the relatives. Someone else contorts in agony and we cajole the doctor into increasing her medications. A man screams and rants, rendered into a mad thing by infection and fever. We try and fail to placate him. Things are as good as I can make them.

Drugs are administered. Beds are changed and changed again. Complex arrangements for discharges home are bartered over. The growing list of tasks builds in my clogged brain, pushing away the thoughts of London and of Sadie that have plagued me all night. The day draws to a close too quickly, my jobs list still epic in proportion.

'There's a girl here to see you. She says it's urgent.'

I put the empty chemotherapy syringe into the sharps bin and smile at the red-eyed woman in the chair before I reply to Charlotte, a slow-moving nurse who rations her empathy.

'Well done, Karen. That's dose three done. Halfway there.' I squeeze her hand, shift my weary muscles back up, a task that gets harder as the day goes on now that I'm in my late thirties. I turn to Charlotte.

'A girl? What does she want?'

'She wouldn't say. I plonked her in the day room.'

The wingback chairs are arranged in a semicircle on the worn vinyl floor, standing around the elderly television like a group of medical students huddled around a consultant. There's a faint smell of illicitly smoked cigarettes. A teenager emerges from one of the chairs and turns to face me. Shocks of adrenaline course through my limbs along with the familiar urge to run.

She's almost the image of Sadie. The same vintage clothes and impractical shoes. The same fuller figure and impressive height. She has Sadie's alabaster skin and red hair but her nose is wrong. Her eyeliner is smudged and her skin looks blotchy with lilac rings framing each eye. The battered vanity case sits near her feet.

'You're Laura Jameson.' I wait for her to say something else. It's as if my voice box and limbs have mutinied against me and I'm stuck here, mute. 'I haven't met you before but I'm Elsie. Elsie Browne. Your best friend Sadie's daughter.'

I nod. Stalling for time, thoughts whirring, my mouth dry and barren.

'You drove away last night.' She looks hurt. Her face is childlike, ready to cry.

'I . . . I didn't see you.' My legs feel like they could buckle at any moment. I grip the back of a chair and force a disingenuous smile.

'But you did see me. I saw you look at me.' She frowns and then steps alarmingly close to me, her eyes running over my face. 'I feel like I know you. All the old pictures that Sadie has. All the stories she tells.'

She steps even closer and I let go of the chair, taking a half step backwards, fearful that she might be coming round to embrace me. 'I don't understand why you're here. Your mother and I aren't in touch anymore.'

'We need your help. Mum needs a nurse and there's no one else.'

The absurdity of the idea that it's me Sadie would want help from makes me want to laugh. It must play across my face because this child looks squarely at me. 'It's not funny. She's dying. My mother's actually dying of cancer and we've got no one to look after her. That's what you do, isn't it? I looked you up online and came here to fetch you. I thought that what with everything that happened . . . that you might help.'

She puffs up with pride at her problem-solving skills. She must have struck lucky to find me. I keep my online presence to a minimum, although there was a grainy photo of me in the nursing press when I spoke at a conference last year.

The word cancer is an unbearable taunt. Half a story that whips up a whirl of curiosity in me, leaving me desperate to ask what type, what staging, what the treatment plan is. I resist. I'm going to have to tell this girl that I can't help. I'm not the right person. The last person who can help.

There's no way I'm going back to London.

To that house.

Chapter Three

NOW

Monday, 12 April 2010

'You're not hearing me. It's impossible.' My voice sounds flat in my ears.

Practically it's not impossible. I'm about to start two weeks of annual leave and my mum and Suzie are away, staying in a borrowed caravan on the Lincolnshire coast. But on every other level it's not an option. 'There must be some professional help you can get. There are people who—'

'And you're still not listening to me. It's only for a few days. Just till my father comes back from Denmark. She needs someone. She's a mess.'

'As I was saying, there are professionals who can help with Sadie. Besides, I don't know if she'd want me there. I haven't seen her for so long.'

'She's too ill to arrange anything. She's got *cancer*. And they've been crap, anyway. The hospital don't see her anymore because she's not having chemo now. It didn't work.' She gets up and walks to the window, looking out at the now empty car park, speaking her words into the glass. 'We've got a specialist nurse but he only comes every few weeks. Mum's getting worse and there's no one else to ask. So I came here.'

'It's a . . . resourceful idea but I'm sorry, Elsie. I can't get away.' I'm managing to keep my voice firm and not show the shakiness that I feel. Thoughts of Sadie are waiting to haemorrhage in.

Her shoulders fall as if unseen hands have pushed them down and her face reddens. She's about to cry. I look down and that's when I notice her shoes. The heel of one of them is broken and there is blood marking the leather where the skin of her feet has rubbed away. Her dress looks like it's been screwed into a ball and put back on, grease stains peppering the front of the bodice.

'Elsie, just sit for a minute and I'll get you a drink. Then we can talk more. I'm sure we can sort something out. I can signpost you to who you need to talk to.' My knotted stomach clenches and a wave of nausea hits me. She's unbearable to look at. This younger version of my former friend.

She does as she's told and sits like a child much younger than the fifteen years she's just told me she is. I glance at my watch. My shift ended half an hour ago so this time is my own. My muscles are tensing again, preparing for me to flee. The kitchen is a welcome escape from that room. I lean back against the chipped paint on the wall and close my eyes for a second, trying to calm my breaths, before willing my unreliable hands to function and make coffee.

She devours a thin pre-packed sandwich while the drink cools. I try not to stare at her but my eyes pull back like she's an accident that I can't look away from.

'Elsie, where are you staying? You're a long way from home.'

'I'm not. I mean, I'm not staying anywhere. I came on the train yesterday. I'd already rung the ward and checked if you were working and they told me that you finished at nine. I thought you'd help me but you drove off.'

'So where did you go?'

She's quiet for a minute, using the coffee as a stalling tactic. 'I got the bus to Derby and I tried to stay in a bed and breakfast but the only ones with any rooms were dodgy looking. So I just walked down by the river and through the streets. Then I hung around on a bench near the bus station but there were some weird men hanging about, so I walked some more.'

'All night? You need to go back home. Have you got a return ticket?'

She slams the coffee cup down on the table. I see Gail, one of the night nurses, peering in through the day room door as she glides by. I'm an object of curiosity to them. Unmarried in my late thirties and unwilling to divulge my past. They'll be loving this. I can imagine the theories that Elsie is my long-lost daughter or the child of a married lover.

'I'm not going back. It's too late now. I'll go tomorrow.'

'And where will you stay tonight?' I feel an urge to put my head in my hands and block all this out.

'With you, Laura. I'm staying with you.' She stands up and faces me, like a defiant toddler. 'You're the person who Sadie keeps talking about. She needs you.'

'What do you mean she keeps talking about me? What's she been saying?' My words are staccato.

'Just old stuff. She's been telling me about when you lived together.' She gives me a look that could be knowing or could just be the defiance of a teenager being denied what she wants. 'She's told me *everything*.'

I fetch my bag and coat and we walk into the night air towards my car. I hope she didn't spot me shuddering.

* * *

Elsie looks with wide eyes around the lane, as I park my car outside my little cottage. When we walk inside, she takes off her shoes without being asked. I can see her trying hard not to stare at my things. The shelves of books and the cheap sofas from Argos that I've tried to elevate with bright Habitat cushions. The framed British film posters from the 1940s and 1950s that I collect. She perches on the edge of a chair.

'Are you hungry?' I excuse myself and walk through to the kitchen. 'I have some beef casserole I can heat up.'

'Is it vegetarian beef or just dead cow?' She smirks as she says this.

I end up raiding the fridge and making a pasta dish.

She balances the tray on her legs and I try not to panic each time she takes a huge forkful of food and gulps it down, tomato sauce splattering across the tray like arterial blood spurts.

Once she's finished she curls her feet up and slumps over to one side on the cushions. Her eyes start to droop. I clear the dishes and fetch a blanket, draping it over her. She must be exhausted after her night wandering the streets. I should go to bed but I can't help but linger, scrutinising her. Everything so familiar but also wrong.

I slide a lock of her copper hair away from her eyes and leave her to rest.

* * *

I barely slept again, watching the clock progress through the hours, my heartbeat pounding in my ears. I hear Elsie moving around downstairs at around six and I go down to the kitchen.

'I can't believe this place. How do people sleep in somewhere this quiet? Way too creepy.'

I make us both coffees. She takes it exactly like Sadie always did, black with three sugars. I have my lines prepared and when she comes down after taking a shower I take a deep breath and go in.

'Shall I drive you to the station when you're dressed? Your clothes should be dry shortly.' The tumble dryer is droning in the background. 'I've made a list of organisations you can contact and a priority list of which health professionals to call for help.'

I hold the piece of paper out to her and she shoves her hands behind her back, leaving it dangling between us.

'Only if you're coming with me.' She stares directly at me.

'Elsie.' I use my professional tone. Practical but empathetic. 'I know this is difficult but you need to go back home and be with her now. She needs someone there with her and she shouldn't be alone. I can pay for you to get back if that—'

'Don't judge me for leaving her. I know that she shouldn't be on her own. I'm not an idiot. I only came here to ask you to help.' She's raised her voice to a level just below a shout. She takes in a sharp breath, trying to quell her exasperation.

'It isn't practical. I haven't seen your mother since the Nineties. And I have a job and a life here. There must be someone else.'

'There isn't. Like I said last night. My father's away with work and he can't come back. It's just for a few days. Maybe a week. That's all.' She says this as if uprooting my life and travelling back to London for a week would be simple, even without the history of what happened there. 'And yours is the name that Sadie keeps saying.'

The use of Sadie's name rather than 'Mum' is jarring. But then everything here feels shrill and discordant. My body has become one giant scream waiting to emerge.

'Surely your father's work will allow him compassionate leave. And what about the palliative care nurses and the—'

'My father is not there.' She speaks through clenched teeth. 'Neither are the nurses when we need them. They're not there in the night when it's just me and Sadie and she's yelling in pain. They're not there when I'm having to deal with her trying to climb out of the bed because she's off her tits on morphine at two in the morning.'

'She needs to be in a hospice. Maybe that would be better for you all.'

A look of contempt crosses Elsie's face. 'She doesn't want a hospice, does she? She'd never leave that house. You must know that. You know how Sadie feels about Laurel House.'

'I don't know anything about Sadie. I haven't seen her since the end of our nurse training.'

'But she's told me so much about you.' Time stops for a second.

'Told you about what, exactly?' I speak slowly, fighting my urge to yell the words.

'Rambling stuff because of the drugs.' She looks directly into my eyes. 'But it's all very interesting.'

The thought of Sadie delirious on medications and unboundaried fills me with dread.

An image of the house floods my brain and I bat it away. I've spent over sixteen years trying to stop that house creeping into my mind. It usually comes when I'm least expecting it, invading idle moments, curdling mindless chores. Vivid images that arrest me into stillness.

I take another long, jagged breath and straighten my spine. 'I can't come. I'm sorry.'

I'd be lying if I said that the urge to run to Sadie's side and help isn't still there after all these years along with a panicked need to check what she's saying about me. But it's just too much. I'm not equal to this.

Elsie gets up and runs out of the room and the bathroom door slams. I can hear her crying, the sound of her shuddering sobs carrying down the staircase. I go and attend to the clothes in the tumble dryer, take my Sertraline pill with a cup of coffee. I'm just moving towards the staircase when I hear the sound of my phone ringing. I rush to grab it, in case it's Mum, before realising that it's not my ringtone. It's Elsie's phone and the name on the screen is 'Sadie'. I feel bloodless and weak. A wave of nausea hits me but I jab at the button and answer.

'Hello, Sadie. It's Laura. Laura Jameson.'

'I don't need an introduction, Laura. I know your voice. How are you?' She speaks as if this is an expected social call. That it was always going to be me answering her runaway teenage daughter's phone. Her voice still has that high, lyrical quality that it always had but it's quieter as if illness has dampened her.

'Elsie's safe. She came up here to Derbyshire and found me on some misguided mission. She thinks that you need me to look after you and that it would be a good idea for me to come down. Obviously that wouldn't be a good idea after what—'

That familiar breathy voice interrupts me. 'Oh but that would be wonderful. She's a clever girl. Very mature for her age.' She pauses and I hear the clink of a glass and it sounds like she's swallowing something. 'Being ill is such a strange thing. I'm spending so much time lying around. And my mind keeps wandering back to our past.'

There's a slight groan and another clunk that sounds like she's put the glass down.

'But we can talk about all that when you're here, darling.'

'I don't think that—'

'So, when are you coming?'

I could never say no to Sadie.

What choice do I have but to go back to South East London for the first time in over sixteen years. To leave this place of space and peace and go back to the sensory assault of London. The place I vowed I'd never return to. Back to who I once was.

The house where death stopped everything.

I walk upstairs to pack.

Chapter Four

THEN

January 1991

The tall woman from the nurses' home is staring at me as I dodge through the London traffic, making my way across the high street, back towards the nurses' accommodation. Her face remains expressionless as I'm almost knocked over by a harassed man on a bike who's weaving between the vehicles. This street is an overload of the unfamiliar. Exotic fruits rotting in cardboard boxes, a window display full of faded wigs, a newsagent with a raft of cards advertising coyly worded services that may or may not be allusions to prostitution. I've failed in my mission to find anything wholesome that I can eat for supper, settling on a packet of Hobnobs and a lurid bottle of Lucozade.

So far London is just the whirr of streets passing by bus windows and this shanty town of a hospital with its hostile surrounding streets. Nothing like the Ladybird picture book images from childhood. This part of South London is colourless. When I was ill the world lost all its shades and nuances. It has a name: anhedonia, the opposite of hedonism, when all joy is sucked from life. The contours of the landscape back home morphed from bucolic countryside into a bleak and desolate scene. Everything was tainted by sadness. The faces of children, old people walking through the village, even inanimate objects. Everything looked as desolate as I felt, as if I was viewing the world through a distorted camera filter.

This isn't that, though. I'm fine. My perspective is grounded. London is just drab on this January day and this area is greyscale. I reach the pavement, dodging an ageing punk with torn tights and deadened eyes. I'm about to shoot across to the nurses' home but the tall woman is waiting, leaning against a shop window. She looks like one of the well-built girls from school who'd have bullied me into playing a game of rounders when all I wanted to do was curl up in the dorm with a book. She gestures for me to walk in with her but I mime having to tie the laces on my trainers. I dip down among the cigarette ends, pretending to do it, indicating for her to go on without me. She rolls her eyes and walks on.

I lock myself in my room. The sound of cheerful goodbyes and banging doors is dying down as the last remaining parents leave. I'm already starting to feel caged in this boxy room with the crescents of chipped paint along the side of the bed. As if someone had spent years lying here, picking away with their fingernails in desperation. I've rearranged my pile of novels three times and hung my sparse collection of clothes in the wardrobe that sways when touched, like it's at sea. I've neglected to bring bed sheets. I'll have to lie directly on the stained mattress and there will no doubt be fresh horrors in the shared bathroom.

A form of quiet has descended now. Not the Derbyshire quiet that I know but a London quiet peppered with distant traffic and occasional shouts. My mum didn't accompany me. She couldn't have spared the money for the train fare and anyway, my sister, Suzie, is 'unwell' again and needs her more than I do. I took the train alone, lugging my bags across town on two buses, squinting at the tiny print of an *A-Z* that I bought at St Pancras station. The fug of cigarette smoke on the top deck of the bus stinging my eyes and permeating my clothes. The bed sags under me. I lie back and write in my journals. I'm never without my notebooks and writing things down grounds me and keeps the thoughts in order.

It's when I dare to venture to the shared kitchen that I'm accosted by the athletic woman from the street.

'Hello! I'm Louise.' Her eyes flick up and down, taking me in as I fold my arms over my T-shirt. 'I saw you just now.'

The latter statement drips with disdain and feels like an accusation. 'I'm . . . Laura. Nice to meet you.'

'Top tip, Laura. Don't use the fridge. Your milk will get nicked.' She wags a finger to emphasise the point. '*I've brought a mini fridge with me.*'

Before I can escape I'm ushered into her room along the corridor where I try my hardest to make appreciative noises as she shows me her matching red kettle, microwave and fridge from Argos. Louise informs me that she and her friends all have similar colour-coordinated electrical sets. I stay silent, unsure what she expects me to say. Her bed is neatly made with fresh polycotton, overlooked by a row of generic Athena posters in clip frames. There's a volley of bragging about what she possesses and what she's done. I listen, smile and nod. My anxiety that she'll single me out as different because of my accent proves unfounded. Louise only talks about herself. I don't get away in time before her two friends arrive. Shazia is squat and sullen while Jane is willowy, a nervous woman with wire rimmed glasses. Louise is effervescent at the thought of starting our training the next day and the other two listen and nod as she chatters away.

I don't tell them how much I'm dreading tomorrow.

How I think I've made possibly the rashest decision of my life. Not that Louise is asking many questions. I don't end up saying much about myself at all, other than that I'm Laura Jameson who was working in the village café and am glad to escape to the capital.

My hopes of finding friends here seem like they'll be fruitless.

* * *

Striking red hair catches my eye as I enter the classroom. It belongs to a woman who's positioned herself at the perimeter staking the corner of one of the tables in the grimy 1960s classroom next to the dust-scented electric heaters. She exudes poise and glamour, like one of the women in the old films that I love. She leans back and surveys the room like a cat, idly scanning the horizon, ready to pounce, occasionally glancing out of the window, as if already bored. The window shows two smoking chimneys and the blackened brick of the original Victorian section of the hospital. I try not to think what the smoke might be from. Whether they burn limbs and organs here.

The room feels unloved. Much like the rest of the hospital, the nursing college is a mongrel mix of styles and eras. I'd wrongly imagined that a London hospital would be a vision of gleaming Georgian refinement with honey-coloured bricks and elegant windows. This place looks hastily constructed and on the brink of condemnation.

I'm drawn towards the red-haired woman's table. The trio of women from the day before are giggling together as they select a space at the back of the classroom. I make the mistake of looking up and Louise catches my eye, pointing frantically to a free seat next to Jane. The threats of their offer to take me out clubbing and the endless cooing over photos of Louise's police officer fiancé yesterday come back to me like returning bile. I try to keep a neutral expression but I doubt I'm pulling it off. I have a face that tends to scream contempt, whatever my inner thoughts are.

I turn my back on them, spurning their offer of friendship. New friends might be what I need but it isn't what I want, at least not with them. And probably not with the other women here who blend into a homogenous mass as they chatter together. When I glance back round I can see by Louise's face that I've made a mistake. That this has been registered as a snub. She whispers to Shazia, holding her hand to her ear. I imagine that she made her suggestion that I sit with them as a charitable act, offering her bounty to someone as awkward and unfortunate as me. I've humiliated her. I sense battle lines being drawn. Our emergence from childhood may be complete but it looks like I'm still not done with the juvenile spite of others that I'm so used to.

I take my opportunity to sit next to the red-haired woman. She's looking at Louise and Shazia, bemused. She places her hand on the table, splaying her manicured fingers and smiles at me through painted lips. Her cat-eye make-up crinkles above her cheeks.

'First rule of college life: be careful who you talk to on day one. Otherwise you'll end up spending the next three years trying to shake them off.' She brushes back a strand of her startling red hair that has come loose from the artfully lacquered confection of curls held up by grips and barrettes. 'That was a deft manoeuvre, by the way. Well done.'

I smile back, glad of the vote of confidence from this older woman. She looks around thirty. Her age isn't the only thing that marks her out in the room of late teenage and early twenty-something students. There are a myriad of words and phrases that could be used to describe her. Rubenesque, curvy, voluptuous. All of those euphemisms uttered by slender young women who have posters of Marilyn Monroe bursting out of dresses in their teenage bedrooms but are living on SlimFast shakes and longing for Kate Moss's cheekbones.

'I'm Sadie, by the way. Welcome to whatever the hell this is going to turn out to become.'

Sadie's presence is further magnified by her clothing choices. Her curves are contained within a cream peasant blouse and a full skirt cinched at the waist with a deep belt. A contrasting handbag in green crocodile skin is propped against the table leg next to her ludicrously high-heeled shoes.

'They don't look happy with me.' I dare to look again and Louise is staring my way.

'They'll get over it.' Sadie smiles at me again, revealing a gap in the middle of the top row of her off-white teeth. Her voice is distinctive. Soft and an octave higher than you'd expect it to be. It'd be a difficult voice to imitate. Something that would take practice.

'So, will *we* be stuck with each other now?' I aim for a

fun little laugh to punctuate this but it sounds strident in my ears.

'Oh, I do hope so.' I can't tell if she's mocking me but I suspect not.

There's something about Sadie that makes me want to stare. It's not lust. Nothing as base as that. She snags my eye and fascinates me.

I want to know more. To explore the details of her life.

I self-consciously smooth out my Topshop shirt and Gap jeans that I saved up for to blend in. A burly fair-headed man and a curly-haired woman with glasses take the remaining two seats at our table. The tutor rushes in, a faint smell of cigarettes trailing after her. She starts to speak but pauses when the door opens again. A surly man with sharp cheekbones and a straight fringe of dark hair draped across his forehead walks in, not acknowledging her. He looks across the room like he's surveying his domain, no apology for his lateness, and slowly makes his way to the last empty seat near the back.

Sadie whispers to me. 'Let the games begin.'

A rush of panic flutters in my limbs.

Adrenaline coursing.

The urge to run and run, an urge I know so well.

Chapter Five

THEN

February 1991

I've spent the last few weeks trying to cope with being away from home and to relish the freedom of being someone new. I'm reborn and reinvented, no longer that stuck-up girl from the troubled family who 'the terrible thing' happened to. I thought that there'd be joy in leaving behind the village with the whispers and stares and that I'd revel in becoming nameless and unremarkable. But this is not how I thought it would be. My head was filled with images of the glamour of London. Me trotting in and out of Liberty or Fortnum & Mason's, watching plays and operas. I'd forgotten that the opulent London I've seen in old films is not one that I'm able to afford on my meagre student nurse's pay.

I hadn't counted on how adrift I now feel. How lonely London is, how threatening and enclosed. Every crowded street sends me into fight or flight mode and electric shocks course through my limbs. Every stranger's face seems to sneer at me. I feel like I'm living in a *Crimewatch UK* reconstruction. The permanent sleepless state due to the noise of the nurses' home makes me leaden and bewildered. I keep my eyes fixed to the pavement as I scurry to the dilapidated row of shops down from the equally dilapidated hospital.

The unsettled feelings that occupy my thoughts and the images that crowd my mind are waning a little, which gives me hope. I'm trying hard, diligently taking my pills and writing my thoughts down. Scrawls of ink across pages and pages of new books. My favourite psychiatrist's voice in my head, reminding me that sometimes distress and worry are just a feature of life as opposed to pathological signs of my PTSD being out of control.

The nurses' home isn't the haven from the hostile streets that I wish it was. It's a cauldron of sounds. The communal payphone rings at all hours with calls from concerned parents or boyfriends who have been left behind. The pad on the wall adjacent to it is a scrawl of crossed-out messages written with a biro on a string. Students work shifts and the doors perpetually bang. The soundtrack of my feverish dreams is raised voices, the clicking of heels and the sound of the nearby road. I haven't seen my neighbour but whoever they are they play trance music on a loop late into the night.

I'm doing my best to avoid Louise, Shazia and Jane. It's been made obvious that the slight from day one has been registered. Louise's eyes narrow to slits whenever I pass her in the corridor on my way to the dingy shared bathroom: a poky room where someone is always banging on the door, asking if you've finished yet. Shazia glares at me, like I'm sure she's been told to, while Jane sneaks me an apologetic half-smile.

* * *

I don't believe that every negative has a positive – how could I, given what happened to me – but there's been a bright spot in this place. Sadie. She's a force of nature. A luminous thing in a dull place. My eyes are still pulled to her every move, receptive to all of her words and phrases. We're sitting together for the eight weeks of lectures that we have to endure before we're ricocheted onto the wards.

Several people have tried to talk to me, including Nathan, the burly man with the fair hair who sat himself at our table on day one. He knows the Midlands, apparently, because his parents lived there briefly. The conversation fizzled out at that. I catch him casting sidelong looks towards me and Sadie when he thinks no one is looking, drawn in by Sadie's glamour, no doubt. His cheeks flush with blood if he catches my eye. He's solid and ruddy, like someone who's played rugby at a minor public school.

The problem with talking isn't the other students, but me. I don't know what to discuss. These young men and women regale each other with tales of foreign travel, CVs of their past care work. They laugh about the headiness of London that they're tasting. I have nothing but vagueness. A hole in my life from the year of darkness. Gaps in my cultural knowledge with the songs I missed, the programmes that went unseen, the fashions unworn during the time of blankness.

They try to engage me in conversation but I make them fail with my curt answers and lack of eye contact. They don't try again, remaining a sea of indistinct faces. Only two people here stand out for me. Sadie and the angular-featured boy with the dark fringe who walked in late on the first day. I sneak glimpses of him, entranced by his ennui and his languid posturing. He's like a Bright Young Thing from another era. He speaks to no one as if disaffected with this whole business, sprawling himself diagonally in the chair or sitting with his head resting on his hands like a feline waiting to pounce.

As the lecture ends Sadie taps her red enamelled fingers on the desk.

'So, Laura. How about lunch? Unless you have other plans.'

I've been scurrying back to my room every day, keen to avoid the chatter of the other students, spending my lunch break immersed in the familiarity of yellowed paperbacks.

'It's time we entered the beast and approached the fabled hospital canteen. If we're going to be nurses then we need to visit that place at some point soon. Do you fancy being my wing woman?' The final phrase seems appropriate for Sadie's outlandish outfit of the day. She's dressed in rolled-up navy overalls with a green scarf holding up her elaborate coiffure, like a World War Two munitions factory worker. 'I'd enjoy your company.'

I feel a swell of unfamiliar warmth at the thought that anyone would want me around.

The hospital entrance threatens to engulf us. The Victorian archway is empty of people, apart from a woman of about my age, sitting in a wheelchair. Her sticklike figure is wrapped up in a dressing gown and blankets as she lifts her sallow face to the brief glimmer of winter sunlight. Her mother kneels at her feet, anxiously readjusting the blankets.

'Watch out.' Sadie gently guides me back against the sickly green wall as a blue trolley rattles by, pushed by two porters with sour expressions on their faces.

'Rest in peace,' she whispers.

'Why did you say that?' I scurry to catch up with her. She's fast in spite of her heels.

'They were on their way to the mortuary. That was the body trolley.' I look at her blankly. 'The one they use to transport corpses from the wards.'

I suppress a shudder.

The staff section of the canteen is full of fierce-looking people. Doctors in white coats, nurses in an array of hats with low-heeled court shoes.

'Will you cope with a uniform?' I quickly look at Sadie again as we stand in the alarming queue for the serving area, trying to imagine her in the distinctly unglamorous polyester uniforms we'll have to wear.

'Haven't you noticed? I love dressing up. Although I'll be sad to lose these.' She waves her crimson talons at me. 'The tutor couldn't wait to tell me that I'd have to ditch the polish and cut my nails.'

I look down at my own nails which I've been desperately trying to stop biting.

I spot Louise and her cronies in the queue before us, laughing with the catering assistants like they've been coming here for years. Louise leading them away towards the tills with their trays at chest height.

'We'll sit apart from that lot, shall we?' Sadie nods towards them.

'I don't think they're going to invite me to go to a nightclub in Croydon, again, anytime soon. But then I don't think I'm really the nightclub type.'

'Or one of that woman's potential followers which makes me like you even more.'

We share a table with four nurses who shovel food into their mouths at an alarming speed, checking the nickel watches pinned to their breasts between bites.

'You don't say much, do you? That's not a criticism by

the way. I'm good with silence and you're a good listener.' Sadie lifts a forkful of the congealed lasagne she's bought and examines it, as if she's trying to work out its origin. 'I've always enjoyed an audience.'

'I'm just finding this all a bit overwhelming.'

'Appropriate. What we're about to do will be pretty mind blowing. All the stuff we'll see and do.' She finally puts a forkful of the pasta into her mouth and swallows, like she's downing medicine.

'I've never done this before. I just worked in a café.' I don't mention that the café job was part of my rehabilitation after my exile and melt-down. 'I needed a challenge and I wanted to do something worthwhile.'

'Oh, same here. Not a minute of care work. I did this.' She points at her overalls. I'm about to answer and say, 'Ah, factory work', thinking she'll be impressed with my guess when she continues. 'I had a vintage clothes stall at Portobello but my business partner wasn't as trustworthy as I thought, so it went under.'

I'm clueless as to what Portobello is. I don't have time to ask before she carries on.

'I chose this job because I wanted to do something that would push me. We're going to be at the sharp end of life and death. The limits of the human experience. Blood, pain, misery and it'll be up to us to try to make people feel better about all the trauma in their lives.'

This is as far from my fantasy of being a nurse as I can imagine. One of the older nurses at the table scowls at Sadie as she pushes past. They leave in a pack, dashing towards the exit. Sadie pushes her lasagne away, barely touched. I gingerly nibble at the sandwich I've chosen, trying not to baulk at the slick of grease from the cheap margarine on the bread.

'But I think the thing that'll break me will be the names of all these diseases and organs. I don't know how the hell I'll learn them.'

Finally, something I can help with.

'It's not so hard. I've noticed that they often come from Latin so you can work out the derivation. It's not always easy to dredge up but my classics lessons help.'

Sadie sits back.

'Things must be different in Derbyshire. We didn't study classics in my South East London comp.' She lets out a teasing laugh. Her pleasure a reward. 'What school did you go to?'

'I . . . You won't have heard of it.' The name of my school is the last thing that I want people here knowing.

'You're cagey, aren't you? I don't think that you're a murderer on the run or in witness protection so I'm guessing that you're hiding something else.'

I draw in a breath, not sure if I can release it again.

'Anything goes with me. You don't have to tell me.' She starts gathering her things together. 'I don't mind if you went to Roedean or a rough school on a sink estate. We can be who we want to be here.'

I force a smile, not trusting myself to speak and she smiles back at me. 'Maybe the biggest challenge won't be learning the names of things, it'll be getting used to this bloody awful food. Why don't you come to my house tomorrow? It'd be nicer to talk somewhere more relaxing. I'm not promising to lay on a meal, though. It'll be a cheese sandwich and crisps.'

I try not to look too eager as I accept her invitation.

There's so much I want to know about Sadie.

I can't think of a better way to learn about the object of your fascination than by examining their home.

* * *

When we arrive back in the classroom there's a new person sitting at our table. A pale woman with short blonde hair is slumped over, resting her head on her hands, her eyes closed. She's emaciated, thin wrists and ankles sticking out from her oversized jumper and jeans, her skin sallow. She looks a couple of years younger than me, maybe nineteen. Cathy, the earnest girl with curly hair, arrives at the same time as us and starts to protest, circling round to wake the woman and move her.

'It's not a wedding. There's no formal seating plan.' Sadie's musical tone makes the words sound friendly, but they're not. Cathy snatches up her things from the table and moves to an empty chair.

I pull my books and notes from my bag and there's something unfamiliar in there. A piece of crumpled white paper is wedged between my loose notes.

There's a single phrase written in thick black marker pen.
I KNOW WHAT YOU DID
I hold it up with trembling fingers.
'What's that?' Sadie peers idly across.
'I don't know. It's . . .'
'Odd. Do you think you picked it up by mistake with your papers when you dropped your folder?' I want this to make sense. I accidentally scattered my handouts when I was putting them in my bag at lunchtime. I could have scooped this up with them, so I cling to this thought.

I screw it into a ball and take it to the bin, ignoring this feeling that someone is watching me and the thought that maybe the note was for me and someone here knows. People *are* watching and gauging each other; we're all new here.

Caroline re-enters the room clapping her hands together briskly, waking the sleeping woman up and making me jolt.

'Ladies and gentlemen. Settle down. We have a late starter. No, not you Anthony. Although your timekeeping could be better.' She waves Anthony, the angular-faced pretty boy, across to his seat, earning a look of death from him. 'This is Amy, who's unfortunately had to miss the first couple of weeks. I hope that you can offer her a warm welcome and help her to catch up.'

Amy becomes animated, like a TV that's just been switched on. She turns and waves to the rest of the room, shooting everyone an effortful smile, before slouching back down again.

The tutor flicks on the overhead projector, revealing a slide with 'Last Offices: Caring for the Deceased' written in green marker. At around the twentieth slide she reaches down and holds up a frilled shroud to dress the dead in, draping it against her body, like she's a corpse.

Amy looks across at Sadie and pulls a faux horrified face which makes Sadie chuckle to herself. I look at them both in turn. I wish Cathy had stayed and Amy had chosen another table to sit at.

Sadie and I don't need anyone else in our friendship group.

Chapter Six

THEN

February 1991

Sadie walks ahead of me, leading me through a series of streets of off-white houses at the back of the hospital. Everything is the colour of sheep in winter. I'm becoming less bothered by the constant hum of traffic and the onslaught of people but I struggle to keep up with my guide. I get the chance to admire Sadie's clothing as she strides ahead on impressive heels, the skirt of her 1940s dress flapping behind her. She's pulled the fur bolero around her shoulders and is toting an immense leather bag on the crook of her arm. She waits at the kerbside of the frenetic road and I catch up.

I feel hot breath on my ear and there's a sibilant hiss. One word. A sudden pressure on my back knocks me forward and my arms flail uselessly for something to grab onto, but there's nothing there to stop me falling into the fast-moving traffic of the high street. I try to yell but the air has been sucked from me. I lurch forward into the clouds of petrol fumes and off the kerb, stumbling onto my knees, hands shooting out and grazing the tarmac. A red London bus is hurtling towards me. The driver is looking up towards the lights of a pedestrian crossing ahead, oblivious to my arrival in her path. I'm level with the immense wheels. The bus is only feet away, moving too fast to stop. I let out a scream but it's drowned out by the noise of the street. I close my eyes, helpless and with no choice but to wait for the impact.

There's a screech of tyres and I lift my head, locking eyes with the driver. I become aware of yelling and turn my face towards Sadie who's standing above me, waving her arms at the driver. The hulking wheels have stopped inches from my hands, which are splayed on the tarmac.

My legs are shaking as Sadie helps me up and guides me to the pavement, ignoring the shouts and florid gesticulations from the bus driver. People swill around us, oblivious, like we're stones in water. Sadie holds me to her and I take in gasping breaths of Chanel No. 5 scented air, trying to get enough oxygen in so that I can speak again.

'I . . . someone pushed me.' My eyes widen as I look into her face.

'On purpose?' Her voice sounds puzzled, as if this is an impossible idea.

'I don't know.' A sudden pulse of people had passed along the pavement behind us. I could easily have been knocked by someone. But the word that I heard is echoing in my ears. I try to slow my breathing down. The sound of my swallowing is loud in my head.

'I'm sure it wasn't deliberate. It will have just been some moron trying to barge by.' She reaches across and squeezes my hand. 'I know we haven't known each other long but I'd have hated to see you flattened by the traffic. It'd be a horrible welcome to London and a downer on the day.'

The imprint of her touch lingers as we carry on walking.

'Here we are.' I've been in a daze, the word that I heard repeating in my mind, my thoughts cycling around, wondering if I could have misheard or imagined it.

I gather myself and look around. We've reached a gap between the houses with their overflowing bins and greying nets. What lies before us is a small cul-de-sac, certainly not grand enough to be called a mews. As we pass through I'm surprised by the crowd of narrow houses lining the street like gravestones. I imagined that Sadie would live in a cosy terrace with bright gingham curtains and chipped teapots, not one of these mausoleums. Hers is a four-storey Edwardian villa in dark brick, caked with the grime of London pollution, set back slightly from the road with a narrow front garden. Dark-leaved laurel bushes strain to escape, pushing through the gaps of the rusted railings, masking some of the scalpel sharp points. She fumbles in her bag and pulls out a set of keys, turning to me before opening the vast door bejewelled with chipped stained glass, flanked by blackened stone pillars.

'Welcome to Laurel House.' The house name is etched into the glass over the door in ornate lettering. 'Shut the gate, Laura. Coco tends to make a break for it and she has no road sense.'

I don't have time to ask who or what Coco is before she unlocks the door. We're immediately assaulted by a tiny bundle of black fur emitting an ear-piercing bark. Sadie reaches down and picks it up. It nuzzles into her fur bolero, blending in.

'Laura, meet Coco Chanel. Her bark is ferocious but she's a pushover. She'll love you.'

I gently put out my hand. I'm used to dealing with animals and I'm not afraid of a tiny poodle. A soft tongue flicks out of her snout and licks the edge of my fingers and I can't help but smile.

'Isn't she gorgeous?' Sadie bends her head forward and kisses her on the snout. 'She's everything to me.'

Sadie's gaze alights on the answerphone on a console table, her eyes narrowing as she glances at the zero on the display. 'Now, we've got about ninety minutes till the next lecture. Shall I show you the house first or do us a quick lunch?'

She places the dog in my arms and marches ahead. I follow, the soft warmth of the animal soothing me.

Once we've passed through the dark of the coat lined hallway, past the age speckled mirrors, we head into the sitting room. I should have guessed what would greet me from Sadie's attire. The room looks like something from forty or fifty years before. Like a scene from one of the black and white films that I used to watch on the battered old TV in my bedroom. Hiding out on wintery afternoons, convalescing after my hospital stay. Until I came home from a walk one day to find that my sister had disappeared again, along with all the electrical equipment in the flat. The TV in my room has never been replaced.

There's a polished wood gramophone, a tiled fireplace and a vast old radio. No sign of anything modern, although I suspect that the strategically placed cupboard hides a television. My eyes dance around the room, unsure where to land. Searching for something to comment on but struggling to decide which china dog or fringed lamp to choose. Sadie throws her bag down onto one of the expansive sofas. I fight the urge to follow the bag and flop myself down, curling into a ball on the piles of cushions. I'm so utterly sleep deprived from living in that nurses' home, averaging about three or four hours a night. The spike of adrenaline from the push onto the road has left me listless and weak.

This place feels like home. Like the home I would have liked to have grown up in. A house from another era that I know well from my TV viewing habits. The kind of place I've dreamed about. Sadie fits into the lead role in this setting. A domestic version of Lana Turner or Marlene Dietrich. The Queen of this tranquil domain. I set the dog down, surprised to see that my hands have almost stopped shaking.

'Do you like it?' Sadie is biting her lip slightly. It's as if she's stripped herself naked in front of me and she's afraid of my judgement.

'I . . . I love it.'

'I shouldn't say this myself, but it's marvellous, isn't it? I'm smitten with this place.'

Sadie lets out a laugh and leads me through to the airy kitchen, grabbing my coat from me along the way and throwing it onto one of the overloaded hooks. The kitchen door has a stained-glass panel that takes up the top half. The distinguishing feature of this is that it's damaged. Red and blue panels have wide fissures across them at head height and the lead that houses the glass is buckled outwards in the shape of a human skull. It's as if someone has been slammed into the door. I push the jarring thought of violence from my head with a shudder. There'll be an innocuous explanation for this. I'm letting my anxiety take over my imagination.

The kitchen is wide and tiled in red quarry tiles, encroached by shelves of plants that seem to push in from the edges of the room. Sadie has gone for the vintage theme again with a battered yellow table, faded to the colour of liver failure. Fabric curtains instead of cupboard doors, old crockery and scratched enamel pans hanging from hooks.

'There's a dining room through there but I don't use it a lot. It feels a bit unnerving when I'm sitting there at the table on my own. My friend, Portia, and her boyfriend lived here for a while, as well as my business partner and his wife. It was glorious. We used to host lavish parties. This house needs people and chatter.'

I nod and try to focus.

'What's wrong, Laura? You look worried.'

'It's nothing.'

'You can tell me. Are you still shaken from the accident?'

I stare at the speckled surface of the tabletop and try to stop my breathing quickening. There's no way of telling her why I'm so unsettled.

'How about some distraction to take your mind off things. I'll start by telling you some things about my tawdry history and, if you want to, then you can tell me a bit about your scandalous past. I do hope that you have a florid one.' Sadie carries on preparing lunch, barely pausing for breath before she launches into a long tale about her vintage clothes business. A torturous story about how she was double-crossed by her business partner and ended up losing everything.

By the time she's finished talking, the table is groaning with food and she sits opposite me. The promised cheese sandwich and crisps are nowhere to be seen, instead there's an array of salads, fresh bread and a quiche. My heart sinks because my fearful stomach is clenched tight but I pick at the food and make polite noises about how lovely it all is.

'So, how about you? I'd be interested to know more.' I study her face as she says this and there's no hint of mockery or disingenuousness. It's as if she might genuinely be interested in me. I tell her the basics. About how my father disappeared with the landlady of the village pub just after I was born and hasn't been seen since. About how my mum worked three jobs and my sister, Suzie, who's ten years older, often had to take over caring for me. I tell her about the people in the small village I grew up in who looked down on our second-hand clothes and our cramped flat over a shop where nothing quite worked. I only make a vague statement about Suzie having some health issues. It's a benign euphemism for the endless cycle of relapse and sobriety that she spins through, the dangerous situations she's been in, the hospitalisations. The times when she goes missing and we're torn apart with worry or worse than that, when she comes back and we cope with the aftermath, all three of us knowing that it won't be long till she falls again, the lure of heroin too strong for her to resist.

Sadie looks up from her plate often, seemingly interested in what I'm saying. She doesn't comment, as if there's nothing tawdry or sad about growing up with no money.

I finish with a brief mention of how I finally escaped home by winning a scholarship and going to a boarding school. I'm careful again not to name it. Incidents like what happened to me there lodge in people's memories. Sadie might have read the press reports.

'People judge me now because of the way I talk. It's like when someone moves from Scotland or Ireland and everyone here thinks that their accent is strong but when they visit where they came from, everyone there thinks they sound English. That's me. I went to boarding school on a scholarship, with a broad Derbyshire accent, and came away talking like this.' The received pronunciation that I returned from school with is like a lingering odour. 'People in the village all think I sound stuck up, especially given my family's financial status, whereas well-to-do people think I sound unpolished and fraudulent.'

'Interesting. There's clearly layers to you that I'll enjoy unpeeling.' She raises an eyebrow and I can't help but smile. It feels like when you exercise after a period of inactivity. There's a tug of underused muscles being activated. 'I like your accent. It sounds classic to me. Very *Brief Encounter*.'

Sadie finishes her food and I've pushed mine around the plate and made a show of enjoying it. What little I ate sits like a mass in my stomach.

'I . . . bought you something to say thank you for inviting me.' I pull the mother of pearl compact that I found in a junk shop down the high street from my pocket. A treacherous trip that involved negotiating with a woman whose South London accent was so strong that I had to ask her to repeat herself three times.

'I love it!' She leans in and plants a kiss on each of my cheeks, leaving behind a scent of Chanel perfume. 'But you didn't need to buy me anything.'

She sits back, admiring the compact and I try to think what to ask, pondering how the girls I was at school with might handle the etiquette of a new friendship.

'Do you live here alone now?' She doesn't wear a wedding ring and there's no telltale groove or tan line on her ring finger; I'm guessing she's single. There are a myriad of other questions I want to ask, mainly how she's afforded this place from running a market stall, but I don't ask that. It'd be crude.

'Yes and no.' There's a brief darkening of her features and she looks lost in thought.

'It's so lovely here.' I change the subject, reproaching myself for being too brash, resolving not to overstep boundaries.

'Thank you. I appreciate that. It's an albatross of a house at times and I do rattle around here like a ghost but otherwise I'm wedded to this place. We come as a job lot.'

'It's beautiful.' This isn't an empty compliment. I'm instantly beguiled by the sense of space and tranquillity. I'd feel free here.

'This house is in my DNA. This is an embarrassing admission but I miss this place if I go away anywhere even for a night. I can't wait to be back again.' Her eyes are unfocused for a moment. 'I was actually born here.'

'Really? In one of the bedrooms?' I've already done a mental calculation and come up with a guess that there's at least four bedrooms.

'In the bedroom I sleep in now. It was my parents' room before they died.'

'Oh, gosh. I'm sorry to hear that.' I can't imagine the death of a parent. My mum's barely present in my life. Her time is eaten away by her jobs and my sister, her mind distracted by money worries but I can't imagine her not being there at all. 'How did they die?'

Sadie is silent for a moment and my cheeks flush with fresh blood as I wonder if I should apologise for my tactless question.

'You're blushing. Don't worry. I'm fine talking about it with you. It's just that it's such a grisly story that I'm wondering if I should burden you with it.' There's a shriek and I jolt in my seat. She pushes herself out of the rickety chair and pulls a whistling kettle off the stove.

'Grisly is fine. I mean . . . I don't mind. You can talk about anything.' After all the hours I've spent reading old crime novels and the daily chaos of the psychiatric unit, I can cope with dark tales.

'My father died here. Right where you're sitting. How's that for grim?' I look down at the quarry tiles that are the colour of congealed blood.

'My parents were both actors. They didn't ever hit the big time but my father was good as background characters. You know the kind of thing. Put upon husband, cuckold, doting father. The sort of person who you never remember once the film finishes but acting is how he paid for this house. He had a steady contract in a TV show for a while as a detective's dull sidekick.'

Sadie pours me a coffee from a tall coffee pot covered in flowers. A pointless touch as she's only spooned Nescafé in there. We could have just used the cups.

'Then my mother became ill with breast cancer. Me and my father looked after her through surgery and chemo, which was tough going. But when it spread, not having treatment was even tougher. Coco, no, darling!' She pushes the poodle gently back, to stop her trying to jump onto my leg.

'How old were you?' Sadie sits down again, resting her manicured hands on the table.

'Oh, eighteen. It was a lot to go through but we did OK. For a while anyway. I mean, he was broken after she died. You'd expect that, but it wasn't just the usual grieving. He was almost catatonic. Like he'd completely shut down. He wouldn't wash or dress for days, wouldn't eat. Then he'd have the odd couple of days where he was almost himself again and I'd think we were through it. But we never were. The GP was one of those old-fashioned types, patriarchal and full of his own importance. He just told me to wait it out so I did. Do you want any more of this egg or shall I finish it?' I shake my head.

'My father was having a run of better days and I needed to get out of the house. It's hard to be contained when you're that age. I was already seeing my boyfriend, Sacha.'

I relish the exoticism of the name, mentally collating the information about Sadie that I'm discovering.

'Are you still with Sacha?' The look on Sadie's face tells me that this isn't something she wants to answer. It's been so long since I've had a real friend. I'm unskilled at this. How it works. What to ask. What the rules of friendship are. 'I'm sorry. I didn't mean to pry.'

Sadie waves away my comment like it's a fly.

'He's working away at the moment. He's a musician.' She draws a deep breath. 'I'll tell you all about him next time you're here.'

Relief floods me. I haven't angered her and the thought of being invited again, of having a real friend, thrills me.

'Back to the parental horror story. So, I thought my father was fine to leave for an hour or two and I went to

Sacha's parents' house. His parents fussed over me and fed me, which was like stepping into a warm bath after the sombre atmosphere here. We went up and lay together on his bed while we listened to the rubbish pseudo punk music that we liked back then.' She stops for a moment and she rests a hand against her powdered cheek. We're a perfect fit. I enjoy stories and Sadie is a born storyteller.

I lean forward, eager to know what happened. 'Next thing I knew I woke up and four hours had gone by. I picked up my things and ran all the way back home, leaving Sacha asleep. And that's when I found him.'

I allow her to pause again without interrupting. There's something actorly about her delivery and timing. Like she's savouring the drama. I think I know what's coming and there's no way I can brace myself for this.

'My father died where you're sitting now. He'd slit his throat. It was gaping open, wet with blood. Like the gills of a fish.'

The room pales before me. My brain is whirring. Frantically pushing away the images of that gothic school building, the drab courtroom, the screams of the hospital ward. The desperate look on my mother's face and the whispers and stares in the village. I breathe away the nausea, pushing my hands flat on the table to stop the shaking. Naming things in the room in my head to ground me back into reality.

'Are you all right, Laura? You've gone pale.'

'Sorry. I'm OK. That must have been terrible. What did you do?' For once, I'm not overthinking what I'm saying. I place my hands square on the table in front of me to stop them quivering. I have an urge to look down, as if there'll still be blood pooling on the floor.

'Well there wasn't anything I could do to save him. He was long dead. But I rang for an ambulance anyway and told the woman on the phone that he was beyond help. She was perfectly nice about it. I still remember her. Then I cleaned some of the blood up with Flash and hot water while I waited.'

I reach across, intending to grab her hand but my manoeuvre is clumsy. I end up stroking her arm.

'It's just life, Laura. Things happen and you have to move through them. Now, do you want some more quiche or shall I show you the garden and the upstairs?'

I refuse the quiche. The shred of appetite I had has now gone.

* * *

The upstairs is exactly as I expected. Sadie's bedroom is a clashing paradise of silks and nylons. Fabrics draped from the cluttered dressing table and the bed and a vast wardrobe looming over the room. Tasselled lamps flank the immense bed. There's no sign of Sacha anywhere, not a trace of masculinity. A bay window overlooks an artfully overgrown garden that stretches down towards a cluster of apple trees.

The rest of the rooms are of a similar aesthetic, but unoccupied, apart from a boxroom that's filled with a dizzying selection of vintage clothes, lined up on clothing rails like soldiers. A long trestle table housing a sewing machine and bolts of fabric. Paper dress patterns, reels of brightly coloured cotton and pins jostling for space. A set of stairs leads up to a third floor. There's a particular bedroom that draws me. It's a square room, just across the landing from Sadie's, with a view over the garden. It looks like a calm place to sleep. I'd be happy here.

Sadie pops in to use the loo before we leave to catch the afternoon lectures and I walk back down the stairs, setting off a volley of creaks and groans from the wood with each step. My legs are still wobbly from the earlier jolts of panic. The dog dances between my ankles, almost making me stumble to my death. I peer at the photographs that line the wall. They're mostly theatrical stills, shots of actors on film or stage sets with two recurring characters: a nondescript man and a woman who bear little resemblance to Sadie.

The shrill ring of the phone in the hall makes me jump.

'Laura, will you get that?' Sadie's disembodied voice echoes down from the bathroom.

My heels click against the Minton tiles.

'Hello.' There's a pause and clicking noises as if I'm being connected to someone through a switchboard, a disembodied voice says something that I don't quite catch. My hand is shaking as it holds the receiver.

'Portia? What the hell are you doing back there with her? Shout Sadie for me. I'm having a bastard of a day. I'm at breaking point in here.' I don't speak. 'Portia? It's Sacha. What's wrong with this fucking line. Sir? I think there's something wrong with the phone.'

A muffled answer in the background above a series of bangs and shouts and the threatening rumble of all-male voices. Someone shouts at someone and calls them a 'fucking screw'.

'Sadie? Speak to me, for fuck's sake. You're the only thing keeping me sane while I'm stuck in this place.' I replace the green plastic receiver. Standing back, I catch sight of myself in the hall mirror. I pull my shoulders up and straighten my spine, standing more like Sadie does. I could belong in this sanctuary.

'Who was that?' Sadie's cloud of Chanel is stronger.

'Oh, a wrong number.' Sadie pauses to kiss the dog on the snout before we walk back to the nursing school.

I lie because I don't want to embarrass her. I know what the background noises were on the call. I've seen enough crime dramas on the TV to know that 'screw' is slang for a prison officer.

Sacha isn't working away. Sadie's boyfriend is in prison.

Sadie has lied to me and I don't mind at all. Shame is a difficult thing to carry. I understand that.

We carry on walking. 'It's such a lovely home, Sadie and so big.'

'It's beautiful, isn't it? But it has been an adjustment being on my own. I'm so used to having a houseful of people to nurture.'

I would be good company for her if I had that empty bedroom. It looks ideal for me. I think back to the nights alone in the box of a room in the nurses' home, listening to the distant laughter of people who don't know or understand me.

I'm besotted. Not just by Sadie but by this house.

I want to come back again and again. To let this place envelop me.

* * *

Sadie holds the door of the nursing college open for me. I'm still contemplating Sadie's house but that's not all I'm thinking about. It's going to be hard to concentrate on the afternoon lectures, with my swirling thoughts and the aftershocks of panic. My mind is spinning. There's a lot to think about.

The word that was hissed in my ear before I was pushed into the road is still resounding in my brain. It has done all through lunch.

'Killer.' The soft hiss of the word as it was whispered by a voice that could have belonged to any gender.

The word that was lodged in my head for so long after it happened.

Sadie isn't the only one with things to lie about.

Chapter Seven

NOW

Tuesday, 13 April 2010

I swing the car off the high street and into the narrow close of eight Edwardian houses. Laurel House looks the same, as if it's been preserved in aspic. The same dark green laurel bushes, only overgrown now and almost covering the windows. The same chipped paintwork on the door but with streaks of London grime staining the surrounding brickwork.

The journey down here was tiresome. We left the sedate green of Derbyshire and hit the grey ferocity of the motorways. The only joy in the dull journey was Elsie. Her bursts of random conversation, snide teenage remarks and constant fiddling with the radio left me unsure whether to laugh or reprimand her.

I lift my bag from the boot while Elsie hovers behind me.

'Home, thank God. Derbyshire isn't for me. Too much grass and hills and not enough shops or phone signal.' This is exactly how Sadie was. She said that she found the countryside alarming and that open spaces made her feel vulnerable to attack whereas she was quite happy boarding a night bus full of drunks. 'You were mad to go back. Or did you go home for a man?'

'I wanted to be nearer to my family.' I swallow hard at the half truth.

'So you aren't with anyone? You're not married, right?'

'You're direct, aren't you.' I slam the boot closed and turn towards the house, head down. Dreading having to see this place.

'Yeah. People say that.' She smiles with what looks like pride. 'So?'

'No. I'm not married.'

Standing at the door makes me feel like I'm twenty-one again, coming here that first day with Sadie. An innocent who was unaware of the devastation to come.

My eyes skim the doorway again. It's flaking in parts and I stare at the frame, as if I'm looking for the bloody fingerprints still caked there after all these years. Those marks that puzzle me to this day. I haul my holdall into the hallway while Elsie walks ahead and flings open the sitting room door.

'Make yourself comfortable and I'll see if Sadie's awake.' She dashes up the stairs, leaving me alone. I force my legs to move and carry me into the room. I close my eyes for a second, not wanting to look.

When I open my eyelids the familiar pictures on the wall are staring down at me. Paintings of sultry women from the 1960s peer seductively over their shoulders and the TV remains hidden in its cabinet, like a dirty secret. Everything the same, only more tired, like the house is a deflated balloon. Rather than shabby chic, it's now just shabby.

The room is dusty and there's a faint smell of damp with cobwebs hanging from the cornicing.

Sadie championed the vintage style way before it was a cutesy aesthetic that a wedding planner might offer up to the bride-to-be or something you'd see in a feature in *You* magazine. She had a strong commitment to the lifestyle even back then, long before there were vintage shops in every town across the country. Striding around dressed like an extra from a wartime film set, not caring about the stares she attracted or the comments that were thrown at her. Or caring a lot about them and enjoying them, which was maybe the whole point.

The sofa looks like it'll collapse under the weight of the cushions. As I push them aside to make a gap for myself a small black snout appears and snaps at my hand, a volley of barks echoing round the room. The head of a tiny black poodle emerges. Two brown eyes staring at me with a contemptuous look. I reel back with shock.

'Coco!' I offer my hand for her to sniff, hoping she remembers me.

'She's called Sophia. After Sophia Loren. Coco died before I was born.' Elsie is leaning in the doorway. She's changed into a different dress. I recognise the geometric shapes and the clashing colours. It's one of Sadie's old ones that we bought together from a vintage shop near Seven Dials. 'Sadie's awake. And she wants to see you.'

The familiar knot is back. The urge to run to my car and screech away from the kerb is overwhelming. I take a couple of deep breaths, trying to focus on the noise from the street rather than my heartbeat.

I follow her up the stairs.

I repeat my mantra to myself: 'This is only for a couple of days.'

I have to be here. As a nurse, as a decent human, I can't leave someone suffering like this when I can help.

And I need to know what Sadie's saying about me.

Elsie keeps changing the story of when her father will be back or where he is. She's now saying that he returns on Thursday night. In the meantime, I need to be professional and try and sort things out for them, call in their palliative care nurse, involve the GP. Reassure this child who's been left to do an adult's job. These are the things I can't leave undone.

The stairs creak and the familiar portraits of the couple stare down at me, their clothes flamboyant in a 1970s way. Their studied poses betraying them as what they were: a pair of actors. There are new photos now. A picture of Sadie holding a baby near Tower Bridge. Sadie and Elsie on Brighton seafront. Elsie in a school uniform. The pictures have metastasised and now cover most of the wall. There are gaps there though. Holes in the plaster, picture hooks still hanging, swinging loose as if photo frames have been prised from the wall in an act of violence.

My hand rests on my stomach, as if I can soothe the anxiety there via touch. Elsie points to the door, like I don't know every inch of this house and then flits off upstairs to the attic. The door opens smoothly and the expected creak of the hinges surprises me by its absence. The room is in semi-darkness. The curtains block most of the light. Shafts of weak sunlight poke through at the sides and along the top where curtain rings have come loose. Swags of dusty velvet droop down towards the floor. The furniture is in the same place. The wardrobe like a doorman, guarding the bed, the brass bed jutting into the spacious room, a barely discernible shape propped in the centre. There's a movement and a tasselled lamp flicks on, half illuminating the space. I force my unwilling body forward. Sadie's hand looks like a claw as it retreats from the lamp switch onto her lap. It's nothing I'm not used to seeing in my job. This sense of dread that's gnawing at me is more to do with what might happen than how disquieting she looks.

My chest tightens. I know she's going to speak and I want her to. There's so much I want to understand now that we're finally in the same room again. But there's another part of me that wishes she'd be silent forever. I can barely see her in here. Only the right-hand side of her face is illuminated. The pools of yellowed light catch in the hollows of her sunken cheeks, her skeletal hands resting on the bed.

'Laura. How are you?' She speaks as if she's only seen me the week before. The way old friends might. But we're not friends. Not now. 'I'm so glad you were able to come. I didn't think you'd say no to my daughter. She's persuasive, isn't she? I thought that sending her up would work better than trying it myself on the phone.'

She lets out a coy laugh, her pitch and tone still high. Still breathy but weaker, as if she's perpetually on the verge of sleep.

I should have guessed that Elsie didn't come up with the insane plan to come to Derbyshire without Sadie's guiding hand. It's such a Sadie thing to do. Always in control even when dying. I clench my fists and turn sharply so that I'm facing towards the door. Sadie knew exactly how to get me here. Sending up a vulnerable child with a desperate story was a masterplan. Sadie knew that I would never, could never, leave someone alone to die in pain.

'Don't just stand there. Come and give me a kiss. I know physical contact was never your thing but I'm ill, Laura.

That's surely an exception, even for you.' Her voice is becoming reedier by the minute. There's a faint wheeze as she speaks, a catching in her throat. I don't go to her. I stay where I am, breathing in through my nose to try to suppress my fury. 'Anyway, more importantly, are *you* well?'

I know what she's asking. She wants to know how my mental health is. Sadie was the only person I told about what had happened to me before I first came here. About the PTSD flashbacks, the period of catatonia and the panic attacks. The reason it all started.

'I'm fine.' My tone is terse. She doesn't need to know about the dark episodes that I've weathered over the last few years. The occasional medication switches when they stopped working for me and the carousel of NHS psychiatrists I've seen over the years.

'I always worried about you. The thing with Jessica . . . Violent death has such a persistent effect on young minds and—'

'I said that I'm fine.' I'm now feeling even further from stable than I did before. I close my eyes for a second and try to centre myself.

I move forward. The bedside table is crowded with things. A water glass that is speckled with dead blackflies, box upon box of medications, a biscuit with a corner nibbled, as if rats have attacked it, rather than human teeth. The bedclothes smell of the old Sadie: a rich rose laden perfume but underneath that is something sour and repellent. The unwashed smell of feverish bodies and twisted bed sheets. A scent of death. This is harder than I thought. There's unexpected pathos to seeing Sadie, the vibrant woman who tended to sick people, now stricken and shrunken.

'While you're here, will you get me some of my pills.

I'm in agony.' I should have spotted that from her body language. Her neck muscles are tight and her hand is bunching up the bedclothes.

'These are a mess. You shouldn't be taking all of this.' I lift one of the packets. There's a variety of opioids. Codeine, oxycodone, fentanyl patches, morphine liquid, morphine pills. 'We need to have a look at these. Rationalise them and evaluate which one works best for you.'

I give her some oxycodone syrup and she knocks it back like it's a vodka shot.

'You don't need to be a nurse twenty-four hours a day, Laura. I didn't bring you here solely to reorder my life.'

'What exactly *am* I here for then?'

'I need more water. Would you?'

I walk down to the kitchen to get fresh water. When I come back up Sadie is asleep. Tendrils of unbrushed hair falling over her face, her body at an odd angle, the pillows not at all right. I stand watching for a while.

I resist the urge to plump and shift and rearrange.

And the urge to shake her awake and ask her what's really happening here.

Chapter Eight

NOW

Tuesday, 13 April 2010

The kitchen is grimier than I've ever seen it. There are bulbs missing and the remaining lamps create random slashes of abrasive light. There's no sign of Elsie. The place is silent, apart from the occasional intrusive shout from the street or the revving of an engine. The empty chairs sitting at the yellow Formica table are a reproach. I can almost hear the clamour of voices and see the four of us sitting there. The five of us once *he* arrived.

I root through a pile of papers on the worktop by the scratched fridge. There's a stack of oncology letters that I skim read. Sadie has pancreatic cancer that has spread to her liver and lungs. She's had doses of chemotherapy but the tumour is still ripping through her flesh, exponentially increasing in size. Her death will come soon.

One of the oncology letters mentions her husband being present in the clinic but not his name. There's no other evidence of her husband in the kitchen or sitting room. No letters, no photographs. I find a number for a palliative care nurse called Tom and the district nursing team but it's too late to call anyone. Their admin staff will have clocked off and there's nothing to warrant me ringing them out of hours.

My skin is pocked by goosepimples in spite of the warmth of the room. An overwhelming sense of exhaustion creeps over me. There's still no sign of Elsie when I go upstairs, no sounds emanating from the attic. I cross the landing and the floorboard creaks exactly where it always did. I don't go up the attic stairs. That room isn't somewhere I want to be.

My old bedroom is exactly as it was when I left. The same gingham duvet and pale blue curtains. The picture of an emaciated woman with oversized eyes still hanging over the bed, only the glass looks grimy now. Sadie always thought it was kitsch and fun but now it just looks sinister. The floor is flecked with balls of dust and a fine layer has settled on the green glass decanters that Sadie bought in Portobello Road market. I stop short at the bookshelves on the wall. Some of my books are still here. Battered old Penguin editions that I picked up cheap at the book market at the South Bank, propped there alongside Portia's paperbacks.

I sit myself up on the bed with pillows, my eyes circling the room. It's effortful to hold my body still, trying to force my muscles to relax and push my body into sleep. Every time I close my eyes it's like watching a cinema trailer of the worst moments of my time living here. Memories flooding in like vertigo. The screams and shouts, cries for help coming from the attic, an unexpected pull as my head is yanked back by my hair.

I keep seeing that bloodstain on the front doorframe again. The bloodstain that makes no more sense now than it did back then.

* * *

I must have fallen asleep at some point. When I wake the room is in total darkness and I flail for where I am. There's a blanket covering me. Elsie must have been in and done that. I can feel something warm against my thigh. I look down and Sophia the poodle has tucked herself into me, just like Coco used to do. I reach down and rub the underside of her chin and she narrows her eyes in ecstasy.

The scream echoes through the house.

'Sacha.' Sadie's yell is hoarse and ragged. That name. It's like a bucket of iced water has been thrown over me.

I run through to her, my bare feet banging against the floorboards of the landing.

'It's OK, Sadie. It's Laura.' She's sitting up in bed. Her wan face looks incomplete in the gloom. Locks of hair hang down like seaweed. She lifts a hand and points across the room. The eyes of china dogs stare back at me.

'There's no one there. There's just us. Elsie is upstairs.' I'm hoping Elsie has headphones on and hasn't heard her. That name has left a residual chill in my flesh. I don't want this word coming from Sadie's mouth. More importantly, I don't want anyone to hear it. 'Are you in pain?'

'Of course I'm in pain. I'm always in fucking pain. Do something. You're here as my nurse, aren't you?'

'Here.' I drip oxycodone syrup into her mouth and follow up with a glass of water placed against her dry lips. 'Come on, let's get you more comfortable.'

I ease her forward and plump up the pillows.

She sinks back into the bed and closes her eyes. 'I'm sorry to be so snappy. I'm just so tired of this.'

I don't respond. Sometimes it's better to resist the urge to provide an answer or platitude.

'Have the spiders and roaches gone yet? I don't mind them but they shouldn't be here. Not now.' She brushes at the sheets as if she's flicking the corpses of insects away.

'Don't worry about them, I'll deal with that. We'll give the oxycodone twenty minutes to work and then if you're still feeling bad, we'll try something else.'

As well as the analgesics, there's a bewildering array of sedatives in this disorderly collection of medications.

'You're a good nurse. There's no one else I'd trust more.' She keeps her eyes closed. 'An improbable nurse, but the job suits you, doesn't it?'

'You were too. Improbable I mean. And good.' I take her hand, easing my fingers between hers. Human touch is a manageable thing when I'm donning my role of nurse like the paper hats we once wore. 'The uniform was never quite your aesthetic though.'

She opens her eyes and mock shudders. Her hands are starting to relax a little. She looks down at the bed sheets, as if she's startled to see that the insects have gone.

'It's a shame what we became.' She locks eyes with me. 'Who'd have thought that it'd end like that? So much death.'

My tongue is useless, as if I've lost the power of speech through a head injury or stroke. The room feels unbearable and I turn to leave, smacking straight into Elsie. She's standing with one hip jutting out, arms folded. 'I heard noises. Is she OK?'

'Just some pain but we're onto it. I'm here now, so you can get some rest.' I need to get her out of here while Sadie is like this. The risk of what she might say in front of her daughter is too great. Sadie talking about the past in front of other people is where danger lies for me.

'OK, nurse!' She smirks and does a mock salute, clicking her bare feet together before exiting.

Sadie has closed her eyes.

I wait a moment and then make my escape, too.

* * *

When I wake up there's a text message on my phone from Miriam, the outgoing matron at work.

Top secret gossip and if you tell anyone I told you this I'll have to kill you. The other applicant has withdrawn. Good news for you.

I've been sitting at the top of the ward sister pay scale for years now and what with helping Mum and Suzie, there's never much money to spare. This promotion looks like it's mine and it will make all the difference. I just need to make sure nothing jeopardises it.

There's a message from Mum, too. No enquiry about how I am. Just a sunny sentence about what a lovely time they're having and how happy Suzie seems. It's a coded missive to tell me that she's still clean. I delete it.

I start making calls as soon as the clock hits 9 a.m. The palliative care team nurse who I speak to doesn't have the sort of calm, mellifluous voice that I expected. She's frenetic but helpful. She calls back an hour later and has arranged for a doctor and Sadie's usual palliative care nurse to visit tomorrow. In the interim she's asked a district nurse to call.

When the nurse arrives three hours later, she's around my age, but with smoker's lines that her pale lipstick has bled into. She's pretty in a jaded way with her hair in a curly bob, dyed a deep chestnut colour. I don't catch her name because Sophia runs into the hall and releases a volley of barks which drown her words out.

She's a practical nurse which is the kind that I like, although she's over familiar for someone I've just met. Sadie's asleep so we don't wake her. We sit at the kitchen table and she talks about home infusion pumps for sedatives and analgesics, suggesting that we wait and see what the palliative care team come up with. She can provide a hospital bed if Sadie will allow that. I suspect she won't, it would spoil her aesthetic. The nurse gulps the coffee down and takes three Hobnobs. It's a relentless job that she does and I imagine that her moments of calm are few.

'I always wondered what it looked like in here. He said it was like this.'

'Do you know this street then?'

She looks puzzled for a second. 'Oh, I thought you recognised me, Laura. It's Cathy. I said when I came in but that dog was barking like a demon.'

She must notice that I still look nonplussed, so she carries on. 'We trained together. But your group didn't really pay much attention to me, did you?'

Of course it's her. I should have spotted that. Another unwanted image. That earnest young woman with the glasses, always on the peripheries, watching the action.

I try to recover the situation. 'I remember you as being quiet and studious with glasses. You're . . . different.'

'I'm wearing contact lenses and I'm haggard! Three kids and us both working full-time does that to you.'

I try not to stare at her. This new version of the earnest young woman with the glasses.

'What does your husband do?'

She pauses and her brow crinkles. 'Didn't you know? I married Nathan. We got together the last week of our training. He's working as part of a drug and alcohol team in Lewisham now.'

Her voice has flattened in tone. There's been a shift in her mood but I can't work out why. Something's nagging at me about what she's just said and I can't think what it is.

'Oh . . . I didn't know.' I think back to younger Nathan and his boyish energy and studious Cathy.

'You were all a bit preoccupied, I suppose. What with everything that went on here. It must have been so hard when that happened to Amy.' She finishes her coffee. 'And I heard about the way it ended for you all, too.'

I try to pull away from her gaze. Her eyes are studying my face, as if she's waiting for a reaction. I'm frozen in place, like a rabbit just before a farmer shoots it.

'I . . .' I rush up the stairs to the bathroom and muffle the sounds of my vomiting by running the taps. She shouts up the stairs a few minutes later.

'Are you OK, Laura? Only, I need to rush off. I've got to get to a case conference over in West Norwood and the traffic is carnage this time of day.'

I shout something back and she responds with a promise to return in a few days.

Although it feels more like a threat.

This is not what I need. If anyone will understand the things that Sadie might refer to then it's someone who was around back then.

Like Cathy.

Chapter Nine

THEN

March 1991

I'm paired with Cathy, who's glaring at me over the top of her glasses. My heart sank when the new tutor, a squat younger man with a reflective bald head, decided to *'mix things up a bit!'* by allocating us into groups. After Cathy, he sends Louise, followed by Nathan. Nathan's continued to stare at me and Sadie on and off. His eyes flicking from my breasts towards my face in a mechanical pattern, his legs never closed. He's a jarring intrusion of masculinity into this White Musk scented room, with its tabletops littered with gaudy stationery from WHSmith.

We've been asked to bring a toothbrush, some soap, a towel and a flannel. It couldn't feel more ominous if they suggested fencing and asked us to bring an epee and foil. My mortification is complete when we're sent to the lecture theatre where we're tasked with washing each other's arms and faces. The embarrassed chatter of the roomful of students reduces and there's an awkward silence between me and Louise as she wrings out a flannel and grips the sides of my head with an alarming amount of pressure.

'I'm sorry if I offended you when I—'

'How could you offend me? I think you're overestimating your own importance.'

The towel scratches as it's dragged across my cheeks, leaving behind an itchy slick of soap. I surrender to it until we swap roles, trying not to look at her face as I lather the soap onto her arms with a shaking hand, crushed by her wordlessness. Louise's eyes shoot round and I see her looking at Sadie, whose meaty upper arm is being dried by a mousy woman who I've never heard speak yet.

Louise's lips form a sneer. 'Beached whale.'

I gasp but I'm not fast enough to come up with a response. I see Sadie glance over at Louise and her cheeks redden beneath her porcelain foundation. She heard the comment about her weight.

'That's not very kind.' Louise smirks and crosses her arms, making sure that her engagement ring is facing out, the cheap H. Samuels jewels flashing in the overhead lights.

'Right, people. Now you know what it feels like to be on the receiving end of being washed by someone, I want you to try something. Swap partners and we're all going for a walk.' The tutor tries to maintain his air of jollity in spite of the obvious gloom emanating from us all. Louise gives him a side-eyed look and makes a tutting noise.

Cathy appears before me and I hear Nathan and Louise making small talk. Her uncharacteristic quietness disappears as she reanimates, laughing with him as he makes a remark that I don't quite hear. The tutor bounds around the lecture theatre, handing out lumpy inner soles for our shoes, glasses smeared with Vaseline and cotton wool for our ears. I'm first up. The ill-thought-out idea is for us to walk around the college and experience what it's like being elderly and frail, with poor eyesight, reduced hearing and a feeble gait.

'I don't feel safe.'

'You're fine.' Cathy's tone is brusque. She's the most vocal during lectures, eager and serious. The one who's always first to answer questions, adding her own astute observations with her arm ramrod stiff in the air as she bristles for recognition. The floor of the mezzanine corridor that skirts the atrium is like rubber under my feet as Cathy's arm guides my almost sightless form through the nursing college. Laughter rings in my muffled ears as pairs of students ricochet off walls. I hear Sadie's voice in the background but not the words. A vein of envy erupts in me as I wonder who she's talking to. It sounds like Amy.

That's when I lurch towards the floor. The space falls away around me. The floor is a smooth expanse of ugly nylon carpet rushing towards my face. I career onto my knees and let out a yell of pain and shock. My hands flap, catching at the top of the staircase, my heartbeat pounding in my ears. Sweat instantly beads on my brow.

The smeared glasses fall from my face and smash as they hit the stone steps below me. I yank the cotton wool out of my ears, sensing the presence of people around me.

'Clumsy.' It's Shazia leaning over me, Louise at her shoulder, her face emotionless. Her voice is singsong, mocking. 'You're lucky you didn't go down those stairs.'

The curved staircase leading down to the atrium is inches from my palm. Cathy helps me up, an exasperated look on her face. I didn't trip. I felt a hand on my back like I did on the road with Sadie. I was pushed again.

'Let's go back in.'

We walk to the classroom. Nathan is sitting on a desk, swinging his legs.

'Are you OK, Laura? I saw you fell over.' He looks genuinely concerned, like he's about to run over and perform a full body check for injuries.

'Someone pushed me!' Nathan makes to speak but Cathy beats him to it.

'You probably just tripped in the crowd of people stumbling around.' I'm about to sit when her hand grips my arm. 'But Laura, I do think that you should be careful.' Cathy lowers her voice to say this, so that no one else hears.

'Careful of what?' I wait for her to tell me what she thinks happened. That Louise or Shazia had deliberately tried to send me falling down the stairs. Nathan leans forward to listen in but she's lowered her voice further to almost a whisper.

'Of Sadie. There's something off about her. You shouldn't get too close.' I don't respond. It's a long wait for the others to start returning, the classroom silent except for the ticking of a clock.

She's wrong. Sadie was the one who saved me when she stopped the bus from hitting me. It's not Sadie who's the danger.

I know now that I was right about that word. I didn't imagine it, like I first thought I might have.

The person who whispered 'killer' in my ear the other day knows what happened to Jessica and wants to harm me.

And they're here in this group of students.

* * *

When we're at Laurel House I tell Sadie what happened on the stairs. I want to tell her the full story about what happened on the high street. But that word. I couldn't repeat it. There'd be too many questions that I don't want to answer.

'Young women can be spiteful.' She glazes over and I wonder if she's thinking about Louise making comments about her weight. I want to tell her that I understand. That I was picked on and belittled all through school and I know how it feels. I don't pity her. It's a feeling of solidarity. 'The best thing we can do is ignore it. They'll stop.'

I don't think this will stop. The other thing that I don't tell Sadie is that I'm weighing up my options. I'm thinking hard about whether to go back home. On the one hand, I need this job and the money will be helpful once I qualify. I can give some to Mum to help with the debts she's run up looking after Suzie. I need a career so much and switching training courses to another place is unlikely to be an option.

But on the other hand, it may be better to just leave and run to safety. I chose London to get away from the person I was seen as in the village but it obviously hasn't worked. Although if someone here wants revenge for what happened, then they could easily track me down wherever I go. It's not like there's anything concrete I can go to the police with.

There's no one to protect me and nowhere feels safe.

My choices are confusing.

There's a third option that I don't want to think about. That the incidents on the road and the stairs are all in my head and I'm losing my mind again.

I pull myself out of my reverie.

'I feel bad about abusing your hospitality.' The warmth

of the kitchen has loosened my limbs and I feel jellied. My body is more relaxed in spite of my racing thoughts. The release of the adrenaline from the almost fall has left my muscles feeling fluid and loose.

'Oh, nonsense. It's good to have someone else here. I eat too much anyway.' She waves a hand down her figure that's clad in a vintage maxidress with a hypnotic print design.

The house smells of beeswax and lemons and lines of fresh laundry catch my eye through the window. Afternoon sunlight catches on the scratched table, making it gleam. Sadie seems even more iridescent here, as if the environment enhances her.

'What do you think of Anthony? The pretty boy who always arrives late?' Sadie isn't looking at me but instead is feeding bits of sausage to Coco, who is standing on her back legs like a circus dog.

'He's arrogant.'

'Maybe he just comes across badly.' Sadie starts clearing the lunch things away.

'No, he was rude to me.'

I outline to Sadie how I'd dashed into the kitchen one night, trying to avoid Louise in the corridor. Treating microwaving an M&S lasagne like it was an urgent mission so that I could avoid talking to anyone.

'I didn't realise until I walked in there that Anthony was there, too, having an argument with a man.'

'Scandalous.' Sadie turns round from the sink and widens her eyes. She laughs but it doesn't feel like she's laughing at me.

'I was already at the fridge before I turned round and saw them and I was too embarrassed to walk away. So I brazened it out and put my food in the microwave, anyway.'

My fair skin had burned crimson as I wished there was a way of turning off my ears as the man spat bitter words at Anthony. 'The man was older and he was absolutely furious but Anthony barely reacted. The man stormed out in the end and I thought Anthony had left, too.'

'Mortifying. And how was your dinner?'

'You're teasing me. It was fine.' I'm blushing thinking about what happened but I laugh with Sadie in spite of my mortification.

'I agree that it sounds horrifically embarrassing.'

'That's not the worst thing. The man was shouting that he'd left his wife for Anthony and it sounded like Anthony wasn't impressed that he'd done that. And after it ended, I thought I was finally on my own in the kitchen but Anthony hadn't gone. He tapped me on the shoulder and asked me if I'd enjoyed the show.'

'How delightfully rude! He was utterly horrible to me today when we did that pathetic exercise. I find him hilarious.' Sadie pushes a cherry cake towards me with a questioning lift of her artfully pencilled eyebrows.

'I'm more interested in Amy. What do you think her story is?' I've started exploring the boundaries with Sadie and realised that there aren't many. She'll discuss any person, subject or part of her colourful history. Except for Sacha. Sacha is off limits. The most joyous thing about Sadie for me is that she doesn't ask many questions. She has no agenda with me. There are no awkward enquiries about my past. Sadie regales me with her fascinating stories and all that's needed from me is that I listen and ask the occasional astute question.

What she does ask me about is how I am. Whether I need more food, more coffee. Whether I'm hot or cold, happy or sad. The questions I'm not accustomed to being asked back home where Mum is always drained after work or worrying about my sister.

Sadie makes me feel like I'm her priority.

'I'm trying to work her out, still. What do you think?' Sadie scoops the dog to her chest and turns towards me.

'She's very thin. I wonder if she might have anorexia nervosa. Maybe that's why she was late, because she'd been having treatment.' Amy reminds me of some of the patients who were in the unit where I was held. Young women who were policed and kept on systems of punishment and reward, depending on their compliance with the dietary regimes. Like they were aberrant children, instead of grown women.

'She is very thin. Unlike me, as Louise so kindly pointed out.'

'But men like curves, don't they? You look great,' I stutter.

'In that case let's gorge on this cake in the sitting room. We've got forty minutes and the sofas are calling our names.'

I delight at the use of the word 'our'. As if Sadie and I are already inseparable.

There's another question that I haven't asked. I want to know if she likes Amy enough to want her as a friend.

Because the prospect of Sadie spending time with anyone else is like a blow to my stomach.

The natural order is that it should just be the two of us.

Chapter Ten

THEN

March 1991

Death finds us quickly. It's been waiting for us in the bricks of the hospital, hiding in the corridor walls, loitering in darkened side rooms. I'd managed to fool myself that death would allow us time to acclimatise but I was wrong.

We've completed eight weeks of basic theoretical training which consisted of ugly diagrams drawn on acetate slides, practical demonstrations and an overload of information that unspooled in my head like strewn bandages. Nothing bad has happened. No pushes or shoves, no whispered words, so I either did imagine it all or they've sated their desire to harm me. I'm resolute. I'm staying here in London.

I've avoided Louise and Shazia, only bumping into Jane, the least offensive of the three. She smiles at me from under her unruly fringe and nods, before creeping back out of the kitchen again. Anthony disappears from the nurses' home intermittently. I've listened at his door but there's nearly always silence. I go back and sit in my room, alone.

We're lined up for our first shift. A thin woman with flowing grey hair sails across the corridor past us, like a phantom, aiming for the door and letting out a wail when a sturdy care assistant ushers her back to her bed. We're shepherded into a cramped office in our polyester dresses, awkward paper hats pinned to our heads. I've been rostered with Jane, Amy and Cathy to work on a women's medical ward. It's a cavernous shed of a place with beds lined along the wall. The inhabitants start awakening in the dim light that filters through the windows and across the metal bedside lights that have been left on low throughout the night. Rustles and whistles mix with occasional groans. I take a deep breath and inhale a sickly air freshener that overlays something more primal.

'I'm absolutely terrified. Is that bad?' Jane's skin is the colour of an invalid's milk pudding.

'I think we should be scared, don't you? If we're too confident we might make mistakes.' Cathy doesn't look at all scared or underconfident. She looks ready to pounce.

Amy stares out of the window, watching a trail of swallows fly past. I occupy myself with the torn flyers on the corkboard. There's a handover by a sweaty-looking staff nurse with terrifying acronyms and obscure jargon that I fail to understand and medical conditions that I've never heard of. Amy and I are taken to one side by one of the kinder staff nurses.

'I'm sorry to do this to you two on your first day but there's a patient who needs laying out. The night staff ran out of time, apparently.' She allows her displeasure to show on her face. 'Will one of you help me?'

Amy looks passively back at her. I'm eager to prove that I can do this job, more to myself than to anyone else, so I volunteer. I follow her, stepping into the darkened room. It turns out that death is prosaic. No contorted features, monstrous grimaces or stretched out hands like in a crime thriller. It's mundane and tragic but it's also a task, something that needs addressing and tidying away. A person, to be treated respectfully, of course but ultimately, to be cleaned, wrapped in white cotton and sent away from us.

Death is something to get used to.

* * *

'Was it awful?' Amy is sitting across from me in the staff room that we share with the next ward. The bad clip art flyers blow in the breeze from the window that I opened in a vain attempt to counteract the oppressive heat that is leaving me dry mouthed and sweating.

'Was what awful?'

'The body. The woman in the bed next to me died while I was in hospital but I didn't see her. And the one after the one after her. She died too. I had to lie there and listen to the relatives crying. Not even my Walkman to listen to because my aunt had forgotten to bring me any new batteries.' I've noticed that Amy tends to do this. Her eyes open wider and she lets out bursts of commentary only to glaze over again shortly afterwards.

'She looked very old and emaciated.' I look across at Amy, who has little flesh on her either. 'I think she must have been ready to die. The saddest thing was putting her things away. Cards, glasses and talc, that sort of thing. That felt more personal.'

Amy rummages in her bag and pulls out a box of

sandwiches, along with a packet of biscuits. 'Want one? They're Fortnum's ones that my aunt left when she dropped me off.'

I shake my head. 'So you were in hospital? Are you OK now?'

'Thanks for asking. No one's acknowledged yet that I arrived here looking worse than half the patients. I'm like a dirty little secret: someone who's crossed over an invisible line from nurse to patient.'

'Do you think you'll be strong enough?' I check each word I speak, conscious that I might be asking too much. Thinking back to how the college asked me the same questions. Their insistence on a supportive letter from my psychiatrist and how frustrating that felt.

'I'm loads better. I had intravenous feeding in hospital for a while and it helped me put weight back on. But I'm eating again, so I'm doing OK now.' As if to demonstrate she takes a bite of sandwich and swallows. 'Some of the nurses I met were lovely but some of them were total arseholes. I hope we don't become the arsehole ones.'

'Who's an arsehole?' Nathan walks in, smiling at us both. The neck of his white tunic looks too tight, like the press studs might pop at any moment. He's carrying a ludicrously large lunchbox and a copy of *Viz* magazine under his arm.

'Maybe you. I haven't sussed you out yet.' Amy says this with a flat tone and he stops dead. 'The look on your bloody face. I'm joking, you idiot.'

The rest of the shift passes in a blur of sheets, counterpanes and bedpans. Aching feet and backs as we lift, wash, record temperatures. Jane drops a thermometer and holds back tears as she has to help an impatient ward sister chase the globules of toxic mercury around the floor with a syringe.

It's a time of mistakes for us all. Spilled urine, unrecorded observations, wrong words spoken.

When it ends it feels like only an hour or two has passed, when in fact it's now midafternoon. A glorious oblivion, a time slip that's stopped my perpetual ruminating and halted the flashing images that haunt me. As we leave the ward Sadie has just arrived for the afternoon shift. The uniform diminishes her. She's almost ordinary. Her make-up toned down, nails bare, hair tied neatly back. Even her posture looks wrong in the low-heeled shoes.

'Look at this.' She waggles her polish-free fingers at me and Amy.

'Oh, you have such long fingers.' Amy grasps Sadie's hand and scrutinises it, before letting go. 'I like them.'

I hold my breath as I watch the two of them.

'Thanks.' Sadie laughs, bemused. 'So, how was it? You both survived?'

I start to speak but Amy beats me to it. I study Sadie's reactions as she listens.

'It was great. Tiring but great. Laura had to lay out a dead body but it was OK, wasn't it?' Amy's voice is starting to slur slightly, her shoulders drooping. 'But you'll be fine, honestly, we'll all be fine.'

She reaches over and embraces Sadie and I wince. Her spindly arms stretched around Sadie's more substantial form. Sadie winks at me over her shoulder and I feel my muscles relax. Maybe this moment I'm waiting for won't happen. I won't be replaced or set aside like I so often have been in the past.

Sadie glides onto the ward and Amy and I stand in companionable silence, donning our coats. I put my hand in my pocket, to pull out my scarf. There's a stiff envelope, the sort that official letters come in, like the ones piled on the side in the ward sisters' office.

I pull it out. My name is written in crude capital letters. I hesitate before opening, curious at why someone would leave a letter in my pocket. My muscles tense. This doesn't feel like it'll be anything good. Amy turns to me.

'What is it, Laura?'

I hold the letter at arm's length, as if it's infected.

'What the hell?' Amy looks puzzled, her eyes squinting as if she can't quite work out why this exists.

The piece of paper inside says:
I'M WATCHING YOU

It's then that I notice Anthony standing just along the corridor, looking at us both. He's leaning back with one knee bent upwards and his foot against the wall.

'Did you see someone near my coat?'

He slowly cocks his head to one side. 'I'm not sure that I like your tone.'

'What do you mean by that? Did you see someone or not?'

'I feel like I'm under suspicion for something here. I've no idea what you think I've done but I'm not amused.' He looks like he's holding back a laugh.

I mutter a half-hearted apology and turn away.

I don't speak on the way back to my room. Amy walks beside me, offering a stream of consciousness of reassurance.

Chapter Eleven

THEN

March 1991

I peer across at Amy and Sadie. The half-light around a diminutive wax figure of Prince is shining on their faces, picking out Sadie's arched brows and Amy's hollowed cheeks. They're laughing together, cackling with glee as they stand in front of another indistinguishable facsimile. We're at Rock Circus, a tawdry Madame Tussauds offshoot, perched high over Piccadilly Circus. I look again at the two of them, waiting to see if they walk on ahead. If they've forgotten that I'm with them.

'Come on, Laura.' Sadie hooks her arm through mine.

It was Amy's idea to come here. The three of us were on shift together earlier, hustled into the back office with a strict edict from the staff nurse that we had twenty minutes precisely for lunch. It was ten-thirty. We're becoming expert at eating at random times. My reddened hands smelled of cheap soap, armpits and talc, in spite of me having washed them twice. I devoured my sandwiches regardless, instantly forgetting the sea of body fluids that I'd faced all morning as hunger banished squeamishness. Amy fired off a barrage of childlike questions at Sadie. Why did she dress like she did, how old was she, where was she from. How come she had a house. I sat back and watched her befriending my friend. My only friend. Amy's gaucheness and youth winning Sadie over. As they talked I imagined Amy in my place at Sadie's table or lounging in my spot on the sofa. I pushed away the images. My place as Sadie's friend is firmly cemented now. Sadie might talk to Amy on the wards but she hasn't invited her back to Laurel House, yet, whereas I've become a fixture. I visit most days and help Sadie with chores while she regales me with anecdotes. She cooks for me in return.

Before we'd finished eating, Sadie, incredulous that neither Amy nor I had ventured outside the local area since we arrived, came up with a plan. Like an indulgent mother offering a half-term treat, she tasked us with thinking where we'd always wanted to go. Amy's choice of the pop star waxworks won out over my suggestion of the Victoria and Albert Museum. Sadie cackled with laughter at the idea of us coming here.

'Are you OK, Laura?' Amy squeezes my hand and I make a conscious effort not to pull it away. I have no way of telling her without sounding deranged. She's the thing that's bothering me, not by her personality or behaviour, they seem innocuous enough. I'm disturbed by her very presence. I want Sadie to myself. I long to usher Amy out into the scrum of Piccadilly, with the incessant noise of the bongo players and the students sitting on the traffic island under the statue. Manhandle her towards the dark mouth of the tube station or through the doorway into Tower Records leaving just me and Sadie.

The café we go to appears to be made entirely of plastic. Sticky chairs and tables, laminated menus, the walls even seemed to be coated with some sort of wipe clean coating.

'Are you serious? That can't be true.' Amy's eyes widen as she stares at me in a way that suggests I'm an alien being.

'It is.' I've made the mistake of telling them that this is the first time I've ever been into central London.

'I know my way around. We could go exploring when our days off coincide.' Amy puts down her menu with its overpriced 'Italian' specialities. The waiter and staff are distinctly un-Italian and all have London accents.

'Thank you.' I force a smile as I run a forefinger down the menu. The idea of making an effort with anyone but Sadie feels overwhelming.

'Laura, I think I may just love you. You're just what I always needed. A naïve waif to teach about the world. Isn't she adorable, Amy? You both are. You two can be my protégées in this wicked city.' Sadie rests her elbows on the table and props her head between her hands, smiling at us both.

'Well, not everyone thinks she's so sweet. Certainly not the person who wrote the note the other day.' Amy starts eating her soggy French fries.

'Note?' Sadie raises her finely plucked brows. 'What note?'

I don't know why I've kept it but it's in my bag. I show it to Sadie, batting away the volley of suggestions from them both about going to the tutors or the police. Telling them that they're overreacting when they warn me to make sure that I don't walk back to the nurses' home alone.

'That's two notes now, after you found that one in the classroom. Do you know why someone would do this?' Sadie's brow crinkles, ageing her.

'That's the problem. I don't.'

The fact that Sadie is interested is good and bad. Her interest in me feels like a warm embrace but I'm having to lie.

Of course I know what this is about.

I just don't know who is doing this and what I can do to make myself safe again.

* * *

Sadie mentions it again the next day.

'So, I've thought about this and I have a list of likely candidates.' For a moment, I expect Sadie to pull an actual list out of her vast handbag, like a detective. She's flopped back in the wingback chair by the bay window, the dark-leaved bushes in Laurel House's narrow front garden pushing against the glass like voyeurs. Everything about her looks in context here. Her clothes, make-up and hair suit the backdrop. Sadie is different at home from how she is in college or the hospital. Her posture is looser and she's more still. It's like she feels she has to put a show on outside of this house but here she can breathe out and be genuine.

'Louise Turner, obviously. She's number one suspect. I mean, she takes up a lot of space and airtime that she doesn't deserve.' I stifle a laugh. Louise has made veiled comments again about Sadie, remarks that Sadie heard. The two of them circle each other like cats when they pass in the corridor, both recognising the potential dominance of the other.

'Then there's her acolytes, Jane and Shazia.'

'Jane is quite nice actually. I worked with her the other day.'

'Don't underestimate the power of friendship. Those two will do whatever Louise asks or whatever they think might please her. She's like a cult leader.'

The speculation feels like a parlour game in which I'm the player who's bluffing. I don't like lying to Sadie but if I told her the truth about my past and what happened to Jessica then things between us would change.

There is an opportunity here, though. I try something to gauge Sadie's thoughts. 'What about Amy? She's a bit odd, don't you think? It could be her.'

'Oh, not Amy. She's a sweetie. But I had thoughts about Nathan? He's a bit of a lech, isn't he? And men have done stranger things to get women's attention.'

'That's silly. Men don't tend to vie for my affections. And this would be a weird way to do it. It's more likely to be Anthony. He looks at me like I'm dirt on his shoe.'

Sadie laughs. 'Oh, hardly. He's so waspish that he'd say anything bad to your face.'

She sits back, as if she's pondering this mystery before sitting forward again and wagging a finger like Hercule Poirot about to deliver his drawing room dénouement. 'Or, and this is the total wild card. Cathy. You know, the one with the glasses. Miss Earnest. Potential Nurse of the Year.'

'I know who she is but . . . no. Just no.'

'Always watch out for the good girls.' Sadie sneers as she says this.

'Sadie, that's not fair. We don't know her yet. She might be really nice.' I haven't mentioned about her warning me that she thinks Sadie is dangerous.

Sadie draws a deep breath and pulls herself upright in the chair. She seems to be dressed as a fortune teller today with scarves and bangles exploding from her.

'I mean you're actually a bit of a good girl but I don't *think* that you're secretly wicked. Although, I think that you may have wanton potential!'

We make eye contact and hold it before we both start to laugh.

This unfamiliar intimacy feels like stepping into a warm bath but I can't remove the thought that Sadie doesn't really know me. That I can't let her in.

There's too much to say. Too much darkness that I can't burden anyone else with.

Chapter Twelve

NOW

Wednesday, 14 April 2010

I've been subconsciously checking my mood for dark patches, like anyone else might keep an eye on the weather outside their window. It's a fine balance between being aware and mindful and being obsessive and preoccupied. The last big episode knocked me off kilter for months. Pill changes, months of dragging my body around, using every shred of energy to pretend I was fine during the working day. Then collapsing into bed the moment I arrived home, hyperaware of every sound and movement in my vicinity. I try to catch the fluctuations so I can be prepared, to avoid triggers and use my knowledge and experience to ameliorate things. I can't ignore how anxious I feel, but I would feel like this, wouldn't I? I'm back here.

I find Elsie in the kitchen. She's listening to Radio 4. A man with a soothing voice is talking about earthquakes in China, deadly storms in India, volcanoes in Iceland. Reminders that there's still a world outside this house. She gets up and turns off the plasticky set. She's dressed more conventionally today. Indigo jeans with deep turn-ups and bare ankles over canvas shoes with a Breton top. 'Here. Sit down.' She pulls out a chair, offering to pour me some coffee like Sadie always did. 'Would you like me to make you some lunch?'

I shake my head.

'Oh, some nurse just rang.' I wait for Elsie to finish but it seems that that's all I'm getting.

'And what did they want?' I measure my words to stop them sounding frantic. It's like trying to hold back a shout when you bang yourself with something.

'She was called Cally or Cathy or something. She said she was coming back on Friday and she wanted to make sure you'd still be here.' Elsie puts down her coffee cup. 'She said she needs to see you. She sounded a bit of a weirdo to be honest. Do you know her?'

I make a noncommittal sound and breathe deeply through my nose. Elsie gives me a puzzled look then sits fiddling with the bracelet she's wearing.

I sit waiting, letting the fear wash over me before I try to drag myself back into the room. I need to be present for this girl. Communicating with sick people or their relatives is all about the right moments. Listening for the lulls, allowing them room to speak. I have a sense that Elsie is about to say something but it's taking her some thought and courage. I can guess what's coming. Years of experience have left me attuned to the signs.

'How do you think my mum's doing?' She starts off casual in tone, her inner workings only revealed by the slight bite of her lip on one side.

'I think that she's uncomfortable.' I choose my words

carefully. By 'uncomfortable' I mean intermittently screaming in pain as the tumour puts pressure on the adjacent structures and nerve endings in her abdomen. 'I suspect it's just a matter of adjusting her medications and finding the right regime for her. Pain can almost always be controlled.' I keep her expectations in a moderate place. There are always anomalies in medicine and I'll lose her trust if Sadie's pain proves intractable.

Businesslike is my starter with empathy as the main course. 'It must be distressing to see your mother like this.'

'I'm fine. This isn't about me.' A flash of annoyance crosses her face and I'm glad, relieved that she hasn't entirely shut herself down and that this glib act she presents is a shield against sorrow. 'I know I shouldn't ask this and that you won't answer me but . . .'

She fizzles out and I wait. I will answer her. I'm not some stuffy old school practitioner who hoards knowledge. She's owed my honest opinion.

'How long do you think she has? To live, I mean.'

'I'm glad that you asked.' She needs this validation. 'The only thing that I can do is guess, based on the information I have and my experience.'

It's there to see in the tinge of jaundice, the sunken cheeks, the hollow eyes. 'We try not to be too specific because there is no exact answer. I'd usually say someone had hours to days, or days to weeks, weeks to months or longer, even.'

I pause to let her process this concept. This is my territory. It's a sad consequence of working on a cancer treatment unit. People die and I deal with it. It's my job and I help them, in whatever way that I can.

'OK. And is Sadie going to die in hours?' There's a squeak of panic in her voice.

'My guess would be that it's weeks or less. Maybe days.'

She nods at me, her face impassive. She looks almost relieved as if knowing that there's an endpoint is consoling.

What I don't say is that I hope that it is quick for Elsie's sake.

And for mine. Given Sadie's fixation with the past and how much she's been rambling when she's high on her medications I may need to stay for the duration.

Or find a way to keep her quiet.

'Should I try ringing my father again? Not that he answers.'

'He's back tomorrow, isn't he?' Please let this be the case.

Elsie looks down and avoids my gaze.

'You said he was coming back tomorrow.'

She looks towards the kitchen window and her cheeks flush. When she turns back I can see from the set of her jaw that it's more frustration than embarrassment that's colouring her face.

'He's been a bit vague and he hasn't answered my texts.'

My stomach lurches. If he's not back then my choices are limited. Sadie needs an adult here with her all the time while she's delirious. Someone to supervise her medications and help when she's in pain. A proxy nurse, or even better, an experienced, qualified nurse. I'm trapped, even if she does stop speaking.

'He has to come back.' Elsie reacts to the vehemence of my words like she's been slapped but her eyes are defiant when she meets mine.

'What do you expect me to do? I'm not in charge of him.'

'OK.' I try to neutralise the situation. 'The specialist nurse is coming tomorrow, so maybe we'll ask them to call your father and update him. They can explain what the situation here is.'

I'm hoping that this nurse is someone efficient who can sort out this unholy mess, find a regime that stops Sadie from hallucinating and talking about things she shouldn't talk about.

My head jolts round at a noise on the stairs but there's no one there. This house was always vocal in its shifts and sighs.

The strange thing is that my first reaction was to expect Anthony or Amy to walk in. Or Sacha, even.

Which is all impossible, of course.

* * *

I try to get hold of Cathy but she's unreachable. The coordinator in the district nursing office refuses to give me her mobile number, as is correct, and Cathy doesn't call back in response to the message that I leave for her.

Sadie sleeps for most of the day and Elsie hides out in her room. I wander around listlessly, unsure whether I want to sit, stand or run into the garden and scream into the ether. In the evening Elsie and I play Yahtzee for a while. She wins every game.

'Has Sadie been talking much about when we were students?' I wait while she finishes totting up her score with a blunt pencil, my heartbeat resounding in my ears. 'Sometimes people in Sadie's situation like to talk about the past.'

'Fuck, yes. She talks about that more than anything.'

'What . . . what kind of stuff?'

'Oh, she talks about the sickly girl. She gets herself really worked up about that one like it was her fault. Which it wasn't, of course. Stuff happens, doesn't it?'

'Yes.' The showreel of intrusive images comes back into my head, along with the lurching feeling in my guts that always comes alongside it.

'And she talks about you.'

I feel a rush of joy. It's a Pavlovian reaction: joy if Sadie wanted me and misery if I felt rejected. But this feeling is tempered with something else. I push down the fingers of alarm that are scratching at my throat.

'You know that she's delirious? That she's on a lot of medication and she might say some odd things? People on strong medications say things that aren't true.' The opioids will work as a weak insurance policy but drugs can only excuse so much of what she says. She might be having confused episodes but they're bordered by periods of lucidity where it's obvious that she's rational.

'I know that.' Her tone is verging on sarcastic.

Elsie passes out new Yahtzee score sheets.

'I forgot to ask.' I affect a casual tone to hide my desperation to know the answer to this question. 'What's your father's name?'

The conversation is interrupted by a crash from the bedroom. Sadie must be awake. Elsie leaps up and then pauses, giving me a beseeching look that says that she wants me to go first.

* * *

'Oh my God. What are you doing here? I haven't seen you in ages.'

Sadie's face stretches into a forced smile. The kind of smile you might try to plaster onto your face through a migraine or childbirth. Her flesh has receded, allowing her teeth dominance and her lips look bloodless, almost albino without one of her signature lipsticks.

'I'm sorry about the state of the place. I've been a bit under the weather. I'll sort things out later. Are they looking after you?'

The bedside lamp is shattered on the floor. Bits of gaudy pottery scattered across the rug. I sense Elsie in the doorway and turn, tasking her with fetching a dustpan and looking for another lamp. Sick people's relatives feel so impotent. They like a task.

'I came to help you and Elsie because you're not well.'

She nods and her eyes blank out like she has no idea what I'm talking about.

'Come on. Let me sit you up.'

The heat of her body burns into my palms as I ease her sideways into a more sensible position.

'Here.' I administer more oxycodone. She swallows and turns her head to the side. Waving to someone, words forming before she realises that there's nothing there but the images of birds on the yellow wallpaper.

I'm concerned that Sadie might be reacting to her medications but I have no choice. Her pain overrides everything else. The important thing is to get that controlled while making sure that she's not overdoing it on the drugs.

I've checked her for signs of overdose. Her pupils are normal sized, not pinpoint as you'd expect if she'd taken too many morphine type drugs. There are other signs, though. Her hands are twitching from time to time, moving in jerks as if she's linked up to the dark recesses of the room and someone is pulling at strings. The hallucinations that she's having are classic too. Spiders and bugs swarming in the room, flitting before her eyes. Turning to speak to someone she's seen out of the corner of her eye, only for there to be no one there.

For now, I have no choice but to work around this. I can't tell which one of the drugs is poisoning her and which one is soothing her. It's guesswork without continued observation.

'It's so good to have you here, Laura. You've always been such a good friend.'

I resist the urge to hiss into her ear that I'm not her friend anymore.

That after it all happened she didn't reach out to me or answer my letters.

'Do you think this lamp will fit here?' Elsie hovers hesitantly by the bed, a rusted Anglepoise in her hands, her back straining against the weight of it.

'Elsie, have you met Laura? She's one of the best nurses you could ever meet.' Her words are honeyed but they sting. An ugly confirmation that the main reason I'm here isn't because she wants me for who I am. She wants what I can offer.

'Laura's not quite who she seems to be, though. She's witnessed a lot of bad things.' The look on her face is painfully familiar. Pure mischief.

'Whatever you're referring to, stop it. It's rude and you're making Laura uncomfortable.' Elsie sounds like the adult in the room here.

'It's OK. Laura knows what I mean.' Sadie stops speaking again and my shoulders fall in relief. 'Now you two. Would you mind leaving me to rest. I'll be down later.'

She closes her eyes and her breathing changes within a minute.

It takes longer for my heart rate to return to normal.

Chapter Thirteen

NOW

Wednesday, 14 April 2010

Elsie has retreated to her room again. I've no idea what she's doing. She's of an age where privacy is vital so I leave her alone. Or that's the reason I give myself for not entering the attic. I don't think I could walk up those steps if I tried.

I wait on the sitting room sofa, idly flicking through the TV channels but the room straight-jackets me. Tiny china dogs' eyes stare at me, these kitsch ornaments that I found so delightful and ironic in my twenties now obtrusive observers. The kitchen is warmer but the vintage chairs are hard on my sacrum. I listen for the impossible sounds of the invasive bass beat of Amy's house music filtering down. Her laughter seeping through the floors, the shouting matches between Sadie and Sacha, followed by noisy make-up sex. The gentle pad of Anthony's footsteps as he slithered into a room. There's nothing to hear other than the distant traffic from the high street.

Back in Derbyshire, I did a brief stint as a night nurse,

working in people's own homes. We'd gather in a damp-smelling office, littered with Post-its and tired inspirational quotations, where the office manager would allocate the patients. As one of the more experienced nurses I'd get the complex cases like the people with delirium or chronic symptoms. Broken bodies wracked with pain and wild-eyed people snatching at invisible demons. The drive to their houses was always the hardest part. That anticipation as my car cruised down blackened country lanes, navigating the terrain of Derbyshire, with its relentless scenic drama.

On arrival I'd be greeted by hand-wringing relatives: blank-eyed husbands, wives, partners, offspring. I'd soothe the sick by calmness, competence and using the arsenal of drugs that had been placed in their houses. Drawing up sedatives or analgesics in dim back bedrooms. Touching skin, holding hands, letting soft, subdued words fall from my lips in fusty bedrooms where the windows were rarely opened. So many dark houses and long nights, fighting off sleep as I sat by the bedsides of the dying.

Tonight I feel like I'm in that car, travelling over the hills and dales again. Anticipating chaos. Things are always worse in the dark especially when someone is dying.

Sadie's screams start up again and my feet flail on the staircase as I stumble on a loose carpet runner. She's sitting up in bed, her hair lank around her shoulders in the semi-darkness.

'Am I on shift today?' She's wincing in pain again. Even the act of speech seems to cause her discomfort. 'I think I might have a bug. Will you call them? I can't manage to get out of bed.'

'It's fine, Sadie. You're off today.'

My presence has made her even more fixated on the Nineties.

'Will you check on Coco? I don't think she's been out.' As if on cue Sophia runs in and trots around my legs, jumping up at the side of the bed. 'The garden will be fine but make sure you keep the front door and gate closed in case she runs out.'

She closes her eyes for a second but they flick back open, like one of those plastic dolls whose lids move with gravity. 'Where's my husband by the way?'

'He's away on business, according to Elsie. She thinks he's back in a day or so.'

'What business? He doesn't work. I need him now. There's something I have to talk to him about. I'm worried about Laura. Or Amy. One of them. Which one are you? I think the other one was just here, too.' She flexes her spindly legs and starts to climb out of the bed. I move to her side, ready to prevent a fall. 'Alex!'

Her voice is surprisingly strong with barely a waver.

'Who's Alex?' My retort is bullet fast.

'My husband, of course. No, hang on. I think that's wrong. It's not Alex, is it? My husband's name is Sacha. Or Anthony.'

These are names that make me want to scream. I hide my revulsion by flipping back to work mode, releasing a steady script of platitudes as I ease her legs into bed, pushing her hair back, arranging the pillows, giving her some cool water to drink. There's no point trying to get a straight answer here as to who Sadie's husband is. She's too delirious.

'Why not get some rest?' I can see that the analgesia is kicking in. Her facial muscles have relaxed and her shoulders have dropped back down. 'I'm sleeping across the hall unless you want me to stay in here.'

She ignores my comment.

'It was fun, wasn't it?'

'Our training. Yes. It was.' It was rarely 'fun'. Satisfying, absorbing, challenging sometimes. But also painful, mortifying and strewn with tragedy. Blood soaked and littered with suffering. Ending in death.

But Sadie can believe anything she wants tonight.

'That. But I meant us. The way we were. The things you did for me. The sacrifices you made.' She squeezes my hand and her eyes lock with mine. We both understand what she means. 'I should have thanked you for what you did for me . . .'

'There's no need.' My words are steady but the inside of my body is a void filled with nothing but the sound of me yelling 'No.'

There's an inevitability to this.

Sadie is going to keep talking about the past.

'All these years and you haven't said anything to anyone, have you? You've kept what I did quiet. I'd have got into so much trouble.'

There's something childlike and naïve about her tone. I flail for something, anything to say to stop her continuing. This talk that could strip me of my career and shame my family. All of the hard-won dignity and respect that I've gained gone in an instant and me, a scandal again.

'Well, I owe you, Sadie. You took me in when things were difficult.' She smiles at me and snatches at my hand and I let her. 'I can't thank you enough for that.'

I eye the sedatives that are neatly stacked on the dressing table.

They may be necessary soon.

Chapter Fourteen

THEN

April 1991

The day begins with blood. I'm working with Jane and Anthony. The shift so far has been peppered with lots of sighing and eye rolling from the staff nurses as they shoot down the ward like ball bearings in a pinball machine. The word 'busy' never far from their lips. I'm frayed by sleeplessness. The woman in the next room at the nurses' home cried all night. The sound of her sobs reverberated through the thin walls. I thought about knocking on her door but I had no idea what to say. Had it been a patient crying, I'd have marched up to her, emboldened by my uniform and status, ready to offer comfort and kindness.

The ward opens up before me like a fever dream, each bed containing a form draped in sheets with the shrouded figures forming an alleyway. The perpetual shout of *'Nurse!'* haunts my dreams. The person shouting this time is a middle-aged woman who was admitted the day before. She has issues with alcohol, consuming three bottles of wine a day. Her skin is yellow with a greenish tinge and her eyes are cat-like, amber irises surrounded by mustard-coloured sclera. Her upper chest is exposed by the dip in the front of a nylon negligee and is covered with broken blood vessels that look like a crawling mass of red spiders.

'Nurse. I need you. I've been sick.' I rush over, not running. We never run. It's forbidden. A pool of blood sits by her bedside, congealing into clots that look like clumps of chopped liver. Streaks of crimson stain the white sheets.

'I . . . I'd better get the staff nurse.' It's too late. A volley of blood bursts from her mouth with a sound like something ripping open, drenching the front of my dress. She sits forward on the edge of the bed, groaning, before another spurt of blood shoots out of her mouth. I reach across the bed for the emergency bell, my lace-up shoe slipping in the slick of blood. My legs slide from beneath me. My knee hits the blood-soaked floor with a sickening crack.

Anthony spots me, looking at me with horror before yelling for help then turning to the patient and taking her blood pressure. The staff nurses arrive and one of them scurries away to page the doctor. I stand back, frozen like one of those waxworks in Rock Circus. The blood seeps through to my skin, my dress already stiffening on my chest. My knees burn where they hit the floor.

I feel an arm looping through mine and there's a gentle pressure as someone squeezes my hand. I look around, dazed, to see Jane. 'Come on. I'll sort you out. I have a spare dress.'

'But . . .' I point at the three nurses and Anthony, then look round at the two doctors dashing towards the bedside.

'I think they'll manage just fine without us.' I follow her and tolerate the indignity as she helps me ease the blood-soaked fabric away from my skin.

* * *

The woman dies but not straight away. They take her to the operating theatre and try to stop the bleeding, which works for a short time. One of the swollen blood vessels in her throat had popped, flooding her gullet with blood, sending it pouring from her body, a consequence of severe liver disease. She's not the only one who died today. There were two elderly women, too. One peacefully and one after a thrashing bout of delirium where she shouted about an air raid. The nurse sedated her and tasked me with sitting by her side to soothe her. I gently stroked the puckered skin on her face and ran my fingers along her forearm. She reached across and squeezed my hand before she slipped into unconsciousness.

This is the first day I've felt glad that the shift has ended and I can leave.

I open the door to my room in the nurses' home.

The red is dazzling. Like stepping into a velvet lined jewellery box.

I become inanimate again, like I was on the ward. My arms drop by my side.

There are sprays of dried blood arced across my walls. It's daubed on the bedding, smeared across the carpet. It settles in puddles on the surface of the battered desk, dripping down the legs and forming thick clots. The only thing not ruined is my pile of paperback books and my clothes.

I step backwards into the corridor and bump straight into Anthony.

'Watch where you're going.' I see his eyes gape open as he spots the room behind me. 'What the fuck!'

His head swivels down and I realise that he's checking

my arms for cuts, making sure that this isn't my own arterial blood that has spurted onto the walls in a frenzy of self-harm. He takes a tentative step into my room, scanning around, firing off questions about what's happened. The colour has drained from his face.

I stand there, mostly soundless.

'Do you have anywhere you can stay?'

'I don't know.' My voice is feeble, childlike.

'You can't stay in that room, Laura. There must be someone. How about that older woman you hang out with. Sadie? Could you stay with her?' I didn't know that he even knew our names.

Anthony leads me to his room which is immaculate with everything lined up in neat rows and piles. It smells fresh, like new soap when you first take the wrapper off. I sit on the navy bedspread and wait while he runs down to the payphone and calls Sadie for me. He rings the college, too. Then he gets an empty Next bag and collects some of my things that aren't soaked in blood. He walks me to the main road and I splutter out an inadequate thank you for everything he's done, which he doesn't acknowledge. I offer him money for the payphone calls and he takes it without a word.

'You'll be fine.' His hand moves forward like he's about to touch my arm but he stops himself, as if the thought of it is too distasteful.

* * *

When I arrive at Sadie's she answers the door in a pink silk dressing gown. Her face is scrubbed clean of make-up and she smells like Yardley's talcum powder. I blurt out an explanation of sorts. My words jumble together as they fly from my mouth.

'You're here now, darling. You're safe.' The honeyed tones of her voice are soothing. I feel like I imagine a child basking in the attention of a loving parent would. She takes my hand and leads me up to the bathroom, guiding me towards a wicker chair under the window. She chats while applying layers of make-up in the mirror, the hot water running into the bathtub.

'You can stay here with me, Laura.'

She leaves me to bathe in privacy. No one interrupts me as I lay back in the scented water. No other students knocking at the door to ask, with tetchy voices how long I'll be.

I'm finally home.

Chapter Fifteen

THEN

May 1991

The room I stayed in that first night is now my room. Sadie's insisted that I stay on, saying that she's bored of living alone while Sacha is 'working away'. This place is like nowhere I've ever lived. Not that I've lived in many places, just our poky flat and my boarding school. This is miles away from living over a corner shop or sleeping in a dorm with a group of hostile girls.

Sadie batted my suggestions away when we discussed payment. She's insisted on taking only the capped amount that I was paying for the nurses' home. This means that I can carry on sending small amounts of money back to Mum each month.

Sadie is fiercely protective of this place. Much like the nurses' home, Laurel House has rules but they're not hard to follow.
1. *No visitors*. That won't be a problem for me.
2. *Always close the front gate.* She's paranoid about Coco

running onto the road. It's a senseless worry as the street is a dead end and largely traffic free.

3. ***No alcohol in the house.*** Sadie imparted this in passing, as if she was trying to evade questions about this final rule.

Perhaps she's had issues with drink, although I can't imagine it. I'm planning to find out but I just need to find the right moment to ask. It will come. Our friendship is going to strengthen. We'll share things and maybe one day I'll even tell her about Jessica. I think that she'd understand.

I've been here a few weeks and there's been little mention of Sacha. There are traces of his presence. I've gone through all the rooms. A near empty bottle of aftershave in the bathroom cabinet, his guitar propped up in an empty room, a section of Sadie's wardrobe devoted to his clothes. Garments which give off an earthy smell that lurks in their bedroom, almost but not quite overpowered by Sadie's sweet perfumes.

Sadie's body language changes if his name is mentioned. A subtle raising of her shoulders and clenching of her jaw. I'm conflicted. I don't want to ignore her distress. If she needs to talk then I want to be here. But equally I don't want to risk my position as houseguest by upsetting her.

There are traces of someone else, too. In one of the drawers in my room there's an Hermès scarf crumpled up at the back. Like it's been pushed to the rear of the drawer and missed when someone emptied it out. There are some mildewed books on the window ledge. Highbrow stuff like Iris Murdoch and John Fowles. There's a name written inside the front cover of each book. Portia McKenzie. My predecessor. I heard her name again when I went on an errand last week to the pet shop on the high street to pick up Coco's specialist dog food order. The shop owner beamed at me when I walked in, welcoming me back and asking where I'd been. It took a few excruciating minutes before I realised that she thought I was Portia.

* * *

We're in the kitchen and Sadie mentions again how awful it must have been for me living in 'one of those tiny little rooms' at the nurses' home.

I take an effortful breath. 'Will you want me to go back there once Sacha comes home? I will, of course if you need me to.' I pretend to busy myself, pouring a drink from yet another elaborately decorated coffee pot.

'Oh, Laura.' Sadie stifles a laugh. 'You are funny. Why would I need you to go anywhere? This can be your home for as long as you need it. I love having people around me. Although, if you're still here buttering toast across from me when the new millennium starts then we might have to rethink.'

We sit in silence for a few minutes. Sadie not eating, instead pouring cup after cup of coffee and spooning in copious amounts of sugar. She walks over to the kitchen unit and opens one of the canary-yellow drawers, ramming it shut with a couple of sharp swings of her hip. It's a drawer that confounds me. Sadie seems to have the knack of bypassing its truculent stiffness. She knows every quirk and foible of the house, like it's her own flesh.

'I shouldn't do this.' She stands at the open back door and lights a long pastel-pink cigarette. 'But every time I think about Sacha I want to smoke.'

I watch her hand glide up to her mouth. She tilts her head

back and lets out a stream of smoke. Sadie doesn't smoke like everyone else does. It has theatre and colour when she does it. I sit back and nod, trying to look sage, as if I have a deep understanding of men and relationships.

'It's been tense with Sacha but I miss him when he's not here.' She takes another drag on the cigarette then holds it up and scrutinises it. 'I used to be able to blow smoke rings but I seem to have lost the knack.'

'Why is he working away?' I know the answer is that he's in prison but I have to play along.

'I told a little white lie, Laura. Can you forgive me? I didn't want to weigh you down with our sorry tale. Sacha has some . . . problems. Tedious little issues with drink and drugs and sleeping with other women. Sleeping with anyone and everything, actually, my former best friend, Portia, included. That's when things got messy between us all.' Coco flies back in from the garden and jumps up at her back legs. I'm learning to tolerate how spoiled the dog is when Sadie is around. 'Oh, Coco. *You'd* never let me down, would you?'

Sadie turns around. Her eyes are damp with prospective tears which don't end up falling. 'He's not a bad person. He's just made some bad choices. There's a distinction. People's actions don't always define them.'

I nod. I'll share with her later about my sister's 'bad choices'. Although, watching her over the years it's never seemed like choice was involved but more of a sad and desperate compulsion. I don't want to interrupt Sadie's narrative, though, and make it all about me.

'He had a lot of things happen at once. He lost his job and the band he was in split up. He plays bass guitar.' Of course he was in a band. This fits my mental image of him.

'And that's when he started drinking more. God, it's a boring story of him saying he'll be better, then breaking his promises.'

I focus hard on what Sadie's saying and push away the memories of smashed crockery, tears and desperation.

Sadie sits back down, bringing with her a distinctive smell of rich tobacco from her Russian cigarettes. 'Something was always going to give one day and it did. He had a fight with Portia. My best friend who he'd been sleeping with behind my back. He slammed her head against the glass of the door there and on the wall. She was in hospital in a coma for a while. Poor girl.'

She pauses as if waiting for me to look horrified, to gasp perhaps but I don't.

'Portia's boyfriend, Seb, made her press charges and that's when it all went wrong. Sacha ended up in prison.'

'I'm sorry to hear that.' I tentatively offer this platitude, searching for something else constructive to say.

'He's an absolute sweetheart when he's sober. It was only the drink that made him violent.'

I lose the battle to stay in the moment. My eyes glaze over and a showreel of events runs through my mind. My sister launching herself at my mum, the theft of my cassette player, the time she smashed up the flat. I can empathise with Sadie about a Sacha. What I can't understand is how blasé she is about him bedding her best friend. The rest of her story, her ennui around his drinking, the casual way she's tried to pass off his imprisonment, pale in comparison. I'm brimming with curiosity about my predecessor. The best friend before me and her betrayal of Sadie. I'm a much better replacement.

'Do you think your relationship will survive this?'

'Oh, I've no doubt that it will. He's always supported me and it's my turn to support him. That's how relationships work.' There's something bright and shiny about her answer, like she really believes this is all going to be fine. 'Wait till you meet him. He's gorgeous. I don't just mean his looks. Let me grab some photos and I'll show you.'

She moves to the drawers and takes out an album. I don't tell her that I've already spent time studying them and am familiar with exactly how Sacha looks. I've wasted no time in sifting through the house, so that I can learn everything I need to know about my new friend. Sacha's black hair and dark eyes are etched on my mind. The evolution of him from sulky teenager to the sullen man that's shown in the pages of the photo album. Sadie always beside him, often clinging to his arm. Some of the photos are torn in two. As if someone has methodically worked through them and erased a person. Another one has a woman's body, standing next to Sadie with her arm round her. They look like they're on the seafront in Brighton but the woman's face has been neatly cut away.

'I shouldn't talk too much about him and colour your judgement. You'll be smitten once you meet him. Everyone is.' Sadie's movements are quick and erratic with excitability as she speaks. 'He was due to go into a residential therapy unit. His parents paid a deposit on a place in Sussex but he went out on a final binge and that's when it all happened. He would have sorted himself out again, otherwise. I'm sure of it.'

My fists clench as I think about how much easier it might be for Suzie if we could afford a rehab place. She's been on waiting lists for years.

'He's not due out yet, by the way. You have leeway before our fireworks begin again.' She laughs and I pretend to laugh back.

* * *

I found out this morning that the crying woman in the next room to me in the nurses' home has been found dead. The rumour is that it was suicide. I can't and won't think about it. My brain is blissfully occupied now. Each day the insane hustle of the wards consumes me, devouring time. Even so, it's a wrench to leave Laurel House. My room here is perfect, like something out of a vintage British film. I have an exquisite view over the long garden, a brass bed that I can stretch out on, watching the sunlight that lazes across the wooden floor. I haven't changed anything. My meagre belongings take up little space.

The fuss had died down now about the blood in my room but for a time it was all that anyone was talking about. I'm waiting for a cruel nickname to emerge. Bloody Laura, perhaps, or something worse. Teenage girls and young women can be cruel. I know that from bitter experience. I had to go to see the head of the college, a middle-aged man with tiny hands who grilled me about what had happened like I'm a suspect in a police drama. Our lead tutor, a pink woman called Siobhan, sat in. I half expected her to reach across and press a button to start taping the interview. I watched the questions fly from the head tutor's thin lips.

Have I fallen out with anyone?

Do I know why anyone might do this?

Have I seen anyone behaving oddly?

I kept my hands tensed in my lap so they couldn't see my tremor. Their final conclusion was that another student had intended to play a harmless prank on me by stealing a bag of blood but had gone too far. The conclusion is that they won't involve the police.

Their final half-hearted comment was: 'We are a little concerned about you, given your . . . history.'

I reassured them and this time I wasn't lying. I'll be fine. I have Sadie to help me.

There was an announcement in class by the tutor. A stern jumble of words about 'appropriate behaviour.' Her eyes carefully diverted away from my seat throughout. Then we moved on to the peristaltic actions of the gut.

I didn't tell the tutors about the notes or the pushing. I'm hopeful that now I've moved out of the nurses' home it will all stop. I'm out of sight at Laurel House.

I'm hoping that it'll be safer here with Sadie.

* * *

The surgical ward is more orderly than the last ward and there's an essential difference: the patients are all men. I'm working with Anthony and Amy and a student nurse called Ramona who's older, a mother with three teenage sons. I feel faceless and nameless. I'm part of a machine, a joyous, anonymous cog with no function other than to serve. I follow the rules, do what I'm told and concentrate hard.

'Let's do this.' Amy winks at me as she fills the plastic bowl with lukewarm water. 'This' is washing someone of thirty-five who had surgery yesterday. An audacious man with gold sovereign rings, reeking of cheap aftershave and past conquests. The sort of person who thinks nurses are something from a 'Carry On' film and that we like having comments made about our *'great tits'*.

Amy is my saviour. She's the right person to dispel my sense of embarrassment and ease any aura of sexual threat. I pull the rattly curtain around the bed.

'Hi Gary. It's Amy. How are you?' He reaches across and scrabbles for the button to the machine that delivers metered doses of soporific morphine. His thumb presses frantically like he's playing a game in an arcade.

'I'm good, ladies. All good.' He doesn't look good. He looks grizzled and vanquished, most of the vigour and bravado gone.

'Me and Laura are going to help you have a wash.' He lifts one eyebrow and smirks, his mouth opening to speak. 'Don't even think about making any saucy remarks. And I'm giving you the flannel to wash your own genitals while me and Laura turn our backs, OK?'

'All right, Miss. Whatever you say, Miss.' His accompanying wink is disturbing. 'Sure you don't want a look?'

Amy rings out a flannel, eases his gown away and starts soaping his chest and armpits. I wait, ready to dab away the water with a towel.

'Right, let's just wash around this. It doesn't look like we need to change the bag yet. We can just empty it in a minute and—'

'Yeah, let's not talk about that, hey?'

He has a colostomy, an emergency surgical intervention to rest his gut that's become inflamed due to Crohn's disease. Another day and he'll be more capable, no longer in need of us. The strange bond of helpless patient and helpful nurse will be outgrown and we'll realign our relationship.

'Shall I empty this now?' He nods and closes his eyes as my gloved hands move towards the base of the stoma bag.

'That fucking stinks.' His face disfigures with disgust. It's only when I've finished opening the bag that I realise that it isn't revulsion contorting his face. He's crying.

'Here. You'll get through this. This is the worst bit. It gets better.' Amy holds his hand. Mine remain at my side.

'How the fuck would you know? Some fucking kid nurse who thinks the world is all happy. Well guess what, love. Sometimes the world is a bag of shite. Literally.'

Amy sprays the air neutraliser again. She places it on the crowded locker top and moves her hand to the top of the zip on the checked polyester dress.

'Do you want me to show you something, Gary?' I stand frozen, wondering whether to grab her by the wrist and stop her.

'Here.' She stands with her dress unzipped to the waist and points to a network of angry scars on her abdomen. 'I've got Crohn's too. I was diagnosed when I was thirteen. I had to have a de-functioning colostomy last year. So I do get it. It's shit. But it's also being alive, isn't it? If that's what we need to do then we need to do it. Now, do you need anything else before we go?'

It's like watching a mask being donned as the vulnerability retreats and he flips back to his usual persona. His face returns to his previous perpetual half-smirk.

'I suppose a kiss is out of the question? I couldn't help noticing that you've got amazing tits, darlin'.' He moves his hand up to scratch his right cheek, wedding ring flashing in the strip lighting.

'And you can also fuck off.' Amy laughs and pulls back the curtains.

* * *

'Why didn't you tell us how ill you'd been?' I spear a piece of tomato. We've given up on the hospital food. By the time we've run to the canteen and bought lunch it's time to run back. Our break system is a recipe for gastritis.

'I thought it was obvious. And nobody's ever asked me for details, even though I looked like a corpse when I arrived. It felt weird to come out and say "Hey, people. I've just spent two months in hospital, half-dead."' She looks smaller somehow as she says this, childlike, even.

'Was it awful?'

'Kind of how you'd expect. My parents are away a lot. My dad works with a chemical company and they send him all around the world. Mum just tags along. We'd been living in Italy for a while, so I didn't have any friends or family to visit, except my aunt.' I understand this. The voids that a person can find themselves contained in.

Her face has a much better colour now than when she first arrived and her cheeks are starting to fill out. 'Are you completely better now?'

'I'll never be better.' She sounds like this is something she's had to recite often. 'Sorry, that sounded blunt, didn't it? I mean that there's no cure. It comes and goes. It's that kind of illness.'

'I thought you had anorexia nervosa or bulimia.'

She pauses, holding her sandwich midway between her lap and her mouth. 'No way! You are so funny. Why didn't you just ask me?'

I'm as guilty as my mum and sister and the people in the village. No one asked me a thing when I came out of hospital. Conversations were forced with people stepping around me like I was an unexploded mine. My mental health a distasteful scar. There'd been reporting, of course: tawdry newspaper accounts of the inquest, coy mentions of me being hospitalised and my mutism. The story of a schoolmistress dismissed for ignoring the plea for help from Jessica the week before it happened. Reductive and sensationalist descriptions of the decision that my friend and I had agonised over for months. The choice that left one of us dead: diminished to a few lines of print.

Amy interrupts my reverie with a question. 'Are you enjoying life at Sadie's? Is her house as amazing as her clothes?'

I don't need to think before answering. I smile and say it's great. I could tell her about the long evenings where Sadie and I sit watching black and white films. Or how we read, Sadie lounging back on the sofa, her feet resting on my lap, listening to unfamiliar 1950s music on her record player. Sadie showed me some dance steps and we occasionally waltz round the sitting room, till we have to stop because we're laughing so much. I could explain how it's like living in a time warp but with technology, modern medicine and no wartime rationing. Like we're both characters in an old film, living in harmony. It's an absorbing charade much like being a nurse in this hospital is with its costumes, mid-century hierarchy and arcane rules.

But my answer to Amy has to be measured. I don't want her thinking she can muscle in. I still have no plans to share Sadie.

'Oh, we're like two boring middle-aged women. You'd hate it. It's very quiet. But what about you? How are you finding it here?'

'The nurses' home is OK, really, because I've got people around me. I've been chatting to Anthony and there's some second years on my corridor who've invited me out clubbing.'

Anthony. He's like this shadow that's always there. We

haven't spoken again since the night of the blood. He's blanking me in the corridors and on the ward as if I'm invisible or not worthy of his gaze. I banish the thought of him and listen to Amy, enjoying her easy chatter. She moves on to regaling me with a long saga about a porter who she fancies. Apparently she already kissed two other porters in the pub so is worried that this might cause complications. She still fluctuates between this garrulousness and the brooding silences when it's like she's behind glass, her face drained of colour.

I'm not going to tell Sadie what Amy's told me today. If Sadie knows her story she'll be more likely to want to take her in and nurture her. She'll find out in time, of course, but my position at Laurel House will be stronger by then.

It's when I open my locker at the end of the shift that I find the next letter.

The smell hits me first. The odour taints my folded clothes, seeping into the fabric of my tote bag.

It's more of the same. A vague threat.

One word scrawled in capital letters. REVENGE TIME.

The writing is messier this time.

But then faeces would be messy to write with, wouldn't it?

The stench persists long after I run to the nearest bin and throw away the paper. Long after the third and fourth time I wash my hands. After I've wiped the vomit from my mouth.

It lingers in my nose well into the evening.

Chapter Sixteen

NOW

Thursday, 15 April 2010

I'm not immune to odours. I'm just good at pretending that I am, even when the raft of vile smells that emanate from bodily waste feel like a slap in my face. Nurses have to be consummate performers.

I spend an hour tending to Sadie. Pushing down my embarrassment at touching her skin as I help her to wash herself. Using my well-honed skills to pretend that nothing revolts me, spraying her with liberal amounts of her favourite Chanel No. 5 perfume.

Sadie looks dazed this morning. She doesn't speak much, apart from to ask me to give her more pain relief. Her silence is calming. Maybe my fears about what she'll say and what this might mean I need to do are unfounded.

'How about some Nina Simone while we work?' There's a whole genre of music that has sent me lurching for the off switch since I lived here. Sadie's mournful women singers and Amy's house music tunes evoke too many memories but I'm reliving these memories now by being here. I put the record on the turntable for her and the usual panic I feel doesn't kick in with the music.

I leave Sadie propped up on pillows, dozing. Elsie is waiting for me in the kitchen.

'He's not coming back.' Elsie's voice is a monotone. I can't see her face. She's bent over the cooker, stirring a pan of something yellowed which I think might be tofu.

'Who's not coming back?' My eyes feel gritty and unfocused after two more visits to Sadie in the night. My mind is fragmented and jagged. I glance over at the pile of medical paperwork, preparing myself for the palliative care team arriving later.

'My father. He's not coming back.' Elsie slams the pan onto a trivet on the side. 'He's stuck.'

The room closes in on me. 'But I need him to be back here. I can't stay indefinitely. He has to—'

'So, no concern about Sadie being left in pain while she's dying. Or me. It's just about Laura, is it?'

'That's unfair.' I feel middle-aged talking in this tone to Elsie, like when I have to reproach the younger nurses on the ward. 'I'm doing everything I can to try to sort things out here.'

She doesn't look at me. Instead goes back to stirring the tofu.

'What do you mean by "*stuck*" anyway? As in he can't get away from work?'

'I mean trapped. Literally trapped. Everyone's trapped.' She walks across to the radio and flicks the dial. I get my answer instantly. The newsreader is talking about a volcano in Iceland that's left a cloud of ash floating in the air, choking the atmosphere and shrouding Europe, grounding planes, creating mayhem at airports. No one can travel. Holidays are cancelled leaving people stranded in lukewarm European resorts, their off-season breaks turning into an aimless void of time. There are no flights in Europe. Wherever he is, he's not coming back in the next few days.

I'm as trapped as those travellers are. Laurel House has closed in around me.

'Hopefully he'll find a way.'

'You don't know my father. He's usually more concerned with finding ways to escape. He didn't exactly sound worried when he rang me this morning. He'll be propping up a bar somewhere. Or propping up a series of his fucking Chivas Regal bottles in his hotel room with an invited guest.' She hands me a plate of singed tofu and a piece of anaemic toast as she says this.

The plate almost slips from my hand. *Chivas Regal*. That drink that he always drank. I suppress a shudder and go to the sink, washing my hands, interlacing each finger, rubbing the palms together in a mass of soap bubbles.

'Like Sadie.'

'Sorry?' I turn my head.

'You wash your hands in that mad thorough way like Sadie. I guess it's a nurse thing.' She dismisses the observation with a wave of her hand.

We face each other at the kitchen table. The lurid patterns on Sadie's 'ironic' vintage plates remain covered as neither of us eat much. Elsie stares blankly out of the window.

'I think the priority for today is to try to address some of the problems that your mother has. Like the pain and the hallucinations.' I stop pretending I'm going to eat and put the fork down. 'The medications aren't suiting her so it'll be good to get her seen by someone. I've made a list and I've gathered the medications up so I can go through them with her team.'

She doesn't answer me. It's only eight so it's a few hours till they said they'd arrive.

Those two words continue to echo around my brain: Chivas Regal. I've only ever met one person who drank that brand of whisky.

Sacha.

And Sacha can't be the man who we're waiting for. It's impossible for him to be Elsie's father or Sadie's husband.

I still can't make myself ask the questions. The possible answers feel too daunting.

There's a tiny shard of something rising in me and I'm unsure if it's hope or rage.

* * *

Tom, the palliative care nurse, isn't what I expected. He looks like he should be a blacksmith or a carpenter. He's around my age, broad and hairy, his legs squeezed into knee-length shorts. There's a woman with him. I know the type well: a doctor in her thirties who was probably captain of the debating team at her minor public school. She could be any one of the many bullies I endured throughout the years. Tom grins through his beard, a wide beam revealing crooked teeth. When he shakes my hand it feels like my metacarpals will snap. For a moment I think that he's going to draw me into a bear hug and that I'll be unable to do anything but yield. Emily, the doctor, stands back, smoothing down her dress.

'Shall we go up? We know the way.'

'I'll come too. Sadie's been delirious and she won't be able to tell you everything that's happened.'

Or rather, I need to be there because Sadie might need censoring.

She's awake when we enter, sitting up in bed with an open make-up bag in front of her. Lipsticks, concealers and eyeshadow palettes are spilling out, marking the sheet. Her face is obscured by a hand mirror. When she rests it down I see that her face is immaculate. The old Sadie with the cat-eye flicks and the lurid red lipstick. There isn't a smudge or a deviation. I suppose it's something she's done so often that it's muscle memory.

I stand and wait like a prison warder.

'Hey, Sadie. How's it going?' Tom slides round me and sits himself on the side of the bed which is a breach of infection control rules. I spot a hint of the subtle lip curl that Sadie does when she's irritated by something or someone. A vague twisting of her mouth that you wouldn't necessarily clock if you didn't know her.

'I'm just trying to get ready to go out, actually, so if you want to come back later, then that would be great.'

I'm relieved to see that Sadie's hand still has the faint jerking that's characteristic of opioid toxicity and that there's something for Tom and Emily to see and be guided by. Emily steps forward and introduces herself. Sadie adopts a fixed grin but the disdain remains on her face.

'We're all fine and my husband is back today. Isn't he, Laura? Sacha is coming back. We won't need you to come here again.' She looks across at me. 'Don't look at me like that, Laura. I know you're not his number one fan but he'll be on his best behaviour.'

'I thought that your husband was called . . .' Emily scrabbles for the name and I hold my breath but she doesn't finish her sentence.

'Laura is a nurse. I'm a nurse. So we don't really need anyone. But thank you, anyway.' The effort of her annoyance creases her face and she succumbs to the pillows, flopping her head back and closing her eyes.

Tom is surprisingly agile in his approach, appeasing her in a couple of quick sentences. They ask the usual questions, slipping them in slyly at first. Making a joke of the more frustrating ones like 'Where are you? What's the year? Who's the Prime Minister.' Sadie's exasperated answers show that she thinks it's 1993 and that the Prime Minister is John Major. The 'where' bit is the easy one. Her head has always been here in Laurel House.

It's obvious why she's wedged so firmly in that year. It's not like it isn't the time that my mind flips back to as well when I'm tired or overwrought. It's imprinted on us both like we're branded.

Emily gently corrects her and starts asking about the pain. Sadie is more effusive about her physical symptoms, eloquently describing the searing agony that grips her abdomen and back, able to recall that the oxycodone seems to be the drug that is helping the most.

'And Laura said you'd been seeing some insects. Are they here now?' Tom rests his hand by Sadie's and she moves hers back a fraction. He doesn't seem to notice.

'Well, if they were there then you'd see them too, wouldn't you?' She looks down and her eyes scan the bed, resting at the bottom of the counterpane.

'There's a couple but they're small and fast. Maybe you missed them. Now, I'm sorry to be rude but I'm really tired and I need to just try to have a nap before Laura and I go out.'

She looks like she's asleep before we even get to the door.

* * *

The doctor leaves, after coming up with a plan. She's rationalised all of Sadie's medications. There's a prescription for slow-release oxycodone tablets to provide background pain relief and a higher dose of the immediate-release tablets for top-up. She's also prescribed some mild anti-psychotic pills for if the hallucinations become distressing. Another useful tool that I might need.

She's confirmed what I told Elsie: Sadie's prognosis is likely to be days to weeks only. I'd hoped that Elsie would talk to Tom and Emily but she disappeared, darting out of the house when they arrived. I shouted her from the bottom of the attic steps, to see if she'd arrived back while we were in Sadie's room, but there was no answer. I'm left with Tom sitting across from me at the kitchen table. Sophia is perched on my lap.

'Has Sadie talked any more about whether she'll go into a hospice?' Tom's thick fingers grasp the hot mug. His knuckles are matted with hair. It seems to be sprouting from his clothes, trying to escape. Tufts showing at the neck and through the gaps where the short-sleeved shirt strains at his abdomen.

'Not to me but she's told Elsie that she won't ever leave here.'

'She's always told me that too. She says she's only happy being here.'

I'm glad that she's here, too. While here'd be less burden of caring on me and Elsie, a hospice is not a good place if Sadie is going to be talkative. Too many listening ears, a chance that someone would unpick the truth during her coherent episodes.

'She was born here.' I'm guessing that she still tells people this story.

'Yeah. She told me.' I see from the corner of my eye that Tom is studying my face. I hope my behaviour hasn't been too shrill or dubious. 'We almost worked together, actually. She was the ward sister on the haematology ward but she left a couple of months before I started. I used to see her occasionally when I had to nip down to the chemo day unit. She always had such a distinctive look.'

I realise that I haven't asked Sadie or Elsie where she'd worked. I hadn't considered that she was doing a job so similar to mine in terms of the speciality.

'She's worn the vintage stuff as long as I've known her.' The amount of vintage clothing that Sadie owns has grown to levels that border on hoarding. When I was checking what was in all the rooms, looking for clues about her husband, I came across her clothing overflow in one of the old bedrooms. Her collection has expanded. The room is lined with wardrobes with two clothing rails down the centre, glittering with jewel-coloured Chanel suits and chiffon gowns. Preposterous clothing that I wouldn't know when to wear, never mind have the confidence to pull off. The most daring dress I own is a second-hand Laura Ashley sun dress that felt too revealing around the neck. I've only worn it once.

'So, how long are you here for?' Tom sits back and crosses an ankle over his thigh. The strain on his shirt buttons makes me nervous. His eyes flit across my face and I start to wonder if he knows something. If Sadie has already been saying things to health professionals. Maybe they've commented on her unsettling words in their handovers.

'Not long, I hope. Sadie's husband is supposed to be

back soon, although Elsie's been somewhat vague and what with the travel . . .'

'Teenagers. I think I must have been one once, although it's a vague memory.' He smiles at me and holds eye contact for a moment before looking down at the table.

I want to laugh. Tom wasn't scrutinising me because he's considering something that Sadie's said about me. He's flirting with me. It's been a while since this last happened. I've forgotten the signs.

'Good luck with Sadie's husband coming back, by the way. The travel news looks grim.'

'Have you met him?' Here's my chance to find out who he is from someone neutral.

'No, sadly not. I did leave a message on his phone to try to arrange a meeting with him and Sadie to go through the care plan but he didn't respond. Sadie said he was busy with work. The nearest I've come to him is the stairs.'

'The stairs?'

'Sorry. That was a bizarre way for me to put it. I mean all the pictures of him, Sadie and Elsie that were on the stairs.'

The pictures that are now no longer there. The only remnants being the gaping holes in the walls where some of the nails have come away when the pictures were ripped down.

Much like the photo albums I've found where Sadie's husband has been neatly snipped out of every photo.

He's been eliminated just like Portia was.

Chapter Seventeen

NOW

Thursday, 15 April 2010

Sadie has been out of it for most of the afternoon. I slide into sleep, too, enveloped by the sofa. I drift away into a world of florid nightmares that I wake up from with a start. I listen for the sound of Elsie or for Sadie shouting. There's nothing. The house feels dead and cold, in spite of the mild weather.

A wave of exhaustion hits me and I steady myself against the wall. The nightmare that woke me comes back to me with the slam of a road traffic collision. I'd been dreaming about Amy. A dream so technicolour that I almost expect her to emerge in a cloud of fruit scented Body Shop spray, her house music thumping away from the attic.

I tidy around, moving like a cat. A skill we all learned as student nurses on torturously long night shifts where we padded around in the near dark, trying to let people sleep in the hostile environment. Although Amy was notorious for being unable to stay quiet, bumping into bedside tables, never learning the subtle art of voice modulation.

Sadie doesn't stir. I check the other bedrooms again. I look in Anthony's old bedroom. There's no trace of anyone except Sadie in her bedroom so this room must be where her husband has been sleeping. Entering here is like travelling in a time machine back to the present day, after the fugue of Sadie's aesthetic. There's an Ikea futon strewn with geometric patterned cushions, a bed that looks unslept in and a cheap bookcase with management books crammed in neat rows. The kind of tedious books about productivity and self-improvement that men in shiny suits read on the tube in the mornings. On the desk there's an old Dell PC that's password protected. A guitar is propped against the wall and there's an empty glass on the desk with a brown slick of dried out whisky. I try the drawers of a small metal filing cabinet but they're locked.

The wardrobe doesn't tell me anything either. It's filled with generic menswear. A sparse collection of dark suits and TM Lewin shirts one side with a few items of bland, designer casual wear on the other, as if half the contents are missing.

There's nothing helpful in here.

I push my nose into the fabrics but they don't smell of anyone I knew, just of washing powder.

* * *

Elsie gets in around eleven. She's more solid, no longer in constant motion. She seems younger this evening. I'm not sure what a parent would do in this situation but I imagine it involves making food, checking in. My knowledge is gleaned solely from TV dramas.

'Have you had a good day?'

'I went to Ollie's and we had pizza. Time passed.' Her voice is world weary.

'I imagine it was a release to be away from here for a while.' She nods and I relax a little. I've never considered motherhood. The logistics of balancing childcare with work always felt too daunting, especially as I'd want to do it alone.

'Ollie's mum and dad are away so we had the whole house.' She has space here but who'd bring a friend to this house with its taint of sickness and death in the air.

'How old is he?'

'What?'

'How old is Ollie? I'm guessing he's your boyfriend. Sorry, am I being too intrusive?' I offer her a thin smile.

'Ollie's my girlfriend. And she's fifteen, like me.'

I don't bother apologising and instead offer to make her some food or cocoa before she goes to bed. A cold feeling like surgical steel runs down my back as something occurs to me.

Her age. I can't believe how blind I've been.

If she's fifteen then that means that she might be Sacha's daughter. Sadie could have been pregnant when I fled from here.

And if the man she's referring to as her father is Sacha and he's away on business then my suspicions are true and nothing that I thought was true is reality. He's living here and drinking his Chivas Regal, playing his maudlin guitar songs, working a dull management job like he was always destined to.

I've wasted my life on guilt, tarred with the taint of a crime that didn't happen.

I feel lightheaded. I excuse myself and go upstairs to my bedroom, shutting myself in. All these anomalies are too much. Elsie's age. The bloodstain that shouldn't have been on the door on the day that I left. Sadie's rage.

I try to make myself remember the heinous things that happened here but my mind blocks most of it. It's like static on that battered old TV that Suzie stole from me. The vivid scene of the blood on the door plays on a reel in my head. I crouch in the corner of the bedroom with my hands hugging my knees to my chest.

* * *

It's the early hours of the morning before I'm able to move. I fetch my phone from my bag and it feels hot in my hand. I push through the tidal waves of nausea and do something that I've always resisted. Something that I should have made myself do when I first arrived here.

My fingers are trying to move as fast as my thoughts, skittering across the screen and I type too quickly, making errors. On the third try I get it right.

SACHA DAVIDSON. The name looks venomous and incriminating in black type on my phone screen.

There's nothing. Not one single result that matches with him. I try changing the spelling. DAVISON and SASHA. Nothing, still.

Next I try Sadie's name to see if there's anything with them together online, maybe a photo of them at someone's wedding or an event. There's nothing apart from work-related things. A picture of her in a local newspaper from a bake sale for the clinic she worked in, a thank you in an obituary for a young woman who died of leukaemia.

I finally try ANTHONY BELL. The page fills with a list of names and I manage to find a profile on Facebook with a picture that might be him. It's hard to tell, as it's small and blurry and the account is set to private. I toss my phone onto the bed and curl into a ball under the covers, my fists clenched.

The urge to run up and shake Sadie awake and demand answers is powerful but I resist.

I feel as naïve and clueless as I did back then.

There's so much I need to think about and evaluate.

Whirling feelings of guilt, resentment and hope come at me like assailants.

Chapter Eighteen

THEN

August 1992

People talk about illness in combat terminology. Fighting cancer, becoming a survivor or losing the battle. It's a flawed analogy but in the hospital it feels like there's a constant fight. A war against disorder and carnage where we strive for structure, neatness and control, trying to stop chaos reigning. We stride down corridors armed with squeaky wheeled trolleys, loaded with sheets and towels.

I mimic the stricter nurses, modelling myself on the ones who you'd call 'firm but fair'. I soothe and anoint with lukewarm flannels and soapy water from plastic bowls. I'm learning how to radiate a no-nonsense empathy. Kindness but with boundaries. I'm thriving here.

I've been in London for nineteen months now and I'm defying the concerns of my mum and the psychologist. I'm more alive than I have been in years. Time is spinning by in an endless procession of faces and bodies. A parade of patients who I care deeply about then have to forget when the next batch arrive. People who I share intimacies with; I bathe their skin, dress their wounds, record the minutiae of their bodily functions. Then I have to consign them to memory and move on to the next prone figure in the bed, the next wound, the next fold of puckered flesh.

It's an education that comes with sore feet and aching muscles. I'm stronger than I've ever been. Ropey muscles have popped up on my arms and legs. I'm becoming someone new, bolder and more able to fight back, no longer the vapid 'stuck-up Laura' who people whispered about and stared at in the village. My metamorphosis is progressing.

I have flashes of the old me, of course. No one ever completely changes. There are moments when I feel myself unspooling again. It's like there's a pool of water in me and I have to keep it from rising. It's a constant labour. The threat from my anonymous note writer is still there, of course. The promise of revenge from the last letter didn't materialise which was worse in a way. Rather than it all coming to a climax it remains open and hangs over me like a cloud. Whoever did this is pursuing me in pulses and waves and I remain on high alert, never quite relaxing unless I'm here with Sadie.

On a positive note, I have this life at Laurel House. Sadie and I live together like two best friends who have known each other for ever. I still haven't told her everything about my past and I didn't tell her about the last note either; the vilest one of all. I know it'd help to talk but it'd entail too much explanation. I can just imagine Sadie now: 'But revenge for what?'

And what could I tell her that wouldn't make her despise me?

I stick to my tried and tested method of filling pages of my notebooks with my neat handwriting, mapping out my thoughts and feelings. I have two new books that I bought from Woolworths and they're already almost full. My thoughts all recorded and ordered.

I've adjusted to Metropolitan life. London is my new home. When I walk through the streets now it feels smaller, provincial in parts. The smell of sweat and animal flesh burning on early autumn barbecues in the unseasonal weather, the sound of traffic and children kicking footballs. I don't miss much about Derbyshire other than the stars. The light pollution here renders London's sky to a feeble display of deadened lights.

This area has become my new village. I know the local characters who wander up and down. The street drinkers and the women in the nearby shelter who congregate on the pavement, indolently blowing smoke from cheap cigarettes, the tired-looking prostitute who replaces her calling cards in the phone booths every day. Shopkeepers speak to me when I call in for crisps and biscuits.

The body trolley passes me on my way to my afternoon shift and the porter with the wandering hands winks at me. I blank him and hold my head high as I stalk down the main corridor. I'm always purposeful in my uniform. People treat you differently when you're dressed as a nurse. They have a label that they can attach to you. The kind of people who would have stared at me and whispered in the village back home are now smiling at me because they see me as something intrinsically good.

Louise is standing in the corridor, outside X-ray, her hand casually resting on the back of a wheelchair. A doctor with slicked back hair is talking to her and their body language suggests that Louise has forgotten about her police officer fiancé. The woman in the chair is caved in, crying into her hands. Louise doesn't even glance her way. As I approach, the doctor's pager sounds and he touches Louise's arm before walking away.

'What are you doing?' She doesn't bother to look at me when I speak.

'What does it look like I'm doing? I'm waiting for a porter.'

I crouch down so I'm level with the crying woman. She lifts her head and tries to smile at me but tears continue to course down her face.

'Can I do anything to help?'

'You could just mind your own business, Laura. She's been crying all bloody day, if you must know. She won't stop.'

'So you're choosing to ignore her?' I look up and Louise's face is flushed.

'I'm choosing to ignore you. Go. Away.'

I look up and the porter has arrived. I think he's one of the ones who Amy was sleeping with last year. Louise glares at me as they wheel the weeping woman away.

Anthony doesn't lift his head when I arrive on the oncology ward and walk into the sisters' office. His eyes stay on the page of the lurid-covered novel that he's reading. I sit opposite him, pulling my book of nursing calculations from my bag and poring over perplexing rows of figures. My breaths sound hoarse and intrusive in my ears as we sit in silence. Two staff nurses enter, laughing about a TV programme that I haven't seen. Anthony discards his book, flashing an obsequious grin in their direction.

I lick my dry lips. The new placement on oncology is daunting. Obscure types of cancer that I've never heard of; crystalline solutions full of noxious chemicals that can burn through skin. The presence of so much tragedy and distress that I'll have to navigate and assist to allay. The last to come in is Nathan. He tries not to look at me but can't help himself. His face flushes crimson as he almost knocks a chair over.

When we leave the office after handover Anthony turns to me. 'You'll never be like her, you know.'

'I'm sorry?' I unintentionally echo the haughty tones of the schoolmistresses at boarding school.

'Sadie. You might be living there but no matter how much make-up you add or how many old clothes you start draping yourself in, you'll still be the same.' My hand automatically reaches to cover my mouth. A habit I'm trying to get out of now that I'm following Sadie's advice and wearing lipstick.

'It's a friendly tip. I've done it myself. Tried to imitate other boys who are more popular. More . . . sporty and masculine. It never works. Try to stop making a fool of yourself, Laura.'

He couldn't be further from the truth. I have no desire to be Sadie.

I'm glad to hear Cathy's voice, calling me over, waving her piece of paper with the morning handover notes on. Wanting me to take over checking a patient's blood pressure and temperature while she has units of blood infused.

The sheep-like woman in the chair looks up at me with a half-smile.

'Were you a public school girl . . . Laura.' She peers at my name badge. 'I can always tell. I was a headmistress, for my sins.'

'Yes. I went to an all-girls school in Derbyshire.' She looks like she's waiting for me to say something else. I fake enthusiasm. 'It was a great education. I loved it there.'

She looks pleased at my untruth. I smile and turn towards Nathan who's hovering to hand over another patient to me.

When the shift finally ends and I leave the hospital, the streets are quieter with people and less traffic. It's almost dark but the pavements are lit by the sickly yellow of the streetlights. I turn off the main street, towards Laurel House and I sense someone walking behind me. I scan side to side and there's no one else around. The houses nearby are either dark or shuttered. I don't turn my head around, relying on my peripheral vision and the sounds around me. The footsteps are heavy but I can't tell whether it's a man or woman.

I keep my vision focused on the house which is seconds away. The steps change beat, becoming staccato. Someone's running at me. I gulp a breath in, preparing to scream and clasp my keys in my fist, ready to scratch at someone's face, if needed. The footsteps stop as I reach the house. I turn, just in time to see someone dart back round the corner onto the road.

* * *

Sadie is fully dressed which is unusual. We've both taken to lounging around in kimonos or silk dressing gowns that smell of lavender and mothballs. She's wearing a navy Fifties dress with a full skirt and white detailing. Her hennaed hair immaculate, crisp with hairspray.

'You look a bit jittery, Laura, are you OK?'

I'm about to tell her that I think this weird thing has begun again, that someone followed me and that my lunch disappeared from the ward fridge. But her demeanour is odd and I can't work out what's going on.

'It's fine. I'm on the new ward with Anthony, which isn't going to be much fun but Cathy and Nathan are there, too, and they're OK.'

Sadie's textbook from earlier is nowhere to be seen and neither is Coco. No doubt she'll be curled up on my bed. She's taken to sleeping in the crook of my elbow some nights, resting her hot little muzzle on my chest. If Sadie wakes, she calls for her and Coco trots back to her room.

'Cathy's a bore but I think Nathan's kind of hot, don't you? That whole rugby playing public school aesthetic.' I shudder at the thought of the entitled schoolboys who would pour out of minibuses and abuse their invites to our boarding school socials. Spending their time trying to dodge supervision and see how many girls they could grope. 'He'd be a good solid boyfriend for Amy, wouldn't he? Stop her chasing after all those grisly older porters.'

I ignore her comment. 'Are you going out somewhere?'

'Of course not. When do we ever go out? I've dressed up because Sacha is coming back.' It's only then that I notice the cloying scent of chemicals in the air and spot the gleam of the furniture where she's been cleaning.

'Coming here?' My sanctuary is about to be breached. I feel suddenly cold in spite of the warmth of the room.

'Don't sound so surprised, it is his home.' She pauses for a second. 'He called me, finally, after his "breathing space" and he's back this evening. Obviously, I'll have some questions.'

Sacha has been silent. He's been finishing off his sentence in an open prison in Derbyshire which, ironically, is not that far from my village. He didn't tell Sadie that he'd been moved. She found out when she bumped into an old friend of his in Camberwell. Sacha stopped writing or calling not long after I moved in here. She had a letter saying that he needed time to sort himself out and then she heard nothing more. Till now.

She's standing in this room, waiting, like a Fifties housewife.

'I . . . do you need me to go out?' I have visions of them embracing and me standing to one side like the secondary character that I always have been, mortified by their affection. No longer a priority here.

'Of course not! He'll be delighted to meet you.'

The feeling of sickness that I have isn't due to hunger from my missing lunch. It's the thought that all this is about to shift on its axis. The place I feel safe in will be altered and marred.

But he doesn't arrive. After a long evening where she cranes her neck at every sound, listens for the phone that never rings and the door that no one knocks at, the night ends. I feel drenched in relief but Sadie simmers with fury. The household is unchanged. It's just us and the dog. The lamplight filters across the walls and onto where I'm lying in bed with Coco at my side. Sadie has gone quiet. There was a noise from her bedroom that sounded like glass being smashed but it's stopped now.

I fall asleep with a smile on my face.

Chapter Nineteen

NOW

Friday, 16 April 2010

Nursing has changed from when I trained. Our values and ethos have, rightly, evolved. We used to take control and were liberal with medications, administering sedatives to the confused or delirious to silence them. Fooling ourselves that it was entirely for their benefit and that we were merely alleviating their distress. Part of it was that we wanted them to be quiet and safe, without us needing to watch them constantly when we were harassed and frenetic. Now, we avoid drugs where possible, recognising that medications carry too many side effects. A heavily drugged patient is likely to feel more bewildered and might get up and fall. We use chemical methods as a last resort.

But there are still times when people need medicating, for their own and everyone else's good, of course.

I'm observing Sadie.

She wakes at dawn and I give her more drugs. The oxycodone seems to be suiting her better but the orderly row of sedatives and analgesics lined up on the chest of drawers reassure me. They're the weapons in my arsenal against Sadie's suffering. The tools of my trade, along with the charts I've drawn up using a ruler I found on the mystery husband's desk.

'Did you ever manage to find love, Laura?' Sadie is applying a slash of scarlet lipstick. It looks like a fresh incision. I've draped a ridiculous chiffon bed jacket over her shoulders. It's like something Elizabeth Taylor might have worn, a pointless garment other than that it will make her feel more like herself. She looks like a tired drag queen in this light.

'I think that being around you and Sacha might have put me off love altogether.' Saying his name is like spitting out bile but I force myself.

She smiles like all this is a joke. I resist the urge to reach across and slap the mirror and make-up from her hands.

'You never really understood us. That was the problem.' She replaces the cap on the lipstick and holds it out to me like I'm the maid.

She shuffles herself in the bed. 'Help me, Laura.'

I move myself to her side and let her push against me to readjust her position.

'Anyway, darling. I was asking about you. We'll discuss the past later. You're too young to be consigned to being alone. What did you think about the nurse who came? Ted was it? If I was better I might have been flirting with him myself but I lay back and let you do that for me. He reminded me of Sacha.' She laughs and it morphs into a series of barks as she coughs.

Any positive thoughts that I might have had about Tom are now soured by this grotesque comparison. I pretend to busy myself with the charts to hide the shaking which feels like it's working through my body. My back is turned to Sadie so that she can't see my face.

'Enough about me. Tell me about your new husband.' The sentence starts off sounding casual but the words are muffled as I finish, like my jaw is locked. There are questions that Google isn't able to offer answers to and I don't want to trouble Elsie with more intrusion into her life than she already has. If Elsie gives me an answer that leaves me reeling then I'm not sure that I'll be able to hide it from her.

There's an excruciating pause before Sadie speaks. 'Oh, he's not *new*. You already know that. And what do you need to know about him? He's an utter bastard, just like you always said he was. But aren't they always? I'd kicked him out for a while but he came back. He does that. We're co-dependent, I suppose.' This relentless cycle of disruption and reconciliation is how Sadie and Sacha always were. 'But he is Elsie's father, which complicates things. Once you've had a baby with someone you're stuck with them for life.'

I turn back around and she's rooting for something in the drawer. I take the opportunity to walk over to the other side of the room and fill my charts out, taking deep breaths and gathering myself.

When I go back to her, a few minutes later, I see from her eyes that she's confused. The last dose of opiates looks like it's reduced her pain but she's flipped back away from reality again. Confusion can be like that. A transient state that flits around like a moth at night. 'Apologies, I've forgotten your name. You must think I'm terrible. Oh, I remember. It's Jessica. It is Jessica, isn't it?'

The name makes me feel like I'm being throttled.

'Sadie, it's Laura.' It's an effort not to yell my words. My fear is morphing into something harder and sharper edged.

'Of course. Laura! My partner in crime. You were the one who was here when I—'

'Sadie!' I stop her from saying it just in time as the door swings open and Elsie walks in.

* * *

When I go back in half an hour later she's asleep. There's a pillow that she's knocked onto the floor and I pick it up, holding it in both hands.

Sadie's breaths are soft and even. Her brow looks smooth. She looks younger and less troubled when she's not in pain. I step closer to the bedside, still holding the pillow in both hands.

It'd be so much easier if she were to just stop breathing now before she says something that can't be taken back.

I stand for a while, barely even thinking, my hands gripping the soft pillow.

There's the shrill sound of a blackbird singing outside the window and I come back to my senses. I put the pillow down on a chair and go through to my room, listening for the sound of Elsie moving around above me in Amy's room.

My mind always flips back to Amy.

Even though she didn't last long in this place.

Chapter Twenty

THEN

October 1992

I've developed strange sleeping habits from getting up at dawn for morning shifts, followed by runs of afternoon shifts where I work late into the evening before we switch over to nights. I get home from a day shift and the house is empty. I unintentionally fall asleep on the sofa, waking up with the TV blasting out *Top of the Pops*, a band I've never heard before hammering out discordant music. There's still no sign of Sadie, so I walk upstairs to my room.

'What are you doing in here?' Sadie looks up when I speak. She has the drawers of my bedside cabinet open. She straightens up. There's no hint of a blush under her alabaster make-up.

'Hello is a more customary greeting. I'm just looking where to put this. It was mixed up in my things in the laundry.'

Sadie holds up a cotton scarf that I haven't worn in a long time and can't recall washing recently.

'I'm sorry. I'm tired and grumpy. I didn't mean to sound off. Where've you been?'

'Tedious errands. I went out to buy new bed linen and did a trawl of the fabric shops.'

Before she leaves, I root in the drawer and pull out the Hermès scarf.

'I found this in the back of the drawer. I didn't know if it was yours or Portia's.'

She takes it from me, without comment. There's a whiff of bleach and lemon polish that comes from her hand. I try to unpick my thoughts through the residual brain fog from the early evening sleep. This smell usually means one thing only. She thinks that Sacha is coming again.

'You smell like you've been busy cleaning.'

'I've been sorting out the attic. We've got a new resident arriving. Hence the bed linen.'

My stomach flips like it did last time she thought Sacha was coming back.

'Is Sacha—'

'No. He isn't.' Her eyes fix on me as she pauses and adjusts her tone back to neutral. 'I thought it was time we populated the place again and used these rooms for something.'

'Use them for what?' I instantly wish I could retrieve the words and soften them. My defensive tone is reflected back in Sadie's raised eyebrow.

'Amy's coming to stay tomorrow. She's not flourishing in that nurses' home like she should be. I saw her yesterday and she was telling me all about her illness. Apparently she's back on steroids for a flare-up. She needs nurture.' My shoulders drop back down from around my ears.

'Oh, I didn't know.'

'That's strange because she said that you knew that she had Crohn's. Why didn't you say?'

I mutter unconvincing excuses about it being private, unable to tell her that the real reason was that I didn't want this to happen. When Sadie leaves the room I check the chest of drawers. My private journals are still all there and they look untouched. I slump onto the bed, not even bothering to undress.

* * *

The day of Amy's arrival is inauspicious. I work a dull shift in Accident and Emergency. Even in that hub of chaos the drama ebbs and flows and there's still mundane routine. I spend the day reassuring crying children while they have stitches put into playground wounds, injecting tetanus boosters or putting compression bandages on sprained ankles.

'It's less scary here than I expected.' Nathan is directly across from me, eating a bag of pickled onion Monster Munch, his legs splayed in their usual right angle.

There's a pause and Cathy walks in, carrying a book and a red marker pen. She looks disappointed to see us in the staff room.

'Do you get back home much?' Nathan continues trying to engage me in conversation.

'Not often.' I've only been back twice. After the comfort of Laurel House, the flat above the shop feels oppressive and bland. There's barely room for the three of us. Suzie is clean again and attending meetings but I'm not optimistic that she'll stay this way for long. My mum's bright and encouraging tones don't convince me that she feels any more hopeful than I do.

I realise that I don't know where Nathan's from. I've been so preoccupied with Sadie that I've ignored most of the rest of my class. I make an effort and ask.

'Surrey, originally. My parents live in Dulwich Village now. But I know Derbyshire well. Great climbing up there.' He smiles across at me, a puppy wanting validation for offering me this gift of a conversational opener.

Cathy has clearly decided that she's not engaging with small talk and is reading her book. I admire her singularity of purpose.

'I hear that Amy's moving in with you?' Nathan's cheeks are getting pinker by the minute.

'She is.' I wait for the inevitable question.

'Do you know if she has a boyfriend?' Nathan's cheeks have moved through an ombre of pinks and reds. I look across and Cathy half-smiles at me before rolling both her eyes.

I actually quite like these two. They're easy colleagues.

I don't need them as friends, though. I have Sadie.

And now we have Amy, too.

* * *

When I arrive home there's a familiar smell of Calvin Klein aftershave that makes my stomach contract.

'Don't panic, I'm just here to see Amy. You can carry on being the lead member of the Sadie fan club.'

I ignore Anthony and push past, down the hall into the empty kitchen. I can hear the sound of laughter coming from the top floor and the thought of Sadie with someone else fills me with dread.

He follows me as I knew he would.

'I don't know what your problem is with me but it's your choice, Laura.' His voice is tinged with amusement.

It's strange how much territory matters. Anthony is on my ground now and I feel emboldened. 'I'm not the one being hostile here.'

'So I've imagined all the withering looks and that time you practically accused me of putting something in your pocket? And how about every time someone tries to speak to Sadie and you almost growl. It'd be funny if it wasn't so tragic.' I'm guessing that Anthony is one of those people who keeps a mental list of whoever he feels slighted by. I suspect I'm near the top of it.

'Maybe withering is my natural expression.'

'Well, at least you're owning up to it.' He lets out a laugh that has a vestige of warmth. 'Do you want to make me a coffee? I'm a guest after all.'

I fill the kettle. Neither of us speaks. I can hear the sound of Sadie and Amy coming from the attic, distant laughter and thudding.

* * *

It's altered the dynamic having Amy here. I'm readjusting to the change in space and telling myself to be more generous. I have what I need here: a few feet to retreat into and drop my façade, read my book or write my journals. Amy can't rupture what Sadie and I have.

These first few weeks have felt like we're the parents of a well behaved but slightly worrying teenager. Sadie mothers us both but Amy is the one getting more time. It's like being back home where Suzie was the vortex who sucked in everyone's attention. Sadie nurtures Amy. Proffering paracetamol for headaches, baking cakes that she likes, offering up sage advice about men.

I hear her heavy footsteps moving about overhead and they wake me at night. Twice I've heard the sound of two sets of feet moving around up there. I peered out of the door when I heard someone on the stairs one time at three in the morning. There was a dark-haired man, handsome but seedy looking, in a denim jacket and baggy jeans, being shepherded down the stairs. I didn't catch who was there the second time. Sadie won't like this rule infraction. I'd tell her about it but it might bounce back on me and I'll be seen as malicious. I'm not risking it.

Everyone else is at work so I'm checking over Amy's room again. It's the opposite of mine, the kind of place I would hate to live in but am fascinated to visit. Stepping in there feels like losing my inhibitions, as if material things neither matter nor have value. She's only been here a week and there are clothes strewn across the floor, as if abandoned during a moment of passion. Department store garments mixed with Gaultier and Chanel, in the egalitarian mess. Teetering piles of CDs fight for attention with rows of cosmetics and well-worn soft toys. Dusty old Steiff bears jostling for space with orange pill bottles.

I spot something in her room that makes me sit up and pay attention. It's a WHSmith notepad. The kind that you write letters on. Or use to write anonymous notes. I pick it up and turn it over, leafing through to check for indentations. I rifle through her pencil case and there's no marker pens so I put everything back as I found it.

* * *

The following evening I change into a sundress that Sadie says suits me. I'm not entirely sure. The blowsy tea rose design reminds me of the women who attend the church in the village.

Sadie turns and waves to me from the oven where she's lifting out a cottage pie, one of her endless supply of garish tea towels protecting her fingers.

Anthony is sitting across from Amy at the table. He's here again. I recoiled when I spotted him and he saw me do it.

'Here she is. My partner in crime.' Sadie beams across at me. 'Sit.'

'Is that what she is? That's not what people are saying in college . . .' Anthony tilts his head to one side as he says this, as if he's casually looking out of the window.

'Are people saying that we're lovers?' Sadie sounds amused rather than horrified by the idea. 'I don't know about Laura but unfortunately I'm desperately heterosexual, which is a bore. It does limit the options.'

'Oh, there was no implication about *you*, Sadie.'

His childish insinuations don't bother me. I don't feel a sexual attraction to Sadie but nor would I be ashamed if I did. I'm too exhausted to allow Anthony's barbs to annoy me today.

'Are you seeing someone?' Amy looks at me with childlike curiosity.

Sadie saves me from answering. 'I think that Laura is already becoming married to the job. She's destined to become one of those old-fashioned matrons from wartime who didn't need a man to be happy.'

'How about you Sadie? Will you marry your boyfriend when he's back?' Amy's voice has a note of childlike hope.

'I'm not sure. I mean, he's asked obviously.' Her left hand is decorated with costume jewellery. No engagement ring. And there's been no mention of Sacha since he failed to show up, thankfully. 'One day.'

The thought of jewellery reminds me that Sadie bought me some vintage bangles last week in Petticoat Lane. I've forgotten to put them back on after my shift so I reach down into my bag where I left them. They're not there. I wrack my brain, trying to recall when I took them off.

My stomach feels leaden as I realise that yet another thing is missing. There's been a regularity to it. More food disappearing when I'm on shift. It's always my lunch that disappears, never anyone else's and it's happened too many times for it be accidental. Trivial items vanish from my coat pockets. A powder compact that Sadie gave me, a pack of cough sweets, a comb, even my coat disappeared one day.

I need to face up to this and share my worries with Sadie but it'll have to wait. I'm not giving Anthony the satisfaction of seeing me upset. So far, I've kept the spikes of panic and the flashbacks hidden from everyone and it's better that way.

* * *

I start night shifts today on yet another new ward. This constant whirl of change that leaves me discombobulated. There was no chance to speak to Sadie about the notes last night. Anthony lingered like a stain. I'll try to snatch some time alone when I get in. Night shifts feel borderless and an unending slog. I've been tasked with keeping an eye on a dying man, tonight. One of the surprising many who are alone or unwanted.

People get better, go home, live happily into an unknown future but it's impossible to ignore the presence of death. The destiny that we try to mask and evade and speak about in hushed euphemisms, as if ignoring it will negate its existence. But death hovers everywhere in a hospital, lurking in organs as a clump of cancerous cells, hiding in damaged cardiac tissue, forming clots or culturing bacteria in the blood. Sometimes ambushing us but more often arriving with a lingering opening act and a drastic finale.

I stop and sit by the old man's bed, holding his hand. He's had no visitors, other than the woman he lives next door to, who came once. My fingers touch his inelastic skin as I watch the light filter through the thin curtains of the side room. His breaths are damp with an alarming gurgling sound, as if his face is partly submerged. I sit for a while until I feel myself falling forward, tipping into sleep.

The sound of Jane's footsteps jolts me upright.

'Laura, can I have a hand?'

I follow her, unable to shake the feeling of being watched that I've had since the shift began. It's an accurate thought, I suppose. We are always being watched in one way or another. Patients checking our manoeuvres as we put on a free show for their confined bodies and staff nurses watching that we don't make mistakes. Nights make it feel worse with every shadowy corner and empty corridor a threat.

I go back in to see the old man but I'm too late. The staff nurse makes me call his neighbour while she nips to the next ward where there's a junior doctor scuttling around. His neighbour is eager to tell me that she barely knows him and that she won't be taking responsibility for anything.

When I've catalogued his meagre property and loaded it into plastic bags I walk to the linen store at the end of the corridor. I reach up for the pile of plasticky shrouds, my dress riding against my thighs with a crackle of static.

The door closes behind me with a slam and I hear the distinctive sound of the key turning. The lights go out.

My hand rattles at the door but it's locked. My knees give way and I sink down onto my haunches. Shockwaves jitter through my legs and arms. I manage to pull myself up. I'm sweating in the heat of this enclosed space. My hands smart as I slam them against the door. The shrill shouts that come from my mouth remain unheard. No one comes. My eyes are pricking with tears of frustration. I'm trapped in the dark with no escape from here till someone notices me gone. Or until the person who locked me in here returns and has me cornered. I stagger in the darkness, banging my fists and yelling till the aftershocks of pain in my hands are too much to bear. I give in and slide down to the floor, wrapping my arms around myself. I don't know how long it is before Jane finds me.

'Someone locked me in.'

'What, deliberately? Maybe someone walked by and didn't know you were in there.' Jane's tone is dubious.

The staff nurse is unsympathetic, labelling it as likely to have been a prank by another student. She eyes Jane suspiciously and discounts her as a suspect before looking back towards me.

'Well, you're going to have to pull yourself back together. You're not going home. We've got too much to do.'

I go to the staff kitchen with its passive aggressive notices about the rules for food storage and cleaning. My face is blotchy so I splash water on it in a futile attempt to look normal again. My skin is as pallid as a corpse.

The rest of the shift is a blur. My thoughts spin like a sample in a centrifuge.

I know that what happened was no accident or practical joke.

They've definitely started again.

The thefts were just an appetiser.

The pit of my stomach is weighed down by the familiar sense of dread.

I want to walk back to Sadie's, climb into bed and stay there.

Chapter Twenty-One

THEN

October 1992

Sadie is quick to spot the new and alien me. The flatness in my tone that I can't hide, the hardening of my features and slowing of my movements. It's like my brain is sloshing in grey water. The flow of attention from her is soft and measured. She sits me down and brings me coffee, batting away my replies that I'm fine. That I'm just tired.

'You do know that you can tell me about whatever's really wrong.' She perches on the mattress. Her hand resting at my side.

It's like I have less skin. My ability to lie and hide is diminished by this mood state. I tell her everything that's been happening. The faeces-scrawled note that I kept quiet about, the thefts, the linen store. They all sound so petty and improbable but added to the other notes and the pushes in the road and on the stairs, I'm afraid. I scrutinise her face for scepticism but there's none. I stare at her, looking for signs of guilt. Paranoia is taking root in me like a parasitic infection. I have no idea who I can and can't trust anymore. Even Sadie feels like a threat today, which is an insane idea. The world feels sharp edged and hazardous. I dig my nails into my skin and remind myself that I'm safe here in this house.

Sadie's brows are raised in shock. Whatever is happening, I don't think that Sadie knows anything about who is doing this. Then the paranoia starts again and whispers to me that maybe she's a good actor, like her late parents. I feel queasy with shame for even thinking these wild thoughts about my best friend. I push the deranged ideas away into the recesses of my roiling brain.

I tell her the things that I can talk about. About how I slid into a depressive episode when I was sixteen. That insidious dive into an unfamiliar world that tinged everything with sadness. Except it wasn't just sadness. That's a misunderstanding people have about depression. It was more of an absence of joy, an absence of everything but dread. A tangible and painful deadening of me that came with an itch of agitation.

There are parts of the story that I skip over. I can hardly talk about the post-traumatic stress disorder without talking about Jessica and I'm not ready yet. I do talk about the psychiatric unit and that blur of confinement. The long road to rehabilitation where my mum didn't know quite what to do with me. About how I recovered, mostly, with the help of a psychiatrist and psychologist and a carousel of medications that left me dry mouthed and groggy. Then the long period of hiding away in my bedroom watching old films on the TV that Suzie eventually stole and sold.

'Has the depression come back before?'

I nod.

'And what do you do to manage it?'

'I take medicines and I . . . I still have a psychologist back home who I can call. And I write things down. That helps a little bit.'

'And what can I do?' I don't make eye contact when she speaks.

'Doing things and being with other people helps. It's like I have to fight my instincts to hibernate and do the opposite of what my body says.'

'Well, maybe you do need to hibernate and rest for a time. You're shattered, Laura. This training is exhausting. You can't just work things away. Let me look after you for a while.'

She touches my hand and I feel tears flowing down my face and I don't feel any shame. I don't feel anything.

* * *

I sleep for a while. It could be for an hour or for a day. I'm unsure how much time has passed before Sadie returns.

'Right, I've rung your tutor and told her you're not feeling good. She's given you a week off, which is kind but it probably won't be long enough. I've also booked in a call with your psychologist for later, OK?'

I carry on looking at her and then realise she's waiting for a response. I don't have one.

'And when you feel up to it we'll go to the police about what's been happening.'

For the next few days I sleep. Strange interludes where I fall into blackness, waking up dazed. Staring my way through early mornings when I jolt awake with a gunshot of dread that lurks in my stomach like a tumour.

Sadie brings me up small meals on a lacquered tray and leaves me alone. Sometimes I sense that Amy is sitting beside me. She's surprisingly good at this and I don't hate her being here. She takes her lead from me and on the rare occasions that I talk she listens. Otherwise she just sits by my bed flicking through copies of *The Face* and *Elle*, listening to her Walkman. She's quieter than usual when she's in her attic room but I still hear her late at night sometimes, laughing with someone.

On the fourth day I get dressed and come down. Sadie puts on a video of *Brief Encounter*. She copies some of the voices, talking like the woman in the café. I find myself laughing, which shocks me. I've always been a good mimic so I join in. Sadie laughs and claps at my efforts, which sends Coco skittering from her lap. She understands what I need and mutters something about walking in the park tomorrow.

On my way back upstairs I bump into Amy on the landing. She follows me through to my bedroom and pulls up a chair as I lay myself down on the bed. She looks well and I tell her this.

She seems taken aback that full sentences are leaving my mouth again. 'I'm better, Laura, but I wouldn't call it well. More of a gap before my twattish body decides to mutiny against itself again.' We're both silent for a moment. 'On the plus side, I'm managing to go out without having to have a strategic plan of all the public toilets.'

She leans forward. Her hand touches my arm and two bangles slide down her thin wrist, threatening to fall off. I stare at them. They're mine. The bangles that were missing from my bag. Some of my many items that have disappeared.

I fight down the urge to roll over and close my eyes, negating her from my consciousness.

'I have major gossip. You won't believe this. Louise has been dismissed.'

'What?' I sit up, the bangles temporarily forgotten.

'Thank fuck! That's the reaction I was hoping for. Sadie barely batted an eyelid.'

'What did she do?' I imagine her getting caught being rude or obnoxious to a patient.

'She's been stealing drugs. Can you believe it? She's the last person I expected. Well, not quite the last. That'd be Cathy.'

'How did they find out?' I'm thrown by this news but secretly pleased.

'Someone tipped them off. She had two strips of diazepam in her handbag and there was a shortfall in the stock. She was called into college the next day and she's been made to leave!'

When Amy goes up to the attic room I think hard, trying to think where she might have put the things of mine that are missing. Wondering when the house will be empty so I can check her things again.

* * *

The police officer keeps looking at Sadie, even though I'm the one who's talking. His eyes keep returning to her cleavage which is on display today in a low-cut crimson dress with a full skirt. Sadie came home from a shift, reapplied her make-up and coerced me into coming here. I can see from her face that she's realising now that this is all a mistake.

The police officer is taking notes in a black book but I suspect that the notes will be the beginning and end of any action. His interest in what's been happening seems minimal. My statements sound vapid and trivial when I say them out loud.

'I was knocked into the road on a busy street and it felt like I was pushed.'

'There was a note daubed in excrement but the rest were in marker pen.'

'Yes, it could have been an accident that someone locked me in the linen store.'

'Yes, the college thought that the blood in my room was a prank that misfired.'

'No, they didn't feel the need to get the police involved.'

'No. I didn't think I should report it at the time.'

'Someone stole some things.'

He nods a lot and makes this little humming noise. His fat fingers writing down about a quarter of what I'm saying. His final conclusion being that this is 'silly pranks' by another student and that these things tend to 'run their course'. I can see that he only half believes me.

His final glance at Sadie's cleavage earns him a look of contempt when he raises his head and meets her eyes.

This was as pointless as I knew it would be. The sinking feeling in my stomach and the heaviness in my limbs is all too familiar.

* * *

On the way back I match Sadie's pace.

'Do you remember those bangles you bought for me from Petticoat Lane?' I've been rehearsing this line but my voice wavers.

'Vaguely. Were they the ones you couldn't find?'

'Yes. They went missing from my bag. I . . . I saw Amy wearing them.' It feels ridiculous to say this about the gentle woman who sat patiently by my bed when I was unwell but I do it anyway. I need Sadie's help. 'I think she might be the one doing this.'

'Doing what? Oh . . . actually. That was me, Laura. I found those bangles in the bathroom and thought that Amy was the one I'd bought them for. I forgot it was you. I put them up in her room and she must have just picked them up thinking that they were hers.' Sadie laughs.

We carry on walking.

'You didn't think that Amy might be the one writing the notes?' I'm glad that Sadie doesn't look around and see the crimson flush of embarrassment on my cheeks.

Chapter Twenty-Two

THEN

November 1992

I manage to return to work after a couple of weeks and no one comments on my absence. I decide to venture into central London, on my day off. Sadie has given me a pep talk. Her view is that I can't let my fears about these sporadic notes keep me imprisoned in the house. She thinks that whoever is messing with me shouldn't be allowed to win. She added in a proviso of 'if someone is still doing anything' with a smile that felt like broken glass.

So, every week I've been venturing a little further into London, away from my anchors: Laurel House and Sadie. As much as I was glad to leave the oppressive hills of Derbyshire, there's a magnetic pull from the natural world. I've taken to exploring the green spaces of London. The landscapes please me. This sense of nature but where the wildness is under control, tamed into something orderly and well behaved. I wander around Regent's Park, listening to the distant sound of the wolves from London Zoo baying as dusk approaches, watching Norland Nannies pushing children. Dogs run around brash middle-aged women who shout greetings to each other.

The ticket hall at Baker Street is crammed with people. I enter the stream of bodies, my portable cassette player headphones jammed to my head, listening to one of the tapes that Sadie made for me. Songs I haven't really learned to love but am trying hard to initiate myself into. It's helpful to drown out the screeches and scrapes of the trains, creating a barrier between me and this alien, underground world.

The escalator carries me down through the hot mouth of the station and I arrive on the platform. I stand near the edge, looking for mice. They populate the tube tracks, scurrying around, unobtrusive and opportunistic. I like that this nest of fellow secondary characters exists, working away, unnoticed by most. The platform is empty when I arrive. By the time the train is due there's a swell of people. The rhythm of the crowd unpredictable. London tube stations beat in pulses with people flowing like blood.

My neck prickles like there's someone watching me. It's not an unfamiliar sensation on the Underground where men leer and ram themselves against you or their hands 'accidentally' skim your breasts or buttocks. I scan the crowd around me, earning a glare from a woman in severe glasses who's standing behind me.

There's a rush of air as the train arrives, scraping noises invading my ears even through the foam headphones. The air whirls around me and it takes me a moment to realise that the new sensation is not just the turbulence from the train. My body is in motion.

I lurch forward, dipping in front of the oncoming train. It happens so fast that I have no time to turn my head to see what or who has sent me keeling over. Not even time to scream. Not that it'd be heard here with the roar of the train.

My hands meet nothing but air. The tracks below pushing up towards me.

The train is fast approaching and I catch a glimpse of the driver. His face is contorted in shock as the moment he has probably spent years dreading arrives and he realises that he's about to hit someone.

Hands drag me back. I feel like someone has dangled me over the tracks, momentarily.

'What the fuck? Be more careful.' A woman in a cheap suit, wearing too much blusher. 'You nearly went in front of the train.'

I open my mouth to speak but I'm winded and have to gasp in air before words can form. My heart feels like it might rupture out of my chest. I'd have been written off as another statistic.

Woman with psychiatric history throws herself in front of a train on a packed platform.

No one would have questioned it.

'Who did that? Did you see anyone?' The headphones have fallen and are dangling by my shins. People either side of me are pushing to board the train and the woman has already been swept away.

I know what happened. This wasn't an accident caused by clumsiness or overcrowding.

Someone dangled me in front of the train.

I want to stand still and yell out. To make everyone stop their trivial routines and pay attention to what has just happened. Wake them up and make them see that there was almost a murder under their noses.

I close my eyes for a second and breathe before fleeing back up the escalator, pushing past the tourists who are standing on the wrong side. The world outside feels oddly mundane and free of drama. I sink down, my back against the wall. Pedestrians and bus passengers carry on with their days, oblivious.

Eventually, I can breathe enough to walk to the bus stop, my legs like jelly. I endure an hour-long journey on an overheated bus.

By the time I get home my heartbeat is slower. Sadie is dressed like a vintage tourist who's holidaying in the South of France. Capri pants in pale lemon and a cream blouse with a spotted neckerchief around her throat. There's nothing ruffled about her that would suggest she's just rushed in before me. This deranged thought again that maybe she's somehow involved, that she could have been there on the platform.

'You look pale. Are you OK?' She's loading cleaning products into a metal box with a handle.

I'm about to tell Sadie what happened at Baker Street so I can gauge her reaction. I stop myself. I'll sound hysterical and paranoid. I know exactly what she'll say. The soft words that'll reassure me that it was an unlucky accident. She'll say that people get knocked on tube stations sometimes. Like she said she thought someone had knocked me when I nearly fell on the road. Which is exactly what Cathy said when I almost went down the stairs in college.

'Laura, if there is something wrong then you know that you can talk to me.' Sadie's face is etched with concern. A look that I was once so accustomed to from the nurses, the counsellors and the psychiatrists. Only Sadie's face looks less disingenuous than theirs always did. 'Shall we sit?'

Sadie leads me by the hand through to the sitting room and onto the sofa. 'I'm worried about you.'

I don't know if it's the thing at Baker Street, the kindness emanating from Sadie or the years I've spent holding this in. Whatever it is I feel something gives and the words I've been longing to say for so long start to become uncontainable.

'I think that the notes and everything that's happened might be to do with . . . something that I did.' My breathing is jagged, making it hard to speak.

'What's brought this on? Have the notes started again?'

I shake my head, trying to think of a way to phrase this but the words feel wedged. There are stories that stick in me like lodged food. Things I can't release.

'You're going to think I'm abhorrent. The first time it happened, when I was pushed in the road, I heard someone say a word.'

'What kind of word?'

I spit out the word like venom. 'Killer.'

'Why would someone say that, Laura?'

I make myself answer. I need to share this or Sadie won't understand my fears. And unless she understands why I'm so afraid, she can't help me.

'Because I did kill someone.'

A brief pause before Sadie regains her composure. Her tone is measured. 'Tell me what happened.'

* * *

Even before boarding school I was a child on the fringes, friendless, apart from the characters from the old films who populated my imagination. The last one to be invited to a birthday party, the person left out of playground games. I imagine that my natural shyness and unintentional aloofness made me hard to like but even if I had made friends, then having them back to our chaotic flat would have been difficult. Childhood relationships are transactional and I had nothing to offer back in return for the sandwiches, Smarties and jellies that their mothers would stand on watching us devour.

Some children respond to a chaotic home life by unravelling while others withdraw into something to find an escape route. My coping mechanism was to hide away in mine and Suzie's bedroom. I'd sit on the edge of the bed or lie on the floor, piles of books spread out before me. Studying was my punishing habit, the magnificent structure I craved but most importantly, my chance of an exit from that place.

When I won the scholarship to a private girls' school I thought that my life would change. And it did, but not in the way I expected. I remained an outcast. Wealthy girls sniff out poverty and they homed in on me like they were rooting out rotten food. They'd sneer at the cheap tape player that wasn't a Sony Walkman, my clothes for non-uniform events that were from market stalls instead of boutique shops, my toiletries that were from Superdrug rather than Clarins. I hadn't accounted for how much worse this would be. Unlike back home there was no escape from the taunts and jibes of my contemporaries as I now studied, slept and ate alongside them. I thought I'd be free but I was even more of a prisoner.

I tried latching onto different girls, picking out targets and then trying to please them. I'd fawn and flatter, dropping words like a gundog depositing dead birds at the shooter's feet. It would work occasionally but they'd always tire of me and my relentless efforts to be everything they wanted and needed. It turned out that too much effort was as bad as none at all when it came to schoolgirl friendships, especially when you're already viewed as something lesser. My nickname was 'The Creep'. I learned this the traditional way: through the thin walls of a toilet cubicle as girls at a sink forensically discussed my failings.

Life was barely tolerable till Jessica came to the school. A late admission from overseas, she was marked out by something, too. Her mental health. Sadness emanated from her like an aura and it felt entirely relatable. The other children rounded on Jessica, like dogs sometimes do when one of the pack is injured. Her blank expression and glassy-eyed unhappiness made her a natural target not only for the bullies but also for my friendship. We needed each other. She just needed to learn that.

She fascinated me, drawing my gaze like a magnet. Here was someone who felt like me, a kindred spirit who didn't belong. Jessica wasn't like the other girls with their New Wave pop obsessions, make-up sharing and neon fashions. Books were her thing. Her features lifted and animated when the mistress talked about them in English classes.

We became friends. She had no choice because I engineered it, watching to see what she liked, sneaking glimpses of her belongings in the dorm. I copied her tastes in books, music and clothes. It took a few months but I was dogged. These things always take time. I'd appear by casual coincidence in the places where she was likely to be. Hiding my eagerness to please her by mimicking the nonchalance that the other fourteen-year-olds were so skilled at. It wasn't my best performance but it worked. My masterstroke was when I pulled a book out of my bag, the same book I'd seen her reading the day before. I'd run to the library and found a battered paperback on the shelf.

'I'm reading that too.' I held up my copy of *Carrie* for her to see.

'Oh, right.'

'Which bit are you on?' I knew the answer. I'd peered over her shoulder and spotted which page she'd reached and placed my bookmark a little ahead of hers. I'd already read the book so it was easy to pull off.

'The bit just after the prom where she sticks it back to them all.' She looked up and there was a faint glint of something in her eye.

'The best bit! I sometimes wish I had some telekinetic powers to deal with this place.'

She looked up, blank faced, and there was a heart stopping moment where I started to second guess whether I'd gone too far. Worrying that she'd be thinking how insane I was for empathising with a heroine who electrocuted and incinerated her classmates.

'Oh, yes. Who would you electrocute first?' Her mouth turned upwards in a smile and her eyes widened. I tentatively offered the name of the worst of the school bullies and she reciprocated with the name of one the meaner games mistresses.

My job was done. I put in my groundwork and our friendship was sealed. By the time we'd finished discussing telekinesis and the symbolism of the blood in a way that only pretentious adolescents would, we were friends. The nicknames the other girls bestowed on us were tired and dull. 'The Doom Sisters', 'The Miseries' and 'The Plaths' (it was an academic school).

Jesscia became my consolation. Our talk soon escalated from books to the tribulations of boarding school to the trauma of being alive. Endless, circular conversations about our unhappiness. Finding an unhappy soulmate was, ironically, the thing that made me happy.

'Don't you just sometimes wish you could sleep for the whole of the term?' Jessica yawned and moved in her usual half-speed way with its balletic grace.

'Yes.' My words emphatic. It was like she read my thoughts.

'I wonder what it's like for people when they take drugs. Like, just being unconscious all the time and not having to think?' I tried not to wince. She didn't know about my sister. She had a different background to me.

Jessica was from a Home Counties family who moved around. A natural misfit in a household of boisterous fair-haired people, with her dark hair, pale complexion and permanent malaise. She had a sharp wit and a wild imagination. We'd spend hours making up scenarios about the teaching staff and our fellow pupils, bizarre and improbable stories that made us laugh.

But the stories Jessica liked the most were the nihilistic ones.

The stories of her own death.

I wanted to please her. She was the first and only friend I'd ever had. So, I reciprocated and did what I always did with peers, dancing whatever jig they wanted me to, and giving her what she wanted.

* * *

'I don't know if I can tell you the rest. It's too awful.' There's been a carousel of professionals who've poked, pried and cajoled and not once have I ever got this far into recounting the story.

Sadie sits back and stretches herself out across the sofa.

'It's a lot to ask of you, Laura, but would you rub my feet. The wards are killing me.' I lean forward and she lands a manicured foot into my lap. 'It's barbarism to expect me to walk in flat shoes. My arches aren't accustomed to it.'

I see what she's doing with this distraction. She's giving me something to do so that I'm occupied and don't have to look at her.

'The worst thing was that I . . . I concocted suicide pacts for us.' I wait for Sadie to say something but she doesn't. 'She loved them. She'd squeal with delight like I'd given her a gift. It actually seemed to lighten her mood.'

Sadie shifts her other leg into my lap and I knead my fingers and thumb into the ball of her foot. 'But she was a depressed child, Laura. And you were a child, too. It wasn't your job to help her to keep her safe and well.'

'But I shouldn't have encouraged her.'

'What about the school? Was there no help? For both of you, I mean.'

'She'd had help, of a sort. I didn't find out till later but there'd been concerns. Medications and therapy but that they'd also ignored some things that she'd said.'

* * *

We wrote down bullet-pointed plans and practised penning mournful notes to our families. We even sat one day trying to work out how to tie knots for a noose. Such macabre and childish games.

The plan that she liked best involved the cupola. It was a plan that I'd invented. The tower was part of the school's folly made up of dark bricks and crumbling staircases that loomed over the grounds. Somewhere forbidden, unsafe, which of course made it all the more appealing to us all. The base of the tower was littered with Benson and Hedges stubs and spent matches where girls cowered in its shadow, shivering in their blazers. The perfect illicit screen from the main building.

I knew that the librarian had a key because I heard her talking to the secretary about what a nuisance it was to cart trolleys to the folly where she stored the dated books. My pilfering skills were impeccable. I engaged her in a conversation about modernist novels and waited till she slipped off to find a Woolf I'd expressed an interest in before sneaking the key out of her drawer.

Jessica looked the happiest I'd seen her in weeks when I presented her with the key. I played along, enjoying our game. This fantasy prospect of an easy escape from our lives.

'Shall we go up there and see? Imagine what it would be like.'

Jessica's eyes glittered at my invite to continue our game. 'Yes.'

We wrote 'final notes' that were peppered with blame and recriminations. Jessica adding in a thank you to me in her notes for my ingenuity in devising the suicide plan and I puffed up with pride at my ability to make her happy. We laughed as we wrote them, revelling in this absurd play act.

My naivety is painful to recall.

The door to the tower was impossibly stiff and I remember wondering how the librarian ever managed to manoeuvre this. The smell of damp, the flickering bulb on the stairwell and the dusty floor of the portico. I could barely contain my delight at seeing Jessica so happy. There was a renewed lightening of her step. Her expression became one I'd never seen before. It was like something had lifted and her musculature had changed. I felt lighter, too, freed by companionship and understanding, enjoying the charade. This was a perfect distraction from the relentless pressure of boarding school life.

Jessica scurried to the top of the stairs, tripping once and laughing it off. The bell tower opened up before us. A square space with four archways each side to release the sound of the now defunct bell that lay like a corpse in the corner.

'Be careful, Jessica.'

'It hardly matters now, does it?'

'I suppose not.' I slipped back into character to rejoin the game.

She rushed forward and for a moment I thought she was about to actually jump and my chest constricted. She stopped at the edge.

'Come on, Laura. There's no time like the present.'

There was a gust of air from the side of the bell tower as we sat holding hands. I waited for her to comment on the drop, to engage in the next step of this fantasy of us tumbling down to earth like the falling man on the illicit Tarot cards that the other girls smuggled in.

'I think we should go down now. This is scaring me a little bit.' My voice was childlike. She turned and smiled at me and urged me to be resolute.

I don't remember her final words clearly. But I know what I said back.

I thought that she said, '*Would you go first or would I?*' An abstract idea.

It was only after it happened that I realised that I'd

misheard her. What she really said was *'Will you go first or will I?'*

A subtle and deadly distinction.

My answer: *'You'd go first.'*

And she did.

* * *

'Did she die in the fall?' Sadie asks me this without her usual sense of drama or urgency. It's more the gentle tone we use with the patients. Her face remains placid but unreadable. There's no sign of revulsion, just a hint of sadness in her brow.

'They said it was instant.'

She looked abandoned. Arms and legs twisted round like clothing that had blown from a washing line. The world gone quiet but for the sound of me screaming. The angle of her neck impossible.

I didn't, couldn't, speak for weeks. If I had I think I'd have started screaming again and never stopped. The images in my head that hit me like fists each time would have become real. It felt like speaking about what I'd seen would send me into a strange loop where I had to watch Jessica die over and over again. Psychiatrists tried to coax me, starting with a kindly approach before their mask would slip to show their frustration. The nurses forced me to swallow pills. My mum came when she could spare time between shifts, looking worn and alone. Suzie was nowhere to be seen and Mum didn't mention her.

The inquest was the worst. I'd expected it to take place in a wood panelled courtroom like from the one in that TV drama, *Crown Court*, that me and Suzie used to watch on ITV. Instead it was in a corporate block in a room with nylon carpets that gave me static shocks when I touched anything. A nurse supported me to a chair. I felt like I was somewhere else, looking in from outside through frosted glass.

There was a damning statement from the librarian who testified that I must have stolen the key and aggressive questioning from the coroner about why I didn't help Jessica or tell an adult. A rightful accusation, gleaned from the suicide notes, that the pact had been my idea. That it was all my fault.

And worst of all were her parents' faces. Cold rage from her father as he stared across the courtroom at me. Her mother beside him, like something deflated. Her face caved and gaunt with eyes like sea glass.

I said nothing.

Then the shouting as her father leapt up towards me and had to be dragged from the room.

* * *

'Laura, you were ill.' Sadie comes to life, lifting her feet from my lap and turning to face me on the sofa. She leans into me and puts her arms around me. I wonder if I should be crying now but I'm not.

'I know that now. But what I did . . . I was so stupid. I should have realised and it was all my—'

'No. It wasn't. You were *both* sick.' Sadie says this with a surprising firmness.

'But you see now? This is why someone is doing this. Someone here blames me.'

More than that.

Not just blames me but is seeking justice.

Someone is going to harm me.

Sadie holds me while I cry, at last, reassuring me that this can't be the reason. That it might well just be some petty jealousy or an unhinged personality and it will stop on its own.

I feel changed already. Reduced but in a positive way.

Like toxins have been released from an infected wound.

* * *

When I returned to the village, my voice finally back but scratchy from neglect, everything and everyone familiar had shifted into something accusatory and sharp. My moods stabilised, to a degree, with medications. The writing helped to take the edge off things, calming my mind with a notebook and pen. Remembering the things that they told me to do to try to cope when the thoughts came. Writing has never been a cure, just a way of communicating even if no one else reads it. I map out when the triggers set me off. Stairs, heights, certain smells. There were too many to list. Learning to cope with simple things like walking up a staircase without feeling like I wanted to curl into a ball and scream was like relearning basic life skills.

Then the months of rest and the job serving in the village café that my mum's friend Helen found for me. A steam filled hell where the villagers could come and scrutinise this strange young woman. That was my life, until I decided to escape here. Nursing was a job that felt entirely correct. Like I needed to atone somehow and give something back. Surprisingly, this job gives more back to me.

I watch Sadie over the next few days for subtle changes.

A tightening of her jaw, a way of looking at me, scrutiny in her eyes. All the ways that people became altered after Jessica died. But Sadie isn't like the small-minded gossips back home. In spite of my revelation, we stay the same.

We carry on talking late into the evenings and playing board games, tending to the house together until it's spotless, eating meals at the kitchen table.

She knows how bad a person I am and still wants me here.

I feel cleaner and more human than I have since I was a child.

Chapter Twenty-Three

NOW

Friday, 16 April 2010

There's a cruel light in the bedroom, illuminating motes of dust and smeary surfaces. There's no sound from Sadie's room nor any footsteps from the attic. I squat down and ease my suitcase out from under the bed, pulling my journal out from the inside pocket.

Sitting on the bed, I turn to a new page making three neat columns in black ink. Being woken so early by Sadie has left me jittery but alert so I make use of this time to try to order my thoughts. I start with the name that recurs so often in my journalling. *Jessica*. I spell it out in neat letters across the top. As usual there's a lurch in my stomach as I write her name, so I pause and take a few deep breaths. Then I write the names of the people who could have been the ones who wrote the notes. I start with Sadie, Anthony and Amy.

I'm methodical. The suspicions and thoughts spool down the page in rows in my restrained script. I add more people to the columns, starting with Louise. It's a pointless exercise of checking and reassurance because I already know who it was who stalked and terrorised me and I think I've worked out exactly why they did it.

I've finally been told the answer I've waited all these years for. I draw a circle round that name three times, almost piercing the page.

For all that I write about what happened when I was at school I never think hard about Jessica's face. She comes at me in flashes late at night or catches me unawares at random moments but her face is nebulous. I need to think about her now and home in, concentrating on the specifics. To remember the set of her features, the curve of her nose and mouth, the angle of her cheekbones.

Because that's the key.

I don't feel any sense of satisfaction when I'm done. There's just a sickening weight that comes over me from this tawdry story of pain and sadness that spread so widely.

I force myself up. There are more jobs that need to be done while I can sneak around the house, unseen. I stay methodical, starting in the office with the whisky bottle and the locked filing cabinets. I find nothing, so I move on to Sadie's dressing room. I'm going through the pockets of her coats when I spot something that I missed before. Nestling under her rail of fusty clothes there's a pile of four vanity cases. Dainty boxes from the 1950s, designed to carry make-up and styling accessories. I was too scattergun in my approach last time and I didn't notice these. The heavy dresses loom over my kneeling form like mourners at a graveside. The first case clicks open and releases a faint tang of floral perfume. There's a speckled mirror on the inside of the lid that divulges a portion of my cheek in the reflection.

My skin looks wan and gaunt in this light, like someone recovering from a long illness. The case is empty.

The next case is full of receipts but the third has more useful things. Old party invitations from the late 1980s, order of services from weddings that have probably now ended in divorce. At the bottom there's a stiff card edged in black. I hold it at arm's length, like it's infectious. The picture on the front is flattering, maybe from late teenage years. The name of the deceased is printed there in black font.

I've got it totally wrong.

There's a groan from the ceiling as footsteps start up overhead. Elsie must be awake. I shove the papers back into the case and push them under the rail of clothes. My knees creak as I stand. Years of hard labour on the wards haven't been kind to my joints.

I'm about to leave the room when there's a flash as sunlight hits a silver car that's parked opposite the house. It's sitting just down the street. The harsh light means that I can't make out who's sitting there, watching Laurel House.

But I don't need to see.

I can guess who it is.

Chapter Twenty-Four

THEN

November 1992

Sadie asks me to tag along with her while she goes to a vintage shop in Seven Dials. When we get back home there's a new letter for me. It's the familiar writing in capital letters, a stamp on the envelope with a London postmark. Sadie peers over my shoulder as I stand frozen in the hall.

'Fuck it. Not again. Do you need me to do it?'

I rip the envelope open, read it and pass it Sadie.

YOU NEED TO SUFFER MORE.

IT'S TIME FOR MY FINAL ACT

'This is insane.' She pushes back a stray lock of hair. 'Don't go anywhere without me or Amy, OK? We need to watch and find out who is doing this.'

I zone out, feeling like I'm sitting on the edge in the bell tower, the world stretching out beneath me. The hideous noises of flesh and bone hitting stone echoing in my memory. Shocks reverberate in my chest like someone's ripping open my rib cage.

'Don't worry, Laura, this is going to stop soon, anyway.' Sadie guides me to a chair and eases off my jacket.

'Why would it stop?' I look to her like a child looking at a parent, hoping she has a solution.

'I got rid of Louise, didn't I? I'm certain that she's the one who's been doing this.' Sadie is smiling and there's an odd look in her eyes that I haven't seen before. 'She was a monstrous liability and a threat to you, so I dispensed with her.'

'What?' I can't understand what she's saying. Her words sound like she's killed her. I stare at her, my mouth slightly open, cold fingers ripping at my stomach.

'I banished her. It's called revenge.' That word. 'Revenge'. It makes me shudder. A common enough word but it's the word that was marked out in faeces on that note.

It takes me a moment to deduce what she means.

'You set her up by putting the diazepam in her bag?'

Sadie's smile widens. 'She's gone now so the notes will fizzle out. She'll get bored of it now she's not near us.'

'You shouldn't have done that.' There's a theoretical part of my mind that sees how morally wrong this is. That Louise, however mean spirited, didn't deserve this injustice. The anxious part of my brain is gnawing at me, wondering what this says about Sadie and just how malicious she could be. Whether this vindictiveness would ever extend my way or if it already has done. I push away these stupid thoughts about the friend who's tended to me, prioritised me and fought my corner. I reach across and take her hand to show her that I support her. I have to. Out of anyone, I'm inclined to agree that deception isn't always wrong if the motives behind it are noble. Her logic is skewed, though. If Louise is the culprit then why didn't it stop as soon as she left?

It's not just Louise who's gone. Jane has left now, too. She was always here as an adjunct to her friends and once Louise was expelled, she exited, quietly. I don't imagine for a moment that she was ever the culprit.

What does this note even mean?

'*Final act?*' It's like someone is planning to kill me.

* * *

Dinner this evening begins as a civilised occasion. Anthony is present again. He might as well be living here. He's slicked back his hair with some kind of wet-look gel which accentuates his sharp features and makes him look like a city banker. I concentrate on Amy, who's regaling Sadie with some long-winded story about a nurse I don't know who's now pregnant by a married doctor I also don't know and has fallen out with a student who even Amy doesn't know. Sadie is doing the whole housewife thing and refusing any help as she juggles between saucepans and chopping boards. She's dressed in a peacock-blue maxidress with a clashing red gingham apron pulled on over her head, rucking the dress up where she's tied it so tightly.

'I'm exhausted.' Anthony interrupts Amy's flow with a performative yawn.

'You do too much. I don't know how you pull all those extra shifts in.' Sadie puts a casserole dish on the table. Anthony is, apparently, working as a care assistant in a care home on his days off. I haven't shared my background with anyone but Sadie but we've all heard Anthony's 'tragic' history about his coming out and being banished from the family farm. I've noticed that the story subtly changes with each telling. A different number of cruel brothers. The farm sometimes arable and sometimes dairy. The only constant is the dramatic incident about being caught fellating one of the farm hands, which is the bit I doubt the most.

I'm managing on the money we're paid and sending a little bit back to my mum. The reason Anthony is having to work two jobs is because of his predilection for designer clothes. He's sucked in by the allure of labels, believing that the tags, crests and motifs on his absurdly expensive garments will give him some kind of status.

Sadie seems off her game and the food is merely adequate tonight. I nod and smile, make occasional benign remarks and ignore the fact that Anthony hasn't once looked at me. By the time we've reached the apricot flan, I'm exhausted. Having Anthony here reminds me of one of the rare times my mum cooked a roast dinner and I found half a caterpillar in the remains of the cabbage I'd eaten. Anthony is the caterpillar flesh I'm having to digest.

'That was great, thanks. I'll wash the dishes.' I move towards the sink.

'Oh, let Ant do it. I'm trying to domesticate him.' Sadie winks at Anthony as she says this.

'Oh, Sadie, I forgot. There was a parcel came for you while you were at work.' Amy points over to the dresser where a padded envelope the size of a book is balanced on top of a pile of cookbooks.

Sadie walks over and opens the envelope. Her back is to me but I see her pull out a piece of paper which she strains to read. I'm sure it's not just me who hears the intake of her breath. She slides the paper back into the envelope and clutches it to her chest, like it's something precious that she fears will be snatched from her.

'Are you OK?' Amy makes to stand and go to her. 'Is it bad news?'

'Oh, it's nothing. I just don't feel well. I'm going upstairs for a lie down for half an hour then I'll be back down.' There's an unfamiliar tremor in her voice and she looks pallid beneath her make-up.

She doesn't return.

* * *

The next day I'm on an afternoon shift that's unremarkable. It passes at high speed in a whirl of chaos. On the way back, the streets are infested with Friday night drunks. Packs of young men who are not quite drunk enough yet to lurch at me but are sufficiently disinhibited to remark on my appearance and shout lewd comments. I scurry up the road, dodging the traffic, my feet passing through puddles that reflect the neon lights from the ungrammatical shop signs.

A stale sickness roils in my stomach, a combination of extreme tiredness, inadequate food intake and disquiet. Turning into the street should bring the usual flood of relief but there's none. My muscles tense like I'm about to enter into a brawl.

My first thought is that someone has fallen from the upstairs window. My head turns around in a neck jolting flick. A shapeless form hangs over the laurel bushes in the front garden, draping onto the railings. The orange streetlight casts a sallow glow making the clothes, *my clothes*, cast shadows on the pavement.

It's not just my clothes draped over the railings and bushes and strewn on the pavement like bodies. My books and postcards are scattered across the front path, my suitcase half on and off the step. My college notes spill onto the dirt of the flowerbed. The door is wide open and I hear shouting from the hall.

I stand for a moment, puzzled at the strange tableau, fingers of dread pushing at my stomach.

The shouting is Sadie.

A strange practicality comes over me and I retrieve the suitcase and cram in my things, fastening the straps with panicked fingers before pushing it out of sight under the bushes. I stand up, my breathing rapid and shallow. The old woman who lives opposite walks by with her dog. She usually speaks but her head is bent towards the dog as if it's communicating something so important that she couldn't possibly look away and acknowledge me and this mortifying situation. I'm glad to be ignored, unconvinced that my voice could come from my mouth.

The hall is dark. I bend down to pick up a couple of textbooks that haven't quite made it to the front garden. Sadie's shape appears over me and I swallow hard enough for the sound to echo in my ears. Her face is pale but with slashes of redness at her cheeks. Her mouth is set in a line. her eyes unreadable.

I don't know which hurts more: the sharp pull of my hair to raise me to her level, the sting of the slap across my face or the slam of my body into the wall.

'Get out of my house.' The words hurt more than the slap. 'I know what you are.'

I snatch my case and run. The adrenaline coursing through my legs is like electric shockwaves.

* * *

The Havana Boarding House is gruesome. It's painted in what must have once been lurid orange but now sports a layer of grey dirt that drips down the outer walls. The landlady shows me to a box-like room painted the colour of Pepto-Bismol. There's a shared bathroom that's like a museum of pubic hair. Mementoes from the fluctuating cast of businesspeople who pass through. I struggle to sleep, sweating in the overheated room on polyester sheets.

I hit a low on the third morning when I catch my foot in the flounced valance on the bed and sail across the floor, landing on the carpet, rubbing my knee and listening to the oily-haired man in the room below shouting at me to '*keep the fucking noise down*'. That's when I give in to it and sit and cry. My mind is a whirr of thoughts about the violence and this cruel exile from Laurel House but I'm determined to continue. I can do this job and I need to keep on with my training. I have to rise above this somehow and find a way to tolerate the remaining time here before I skulk back to Derbyshire.

I go back to my old habit of writing in my journals. I prop myself up on the misshapen mattress and lay out my notebooks, ready to puzzle through recent events and my emotions and actions. As I arrange them on the bed I spot something. The ones that I've been using most recently aren't there. I kneel on the floor, frantically looking for them. They're not in the case when I tip the contents out.

Two are missing. There are six and there should be eight.

They weren't there in the chaos of my belongings that night. I'm sure that I didn't leave them behind by accident.

Sadie must have my journals. It hits me like a fist. That's what must have been in the book-shaped parcel that she reacted so oddly to when it came the day before I left.

My malicious note writer stole my journals from my bedroom.

There are only three people who could have accessed that room: Sadie, Anthony and Amy. My skin freezes at the thought of the journals being sent to Sadie and her reading them. This explains why she was infuriated.

She knows the whole truth now. Not just about Jessica but the rest, too.

* * *

After a week in the guest house I come home to find the proprietor hovering in the hall with an air of general disapproval. She leads me into the dining room where a single cardboard box sits on the table. The remainder of my things. My clothes folded and laundered, the rest of my books and papers neatly stacked. I lug them up the stairs. Apparently a 'thin man, nicely dressed' but 'not especially polite' brought them round. The landlady looks more cheerful when she tells me about her reduced rates for long-term lets.

My missing notebooks aren't here. Sadie must have kept them.

Sadie is hard to avoid in the hospital because we're working on the same ward but a stroke of luck has put us on opposite shifts. I only see her at handover. She's a masterclass in strained decorum, never quite meeting my eye or speaking about anything other than work. Her voice has no trace of warmth. I can see that it's pointless me trying to speak to her.

I'm quieter now. More like the Laura I used to be, sitting silently waiting for handover to begin. Batting away conversational openers, taking my breaks alone and keeping to myself with my head held high, which takes effort.

Alone again, ignoring the whispers and gossip that rustles like leaves when I walk past.

I've ruined it all.

There's a final note pushed through the gap of my locker in the staff room: *FINISHED*

Chapter Twenty-Five

NOW

Friday, 16 April 2010

It's ironic how much time I once spent wishing I could be back here. Only now that I'm here I'd happily pay money to stay somewhere else. This place is rottener and more dangerous than any grimy guest house. But I'm imprisoned here with Sadie.

I peer out of the condensation-marred window. The once orderly vegetable patch is sprouting weeds and the paths are swallowed up by woody lavender bushes. I try to think what day it is. My sense of time has long been dictated by hospital routines and rhythms. Consultant ward rounds, operating theatre lists, planned admissions instead of the names of days of the week. There's an inaudible hiss when I turn the switch of the wooden radio near my bed. Twisting the dials brings me nothing but a station in French. Sadie's house is burdened with useless objects.

The kitchen is deserted when I walk down. The surfaces wiped clean, as I left them. The chipped fridge full of untouched food. Elsie has been trying to tempt Sadie with full-fat yoghurts and pots of custard that sit uneaten, slowly reaching their spoil dates. I find some eggs and a punnet of shrivelled mushrooms. The olive oil is spitting and I'm about to crack the first egg when I feel someone behind me.

'Morning, Elsie. Do you want me to make you something?'

'It's not Elsie. It's her haggard old mother.' I jolt around, flinching.

This isn't the Sadie who haunts my thoughts. She's leaning in the doorway, her stick thin legs looking like they can't possibly support her body. Her face is sepia toned with encroaching jaundice.

'How did you get down the stairs? You should have shouted for me.'

'Yes, Nurse Jameson. No, Nurse Jameson. You don't change, do you?' She smiles at me, her skull too close to her skin. 'Actually, don't change. I like that you're the same.'

A bubble of outrage swells in my gut. Sadie knows nothing about me. I'm altered beyond all recognition. Every cell and fibre eroded by the years spent trying and failing to not think about the things that happened to me here. I push away my frustration.

'Come on. Let me help.' I give her my arm and she reluctantly takes it, her gait an inebriated wobble as I guide her to a chair. There's a rush of activity: running to fetch analgesia, offering a drink, opening a yoghurt that she swirls with a teaspoon but doesn't eat. Finally we sit, alone, no sound but the tick of a wall clock.

'I feel like I've been in a terrible dream for days. Something about a hairy man in shorts and a volcano.'

'That wasn't a dream.'

'You mean that a hairy man in shorts saved us from a

volcano? Things have certainly livened up around here.' I try to laugh but it won't surface. I fill her in on the previous days and explain about the ash cloud that's left her husband abroad. There are no more questions about him on my mind anymore. I know as much as I need to.

'What's going on with the planes now?' I get up and switch on a grease-spattered reproduction radio and find the news. The situation is no better. The cloud of ash persists with the airports, the railway stations, the boats all chaos and people stranded all across Europe. Wherever her husband is he's not coming back yet. I'm stuck here.

'It's a good job that I sent Elsie up to Derbyshire to fetch you. She needs someone.' I feel a flash of rage at the thought of how much danger she put her daughter in.

'It was a stupid idea. She's fifteen. She had nowhere to sleep. She was hanging around the bus station all night. Was that all part of your plan, too?'

She screws her face up as if I've said something puzzling. She might be brighter today but she's still fogged in her thinking.

'She wasn't meant to be there overnight. And she's not—'

'What if I'd refused to help her? Do you think I even wanted to come back here?'

Sadie reaches across and her blanched fingers touch my hand. The cold of her skin emanates through my hand.

'But you needed to help me. I knew that you'd want to look after me.'

I close my eyes for a second, breathing through my nose.

'Well, maybe it would have been better if you'd called me sixteen years ago.'

'But I didn't need you sixteen years ago.' Her brutal logic can't be argued with. I have no reply.

This is it. Sadie didn't call me back here for any other reason than that I'm a competent nurse. Which is exactly what she did when Sacha needed help. I'm a nurse who she can relax around without having to worry that she'll say something incriminating when she's wild on medications.

There's a noise on the stairs: Elsie's teenage feet. She runs with a zest that I lost long ago. Once she's calmed down from her glee at seeing Sadie out of bed, she starts planning lunch for us all. Overambitious lists of things that she could cook for the three of us. Her flutter of hope is endearing. Sadie sits and smiles benignly and I can see that she hates that someone is doing the job she thinks is hers.

'What shall we do now. How about a film or something? Or maybe some music?' Elsie flails for some normality in this twisted new world that they're in.

Sadie doesn't answer. Her eyelids are drooping and she's slumping over the table.

'I think what we might do is help your mother move to somewhere more comfortable.' Sadie nods. 'Oh, and the palliative care nurse is coming later as well as the district nurse at some point.'

I push away thoughts of Cathy for now. I'll deal with her later.

The stairs are a struggle and by the top third we're having to manually lift Sadie's stick legs. When she's on the bed I send Elsie on an errand, reeling off a quick list of groceries that we need. She writes it down with keen attention, like she's taking dictation.

I tidy the bedroom but it's impossible to rid a sick room of the taint. This house that always smelled of polish, baking and laundered clothes is now rich with the odours of illness. There's a waft of perspiration and a sweet chemical tang that invades my nostrils. Nothing will mask it, so I don't try.

I rest the bowl of water on the bedside cabinet that I've cleared and reach for the flannel and soap to wipe away the cold sweat that's coating Sadie's skin. I'm doing the job I was brought here for. Sadie has the dedicated personal nurse that she wanted. I'm stuck with this role and I'm taking it seriously.

I have three jobs, all of which I'd rather not have to do. Task one is to be here for Sadie. The dying can be content, happy sometimes, even when people are dying young. There are a few people who leave the world in a more turbulent state and that's when I need to step in and soothe. I'm guessing that Sadie won't go peacefully. Her periods of agitation are a portent. She has too much at stake here with the motherless child. I'm guessing that she'll scratch and claw onto life, dying in a frenzy of flailing hands and yells as her body gives out.

My second job is to support Elsie. She's as important as Sadie in all this. I'm chipping away at her teenage armour and breaking down the pre-adult truculence. She walked across and hugged me in the kitchen earlier. The unfamiliar warmth of flesh that isn't lying prone in a bed or sensed via a barrier of plastic gloves sent me reeling momentarily.

My third job is to observe. I'm a nurse; I chart, quantify and report abnormalities. This is different, though. There's an observation that there's no chart or measuring tool for. I need to observe Sadie's speech and watch what she says. There's risk here. Whatever happened back then needs to stay between us. I'm not having everything I've achieved and worked for stripped away. People rely on me.

I need this to be done so I can go back to my cottage,

to Mum and Suzie, get this promotion and continue my uneventful life.

Sadie definitely has to be watched.

* * *

When Sadie wakes up later, the light in the room is hitting the wall behind her, showing up damp patches that have bubbled through the wallpaper.

'I don't want my story to be this.'

'Don't want it to be what?' I speak in the tone that I use with patients, soft but never patronising or singsong. I sit myself down by the side of the bed.

'A sick woman's story. They don't end well, do they? Like the bedridden wives who get poisoned in those old crime films that you used to watch.' She tries to reach for the glass but I'm quicker, putting it firmly in her hand and guiding her to take a sip.

I stroke her hand and sit. Not exactly waiting, more allowing a pause.

'I know what's wrong with me and they say that there's no cure. But they're wrong. I won't . . . I can't die. Elsie needs me.'

'Whatever happens, she has her father, too. You're not alone with her.' The nausea that engulfed me before when we alluded to this random man has gone. I don't care who he is as long as he comes back here soon.

'He's an unreliable dick.'

She turns her face away and her eyes close.

The doorbell rings and I leave her.

Cathy is back, her clothes letting off the taint of cigarettes. I hope she had her uniform well covered if she was smoking.

She's brisk and efficient, flipping through Sadie's care plan, like the student she was back in the 1990s. Only this Cathy is harder edged and nervous with a catch in her voice. I allow her to go upstairs on her own. I trust Sadie today. She's safe when she has these lucid and contained moments.

Cathy comes down after an excruciating ten minutes. I'm not looking forward to this. I'm not sure which one of us will instigate the conversation. When she appears she's jittery but putting on a front of faux cheerfulness. She suggested ordering a hospital bed to Sadie and was refused and dismissed. She makes calls to try to get a Marie Curie nurse to come to sit with Sadie at night. There's no one available. Death must be sweeping this part of London this week.

I sit and wait, watching her, while she does this.

She thinks it'll be soon, days only perhaps, till Sadie dies and I agree. There's comfort in knowing that there's an endpoint to this danger, that there'll soon be silence. Maybe she'll be gone before her husband even returns. But I'm not sure that I could even leave before he does return. The prospect of Elsie being alone after they've carted Sadie away is unthinkable.

I pull myself back to the present moment. It's time.

'How's Nathan?' I'm standing by the kitchen worktop with my back to her and she's hovering. I've become as ridiculous as Sadie and I'm decanting instant coffee into one of her pointless coffee pots.

'Can we sit somewhere, Laura? I need to talk to you about something important.'

Whatever the intervening years have done to her, Cathy still has a pompous superiority that breaks through her veneer. I lead her through to the sitting room and she sits back on the sofa, adjusting the skirt of her uniform.

I lower myself onto the armchair. I'm higher than her.

She makes a performance of setting her coffee cup down on the table, stirring for longer than is needed, failing to mask her shaking hands as the spoon hits the crockery and makes discordant notes.

I lounge back in the chair and cross my legs, taking a sip of my drink.

'I can see that you're finding this difficult.' I keep my voice level. 'I'll save you the trauma. I already know what happened.'

Her face freezes.

Chapter Twenty-Six

THEN

December 1992

I've been using the bulk of my wages to rent a boxroom in Battersea with a tiny window and barely enough room to turn around at the side of the single bed. I can't afford a place closer to the hospital so my trips to and from work are torturous. I sit wedged in for an hour on the top decks of buses that drip condensation, coming away with my hair smelling of cigarettes.

The two women I share the flat with communicate with me by passive aggressive notes on the fridge. They whisper together and stop talking when I walk into the room, arranging nights out that I'm, thankfully, not invited to attend. When they burst back into the flat in a riot of sound in the early hours, they wake me, then complain about the noise that I make boiling the kettle when I get up at five in the morning for work.

I feel friendless, untouched and unconsidered. My flesh misses the easy pressure of Sadie as we slumped together on the sofa, her legs flung across mine as she lay back. The way she would reach across and touch my hand. Even my mysterious enemy has gone. Hatred is a type of attention, too. I'm not even important enough for that now. As promised, that was the finale. There's been nothing more. There's no one to take an interest in the minutiae of my life. Apart from work-related exchanges with other staff, I talk to no one except the patients. This is my penance.

I've enquired about transferring my training up to Derbyshire but the answer was what I expected: they've told me that I can't. I'd have to start again and all my efforts will have been a waste. Other than work, there's nothing to keep me in this city now that I don't have Sadie and Laurel House. I stay in my room and read or I'm at the hospital, putting in practice hours. The responsibility I'm given increasing exponentially, the wards my home but also a threat. Anthony and Sadie prickle with hostility when they pass by so I maintain my impassive look as they blank me or I speak with pained politeness. Amy is a different story. She smiles and grabs my hand when she sees me, whispering 'It'll be OK, matey.'

I pull my hand away, still unsure if she's the architect of this.

* * *

It's Cathy who delivers the summons to me. She approaches me as I walk onto the ward and hands me a pale lilac envelope with my name written on it in flowery writing. Sadie's handwriting.

'I passed Sadie on my way in and she asked me to give you this.'

'Why did she give it to you? She's working on the same ward as me. She couldn't even give me a note?'

'Don't shoot the messenger, Laura. I'm not involved in this.' There's a flash of misplaced rage and I want to slam her against the wall.

I sit through handover, the note stuffed into my uniform pocket, unread. It whispers to me as I listen through the list of names and conditions.

'Laura, are you with us?' Sister Bronwen smiles across at me. 'Karen asked for your opinion about Mrs Green and you haven't answered.'

The remark from Sister Bronwen is mild but stinging for me. I need to do this well. There has to be something that I can't mess up.

'She's much more placid when her husband is here so it might help if we relaxed the visiting hours for him.'

Sister Bronwen's nod is validating.

The first chance I find I run to the bathroom, leaning against the flimsy cubicle wall. The note is written in smudgy ink. It tells me nothing. It's merely an invitation.

We would like to resolve these issues. Please call round after your shift today.

I screw it up and flush it down the toilet, banging the lid closed.

* * *

Whether it's for a parental discussion, a teacher wanting to talk about your bad behaviour or a manager, dissatisfied with your work, being summoned is not a pleasant experience. Being called in by a so-called friend to dissect what I've done wrong is far worse. The '*we*' of the letter puzzles me. I have visions of a panel that consists of Sadie, Anthony and Amy. Maybe even Sacha, who knows. A jury of my peers sitting along a table, judging me. Reading from the notebooks where I've recorded my every aberration. Another inquest to attend.

I make no effort with my clothes. I'm determined that this isn't going to be an occasion. The muted vintage dresses that Sadie says look good on me stay in the case. Instead I pull on a Debenhams jumper that my mother bought for me one Christmas and a pleated skirt. Me before I met Sadie.

'You came.' This isn't the Sadie of the night she slapped me or the coolly polite Sadie of the wards during the last two weeks. But she's not quite the Sadie I was living with either. She's a staged version: a Doris Day film Sadie with a forced smile.

'Come through.' I follow her into the kitchen. I'm a guest here now.

Amy sits in her usual place, her head propped up on one hand, both elbows on the table. Anthony has taken my seat. He sits straight backed, refusing to acknowledge me. The urge to laugh rises up. Pomposity always does that to me. His slender feet are bare under the table. No footwear nearby so I'm guessing that he must be living here now.

'Sit down, darling.' The 'darling' gives me hope. 'Do you want coffee?'

When she passes me the coffee cup her hand causes ripples in the black fluid. Sadie sits facing me. Anthony leaps up and places himself behind her, giving her right shoulder a reassuring squeeze. She lifts her immaculately manicured hand and rests it on his. They're a twisted tableau of a husband and wife straight from a Norman Rockwell painting with Amy as the good child and me as the wicked one.

'I need to apologise. I shouldn't have hit you. Violence is never acceptable. I'm deeply sorry for doing that, Laura.'

'You also pulled my hair.' My hand automatically reaches to the back of my head.

'What?' Sadie moves her chair in towards the table, the metal feet hitting the tiles with a bang. She didn't expect me to interrupt. My role here is to be judged, not to offer retorts.

'You didn't just slap me. You pulled my hair too. We should mention that.'

'Well, OK. This isn't a court proceeding but you're entitled to take the higher ground. To an extent. I'm sorry for all of it. I've been under a lot of pressure worrying about Sacha, working, studying and trying to keep the house going. Which isn't a justification, of course.' Sadie waves a hand to Anthony and he walks over to the kitchen drawer, pulling it open with a flourish, like some hackneyed magician at a children's party. He walks back holding my notebooks. 'But there *are* things we need to talk about.'

Sadie rests her hand on my journal. 'Laura, why did you lie?'

'She didn't just lie. It's been a large scale manipulation.' I knew it wouldn't be long before Anthony spoke. He's been twitching away like a child trying to keep a secret.

I'm silent. I know exactly what's coming.

Chapter Twenty-Seven

THEN

December 1992

Some religions classify sins by severity, grading them like nurses classify patients' wounds. My crimes are about to be judged and recorded.

With Sadie, my need for a friend pushed me over an invisible line into duplicity. So let's call these sins of desperation. Lies that made life better for me. Who hasn't done that? Shaved a couple of years off your age when it suited you, exaggerated your qualifications or achievements for advancement, pretended to have read a particularly impressive novel. We all lie a little.

But I've only ever lied and cheated with one goal in mind: finding somewhere to belong and someone who I could be with. Someone who would see me as their priority. A friend to banish my loneliness. Sadie was my aim from the moment I set eyes upon her. Her and Laurel House. These safe havens where I could finally settle and expand and develop without judgement.

'Anthony had already guessed about the notes. And the blood. But I refused to listen.' If I had to describe Sadie's look, I'd say it was mortification.

'It didn't really take Miss Marple. I guessed that you'd stolen the discarded blood bag. I saw you from the window of my ward, walking back from your room.' Anthony's smirk is well-earned. He has every right to scorn me, for once. 'But I dismissed it as harmless. Much like the stupid anonymous notes that you sent to yourself.'

'I—'

'Let me speak.' There's a weariness in Sadie's voice.

I glance across at Amy. Her head has slid further down her arm and she's staring intently at the table. As if the Formica holds the answer to a hidden code.

I did lie about the blood.

The mistake I made was writing down exactly what I'd done in my therapy journal. The one that Sadie now has. I write down any incidents that leave me feeling fragile or wounded. A rude shop assistant, another student snubbing me, a mistake on the ward that leaves me feeling bruised and inadequate. These minor incidents that lead to rushes of self-loathing. More importantly, I use my journals to work through my triggers, analysing the moments when I have flashbacks to Jessica, trying to reduce their power with words. The blood thing needed processing. There were twinges of guilt about what I'd done and the reaction it caused. The nerve wracking trip into college to be interviewed and the wafts of unearned sympathy.

I made that macabre tableau in my room. A theatrical set, both facile and dramatic. All it took was a discarded transfusion bag waiting to be sent back for disposal and a large syringe to do the job. I sneaked back to my room when the ward was especially chaotic and turned it into a bloodbath. No one on my ward noticed that I was gone. If the blood didn't get me a room in Laurel House then I'd planned to fake an attack on myself next. It would have been easy enough. A few rips to my clothes and a strategic self-inflicted bruise.

But I didn't need to do that because Sadie took me in, like I guessed she would.

I had what I needed. Someone cared about me. Pathetic, isn't it? Most people earn that on merit but I've never quite worked out how to do that.

The beauty of it all was that Sadie needed me as much as I needed her. She just required a push and I happened to be the one to exert that force. We were happy together, content and symbiotic in our two-person household, albeit a household with the threat of her boyfriend returning and disrupting everything we'd built. One with Amy and Anthony looming on the peripheries.

'I can forgive the thing you did to your room, Laura. It's flattering really that you were so keen to be here. A bit pathetic, perhaps.' She swallows and it sounds too loud in the room. 'But it's the rest of it.'

I don't bother to pre-empt her. I wait as Sadie flicks through the notebook, Anthony peering over her shoulder like a ghoul.

'Can I go? I don't want to be part of this.' Amy addresses Sadie but she can't keep from glancing at me. Her eyes bearing no hint of the darkness of the other two.

'I'd rather you stayed. It's better if this is a group discussion.' Sadie's tone makes it clear that this isn't a request.

There's a pause and I jump in. 'It was one time. The

blood I mean. The notes weren't me. And the thing at Baker Street. They—'

Sadie freezes, her finger on an open page.

'Enough lies.' There's a note of exasperation.

I *was* manipulative. I own that.

But I didn't send the notes. Not one of them came from me.

And I *was* pushed, tripped, followed and locked in a cupboard.

All of that is true. Someone hated me enough to do it.

Maybe even someone in this room.

'I'm not lying. Why would I send you the notebooks when they've caused all this? And you won't have found anything written in there about me writing the notes. Because I didn't do it. I've been in danger.'

'I don't believe you. I think . . . I don't know what to think. I think that there's a chance that you're telling the truth about some of it and you might have received a few childish notes from someone but the rest is all in your head. Nothing happened at Baker Street. That thing with the linen store was just a silly accident.' Sadie presses against one side of her forehead.

'Someone wanted to harm me.' My voice sounds like that of a petulant child.

The silence is too long, long enough to tell me that Anthony and Amy don't believe me either. That this slice of truth in my deception has failed to impress them.

And why should they listen to a word I say? I'm the girl who cried wolf. The opportunist who they think wrote a series of silly anonymous notes to myself for attention, added on a blood drenched coup and some extra drama with a few staged incidents like that linen cupboard.

'You liked it, though, didn't you?'

'Liked what?' Sadie locks eyes with me.

'Being my rescuer.'

Anthony pulls up a chair and sits down. 'You're not even repentant, are you?'

'I think that's between me and Sadie, don't you?'

'For fuck's sake, she's—'

'Enough.' Sadie covers her face with her hands. Her voice is just above a whisper. 'You can leave now, Amy, if you want to go. And you too, Anthony. Maybe it's better if Laura and I go to the sitting room and speak about what else she did.'

* * *

Sadie doesn't need to turn the rest of the pages of my notebook. We both know what's there. The litany of my further crimes written in orderly ink. The record showing that my skill at manipulation was further employed with painful consequences.

'Did impersonating me amuse you?' Sadie leans back on the sofa, her dress riding up over her knees. 'Am I so ridiculous?'

I don't answer. I sit and stare at a painting on the wall opposite, tracing the outline of the mournful-looking woman staring out from the frame, wondering what she had to be so unhappy about.

'Did you go full method?' She smiles and her hand sails gracefully across and settles on top of mine. Her rings scratch into my flesh as she grips down hard. 'Maybe you could take over being me for a while and I could finally get some fucking rest.'

I dare to look up, confused as to why she's touched my

hand and where this is going. Unsure whether her face will still be shuttered down or whether the familiar warmth will be back.

'It's flattering, I suppose that you were so desperate to be with me that you engineered all that. I just wish you hadn't interfered with the situation with Sacha. It was all under control.'

'I'm sorry.' My voice is no longer weak.

'I have plans with Sacha and you've inadvertently done your level best to royally fuck them up.'

I stare down at my legs.

'Do you want to come back home?' This is unexpected. I'd thought that this was something I'm going to have to work on. That there'd be a period of atonement, maybe some further manipulation and conniving before Sadie and I could be friends again.

I nod, not trusting myself to speak. I want to be back in this house more than anything. To sink back into the hum of domesticity and the quotidian tasks.

Sadie reaches up and touches my face. 'I don't know if I can forgive your lies. But I do want you to come back. I have something that I need help with.'

'Yes.' I look across at her, not asking or caring what it is she wants. She squeezes my hand tighter.

'I have to ask this. Are you in love with me, Laura? I mean in a sexual way. I won't judge you.' She sits more upright, her chest puffed out like a preening bird. Finally smiling in a way that I recognise with a soft widening of her painted lips. 'I don't mind.'

I shake my head. 'Not in that way.'

I don't have sexual feelings for Sadie.

That wasn't why I tried to get rid of Sacha.

* * *

Living with Suzie has shown me the effects of addiction. I don't mean the effects on my sister. Her suffering is impossible to watch but regardless of the empathy I feel for her, I've had to harden myself and look away. It's what it did to me and my mum and our relationship. The constant worry and strain, the sense of shame, the never knowing what's coming next. All of this ate away at Mum and left her no time for anything or anyone else. We lived a tense and sparse life.

It wasn't long after I'd moved in that Sadie shared with me that Sacha had issues with alcohol. She played it down but the subtext was obvious. I didn't want Sadie to end up like us. To become worn down from staying caught in the cycle of someone else's addiction. I decided to help her. The additional effect of this was that I'd have Sadie to myself, of course.

I took another of Sacha's calls not long after I'd moved in. His tone was abrupt, words spat out with vehemence. He showed no interest in who I was, demanding that I run to fetch Sadie, treating me like a servant. His voice made my skin feel like it was caked in dirt.

I loitered on the landing, eavesdropping on Sadie's side of their conversations, occasionally picking up snatches of his speech through the receiver. It seemed obvious that their relationship was hopelessly flawed. An entirely different picture from the one Sadie painted of her being the faithful woman, waiting patiently for her beloved partner to return. Sadie fawned down the phone line, reduced by him. Her sentences never finished as he butted in, bulldozing over her.

I listened eagerly for clues in Sadie's words when we discussed him, picking at fragments and single words. Noting when she used words like 'hot-headed' or 'opinionated' and translating that as 'violent' and 'controlling'.

I decided to repel him. I devised a plan to save Sadie from her delusions. Long hours practising in my bedroom, whispering words in her honeyed tones. It wasn't difficult to mimic her after the hours I'd spent listening to her stories and anecdotes. It only took two more calls from Sacha before he stopped ringing at all. I delivered a stern monologue whereby 'Sadie' deflected all his interruptions. My version of Sadie told him that she didn't want to hear from him for a while. That it was all too much and she wanted time to think.

The letter was tougher. Sadie kept Sacha's correspondence locked in a drawer and endless searches failed to reveal where the key was. I knew that they arrived in torrents; nothing for weeks then an outbreak of mail over a period of days before the next void. Letters that made Sadie's neck redden and sent her into periods of silence where she consoled herself by smoking more and retreating to her bedroom, playing her scratched records on the Dansette with the toneless speakers.

Once I'd made my decision to ward him off, I started intercepting any new letters that arrived. I loitered for the first post. Three letters arrived on consecutive days, stark missives filled with self-pity. Scrawls of handwriting stating that he wanted to be back here, to sort his life out once and for all and fix their relationship. That he loved her and wanted to be a better man. I banished the letters to the bins on the high street on the way to the hospital.

Then, I hunched over the desk in my room, practising repeatedly till I got his handwriting right, printing the prisoner number on the top of the page in ink and sticking the letter in one of his envelopes that I'd steamed open.

I didn't end their relationship for good. I'm not that harsh. I just told her that he needed time apart from her when he left prison and was asking for her to not contact him until she heard from him again.

Then I wrote a similar one from Sadie to Sacha. I bashed it out it on the old typewriter in the dining room that she keeps mainly for show and ended with her usual dramatic flourish of a signature. Their letters would have crossed in the post. I was poised, ready to comfort her when she read the missive from 'Sacha'. Naturally, I didn't like to see her upset. She showed resilience and bounced back after a few tearful days. My gamble paid off. Sadie stopped mentioning his name and told me one evening that 'Sacha is taking some time out, to reflect and try to become a better person'.

There was a flaw in my plan which I was painfully aware of. He'd turn up eventually but my hope was that Sacha would be deterred enough by my Sadie impersonation and his ignored letters to stay away for a period of time. Sadie and I would be safe. My naïve dream was that my meddling would go unnoticed in the carnage of their chaotic relationship.

And Sadie would still be mine.

The right outcome for us both.

* * *

'Does everyone know about this?' I don't care what Amy thinks but I worry about Anthony having ammunition against me.

'I don't think that what anyone else does or doesn't know is relevant.'

'I'm so—'

'I've been processing it all and I think that I understand. I can accept why you did it. Even though it was abhorrent behaviour.' Sadie stands up and walks towards the mantelpiece, her fingers brushing along the long necked ceramic dogs that stare at me with saucer eyes. 'It's flattering, really.'

'And has Sacha been back?'

'He's on his way now.' Sadie's face hardens. It isn't the look you'd expect from someone whose lover is finally returning to them. 'I need you to help me with something. You're the only person who can do this for me and Sacha.'

I nod eagerly. I can make Sadie love me again. In time, she'll understand that I'm not as messed up as this makes me look and that everything that I did was for our friendship. I also need her to believe the whole truth. She has to know that I didn't send the notes. That I really was in danger.

Sadie's head jolts round as the front door slams hard, making me start. Unfamiliar footsteps cross the hallway.

'Fuck.' Sadie shoots out of the room and I follow. 'He's early, for once.'

A man stands against the kitchen sink with his back to me, staring out across the garden. His black hair is cut shorter than in the photos. His face in profile looks puffy and puce and his clothing hangs off him; crumpled garments that look like he's slept in them. The stale alcohol smell exuding from him taints the room.

Sadie rushes across the room to him.

'Sacha!'

He's back.

Chapter Twenty-Eight

NOW

Friday, 16 April 2010

I look up as something catches my eye through the sitting room window. There's a man pacing the street in front of the house, walking up and down in the way people sometimes do when they're smoking. Only he doesn't have a cigarette.

Nathan doesn't look like I thought he would. I'd expected weight gain, incipient hair loss and puffiness but he's lean, like one of those men in his thirties who's discovered cycling and lycra. He's attractive and wholesome in that way that enthusiastic fathers in their thirties sometimes are.

'You might as well invite him in.' I put down my cup and lean forward in the chair. It's me who's trembling now. A slick of coffee lands on the table.

Cathy goes to fetch him while I walk around the room, straightening my clothes and hair. I catch sight of my drawn face in the glass of one of the pictures. He walks in and Cathy snatches at his hand, leading him to the sofa like she's herding an animal.

'Thank you for letting me in, Laura. I just want to explain . . .' His public school accent is still there but there's a lack of authority in his voice. He sounds meek and beaten.

'You were grieving. I understand where things can take you to.' He looks across at me. It's still there in the way he looks at me. That eagerness to appear friendly. Only now it's real instead of the elaborate act that it was when we were students. The way that he'd stared so intently at me when we first arrived that I'd assumed was him being lecherous. It all makes sense now. He wasn't attracted to me. He was studying me and masking his justified hatred.

Cathy looks across at me with sheepish eyes. 'How long have you known?'

'Only since you came here earlier this week. You said something about the house being like he'd told you it was. You'd never really spoken much to Anthony, so the only man who could have told you what it looked like here was one of Amy's nocturnal visitors. Which had to be Nathan.'

'I see.' She squeezes Nathan's hand and turns to face him. 'Whoever was writing the anonymous notes stole my journal, so they had to have been inside the house. I remember Amy and Nathan talking together and how keen he was on her. It all added up.'

I don't mention all the other memories that have come rushing back. Thoughts melding together to form a truth that makes sense to me. Nathan's public school accent. His references to knowing Derbyshire well. Jessica talking about her hardy, fair-skinned family.

Nathan lets go of Cathy's hand and walks to the window, looking out onto the street as he talks.

'I hated you so much.' I'm glad I don't have to see his face. Now that I know who he is, I'm having flashbacks to the courtroom. Nathan wasn't there but he sounds like his father, that scarlet-faced man who was screaming at me as he was dragged out by the security guard. 'My father had a lot of rage after Jess died and he didn't know what to do with it. It became his obsession. Hating you became a reason to keep on living for him.'

I have this urge to draw my limbs up to my torso and curl in on myself, making myself as small as possible. I force myself to be still.

'I don't know if you can imagine what that was like to live around. I came to London to start a new life away from my family. But there was no escape, I recognised you on the first day.' He turns away from the window and faces me. 'I hated you for being here. For being alive.'

My posture slips and I deflate back into the chair. 'And I deserved it.'

'No, Laura. That's not true.' His voice rises in pitch. 'It's really not. I should have contacted you years ago to apologise. What I did was unforgivable. You must have been so afraid.'

'He's been haunted by this, Laura. He really has. This isn't what he is.' Cathy looks at Nathan, rather than me, when she says this.

'But you were right to want to hurt me.' I feel the prickle of tears forming in my eyes 'Jessica—'

'No!' His shout sends echoes of adrenaline through my body. 'I was an absolute dick. I couldn't accept that my sister was sick and that my insensitive parents were too wrapped up in their fucked-up marriage to notice it. I wanted someone to suffer. I wanted you to feel as scared as I thought Jessica must have been. And the years of listening to my father had programmed me to hate you.'

The tears run down my cheeks, a mirror to Nathan's.

'When I first recognised you, the rage I felt was like something unstoppable. I went to the toilets and wrote that first stupid fucking note that I put in your bag. I was ripped up. Like, really fucked up by my family and I just wanted to see whether it made me feel any better to see you being scared.'

'It's OK.' There's an enviable compassion and affection in Cathy's reassurance to him.

'Then I saw you with Sadie on the road and something gave in me, so I pushed you.' He lowers his gaze and closes his eyes. 'And you nearly died, which I didn't want. I just wanted to scare you.'

'It's done now and I—'

'No. I have to say it. I did so many shitty things. All those notes and thefts and then I went in your room.' He flushes when he says this, making his reddened face flush more. As if invading my privacy is worse than dangling me into the path of a tube train or leaving me a note written in human waste. 'I'd spent the night with Amy and on my way out, I spotted that your door was open. I went in to leave a note in your room to really freak you out and I rooted about while I was there. I'm sorry. You already know that I found the notebooks. I read all the things that you'd written about what really happened with Jessie.'

'It was work I did for therapy.'

'I know, I know. And I didn't expect what I found. Pages and pages where you . . . where you set out everything that happened over and over. It helped me understand that it wasn't your fault or my sister's, regardless of what my messed-up father chose to believe. I finally saw that Jessica wasn't scared. She was happy, at last.'

He tries to smile but it doesn't quite land. His voice is

softer again. I imagine he's a good nurse. 'I felt so much shame at how I laid the rage at your feet but even then I still did something unforgivable. I got drunk and sent the books to Sadie, to hurt you one final time.'

'It's OK.' There's something unspoken in the air and I'm guessing that he's not saying the full reason that he sent them. I suspect that part of him wanted to warn Sadie about how toxic I was.

'But I knew then that you hadn't done anything to encourage Jessie and I still did it.'

There's a period of silence and I can hear Nathan's breathing.

'There's something that still puzzles me. Why were there so many gaps? It was all so sporadic. I was always waiting to see what you'd do next. That was the worst part in a way.'

He colours now, redness creeping up his cheeks and forehead in the way that happens with fair-skinned people.

'Can I tell her?' Cathy stands up and goes to his side, the two of them looking down on me from across the room. 'He had a drink problem. He's been dry since we finished college and we've both worked at it but he was a mess back then and—'

Nathan interrupts her. I imagine he has to do this often. 'I could control what I felt about you when I was sober but then I'd go on a massive bender and it would start up. I was in the midst of a crazed vodka bender when I pushed you forward at Baker Street. I pulled you straight back. I wouldn't have hurt you and—'

'Nathan, stop. There's no need.' I get up and walk over to stand facing him and Cathy.

'Do you forgive me?'

'There's nothing to forgive.'

None of it matters. I accept that he wanted to punish me, to make me feel as bad as Jessica did. I feel a weight of sadness wash over me at the thought that Nathan was so tortured and twisted that he did what he did. That his life became so intolerable that he had to annihilate himself with alcohol. I understand his need to avenge. He arrived here to find the woman who helped his sister kill herself was sitting across from him in the classroom. No wonder he did what he did.

I understand the insanity of wanting to hurt someone and how that can overtake you.

We're not that dissimilar.

The room feels oppressive, like we're in an impossible impasse. I'm stuck for what to say next. Should we revert to cocktail party chatter, asking banal questions about careers and how many children they have? Nathan brings resolution by saying that he has to leave to prepare for a clinic.

Cathy touches my arm but her eyes are still shooting across to his face, checking in on him. 'You went through a lot here, Laura. It must have been hard to come back with what happened at the end. Sadie's fortunate to have you.'

I have a sudden thought.

'Was it what happened to Amy that made you start again?' I don't allude to what he did later on. To the violence and destruction.

Nathan looks confused. 'Start again? I didn't start again.'

* * *

Sadie's pain has flared up. It bites into her, grappling with her breathing, contorting her face. She looks pallid and drained. The dull bulbs of the bedside lamps enhance the yellowing on her sallow skin. Her eyeballs are protruding now, layers of flesh devoured.

'It's OK. Just sit tight. The oxycodone always works. It'll just take a little while.'

'I'm a nurse, Laura. I know that.' The flash of irritation soothes me. It's an indicator that Sadie is still there, behind all the pain and exhaustion.

I tell her about Cathy coming. About how she looks like a different woman. That the class swot is now as human and flawed as the rest of us. When I get to the part about her marrying Nathan Sadie's eyes shoot open.

'Nathan? Good for her. She had a crush on him all through college.'

I start to tell Sadie about Nathan being the one who hated me so deeply that he terrorised me but she can't stay awake to listen. I don't suppose that any of that even matters now.

I sit and wait till it's dark and Elsie comes to join the vigil.

Chapter Twenty-Nine

THEN

December 1992

We often think about when love begins. People eulogise about romantic love, with poetic words about the moment their partner first said or did something that made them unspool. We recall the first glimpse of a newborn baby that marks a lifetime of love and anxiety, the first time we walked into a new home or the day we adopted a new pet.

We don't think about hatred as often. Hatred has to commence too, rarely announcing itself fully formed. It has an evolution, spreading like bacteria, starting off as a microscopic clump that then multiplies and proliferates. Crushing healthy emotions and depleting the hater. That's the other thing. People rarely have sympathy for the one doing the hating but hate is exhausting.

I've disliked Sacha from the moment Sadie first mentioned his name. I've been revolted by the tales of his pseudo rock star excesses that she's recounted. I loathed his words coming down the telephone line and recoiled from the pathetic and needy responses that he elicited from her. Hatred festered in me from the first time I sneaked a look at the photo album and saw his sullen posturing. Now I see him before me and the loathing becomes flesh and bone, tightening my throat and burning my chest.

He shrugs off Sadie's embrace and bends down, rooting through the kitchen cupboards.

'There's nothing in there. I've removed it. Every bottle.' Sadie folds her arms.

'Fuck you.'

'You promised, Sacha. You said—'

'Tomorrow. Where's it hidden?' His eyes scan the room and alight on me, as if he's only just noticed that I'm here.

'Who the fuck is this? Another parasite?' His eyes eat into me. 'You managed to find someone who looks and sounds like Portia. I'm not sure that's going to end well.'

'Don't be so rude. This is Laura. I've told you about her.'

'Oh, the meddling twat. Well, hello, Laura and fuck you. Are you going to be as much of an arsehole as Sadie or will you find me some fucking vodka?' He lurches forward as if he's going to run at me but Sadie intercepts him and pushes him towards a chair where he slumps inelegantly.

Sadie's eyes scan down his legs and I follow her gaze, looking on horrified as one leg of his trousers starts to darken, a puddle of urine forming on the floor. Sacha slaps his leg and lets out a roar of laughter before jumping up and grabbing Sadie into a bear hug. Pushing his urine-soaked legs against her vintage kimono.

She disentangles herself and reaches down behind the cleaning products and pulls out a half bottle of vodka. He snatches it from her and swigs half of the bottle before she has chance to pour any into the glass she's placed on the table.

'I want you out, by the way.' His eyes drift across, settling on Sadie who's now standing next to me. Then on to me and back to Sadie again. 'You can get the fuck out of my house.'

I feel a rush of indignation, opening my mouth automatically to challenge him and remind him that this is Sadie's house and he's lucky that she's letting him stay. That he can't decide what happens here. He pours the rest of the vodka into the glass, holding his wrist as he does it to quell the shaking.

Sadie beckons me to follow her out of the room and leads me up the stairs to her bedroom. The usual orderly calm is gone and the air smells faintly of cigarettes instead of the usual undertones of Chanel perfume and talcum powder. Dresses and elaborate undergarments are strewn across the counterpane. She bends down, scooping the clothes up and begins hanging them. I stand beside her and pass her the lilac quilted hangers. When we've finished she sits on the edge of the bed, beckoning for me to sit on the dressing table stool.

'I'm sure you can see that Sacha needs our help.' The word 'our' sparks a febrile warmth in me. She still needs me. Me, above Anthony and Amy.

On the occasions when Sadie has talked about him, usually late at night when we've shared a bottle of wine, she's confided about his substance misuse. About how scared she is that he's going to end up dead because of his recklessness. She's never referred to it as a full-blown addiction in spite of the fact that she's alluded to him needing alcohol to get through the day, supplementing this with benzodiazepines and cocaine, even smoking heroin on a few occasions.

'He seems . . . ill at the moment. Has he been this messed up for a long time?'

'On and off. He's been troubled since I first met him. He has these dark periods where he turns away from me and uses. But then it calms down and he's a delight again.'

I can't imagine the Sacha that we've just witnessed ever being delightful.

'Obviously he didn't drink in prison. Being incarcerated was a compulsory detox for him.' Sadie's lip curls slightly at this sentence. 'But he's gone on a massive bender since he was released and I've been trying to get him back here. This is the worst he's ever been.'

I nod with one of the empathetic expressions that I've learned from the ward nurses. I'm not convinced by Sadie's assessment of him. I think back to her telling me that just before he attacked Portia his parents had arranged a rehab placement for him, so he must have been pretty messed up. She'd later mentioned in passing that he'd been in rehab once before in his late twenties.

'So, Laura. We're going to help him.' Something crosses Sadie's face. I can only describe it as the look a child has before they tell you that they've done something naughty. 'He's scared to go to rehab again because it was so awful last time, so I've managed to persuade him to agree to be detoxed here. And he's going to go to meetings. Alcoholics Anonymous and all that.'

'That's . . . promising. Are the mental health team going to help to dry him out?' I've seen people withdrawing from alcohol on the wards. Some glide through it but others are red-faced and sweaty, hands shaking, wracked by hallucinations. Men and women who claw at their own skin, thrashing around, lashing out at people around them.

We're on hand with sedatives and vitamin drips, bags of intravenous fluid if needed to compensate for the fluid loss.

Then there's my sister. I've spent countless hours sitting holding her hand, changing sweat-soaked sheets as she clutches her abdomen, fetching bowls for her to vomit into. Listening to her crying out while we wait for it to pass.

'There isn't any help to do it at home. Which is where you come in.' She eases herself up with a grunt and walks across to the largest chest of drawers by the window, pulling open the bottom drawer. Inside is an array of vitamin pills, injections, bags of glucose, cannulas. There's a set of charts and a neat pack of pens held together with an elastic band. My first stupid thought is that the pens are blue. We're only allowed to write in black ink.

'You can't do this. You'll be caught. It's dangerous.'

'I've been collecting all this for months. I slipped things into my pocket when I was helping the staff nurses to check the IV drugs, then sneaked them into my bag. You can get a lot in a vintage handbag.'

'It's not safe.' Safety is always on my mind. We're around desperately sick people giving treatments with potentially deadly side effects. Mistakes and misjudgements can end in death. It's a thing a nurse has to learn: to accept that we live with the risk of causing major harm. 'People can die from alcohol withdrawal. They have fits or sweat so much that they become dehydrated and we don't know how to cannulate if—'

'But I have you. You know what to do because of your sister and you're also one of the most competent nurses I've worked with.' Her words are like cold water. I'd thought that she wanted me back because she valued our friendship but it turns out that what she values is my ability to do a job and my experiences of living with someone with an addiction.

'He's going to die anyway, Laura, if we don't do something. You saw him. He's killing himself. And this is the only way I can get him to do it.' Sadie slams the drawer closed and steps back, facing me. 'I've thought about this and I know what I'm doing. I've watched the doctors put IV needles in. I can try to do that if we need to and if anything goes wrong then I'll call an ambulance. The medics won't know what we've been doing. If they see injection marks or work out that he's had sedatives then they'll attribute it to his drug use, not to us. But nothing *will* go wrong.'

I hug my arms across my chest and stare back at her, our eyes deadlocked.

'So, will you help me? It has to be you. You're the only one I can trust to be discreet.'

'What do you need me to do?'

'It's just minor things. Step one is that I need some Librium. We don't have any on our ward, but your ward is adjacent to the liver ward. All you have to do is go and ask the staff nurse if you can borrow the keys to get some pills out of the cupboard. Tell her you've got someone starting with the DTs and you can't wait for the pharmacy to send up the pills.'

What she's asking is illegal and dangerous. I'd lose my place on the course and wreck my future if I was caught. It's too much.

Sadie is watching me, as if she's mapping my buzzing thoughts. 'I stole those drugs and got rid of Louise for you.'

Sadie has chosen me. Not Amy or Anthony. She trusts

me more. After everything I've done she still wants me back, even if it's just as a nurse for Sacha.

She steps nearer to me and I can feel her breath on my face. She raises one hand to my cheek and gently runs a finger down my face, as if I'm a precious work of art.

I owe her this. Here it is. My chance to atone.

I'll bring some black pens. The blue one wouldn't be right.

Chapter Thirty

THEN

December 1992

Sweat isn't something I'd thought about before I became a nurse. There was a woman who worked with me in the café who had a faint taint to her, like onions frying in another room and the man who delivered the supplies had this earthy smell that crept out from under his liberal sprays of Old Spice cologne. A scent both unappealing and alluring.

Nursing has taught me about sweat. Another lesson I could have happily lived without learning. A medley of aromas comes from a ward full of people as they spend days and nights prone or writhing on plastic coated mattresses, leaving behind their mark like dogs spraying urine. The individual odour of each person has subtle variations. The taint of it seeps into my hands and wrists, haunting me, impossible to wash away and lingering in my nostrils.

Sacha smells subhuman, undomesticated. Below the fumes of the vodka is this wild smell. It invades my nose as Sadie and I guide him up the stairs. He's benign now, thanks to the alcohol. There's no more swearing and insults, his near-black eyes now blank.

Sadie and I stand either side of him, no longer two friends in our home but two nurses, getting our job done. We strip him down, his sexuality not of interest. I note his firm musculature as if I'm assessing his fitness for a procedure. This is a task to be treated respectfully and with as much preservation of dignity as possible. I squat down and loop the wet trousers over his blackened feet. He lifts each leg like an obedient child. His bare genitals are uncomfortably near my face. Things like this no longer bother me. It's work.

We wash him, put clean pyjamas on and leave him to sleep on top of a waterproof cover and clean sheet. Sadie has an old metal trunk in the corner that she uses for scarves. Locked in there is a further supply of vodka. Enough to keep him settled till the next evening when I return from work with the medications.

* * *

I do as Sadie asked. It was easy to pocket the Librium tablets. A chaotic hospital ward is a perfect cover for crime. No one suspected a thing, although the bottle was fluorescent in my thoughts. The risk of losing all this, to have to forsake my career for an act that isn't even for my own benefit. But what choice do I have if I want Sadie to forgive me for my deceptions and interference. My penance needs to be completed in full.

We begin as soon as I arrive home from my shift.

'He's not drunk any alcohol since last night. He should wake up soon and we can start.' Sadie is waiting in the hall.

Her hair is held back with a green scarf, her dress the colour of dried blood with a full skirt tied at the waist.

'Where are the others?'

'Oh, don't worry about them. I've told them that he has diarrhoea and vomiting. They think he's infectious and are keeping well away.' She holds out her hand and I pass her the pills. There's a yell of '*Sadie*' from the bedroom.

She lets out a sigh. 'And so we begin.'

When we go in to him Sacha is strangely compliant. He's woken from his stupor, clamouring for drink, again. Instead Sadie gives him a handful of the pills. He weighs them in his palm, as if deciding whether to swallow them or throw them across the room. The sound of him gulping them back is a relief. He looks up and scans around, as if unsure of where he is. His eyes alight on me. I brace myself.

'I'll say one thing for you, Laura. You're a lot more fuckable than Portia was.'

I don't speak, instead I walk over to the dressing table, cleared of all the vintage perfume bottles now, and I lay out the tools of our work. Pill pots, charts, the black pens.

* * *

It's hard to read in the half-light but the charts must be correct. We measure Sacha's fluid intake and his urine output, now that he's mostly continent again. We're a day and a half in, scraping through this, hoping that we know what we're doing. I've consulted my textbooks and read how many ways Sacha could die. Seizures, fluid imbalances, a poorly judged sedation dose. Vitamin deficiencies that could damage his brain. I try to banish these thoughts. Things changed once the last of the alcohol left his system and he flipped from the random mood swings of a drunk person and became a feral creature; delirious and uncontained. We're trying to manage him, loading his system with brightly coloured capsules of sedatives and yeasty-smelling vitamins that turn his urine fluorescent.

The sweating is relentless. Beads of it appear across his scarlet forehead, rolling down his cheeks like raindrops on a car window, dripping from the end of his prominent nose, soaking his back and pooling in his sternum. I've been running up and down to the washing machine, dodging the quizzical glances of Anthony who seems to be forever conveniently passing by the bottom of the stairs or on the landing.

There's a medical term for this: insensible losses. Like the name of a mournful romance novel. It means the fluid losses that can't be recorded, like tears, sweat, fluid lost through respiration. We keep forcing glasses of water down him when he's awake to account for the copious perspiration. His hairy knuckles clutch the glass with a force that I worry will cause it to shatter.

Sadie sent me in to speak to Anthony and Amy yesterday, to tell them to continue to keep away as Sadie and Sacha are now both unwell. I explained that as I've already been near them I'm likely to be brewing whatever virus Sacha and Sadie have, so I'm helping them. Amy has offered to shop and do laundry. Anthony merely pursed his lips and raised an eyebrow.

* * *

Another night and Sacha and Sadie look peaceful in sleep, curled up on her bed like commas. His arm is thrown across her chest and I can't decide if their pose looks confining or blissful. He's calmer when the benzodiazepines kick in, his skin loosening, his scarlet cheeks receding into something less demonic.

Sacha's arrival has been well timed as it's my days off. Had it not been then I'd have refused to help and I'd probably be back in the guest house. I wouldn't pretend to be sick. Work is sacred and has to be placed above anything else.

Sadie and I take turns nursing him but she's insisted that I only do two-hour blocks while she does four-hour ones. Merciful periods when I scuttle across the landing and lie on my bed, sometimes sleeping, sometimes not. I ease my bones out of the chair, tiptoeing across to watch Sacha's chest move up and down. Making sure that the copious amount of drugs we've loaded him up with aren't affecting his breathing. Sadie has set me the task of counting his respiratory rate every fifteen minutes. I do as I'm asked, pushing down the constant urge to beg her to give this up and send him to hospital.

His skin has a greenish sheen in the light of the lamp. His black eyebrows sit like caterpillars on his heavy forehead, his thick head of hair matted. He's objectively handsome. I can see the man he might become again if he can manage this sickness that he has. I jump back as his arm moves, rising in the air before flailing around and settling on the cover. The size of his biceps a reminder of how much effort it's taken me and Sadie to hold him down and force the last dose of pills upon him. His compliance is starting to waver.

His eyes flick open, two earth-brown irises staring straight at me. He eases himself up, looking around the room, his eyes locking with mine. 'Fuck it, Portia. Does Sadie know that you're back here?'

I turn away and he shuffles up the bed, turning his

head as he looks around the room. His gaze alights on the makeshift hospital. The rows of injections and pills on the dressing table, the urine bottle, the poorly fashioned drip stand made using a mahogany coat stand. He frowns as if trying to fathom the rationale for this before glancing over his shoulder and at Sadie's sleeping form.

His eyes are gaping and wild. He springs to his feet, dashing towards me. I try to ignore how close he's standing and his nakedness, his bare flesh about to collide with my clothes. My urge is to dart away from this man who's alternately showered us with insincere compliments and spat invectives at one or both of us, almost landing punches. Luckily we've been quicker than he is.

His voice drops to a whisper and he peers over his shoulder again. 'We have to get you out of here. Sadie is going to blow a fucking gasket. You know how she is.'

I recite the words I've said over and over. 'I'm Laura and I'm a nurse, Sacha. You're not well and you're being looked after. Try and sleep again.'

He's too quick, striding across the bedroom in an uneven line. I chase after him into the bathroom, scared that he'll fall and injure himself. I peer back at Sadie. She's turned in her sleep and is on her side, tresses of her hennaed hair obscuring half of her face.

'Hey. Calm down. I'm just having a piss.' He stands over the toilet holding his penis in one hand. 'You were already here, weren't you?' His voice is hoarse. I keep my eyes level with his face as a stream of urine hits the water. 'You're that woman, aren't you? The creep who tried to split me and Sadie up.'

'I'm Laura.' I wait for a beat, ready to run if he moves towards me. There's nothing. He looks down at himself, as if noticing for the first time that he's naked, not seeming to care, making no effort to cover himself.

'You know about Portia? Maybe you should get away from this house, while you can. It's not a safe place for a girl like you.'

'Shall we put this around you?' I hold up a towel for him but he bats it away. He steps towards me and I realise my mistake. I've let him get between me and the door. I should know better than this and I've been stupid. I lift my shaking hands to my chest, ready to push him away as he closes the gap between us.

The stubble on his cheek brushes against my face like wire wool as he leans in to whisper in my ear.

'You're crawling with lice, Laura. All over that pretty face. Don't move. There's one coming out of your nostril.' His hand shoots up and plucks an imaginary bug from my upper lip.

There's an unexpected slap at the top of my arm as he aims at another phantom insect. I try to pull away but hit the wall behind me, knocking my shoulder on a shelf, Sadie's kitsch ornaments rattling as it wobbles precariously.

'Come on, let's get you back to bed.' My assertive words are pointless as he drops to the floor and crawls around on the tiles, plucking more imaginary creatures from the grouting and throwing them into the bath. My eyes flick to the exit as the bathroom door opens. Sadie squints against the light. Her skin is pallid and greasy from sleep deprivation. Her eye make-up is smudged like bruising.

'I leave you two alone for five minutes.' She fake laughs and steps towards him, linking her arm in his. 'It's better if you use the urine bottle, Sacha. You're wobbly. Come on back to bed. It'll all be fine.'

I'm not sure who she's reassuring that it'll be fine. Me or Sacha.

It's not my practice to remind delirious people what they did once they recover. It serves no useful purpose to do that. I might make an exception for Sacha, though. I'll delight in telling him every aberration, every act of violence, every inappropriate word.

Like I said: hatred grows.

I'm ignoring the words that Sacha said in the bathroom. The only danger here is him.

Part Two

Chapter Thirty-One

THEN

October 1993

London is home and Derbyshire feels like a distant memory. Hard pavements to walk on instead of the muddy lanes and fields around the village, traffic noise instead of birdsong, people everywhere. I've only been to see Mum and Suzie a couple more times, even missing Christmas last year because I'd been rostered to work evening shifts. Apart from the nauseating amount of boxes of Roses and Quality Street at the nurses' station and some sad-looking tinsel it was an entirely un-festive occasion.

My life here passes in a whirl of two-month blocks. I'm constantly uprooted and moved from medical ward to surgical ward to speciality ward. The recurrent pattern is that the new staff don't speak to me much for the first few weeks but by the time I leave they warm to me, becoming kinder once they see the value in my work ethic and willingness to learn.

It's nearly a year since Sacha arrived and we're all still

here in Laurel House. Amy and Anthony are as moored in this place as me and so is Sacha. His delirium ended after four days and was replaced by something equally wearing. For the first few weeks he sloped around the house with a morose look on his face. The household order was upended overnight, the centre of the action shifting away from Sadie and her attention moving away from me. 'Post-illness' Sacha became the new leader with Sadie, Amy and Anthony as his eager acolytes. Members of a new cult that I'm not part of.

Amy gleefully questions Sacha like he's a wise older sibling, squealing in delight when he teases her and fires retorts back. Anthony's eyes follow him around the room and he slides into whichever seat is closest to him. Anthony always liked us to be waiting on him but is now servile, rushing to offer hot drinks and snacks to the new demigod. Sacha sits back and preens under his gaze, like he's deserving of whatever adoration comes his way.

And through it all Sadie plays her new roles. She's the patient wife whose husband is finally back from an epic sea voyage, the desperate girlfriend, elated that her fiancé is back from the wars. The loyal housewife who's tended a stove all day while her husband toils at his office desk. Sadie's laughter fills rooms. She radiates glee, acting like looking after this house and Sacha is her only vocation and going to work is an inconvenience.

I'm back in my secondary role. The perpetual supporting character, the willing aide who bolsters Sadie up, scurrying behind her, helping with household chores. I'm invisible to the men and taken for granted by Amy.

My eyes flit up towards the kitchen ceiling as I run the tap, rinsing the last of the pans. There's laughter coming from upstairs from Sadie and Sacha's room, followed by the sound of his footsteps on the stairs as he rushes off to another AA meeting. He lets the door bang which sets Coco off barking. Amy's sprawled across the kitchen table, like a disaffected teenager. Anthony sits upright adjacent to her.

'I wonder if I'll have one of those lifelong things like Sadie and Sacha have.' I don't bother to keep track of Amy's boyfriends. They're interchangeable and indistinct.

Anthony flicks his eyes towards the door and then back, speaking in a lower tone than usual. 'Don't believe everything you see. This, whatever this is, won't last forever.'

'Don't be such a cynic. Why wouldn't it?' Amy sounds indignant.

'It's all a bit too good to be true, don't you think?' As usual he's addressing his comments solely to Amy, as if I'm invisible. Even living next to me in the same house hasn't made me exist. I was right with my theory that Anthony holds long grudges.

He's right, though. There's something cloying and saccharine about Laurel House now. I feel like I'm living in a stage play where no one has total conviction in the parts that they're playing or the lines they've memorised. We all walk in and out of rooms pretending to be people that we're not and knowing that we're not convincing the audience of each other.

* * *

I relish my escapes to work. Even the bad days, like today, are a respite. The ward has been sweltering. The cast iron radiators scorching to the touch and the windows sealed shut by years of magnolia paint and rust. I've worked at velocity in my polyester uniform and tights, a paper hat clipped to my hair, my feet pinched and rubbed by leather shoes. I'm like a worker ant, scurrying between the linen cupboard, the storeroom and the commode store. After eight hours of this I'm rendered mercifully senseless.

On my way home, one of the street drinkers on the high street who I sometimes speak to nods and toasts me with a can of Special Brew in her grimy-nailed hand. I wave back.

The house is gaudy and loud. The noise from the kitchen tells me that they're all here. I stand in the hall, deciding whether to go in to them or sneak up and hide. The choice is removed when the door opens, releasing a scent of fried meat and garlic. Sadie steps into the hall.

'Shh, darling.' Coco is under her arm and she's letting out sharp, piercing barks that land like body blows. 'I'm just taking her round the block and then dinner will be ready. We're all here.' She beams at me. Even her mannerisms have changed since Sacha returned. Under the cloying performance of joy, she's like a dialled down version of herself. She steps out into the street, pulling the door closed behind her.

Sacha is leaning back, his chair tipped precariously. He glances at me, not concealing the contempt in his eyes. I resist the urge to tip him further and watch the glorious moment when he passes the moment of balance. Imagining his face as he registers that his head is about to slam on the floor.

'Hi.' Amy is wilting. She looks as if every hour of the late shift has registered on her body.

'How are the lies today? Oops. Slip of the tongue. I meant to say how's it all lying with you today?' Sacha smiles at me like a shark, smirking at his clumsy allusion to what he knows about me. Sadie told him everything that I did.

When I said it was a house pretending to be harmonious I failed to mention Sacha's attitude to me. He lets the grand performance slip where I'm involved. He keeps this up with a regular acidic drip of words and I mostly ignore them.

'Come and sit down.' He places a hand on the back of the seat next to him and offers a sycophantic half-smile.

His mood this last week has been darker. He's been snapping at me and pacing the house at night or sitting silently with his head in his hands. It's like this place has become stained with him. I've considered whether I should leave. I've often looked at the small ads in the local paper and peered at cards in shop windows but there's nowhere that I can afford, other than grim-sounding flat shares on the outskirts of London. Not if I still want to send money back to Mum. The nurses' home isn't an option either with the rooms there reserved for first-year students.

I have a spacious room to retreat to. Besides, Sadie might not realise it yet but she needs me here.

'Sacha was regaling us with tales of being on tour, before you arrived back, Laura. But he's been coy about it. So, I'm asking for a second and final time. Did you have groupies?' Amy looks across the kitchen table at Sacha. A playful smirk lifts her mouth.

'What do you think? I was in a band. There are always women. But I had Sadie back at home of course. Why would I need anyone else?'

I want to scream at the repulsive hypocrisy of this statement and tell him that he's fooling no one with this faithful partner act. Although maybe he is fooling Amy, Sadie even. She seems to be living in some strange, loved-up fantasy.

Anthony lets out a coquettish laugh.

Sadie's voice sounds across from the doorway. 'You mean that you had me in the audience of every gig, keeping you in line.'

Her statement is playful but there's a hard edge beneath it.

By the time that dinner is served I've lost my appetite. I slice into the steak on my plate and a trickle of blood oozes out. I push it to one side, uneaten.

'So how was work?' Sadie is sitting to my left. The kitchen feels impossibly small when the five of us are here.

'Oh, hellish. The usual cacophony of wants and needs that all coincide.' I spear a piece of broccoli with my fork.

'Tell me about it. I'm fucked.' Amy looks sick again like she did when we first started. I've heard her making frequent trips to the bathroom during the last few days and watched the waves of pain that occasionally cross her face. I know better than to make any suggestion that she sees her medical team. She becomes irritable and accuses us of trying to manage her condition. She's been burdened by people's advice too often.

'Right, I'm off upstairs, chaps. My bed is screaming for me.' Amy leaves behind a plate that's still three quarters full. Sadie frowns, her maternal concern not entirely extinguished by her overriding obsession with keeping Sacha happy.

'Anyone want more water?' The alcohol ban is still in force. Now that Sacha's been illicitly detoxified they're happy for people to know about his 'valiant struggles'. But in their version his addictions are sanitised and couched as something minor and in his distant past. A narrative threaded with bravery and resilience.

I push my plate away. 'No thanks. That was lovely.'

'My pleasure.' Sadie sweeps a hand around the table. 'This is lovely, isn't it. You three eating with Sacha and me. This place needs people.' She puts herself last on any list of names now. 'Long may this last.'

Sadie lifts her water glass as if in a toast but no one else joins in.

I don't believe that she's any more convinced than the rest of us that this will last.

Chapter Thirty-Two

THEN

October 1993

Coco has tucked herself into my arm on the side of the bed. I listen for sounds, my paperback novel ignored. The heavy tread of Amy's footsteps from the attic are brief tonight before I hear the creak of her bed springs. Next is Anthony. I hear him shout an effusive goodbye as he leaves the kitchen. His sycophancy jars in my throat. I try to read again but my eyes keep sliding from the pages. I lay my head back and listen to the dog's soft breaths.

'Quiet, sweetie. Don't wake the children.' Sadie's voice is a soft whisper from outside my door.

'For fuck's sake. Children? They're more like—' The final part of his sentence is curtailed as they walk into their bedroom and the door closes.

When I get up to go to the bathroom I can hear voices coming from Sadie's room. I yield to my base instincts and press my ear against the door, my eyes fixed towards Anthony's room so I can spring away if he appears.

'I'll give you that one. Amy is fun, when she's awake, and I'm not averse to having your pet gayboy leering over me. But Laura is—'

'Sacha, stop it. You weren't here and she's been an amazing friend.'

'Well they're all going soon.'

I wait for Sadie to correct him. It's her house, her decision who's here.

'I think that this has gone on too long and things are going to have to change.' The voices peter out and the sound of kissing begins. Softly muttered terms of endearment. I retreat to my room, ignoring the animalistic noises now coming from the room. I push my face into Coco's fur and wait for it to stop.

* * *

The shift shoots by like the view from a car window. My adrenaline levels are peak. There's a strange feeling that comes when I've been rushed off my feet for eight hours. Everything around me feels too slow, like I'm an exotic insect that survives for a few days, living with a different heartbeat, a frenetic pace. Lifts become painfully tardy as my fingers press the buttons of the crossing in a tattoo, vending machines are absurdly lethargic, even the cars on the road look like they should accelerate.

Nothing exists but this artificial world where people are confined to bed spaces so small that they could reach across and touch their neighbour. Where the outside world feels negated by neon lights and hissing radiators. On leaving I'm often shocked by the time of day or the weather. Seasons could change, cataclysmic floods or hurricanes could happen, the streets could be full of rioters. It feels like nothing can permeate this world.

I'm scooping things from the floor into a yellow clinical waste bag. Alone behind the curtains, just me and the dead woman on the bed. A middle-aged woman who collapsed and was the victim of a brutal resuscitation attempt. Shouted orders, needles piercing her veins, the crack as chest compressions snapped ribs. Now she's sightless with eyelids that won't close and stare up at the polystyrene tiles, her body covered by a pristine white sheet. The room looks like a crime scene with smears of blood and random bits of plastic scattered around. I try to restore some dignity to her before her family come in to view her.

I leave the altered reality to go back home.

* * *

'Look at you. The cool kid.' Sacha's grin lifts his face.

'What, this old thing?' Amy twirls around like Kate Moss on a catwalk, holding out the bottom of her baggy Nirvana T-shirt. Her jeans are carefully ripped and faded, wide legged with engineered wear at the knee. Her thin legs show through the slits.

'You look great. And you, Ant. Loving the monochromes.' Sacha places his hand on the tabletop and I instinctively move mine away. No one else is allowed to call him 'Ant'. If we tried it we'd be met with a snarl.

Anthony smiles back at Sacha and sits down while Amy sidles over to the fridge and pours herself a glass of milk.

'Is that bread from the continental food shop?' Anthony has abandoned his usual snideness and sounds enthusiastic as he points to the dark brown loaf in the middle of the table. 'Your family's Russian, right?'

Sacha looks at Anthony with a bemused expression and lets out an abrupt laugh. 'Has Sadie got you believing her delusions? Sacha is one of her exotic inventions. My parents came from London.'

'What did I do this time?' Sadie marches into the kitchen in a waft of Chanel. She's dressed down. A sedate two-piece in dun tweed with no accessories.

'Do your parents still live nearby?' It always feels like an effort to make conversation with him but I try, on and off.

Sacha freezes, his fork hovering over his plate. I feel Sadie stiffen beside me. The sound of the tap dripping, broken only when Coco lets off one of her volleys of heart stopping barks to alert us to a fox that she's sensed sloping across the lawn.

'We'll maybe discuss it another time.' Sadie places her hand on top of Sacha's and he doesn't move.

Sacha's expression is blank and he doesn't move for a few seconds. He lifts Sadie's hand from his and turns to Amy and Anthony. 'So, tell me exactly where you two are going tonight and exactly how much you're going to drink. I want to live vicariously.'

'Sacha, no.' Sadie bangs her cutlery down onto the table, startling the dog again who sets off on another round of yapping. 'That's not appropriate.'

Sacha carries on eating. I notice him smirk at Amy and she crosses her eyes at him.

I feel my muscles soften when they all go through to the sitting room, leaving me and Amy to wash up.

'My bloody nose! Always happens when your hands aren't free. There's a tissue in my pocket. Will you dab it for me?'

I pull the tissue out and a small packet falls from her pocket. The kind that buttons come in on a new jacket. There are two crude-looking pills in there. One of them is yellow with a smiley face stamped on it, the other is pale pink with a bird embossed.

'Oops.' Amy strips off her rubber gloves and scoops down to pick them back up, taking the tissue from me and wiping her nose. She slips the gloves back on and starts scrubbing at a pan.

'What are they?' I try to sound neutral but the thought of illegal drugs strikes a note of alarm in my chest.

'Nothing to worry about which is why I don't want you to tell Sadie.'

'Amy, I don't think—' I sound middle-aged and parental.

'I don't need a lecture about drugs. We did that in college last year.' Two police officers with monotone voices had come to lecture us about the evils of street drugs.

We finish the dishes in silence.

* * *

This is the time I like best. Sadie to myself, which makes it worthwhile still living in this place. Sacha has gone up to bed after falling asleep in front of a film. He'd been flicking through the TV channels, a perpetual white noise as he vacillated between the four stations, never settling on a programme. Sadie turned the TV off the minute he left the room and closed the doors of the cabinet, restoring the room to 1958 or whatever year it's supposed to be in her mind, the soft sounds of music coming from a warped record.

'You'll soon forget all this and start living in modern times again.' I don't remind Sadie that we're already living in 'modern times' with the washing machine, fridge freezer and covert television. 'Do you think that you'll miss me and my silly ways when you go back?'

A note of alarm sounds in my head. It's less than three months till we complete our training and, stupidly, I haven't told Sadie that I'm hoping to stay on in London. There's a temporary vacancy coming up on the oncology ward. A staff nurse is starting a secondment in January. The ward sister took me aside and spoke to me about applying, telling me that she was impressed by my sense of calm and efficiency.

'Go back where?'

'Back to your village in Derbyshire. Why would you want to stay here with decrepit old me when you've got a sweet little village to live in?' She eases herself up with a groan, as if to demonstrate her great age.

The comment is wounding. Sadie knows about my home life and the issues with Suzie. Her reduction of my history to a romanticised idyll from *Country Life* magazine smarts.

'I always knew that you'd all leave me in the end. Amy's planning on going to live with her aunt when she finally finishes and I'm not sure that Anthony even knows what he wants, except to never go back to where he's from.'

Amy already has an extra month of training to do. Her frequent sick days, along with a failed assignment, means that she has to make up for the missed time and work. She'll linger here for a few weeks before moving on.

'I don't know what I'll do.' I turn to look directly at her, hoping that she might see the desperation in my eyes and ask me to stay. Amy and Anthony will move on and Sacha will be gone, without me needing to interfere this time. I won't make that mistake again. I'm certain that their relationship will implode of its own accord. I've been watching and the early cracks are showing. Whatever it is that fuels Sacha's addiction is still there, waiting, unaddressed. This happy couple act is going to end soon.

'I thought I might stay in London a bit longer. But now that you've got Sacha back I wasn't sure . . .'

'Just listen to that voice.' Sadie leans back and waves a hand in time to the jazz music, not responding to my comment. She doesn't close her eyes, thankfully. I hate it when people close their eyes when other people are around.

I'm about to speak again, to try another angle at seeing where I stand, but Sadie speaks first. 'Things with Sacha are more complicated than they seem. You don't need to worry about him.'

I wait, my breath frozen in my chest, but she doesn't elaborate. She sinks back into the sofa and this time she does close her eyes to listen to the music. I don't hate it.

I lie back and close my eyes, too, a bubble of hope rising in my chest.

Chapter Thirty-Three

NOW

Friday, 16 April 2010

Sadie's eyes are closed as I sit with Elsie and wait for the approach of death. It's a strange thing to watch someone who I once loved in this state. I'm accustomed to putting my emotions aside at a death bed. Tonight, my skills of detachment and neutrality are failing me. I thought they were ingrained but it turns out that my neutrality can leave me in a flash. I feel like I'm back at the start, like a newly registered nurse.

When I managed to centre myself enough to find a job in a Derbyshire hospital everything felt new and raw. A mantle of unbearable responsibility had been thrown over me and I was obsessed with the perilous powers that I now had and wasn't sure that I wanted. I lived in a state of terror, conscious of the fact that I could kill someone by my actions, errors or omissions. An unbearable thought.

Patients' relatives often ask me to kill someone. It's usually the ones who've sat by the beds of the dying through torturous days and nights. Their buttocks dented from hard plastic chairs and their emotions eroded by wakefulness as they watch their incoming loss inch closer. They note every twitch, every gasp and stutter. For the unlucky ones it's a protracted process and that's when they sometimes ask. They start alluding to euthanasia with talk about animals and vets. On a handful of occasions people have been so bold as to ask directly whether there's a way we can expedite things.

I understand. Their pleas come from a place of compassion so I do everything within my power. I mouth empathetic words, alleviate symptoms, offer support.

But the thought has never entered my mind.

I've always had the power to kill.

But I've never considered killing a patient. That's always felt abhorrent.

Although my thoughts this week are a maelstrom filled with pockets of darkness.

History has taught me that you sometimes need to take radical action to survive.

Principles sometimes have to be abandoned.

* * *

I don't know what Elsie's thoughts are and if she dreams of a speedy death as we sit here watching her mother. Maybe she wants to cling to every moment or harbours false hopes of a miracle.

We're both shrouded in shadows tonight. The dim lights from Sadie's ridiculous lamps mean that I have to strain to see Elsie across the room. I'm standing back from the bed, allowing Elsie a semi-alone moment with her mother.

I don't leave them. Sadie has been fretful and pained and she's needed additional doses of oxycodone. She's asleep but her movements tell me that the pain is coming back.

'Is she worse?' It's the third time that Elsie has asked me this today.

'I think that she's stayed the same today.' I rest my hand on the ache in my lumbar spine. The thought of my uncluttered bedroom back in Derbyshire taunts me. I imagine myself ringing the palliative care team and telling them that I can't do this anymore. That they need to do something. Anything. Then I'd get in my car and never look back.

I won't, though. How can I leave while Sadie still needs me?

While she's still speaking.

Elsie leans forward and rests her face on the bed. 'I'm scared, Laura.'

I do the right thing and move to her side, placing my hand gently on her upper back.

'You're doing fine.'

'Do you think so?' She turns her face to me. She's puppyish in her bid for approval and I'm reminded of how young the age of fifteen is to be going through this without any other family here.

'I honestly do.' She smiles at me and squeezes my hand. Her palm feels comforting against mine.

'There's nothing wrong with being scared.' Sadie's croaky voice takes us both by surprise. She doesn't open her eyes but lies there, perfectly still. 'But you'll get through this and your father will be home soon.'

'I haven't even heard from *him*.' There's a note of contempt in her voice. 'How am I going to be the one who looks after everything here?'

'You don't have to do anything. Don't worry.' Sadie still doesn't open her eyes. Her voice is soft but we both hear her.

Elsie's face remains set into a frown.

'Anyway, scat! I need Laura to help me with something private.'

Elsie stands back up and surveys her mother. Like she's the parent and she's looking on at a lying teenager. She leaves the room and the door to the attic slams.

'I need something, darling. Badly need something but I know you'll say no.'

'Let me guess. One of those absurd cigarettes?' I make a tutting noise while trying not to laugh.

'Yes, Mother.' Sadie makes sad labrador eyes at me. 'I'm desperate. I haven't had one for so long.'

I let out a pantomime sigh and roll my eyes.

'Where are they?'

'The drawer on the left. No, the bedside cabinet. That's it.'

I pull out the distinctive pastel packet and a hideous Perspex lighter that looks like a fish tank.

'There's a shell in there that I use as an ashtray.'

'Where do you still get those?'

'Oh, I have my suppliers.' She winks at me. She coughs as she inhales the first drag of foul-smelling smoke but with the second she closes her eyes in a dramatic reaction of ecstasy. It's reassuring to see Sadie still manging to imbue everyday actions with her usual flair. I stand by the bed, ready to catch the lit cigarette if necessary, mindful that she drops off to sleep at inopportune moments.

When she's smoked half and stubbed out the lurid pink cigarette butt on the clam shell she wriggles herself round in the bed so she's half facing me.

'I've done my best for Elsie. For the future I mean.' She starts shuffling again and I instinctively rearrange the pillows. 'It's all set up with the solicitors. But I've also spoken with that man. The palliative care one who flirted with you. What's his name?'

'Tom. And he doesn't—'

'Yes, him. He's going to make sure she gets bereavement counselling. But she worries me. Losing someone can do terrible things to a person.'

A random thought comes into my head of Sadie that final day. The sound of her grief-stricken sobs from the kitchen. Her face as she stared at me. Her clothes inexplicably daubed with blood.

'However mature for her age she seems, Elsie's still a child. Hopefully she's inherited more of my character than her father's.'

I'm going to have to say it. The word feels like a lump of food stuck in my throat that I can't cough out. The syllables are distasteful on my tongue.

'Sacha?'

'What!' Her tone is somewhere between shock and amusement.

'I worked it out. If Elise's fifteen now then I'm guessing that Sacha is her father.'

'Are you asking if I was pregnant when you walked away and left me with this mess?' Her eyes are open wide now. Her face more alert than it has been all day. Anger is reviving her.

'I left you?' I surprise myself with how assertive my tone is. 'That's not how it happened at—'

'You want to know if I was pregnant when he was killed?' She laughs and it feels ugly and cruel.

I look around to make sure that Elsie hasn't crept back, lowering my voice to a whisper. 'Yes. Tell me.'

Sadie speaks again. 'You always thought that you understood everything, but you were wrong. I've never known anyone less perceptive.'

Her words sting like salt on an open wound.

'And what makes you think Elsie is fifteen, anyway?'

'She told me she was.'

'Have you met a teenager before? All teenagers want to seem older. She's thirteen.' Her eyes close and I see her face changing as the last dose of oxycodone starts to kick in.

I'm about to walk away when she laughs again. It's a weak sound, a poor relation to the laugh I once knew.

'Elsie's like you always were, Laura. A liar. You make a good pair.'

Chapter Thirty-Four

THEN

October 1993

Amy and I walk back in companionable silence, our voices overused after eight hours on the wards. The house has a curious smell when we open the door. It takes me a moment to recognise it as whisky.

'Sacha's not in great shape, I'm afraid.' I look behind Sadie but he's not there.

'It smells like a pub in here.' Amy laughs, unaware of the trauma we've gone through to get Sacha to this point of sobriety. 'Someone's had fun.'

'We had a bit of a big day and he's stupidly had a couple of drinks, I'm afraid. I've put him to bed.' Sadie catches my eye, as if daring me to comment.

'Fair play. What are we eating? I can go and get chips if you've been too busy to cook?' Amy pulls a battered five-pound note from the pocket of her baggy jeans.

Once Amy has left and we're on our own in the kitchen, Sadie's façade crumbles.

'I've tried so hard to keep him sober. I just can't do it with him anymore. I might end up just having to leave him to it here.'

'It's your house. You could just kick him out.' I don't see a problem. I'd gladly help to pack up his meagre belongings and send him on his way to a hostel. My compassion for Sacha is thin to non-existent.

'It's not that simple.' Sadie turns away. Her usual tactic when she wants to change the subject. Her hands become busy pulling plates from the cupboard and smearing slices of bread with thick layers of yellow butter.

A glint of gold on Sadie's hand catches my eye. She's wearing a wedding ring. 'Have you . . . Oh, God, Sadie. Do you think that was wise?'

The insanity of this makes me want to run up the stairs, grab my things and flee. Or take Sadie by the shoulders and shake her.

'I don't need my choices questioning.' Her words are over defined and cold, designed to leave me in no doubt that I've overstepped the mark. She turns to me, her forehead lined. 'Look, I can't explain yet. Just . . . just don't ask. You'll understand the reason in time.'

'But I—'

'It was nothing lavish. Just a registrar's office thing. That's why Sacha decided that today was a perfect excuse to go on the piss again. I mean, who doesn't get drunk when they get married. He'll be fine tomorrow.'

I'm mute. I can't think of a sensible response.

* * *

Amy rests her fork down on the plate. 'So, what are you two old ladies doing tonight?'

'The usual. Reading, music. And listening out for Sacha waking up and then sitting feigning interest while he regales me with his remorse.' Sadie's voice sounded strident and unconvincing in my ears.

I can't envision Sacha succumbing to remorse. Instead, I foresee this being the beginning of a bender of mammoth proportions with all the associated carnage. The stench of alcohol on breath, the sound of stumbling in the corridor, shouting and breakages.

'Rather you than me. I've had enough books to last a lifetime. I don't think I'll pick up another one until I'm old,' says Amy, who has barely touched a book for the length of the course.

'Where are you off to? Go on. Titillate us old ladies with a glimpse of the high life.'

'There's a rave on in Brixton. Naomi said she'd meet me there. You remember Naomi, don't you?' I nod, pretending as usual that I know who any of her fluid circle of friends are. 'I'll probably be back late.'

I'm relieved that Amy is looking better again. The fluctuations in her health have felt dizzying.

'Be good.' Sadie gives Amy a knowing look.

'Yes, Sir.' She stands to attention and mock salutes. 'Right. I'm off to get changed.'

'And close the garden gate when you go out. Someone left it undone yesterday.'

Amy's feet pound up the stairs. I listen out for Sacha waking but there's no sound from him.

'I don't know why she needs to change. She'll replace one pair of baggy jeans and a Nirvana T-shirt for another.'

Sadie looks to me for a response but I'm silent.

'There's no need to look so worried, Laura. He can't get out.'

'I'm sorry . . . what?'

'Sacha. I've locked him in the bedroom. Now, what do you think we should listen to tonight?' She eases herself up with a groan. 'Peggy Lee or something else?'

* * *

Amy leaves the house ten minutes later. The slam of the front door sets Coco off barking. I stiffen, waiting for the sound of Sacha's footsteps above, relaxing back when there's still nothing apart from the click of dog claws on the tiles as Coco noses her way into the room.

It's another ten minutes later when three loud bangs send me lurching forward, my book dropping to the floor. The sound of splintering wood. Muffled shouts and volleys of swearing.

'Oh, dear.' Sadie has laid herself back on the sofa, her feet stretched across my lap. 'Looks like he's up.'

In spite of her bravado her eyes are darting around and her mouth is pinched shut. She stands up, straightening her skirt, tucking a strand of loose hair back in. Her shoulders droop down, an air of resignation hanging over her, as if she's about to embark on a troublesome household chore, like an exhausted mother who overhears a row between her children and is about to intervene yet again.

I push myself forward, forcing my tired limbs to move. A swirling nausea begins to rise. My eyes scan the room for escape routes, as if I haven't been living here for almost three years and don't know every inch of the house.

Another crash and footsteps along the landing, lurching and stumbling down the stairs. Sadie wedges the door shut, her back against the wooden panels, but the force of Sacha's bulk against the door sends her stumbling forward as it flies open.

'Get out!' The violence of Sadie's yelled words takes me by surprise, making me recoil. Coco jumps up on the sofa and leans into my side, her torso quivering, tail tucked beneath her body.

'The fuck I'll get out. You don't have a right to tell me what to do.' Sacha's drunken logic again. The alcohol making him think he's invincible. The stench of stale vodka coming from him.

'What do you want, Sacha? We had such a good day. Why are you being like this?'

He pauses, stepping back, lurching slightly towards the wall of the hall but righting himself in time. 'I'll tell you what I want. To not be locked in a room like a child.'

Sadie blocks the doorway, her arm raised against the frame. Sacha's eyes rove beyond Sadie and fix upon me and the dog. I hold his gaze.

He turns his eyes back on Sadie and his shoulders fall, his fists unclenching like he's been punctured. He moves backwards and stumbles again.

'You're pathetic.' Sadie's voice is quieter, more resigned. She steps forward and grabs his bicep, guiding him into the room, towards the sofa. I jump away and Coco follows. 'Sit down. I'll make some coffee while you decide whether to fuck your whole life up again or not.'

He flops onto the sofa, his body collapsing inwards as he rests his head on his knees. He's dressed himself in clean clothes and is doused in aftershave. His face is starting to grow a hint of beard that emphasises his bone structure. As a specimen, reduced to a still life without the pitch and flail of his inebriated gait, then he'd be handsome. But he isn't. He's ugly and grotesque.

'I'm sorry that I'm being such a stupid bastard.' His voice is muffled by his posture.

I can hear Sadie clattering around in the kitchen and wish she'd hurry.

'It's not been easy for me and Sadie, you know.' He sits upright, leaning back and closing his eyes. His face catching the light from the standard lamp, casting shadows down one cheek. 'With what happened.'

'I can imagine.' What I can really imagine is that whatever happened between them was because of his actions. Sadie's life would be better without him in it.

The sound of Coco barking as Sadie lets her out in the garden echoes through to us.

'I'm not a bad person.' He looks up at me and his face is quivering, ready to release tears. Drunken self-pity or rage is what I expected. His eyes close again and I gauge the distance to the door, judging how fast I can slip out. Given how glazed his eyes are, I suspect he'd carry on talking, my exit unobserved.

'I sometimes think I'd have been better without this house. It's like a stain, the stuff that's happened here. I should have sold it.' His eyes flick open and he sits forward. 'I imagine Sadie told you about my parents?'

'Your parents?' Sadie has told me nothing about them.

'It's hard to live up to people like them. They were really talented actors. But I lost them. Such a shitty phrase for what happened. My mum died of cancer and my dad killed himself right there in the kitchen after—'

'That was Sadie. That's Sadie's parents. She told me.' The words fly from my mouth before I have time to regret contradicting him while his moods are changeable and uncontained.

'Oh, of course it fucking was. It was Sadie who walked in and found her father in a pool of blood. I forgot that twisted little fantasy.' His tone has changed into something more urgent. His words are staccato. 'Wake up, Laura. This is my fucking house. Sadie's parents are . . .' He stops dead and turns his head when he hears Sadie coming back, her footsteps sounding out a rhythm on the tiles. He shoots up and staggers out into the hallway. The tray she's carrying crashes to the floor, a slick of coffee splashing across the tiles like blood, shards of crockery scattering. The two-handed push from Sacha takes her by surprise. Her head ricochets off the mirror, a large crack forming down the glass. Sadie slides to the floor, her legs sticking out awkwardly like a toppled mannequin in a dress shop window.

'Fucking liar. You're a liar!' He bends down and screams into her face. I look round for something to defend myself with, impotent against his strength and rage.

When I turn my head back, he's gone. The front door slams behind him.

* * *

'Head wounds always bleed a lot. They look worse than they are. It's nothing.' Sadie says this as if I hadn't been working with her in A and E, cleaning up children's playground wounds.

'It's stopping now.' I lift the gauze from the back of her head. A small cut nestled in her hair. A line of red from the glass of the mirror. 'Sit still.'

Sadie is leaning forward, both hands on the kitchen table

as if she's about to get up. 'I want to clean all this up before the others return.'

'I know you're an amazing housewife but you can't clean this away. I think Anthony might notice the broken mirror and the smashed bedroom door.' I carry on pressing on the gauze as I speak. The blood has almost stopped flowing. 'Look, why don't you just sit here and smoke one of your cigarettes while I keep applying pressure. I'll sweep up the glass in the hall and then we can both go and look at the bedroom door.'

Sadie smiles as I open the drawer for the cigarette packet.

'Sacha said something strange.' I pass her the cigarette packet with a shaking hand. 'He said that it's his house.'

'Oh, did he?' She lights the cigarette and blows out a plume of smoke. 'Has it stopped bleeding?'

'Do you think we're safe here? Should we leave now?'

'You worry too much. We need to make sure the others are OK, anyway.'

I wait but she doesn't say more.

The quiet of the kitchen fails to beguile me. It feels like the beginning of something. Like a stage set waiting for something more to happen.

Chapter Thirty-Five

THEN

October 1993

I claw myself out of sleep and am alert straight away for the sound of Sacha rampaging about in a drunken state. There's no noise except the familiar hum of traffic. A reassuring moment of peace in this war zone.

His words from the night before return to me. His parents owned this house and Sadie's story belongs to him. If he's telling the truth then Sadie has been lying to me and my position here is even more insecure.

Anthony barely commented on the damage to the house when he arrived home last night. He raised an eyebrow at Sadie and then sloped off to bed, telling us that he'd seen Amy and Sacha together on his way home, through the window of the pub round the corner. I think Sadie's expression was enough of a sign to him that saying anything about the mirror would be a mistake.

I scurry to the bathroom averting my gaze from the splintered wood of Sadie's door, washing myself quickly in the temperamental shower and dressing before I go downstairs. Sadie is already sitting at the kitchen table. There's a faint top note of old cigarette smoke in the air otherwise the kitchen has the caustic tang of bleach. Sadie is uncharacteristically sombre in her attire, sheathed in a high-necked black dress that clings to her hips. She's wearing her signature make-up, of course. I scan for discrepancies, shakily applied lines, clumsy streaks of blusher, but she's immaculate. If it hadn't been for the door and mirror I'd doubt that any of the night before happened.

She's still wearing the wedding ring.

We're slow to react at first. We've grown accustomed to screaming. The constant wailing of confused patients and the cries of pain and distress that are the soundtrack of the hospital. This low noise hovers on the edge of our collective consciousness. I look up, cocking my head to listen for if the noise is coming from the street.

Sadie darts up before me. As she opens the kitchen door, I recognise Anthony's voice and the familiar clarion call of 'Cardiac arrest!' Repetitive shouts for help. A gross intrusion of work into our home. This phrase that feels controlled and manageable at work is an impossible insertion here.

Anthony is crouching on the attic room floor, stiff arms moving to the hideous counted-aloud rhythm of his movement as he pumps at Amy's bare chest. Amy is on the carpet, diagonal to the bed, arms splayed out, away from her sides like she's dancing. Her eyes are glassy as they stare up towards the ceiling rose. Her fingers are impossibly blue at the tips, the inky colour staining her lips and nose. Anthony moves up and pushes his mouth against hers in a sick parody of a kiss. The familiar Nirvana T-shirt is pulled up, the harsh scars looking uglier, more puckered, against the waxy yellow white of her skin. Her breasts are on show.

'Help me. I walked in and she was on the floor. I was trying to wake her up and she stopped breathing.'

Sadie moves Anthony's hands away while she stops and feels for a pulse in her neck. I run down to the phone, leaving them continuing to resuscitate her.

Talking to the emergency services operator is jolting. The call handler is disconcerting in how unflappable she is when I tell her that I think that my friend is dead but that we're trying CPR. I garble something about us being nurses then back it up by a stream of consciousness where I try to explain that we're still students. She has a regional accent that I find myself trying to place. There's a barrage of questions; intrusive words, bizarre, and impossible to answer enquiries. Then the surreal moment when I put down the receiver and run back up the stairs.

I guess that they couldn't bring her back when I see Sadie holding Anthony while he cries. The unexpected intimacy makes me want to turn and run. I avert my eyes, unable to bring myself to look at Amy's dead body. Sadie breaks away and assumes her usual role of competent adult, ordering Anthony to go and find his dressing gown, touching his face gently with her fingers like a lover would. He scurries away.

It's her next words that shock me the most. 'Laura, will you just re-check Amy's pulse for me while I grab a blanket off the bed.'

Her pulse is thready and rapid under my fingers. Amy is breathing, her colour now more Victorian invalid than cadaver. She's laid on her side and her T-shirt is covering her breasts and abdomen now. Anthony arrives back in a ludicrous dressing gown that looks like it's made of silk.

Sadie lays a blanket across Amy and props a pillow under her head. We sit around her on the floor, in silence. We guard her, watching her erratic breaths while we wait for help to arrive.

When the paramedics arrive they ask repeatedly whether Amy takes illicit drugs. I open my mouth to speak but Sadie is quicker, louder.

'Never. She was anti-drugs.' They defer to Sadie, treating her as though she's mine and Anthony's parent.

I don't say anything. Make no mention of the packet of ecstasy tablets that were in her pocket that day.

They cart her fragile form down the stairs and the door slams behind them. I feel like every bone has been removed from my body. A ridiculous urge to just lie down on Amy's bed grips me. I hear Sadie say something to Anthony and her words sound like she's underwater.

'Where's Sacha?' She looks around, as if she's only just realised he's not been woken by all the mayhem, hasn't run up to see what's happening.

'No idea. Maybe he went to the rave with Amy after the pub.' Anthony's voice is back to his usual volume and rhythm.

'Well, he can stay wherever the fuck he is. We're probably better off without him here.' Sadie stands firm and puts her hands on her hips. 'We'd better try and find a number for Amy's aunt.' I go down and stand by the kitchen sink, inert. My eyes look out across the garden but see nothing. When Sadie comes back down we begin clearing the bottles and glasses that Sacha left behind and the ubiquitous coffee cups that litter the aftermath of any British crisis or tragedy. Sadie's face is worn and she looks a decade older than she did last night.

'Anthony's gone to lie down.' Sadie passes me a cup and I slide it into the soapy water. 'What do you think happened?'

'I suppose she choked or something. That happens, doesn't it? She sounded messed up when she came in, but I didn't think anything of it. She must have been drunk because she had to be helped up the stairs.'

'What do you mean? Who was with her?' Her tone is sharper.

'I . . . I thought I heard a man.' Sadie is filling the kettle as I say this but she stops and rests it down. 'At least, I think I heard a male voice with Amy. But she sometimes brings men back, doesn't she.'

'Tell me exactly what you heard.' Sadie places her hand on the back of her head, where the wound from the mirror is.

'I couldn't sleep. I heard Amy come in and walk up the stairs but there was a man's voice, too. I thought it must be Sacha but it can't have been because whoever he was, he went straight back down the stairs again. I waited for the front door to slam shut, but I didn't hear anything so I thought that he must have closed it quietly. There were no other noises and I fell asleep after that.'

* * *

It's Coco's barking that alerts us to who the man from the night before is, telling us who'd brought Amy home and why he stayed. We hear her whining and scratching at the sitting room door, her claws scrabbling at the wood as she lets out a musical howl. Sacha is lying on the sofa, fully dressed. His cheeks are deathly pale above the blackness of his stubble. His chest rises and falls in a painfully slow rhythm. Sadie kneels forward and digs her knuckles into the muscles above his shoulders, then moves her hand down to push her fingers hard into his sternum. For a moment, I'm alarmed at what she's doing, thinking that she's carrying out an act of violence on him rather than trying the customary methods of rousing someone.

'Oh, fuck.' She looks up at me. 'Laura, there's something badly wrong. He's unresponsive. Ring an ambulance, now.'

With a sickening repetition, the same ambulance crew arrives. The same green boiler suits. The same woman with the ponytail and the man with the tattooed hands. Syringes pop, veins are slapped, the Velcro scrape of a blood pressure cuff opening scratches at my nerves. Anthony appears in the doorway. The horror on his face from earlier replaced by an air of impassivity.

Coco clutches a used syringe in her mouth and runs off, enjoying the game as I chase her, to get it back. This time, Sadie disappears entirely, going along with Sacha to the hospital in the back of the ambulance. Anthony runs up and reappears a few minutes later, fully dressed, shouting that he's going to the hospital to support Sadie. That should be me doing that.

I'm left alone here.

* * *

I stand still by the kitchen window. The house vast and unnavigable. I'm unsure what to do or where to be. Hours disappear in silence. I'm in my room when Sadie bursts into the hall at around teatime, filling the house with noise again. I hear Anthony's footsteps as he makes his way to his room, Sadie follows behind him and the bathroom door closes behind her. When she reappears at my bedroom door half an hour later she's refreshed. Her hair towers over her head, the dark circles under her eyes are masked by concealer. She's wearing a neatly ironed summer dress in blue and white, a discordant choice for the weather.

Her eyes search the room, looking for the dog. She spots her lying on the bed and bends down and strokes her before easing herself back up.

'Do you feel up to coming down? It'd do us all good to have something to eat.'

We cook and then make a show of trying to eat, sitting in near silence. One of us occasionally starts a sentence that fizzles out.

Sadie tells us what she knows. Amy and Sacha are both on ITU on breathing support. The doctor said Sacha's critical and they're running tests to try to elicit the cause of this.

We know nothing about Amy's condition. We're not her family so no one would tell Sadie anything.

* * *

Anthony somehow managed to charm the tutors and we've been given three days off by the hospital on compassionate grounds which feels like a punishment for me. I want to be back at work with frenetic task lists that block the thoughts in my head like they always do. Instead, I'm stuck here.

Sadie called Amy's intimidating aunt again. She refused to tell us how Amy is but coldly informed Sadie that she'd visit the next day to collect Amy's things as she would never be coming back here. She arrived yesterday and batted away any questions that Sadie had. Her visit was a brief but taut occasion where we talked across the kitchen with violent politeness. The aunt's eyes bored into us as she shot accusatory questions out of her pursed lips. The implication being that we're a house where midnight raves and orgies of drug taking happen. That we harmed Amy.

She left with all of Amy's belongings. Sadie and I had already taken on the grim task of folding clothes and books into neat piles. I only found one bag of pills. Two tablets that were the colour of Elastoplast and shaped like the Superman symbol. I pocketed them before Sadie saw them and flushed them down the toilet later. It's kinder for Sadie to continue to believe that Amy was a naïve innocent. If she wants to think that Sacha is the villain then so be it.

I guessed that she would blame him and her rage is both a horror and a joy to behold.

She keeps up a monologue in which she berates him, blaming him for the shame he's brought upon the house and upon her. For the harm that he's caused to Amy when she should have been being nurtured and supported by us all.

'He's given that poor naïve girl something. She wouldn't have taken stuff, not with her health being so fragile.'

I've had a thought. If Sacha does die and Amy is gone then Laurel House will be Sadie's. Once Anthony goes it'll just be us two again and I'll be here to help her recover.

Chapter Thirty-Six

THEN

October 1993

'How is he?'

Sadie left me reeling when she told me today that she was going to go and visit Sacha in hospital. He's been there three days and she hadn't so much as rung to check on him. I was poised to advise her, to help her find out if she could annul the marriage. I'm hoping that she can rid us of him somehow. Maybe we'd even get to stay on here.

'Rough. They say he might not survive which gives us something to hope for.' There's no emotion in Sadie's voice as she says this. 'That poor girl. I sneaked a peek at her when I walked by her bed space and she looks shocking.'

Apparently, Sacha is now semi-conscious, skin tinged yellow. Sadie tells me that his eyes are swollen like jelly and brackish urine drains into a catheter. The theory of the hospital doctors, while they await toxicology tests, is that he and Amy both took something noxious, maybe MDMA, probably a bad batch of ecstasy along with some form of opiates. Amy's thinner frame and underlying illness may be the reasons that she fared worse.

'This is all his fault.' This is the mantra that Sadie utters at regular intervals. Sometimes as a lone statement, other times as part of a longer monologue. I stay silent while Anthony makes non-committal noises. I watch her rage fester and grow, choosing not to reveal the truth about Amy's drug use. Never saying that it's more than possible that the reverse of what Sadie believes might be true. Amy could have been the one who provided the drugs for them both.

* * *

The concept of returning to the wards is delicious but daunting. The absorption of work calls me but I loathe the thought of being in the spotlight of people's performative empathy. It's nothing but an unsubtle mask for prurient curiosity about this drama that I have a sideline role in. We have a few months until our training ends and I'm desperate to get through this final part and to no longer be whispered about because I'm one of the student nurses who was there when '*that student OD'd*'. Only I suspect that it'll always follow the three of us, like fading tattoos.

Memories of the times when Suzie's chaos spread beyond the walls of our flat and onto the streets of the village hit me like sound waves. My brain is a roll call of the villagers' faces, tinged with faux concern that masked contempt and disgust. This is nothing new for me. I'll push through this. My new life spreads before me. I've been offered the job on oncology for when we finish and I've said yes. I try to think about the future but it feels as improbable as thinking about marriage or children. My mind is like the static on the television at night if I try to plan any further.

* * *

Sadie knocks at my bedroom door and walks in without waiting for me to speak. She hasn't been here much. She's either working or on one of her daily visits, sitting beside Sacha on the intensive care unit. She dresses in tailored suits: tweeds in muted colours, a handbag swinging in the crook of her elbow, sometimes a small hat pinned onto the crown of her head. Full pantomime of a distraught wife. It's like she's in a black and white film.

'He looked awful yesterday, Laura. I don't think he'll survive this.' I was lying on my bed, reading, lost in a better world before she burst in and brought me back to ugly reality.

'I'm sorry.' I blurt out the expected reply before I realise that Sadie is on the brink of gleeful laughter.

'Sorry? We shouldn't be sad about it.' Her laughter feels cruel and not the kind of amusement that makes you want to join in. 'I think that if there's any justice then he'll die.'

'You don't mean that.' I scour her face for softness but there's none.

She walks out of the room and I throw down my book, following her retreating form down the stairs and into the kitchen.

'This rage, Laura . . . I can't even begin to describe my rage. This is a twisted admission maybe, but I want him to properly suffer. I don't want him to die like he is, all tucked up in bed, happily delirious. I want him to know that he's almost killed that sweet young woman.'

'I understand.' I walk over and consider forcing myself to hug her but she looks rigid and unyielding.

'I don't know if you can. Understand, I mean. I've had years of his chaos. His fucking me about. I took all that because of our history and how he's supported me. I loved him. But to wreck her . . . To wreck all of us. To take us all down with him. Like he nearly took me down with him with the thing with Portia.'

'Sadie, we're not wrecked. We'll get through this.' My shock at her revelling in his sickness gives way and I feel a moment of shameful glee at the word 'love' now being in the past tense.

'Will we? And how will we do that? By working away our sorrow with this glittering fucking job? This pathetic little career that you thrive on. I don't know where you get your protestant work ethic from but it's pitiful. You can't work away all your past guilt.' Sadie's words are like scalpels. 'This was my fault as much as his. I shouldn't have exposed her to him.'

She gets up and walks to the back door, snatching her cigarettes on the way. I hear the spark of her lighter. I look at the clock and I have an hour till my shift begins. I'm about to speak but Sadie carries on.

'Maybe you should move out and find somewhere calmer. Latch onto someone else's life.' Sadie pauses as if she's wondering whether to stop at that. She doesn't. Her ensuing words are colder, more emphatic. 'Perhaps you'll be able to get enough kicks from your voyeurism by spectating people's pain and suffering on the wards, rather than watching mine.'

'Sadie, that's not—'

I can't see her face but the back of her neck is scarlet.

'Enough.' She finally turns to face me. Bright blooms have appeared on her cheeks 'This is about poor Amy. The fucking life she had and then we did this to her. Look what we did to her. What he did to her by sharing his fucking pills with her. This is on us all.'

She turns away again and I sneak away, upstairs. When I leave for my shift Sadie is sitting at the table in a cloud of cigarette smoke.

I close the front door softly. Latching the gate behind me.

Chapter Thirty-Seven

THEN

November 1993

Sadie's knock is unfamiliar in its urgency. Her eyes are brighter, her movements twitchy. I've avoided her and Anthony for days. I shoot down to the kitchen at night and gather enough food for the next day, pushing my ear against the door so that I can check for anyone on the landing before I dart into the bathroom. Sadie has knocked on my bedroom door twice and I've shouted back that I'm fine. She left it at that.

This time feels liminal, like I'm in purgatory. My thoughts of the past are eclipsed by this horror around me but a sense of panic remains. Sadie's been going to work and she still visits Sacha every day after her shift. I'm faking normality at work, fielding the frequent questions of the other students. At home, I spend my time lying on the bed, trying to read, often barely taking in plots and characters. My eyes skimming on by default. Re-reading thrillers where I already know who the villains are feels safe. In the moments when inactivity feels impossible I scurry about the room, walking in circles.

'I need to talk to you both now.'

It's dark outside. I want to turn off the lights and hide in here. Instead I follow her to the sitting room.

I opt for the armchair, pushing myself back into the unfamiliar space, leaving the sofa for Sadie. She sits forward, Anthony perching on the floor in front of her. The negative space next to him is like a punch. My eyes stray down to the gap where Amy should be.

'I had the most terrible shock today. Amy's bed space was empty and I thought she must have died.' Sadie recounts this without emotion. 'I had to beg the nurse to tell me but apparently she's improved so much that they've transferred her to a hospital near her aunt's house.'

'Oh, shit. That must have been horrible to see the empty bed. Are you OK?'

Sadie ignores Anthony and continues. 'Sacha's bloods are getting better, too. He might be able to move off the intensive care unit soon.'

I still haven't broached with Sadie about the stuff Sacha said that night about him owning the house and her lies about her parents. She's not exactly approachable at the moment.

Anthony closes his eyes, reaching out for Sadie and gripping her hand.

'We might need to rethink our living situation.'

'Why are you even visiting?' Sadie looks at me with puzzlement when I ask this. 'I mean, isn't it better to just leave him there and cut all ties now?'

'Isn't it obvious why? I've reached my limit and I want to watch him suffering.'

Anthony looks across at her but his face is blank. There's none of his usual sharpness.

'Anyway, that isn't what I wanted to tell you.' She shuffles on the seat. 'Someone tried to kill Sacha today.'

'What?' Anthony almost shouts this.

'He had a massive hypo but they stabilised him with glucose.'

'What makes you think someone deliberately caused that?' Anthony's right to question her. People with liver problems can have drops in their glucose levels. It's part of the illness.

Sadie flops back onto the sofa, lowering her head and looking at us with Princess Diana eyes.

'Can't you guess how I know?' She laughs and puts her hand in front of her mouth as if she's saying 'Oops' after almost knocking over a teacup and not hinting that she injected her husband with insulin.

I surprise myself with my vehemence when I tell Sadie my thoughts about the madness of her actions.

'You'll be caught. And what's the point of that? *You'll* be in prison and—'

'But I wouldn't be caught.' There's something petulant and childlike about Sadie's response. 'And there's a side benefit. I'll have the house, won't I. I'm his wife.'

'Insulin would show up on a post-mortem. He'd have to have a post-mortem because he's ill from taking illicit drugs.' I try and fail to hide my exasperation but my voice rises further in volume.

Anthony looks like he's thinking hard and I wait, hoping that he'll say something sensible to bring Sadie back to reality but he doesn't. 'Good for you, Sadie. You do what you need to do.'

'Anthony! You must see how mad and dangerous this is. It's beyond dangerous. He's on intensive care for God's sake. You can't be more watched and—' My voice sounds shrill in my ears.

'Sacha almost killed Amy. He must have been the one who spiked her drink with drugs.' Sadie's words stop us both and there's an uncomfortable silence for a few seconds. It's on the tip of my tongue to shout out what I know. To tell them about Amy dropping the bag of pills in the kitchen and about the pills that were in her room. I'm incredulous that Anthony doesn't know about Amy's recreational drug use, too. I should tell her what I know but I'm also convinced that she won't listen to me.

Anthony levers himself up and sits on the sofa next to her putting his arms around her. I would have done the same but from me it would have been stiff and awkward.

'Maybe just leave me and Sadie, OK? You're not actually needed here.' Anthony's voice is back to its usual pitch.

'Sadie, promise me you won't try anything else. This is madness.'

'Of course.' Sadie bats me away, like I've said something childish and she's humouring me. 'Would you go and find Coco for me? I think you scared her off by your shouting. The poor thing.'

* * *

I sneak back down later that evening to fetch food, counting on them both still being in the sitting room. Sadie is alone, standing by the cooker. She hands me a ludicrous apron that's more frill than anything else. We don't speak but just start to cook together. There's no sound from Anthony's room. I've no idea what he does when he's alone.

'I'm sorry about what I said the other day about you. I didn't mean it. This whole business has sent me spiralling down.' Sadie doesn't seem depressed. If anything her movements are quicker and lighter.

'It's fine.' I try to put warmth into my words but it doesn't quite land.

'It's such a strain. Holding my face in that sombre expression when all I've wanted to do is rip out his tubes and watch him bleed to death.' Her words are discordantly cheerful.

We stand silently for a moment.

'I'm scared, Sadie.' It's only as I say it that I realise just how terrified I am. 'I don't like all this.'

'Don't worry. It's all in hand. We'll be fine.'

'How?' I try to hide the note of alarm in my voice. I'm worried that Sadie is thinking of doing something else stupid. I reach round and place my hand on her arm. 'The only sensible plan is to keep away from him and stop visiting.'

Sadie unfurls my fingers from her forearm and takes my hand, squeezing it. I don't know if this means she's agreeing with me or not.

* * *

The next afternoon, Anthony shouts up the stairs to me. I hadn't expected the phone call to be for me. It so rarely is.

'I don't feel so good, Mum.' It goes against my instincts to admit this to my mum when she asks how I am. I've worked so hard to be OK. To not be the one who causes her brow to crinkle in worry and keeps her awake at night. She's had enough to worry about with Suzie so since I came out of hospital I've done everything I could to try to appear to be coping.

'These things pass. They have before, haven't they?' I hear a note of panic in her voice and I can visualise the way her hand will be gripping the phone receiver until her knuckles whiten. This feels less like reassurance and more like an instruction telling me to be OK.

There's a pause and I falter, taking the easier option. 'Yes. You're right. It's maybe just exam stress.'

'I'm sure that's all it is. Anyway, I can't talk for long. I just phoned up to tell you the good news. Suzie has a new boyfriend and she's got a job interview next week.' She regales me with all the details, her voice glowing with pride. 'Things are looking up and it'll be easier once you get back, too. It's been hard on my own with everything.'

I want Suzie to flourish. I can think of nothing that I'd like more but my hope is less hardy than my mother's. It shrivelled and died after the third time she failed on a methadone programme. After the first job, where she was sacked for stealing after a week and the second one where she, miraculously, lasted a month. The string of hopeless boyfriends like the one who turned out to be a dealer or the one she met in rehab and the one she met at a Narcotics Anonymous meeting. The chances of her relapsing doubling each time as she would fall back into addiction if he did and vice versa. I'm exhausted by it all.

What I haven't told my mum is that in spite of everything that's happened here, I want to stay in London. I will stay with Sadie, I'm sure of it. Things feel bad now but I can make them better. A return to harmony is within touching distance and it'll be me and Sadie again. Her rage worries me but the unhinged thoughts are part of the shockwaves from recent events and they'll dissipate. She'll see sense once Sacha is out of hospital. There's only one solution to this and that is that we'll have to leave Laurel House together. We'll pool our resources and find somewhere peaceful to live. Sadie will be able to make a home for us, wherever we end up.

* * *

I'm working a night shift with a truculent care assistant called Michelle. She looks at me suspiciously from under a frazzled blonde fringe. The staff nurse is an older woman called Sue who has a disciplinarian stance due to her having trained in the army. I couldn't avoid finding this out. Her anecdotes about life in the forces stretch into each night. Michelle ignores her, flicking through magazines, tutting to herself if anyone dares to ring a buzzer for a commode or pain relief. Always eager to return to sitting behind the nurses' station, while I'm perpetually keen to be away from them, enveloped in the darkness of the bays on the ward, creeping around, checking on patients.

'You don't sit much, do you? Try to calm it, will you? I'm not sure that my nerves will take three nights of this.' Sue's oversized teeth munch into an apple with unsettling vigour.

The dim light of morning brings the usual flurry of activity and Michelle reanimates, asking me a barrage of questions about my life, mostly about my romantic aspirations or lack of them, seemingly disappointed with my chaste answers. The shift ends with the usual intense flush of morning activity, just when I'm so tired that I can barely recall my own name.

Sadie appears as I'm putting my sandwich box and

book back into my shoulder bag. Her face is exactly as expertly painted as it had been when she left home the night before.

'You look as knackered as I feel.' Sadie doesn't look exhausted. There's something discordant about her like she's wired. She talks non-stop as we walk, asking how things are and telling me anecdotes about the nurses she's working with.

'Oh, and I've got some news that you may not like. Sacha is coming back home this morning.'

I stop dead. The street around me receding.

'Sadie, I don't think this is a good idea for us to be there with him. We need to get out of there.'

Sadie carries on walking but I'm frozen in place temporarily. I scurry to catch up, breathless as I near her.

'Don't be so defeatist and don't look at me like that, Laura. I need your support. You know how much I've relied on you these last few years. I promise you that he won't be around much longer.'

My stomach lurches at the thought of what she might mean.

* * *

Sacha looks alarmingly yellow still, his eyeballs tinted a pale lemon. The transport crew set down a bag on the sitting room floor. Books and magazines, packs of biscuits and bottles of squash spill out of the cheap white plastic. Gifts from Sadie, I suppose. Part of her campaign to make the hospital staff think that she's the devoted new wife.

He pulls his swollen legs up onto the sofa, wincing and lays back against the pillows that Sadie has arranged for him before she shot off into the kitchen. He turns his head away and closes his eyes.

'I'm sorry, Laura.' His voice is unfamiliar, languorous, and slightly slurred.

'Sorry for what?' I want him to say it. I have a perverse fantasy that he'll admit culpability and say that he'd coaxed Amy into taking drugs that night. That the fact that Amy was taking stuff didn't mean that this rogue batch was her doing. As dangerous as this is for Sadie's mental state, I also want him to be the villain that she's making him out to be. That way she will give in and leave here and we can begin somewhere new. We'll go back to how we were before the others arrived and he came back.

'I'm sorry that I've not always been kind to you. I wasn't in a good place emotionally.' There's a taint of self-pity to his tone.

I snatch up the bag of his belongings and start sorting it into piles. Dirty laundry to wash, things he might need now. My failsafe strategy for discomfort around patients is tidying things.

There's a battered James Herbert paperback with a lurid rat on the cover. Wedged inside is a stack of folded notes. Red ink has bled through the paper. I try to open them but my hands shake and they fall from my fingers onto the floor.

Sadie walks back in, smiling, until she spots the notes lying on the floor.

'What . . .'

They're exactly the sort of notes I had. Marker pen, capital letters, threats. Only Sacha's notes are more explicit than mine. There are seven in total, detailing ways that they'll kill him.

She takes them from me and reads them.

'What are these, Sacha?'

'Someone's taken a dislike to me. I was a bit of an arse with some of the nurses when I was out of it. I think one of them must have gone psycho.' His laugh is hollow.

'I think it's more than that. These are worrying, don't you think?' Sadie looks at him expectantly. It's as if she wants to see him afraid.

I need to get out of the room. The air feels toxic and I can't be here. As I walk through the hall I bend down to pick up a postcard that's been delivered to the wrong house. Grim vistas of Margate looking gaudy and unloved, meant for the neighbour with the dog. Sadie's words are hissed but audible through the crack in the partly closed sitting room door.

'So, what happens now, Sacha?'

'Well, I still think it'd be a good idea if you three left *my* house.' His voice sounds weary.

'Oh, darling. What makes you think that *I'm* going anywhere? You might own this place but I'm the one who's loved it and looked after it. It's my home now.'

I don't hear his reply if there is one. Sadie speaks again. There's a steeliness that's crept in.

'I've been thinking. I'm not content to let what happened go unpunished. You almost killed that girl.' Her words are cold and businesslike.

'Oh, fuck off Sadie. I didn't force feed her any drugs, did I? She must have taken it by choice. The police interviewed me and they believe me that I don't remember anything. There's no case to answer. They aren't pursuing anything, so fuck off and let it go.'

Sadie's tone remains cool.

'But you should be punished.'

'Well, tough shit, Sadie. I'm not being fucking punished.'

'Aren't you? Maybe I'm the one in a position to decide that.'

'Grow up. It's time you faced the real world instead of play acting this shitty little life that you've built.'

'Someone nearly died because of you.' There's no rise in pitch or change in tone. Sadie's voice stays level and calm.

I hear the click of heels and the door closes with a thud, muffling the rest of the conversation.

I creep up the stairs of this house that belongs to Sacha. I make a list in my head of arguments I can present to Sadie to get us away from here and to safety.

Chapter Thirty-Eight

NOW

Saturday, 17 April 2010

The house is restless tonight. Creaks and groans echo from the staircase. Sadie shouts out for more pain relief. Elsie paces the attic, flicking her TV on and off with the volume too loud. I know I should go to her but I can't. That room has felt tainted since the morning Anthony found Amy, as if the shock of the events lodged in the rafters. I stand on the bottom step and call to her, hoping she'll come down and we can talk. But she doesn't hear me. Either that or she chooses to ignore me.

I give up the idea of sleep at around four and wait in the kitchen for the light to begin to filter through. There's a promise of springlike weather but the sitting room feels as cold as a mortuary. I tidy the coffee table, putting away the Yahtzee game that we left out. The drawer is stiff but I manage to ease it out with a few sharp tugs. It's stuffed with the chaotic detritus of Sadie's life. She clings onto things, as if the past can save her. I push aside old theatre programmes with yellowed edges and a dozen or so curled-up concert tickets. There are photos but not of anyone that I recognise. Lines of earnest girls on nights out with Sadie always hovering at the edge, looking like she'd rather be anywhere but where she is.

Sadie always kept detritus from the past, whether her own or other people's. There's a letter that I missed when I looked the first time, tucked right at the bottom, wedged between an old sewing pattern from the Sixties and an empty sleeve for a vinyl record. I pull it out and flatten it down. It's a hospital appointment from January 1994. The patient didn't stay alive long enough to attend. It's addressed to Alexander Davidson. The same name that was on the order of service from his funeral that I found upstairs. This is the Alex who Sadie shouted for. The one she usually called Sacha. I should have remembered when I tried to search for his name online. Sacha said that his name was a silly nickname that Sadie bestowed on him. Part of that pretence that his dark looks meant that he had exotic ancestry. I remember from reading Russian novels at school that Sacha could be a nickname for people called Alex. That's the reason why there was nothing online under Sacha when I searched on Google.

Sadie's yells bring me back to the room. The drawer sticks as I slide it back in and I bang my hip on it in my haste, bringing tears to my eyes. Elsie is hovering at the bottom of the attic stairs, chewing at a finger, looking, for once, younger than her *real* age.

'It's OK. I can see to your mum.'

Sadie is on the edge of the bed. I've no idea how she

managed to get herself there. She has so little muscle left that it's a wonder she can even lift a hand.

'I need my laptop.' It feels incongruous that she should have one in this faux time capsule. She gestures a bony finger towards the wardrobe. The laptop is hidden away like some dirty old man's 1970s porn stash, slid under some moth-eaten jumpers at the base of the wardrobe.

'I need you to check something.' There's a note of panic to her voice. 'It's important.'

Her hand is uncoordinated so I navigate to her Hotmail account. There's a chain of three emails from her solicitors with attachments and she asks me to open one which remains unread. Her finger moves along the screen as she mouths words.

'I needed to check all this was finalised. I'd forgotten.'

I catch sight of the document and I freeze for a moment. 'Why did you do that?'

'Because I always knew you'd come back when I needed you.' Her speech is matter of fact. 'It was fated.'

She's right. She's still in control here. She always was.

* * *

I'm helping Sadie to change her nightdress when the doorbell rings, making my arm muscles jump. The expected sound of Elsie running downstairs to answer doesn't come. She's either sneaked out or she has her headphones jammed over her ears.

The bell shrieks through the hallway again, as if someone has their finger held down on it. I almost slip on the rug as I rush down. There's no one expected and I won't have forgotten an appointment.

There's a man standing on the doorstep. Thinning hair and high cheekbones, the flesh of his cheeks sunken. His jawline puffy.

'Are you going to stare at me all morning? Grab one of these bags, Laura. My keys are in there somewhere but I couldn't face rooting about.' His voice is unchanged. Still as sharp edged and lacerating. 'Elsie told me that you were here.'

'Anthony. What . . . what are you doing here? I didn't know you still kept in touch with Sadie.'

'Kept in touch? I've come home. I'm back to help my daughter to look after my wife.'

Anthony doesn't go up and see Sadie. He marches into the kitchen while I carry his holdall and dump it in the hall before going through to him. His back is to me as he fills the kettle. He doesn't offer to make me a drink.

'How did you get back?' It's a mundane question but it's all I can think to ask.

'Trains and boats and planes and all that. Total bore.' His tone is dismissive.

I wait for him to ask about Sadie but he carries on making a coffee.

'And are you going to ask how she is?'

He turns to face me. His face is both leaner and fatter. Gaunt cheeks with deposits of flesh that have appeared around his neck and jaw. 'Still dying, I expect. But I suppose you were going to tell me that anyway.'

I feel an urge to grab him by the shoulders and shake him. I turn away, sucking in air before I sit myself down at the table.

'How long have you been married to Sadie?'

There's a long pause as he studies my face.

'Marriage? I always think it's ridiculous to use that to mark the length of a relationship. I've been here since you left. That's what matters.'

'But marriage? I thought you were . . .' My words trail away.

'Go on. Share your insights, Laura.'

Sophia trots into the room but she takes one look at Anthony and walks back out, her tail down.

'Popular as ever, I see.' I take pitiful pleasure in finding something to taunt him with. 'I thought you were gay.'

'It's not really any of your business but Sadie and I have an unconventional marriage. We've never been together as in *together*. But we were close. Sadie always said *I* was the best friend she ever had.' He tilts his head back, watching my reaction to this.

'That doesn't explain why you got married.'

'Sadie wanted to have a child and I liked the idea of continuing my genes. So I donated.' He looks at me as if expecting some sort of reaction to this. 'But, you know Sadie, that wasn't quite enough for her vintage fantasies. She wanted an excuse to wear a dress. Her last marriage was shabby and rushed. So we got married. A play act of a wedding to keep her happy. It was fun, in a campy sort of way. I'm sorry we forgot to invite you.'

I have a choice. I'm free to grab my case, get in my car and drive away. I don't think that I can trust Sadie and Elsie's wellbeing to this man, though. Anthony sets down his mug. I hear footsteps above, a few creaks then nothing. Elsie must have gone into Sadie's room.

'It's funny, Laura, how much you tried to make Sadie

like you. All the silly stunts and the ingratiating actions. And you actually ended up making her hate you more than she ever hated anyone.'

'Yet she brought me back here.'

'Her grudges are selective when she needs something.' He pronounces his words like an actor in a bad am-dram show. 'It's convenient to forgive the woman who ruined everything when you need a discreet nurse.'

'Ruined what exactly?' I stand, my body primed to rush across to him. My hands itching to shake him. I manage to stop myself.

'You still don't know what you did to her, do you?' His facial expression makes me want to slam his head into the sink. His eyes roam my face as if he's gleefully looking to see how agitated he can make me feel. I breathe deeply and force my fists to unclench. I'm not engaging in his games. I won't beg him for answers and give him the satisfaction of seeing me lowered. I know how he operates. If he has something he wants to punish me with then it'll come soon enough.

'Anthony, things have gone downhill while you've been away. Sadie's not so well.' I pause to allow this to sink in, waiting for him to question or comment. 'It looks like time may be short.'

Still nothing, other than a fleeting look of disappointment that he's not roused me to argue or plead with him for more information. He stares at the floor and continues to drink from his mug. I walk towards the door.

'I'd better say this now then if there's not much time.' His voice is quieter and I turn back to face him to catch his words. 'Thank you for doing what you did. For enabling me and Sadie to have all this.'

My chest constricts. The room feels like there's no air.

I have no memory of walking up the stairs. I lie on top of the bed, listening for Sadie calling me, expecting to hear Anthony walking up and into her bedroom.

There's no sound at all, other than the low thump of Elsie's music.

Chapter Thirty-Nine

THEN

November 1993

Sacha's period of self-pity and atonement was brief. Now he's stumbling around the house day and night. Frequently emphasising his own benevolence, reminding us that he's 'allowing us' to live in his house, for now. His comments are spread evenly between us but he aims them most pointedly at Sadie. 'In *my* house' is a phrase he uses several times a day, words dangled like a taunt. I haven't confronted Sadie about her lies about owning Laurel House and about her stolen family history. How can I when I've been shown to be the liar in chief in this group. It's not like I can claim to be a stranger to manipulating people. I deserve this.

Sacha and Sadie have entered an insane cycle of tenuous reconciliations followed by prolonged bouts of violent arguments. It's dizzying. His sobriety varies day to day. There are no more AA meetings, just days where he's hungover and morose, haunting the house. Saying he won't drink again before he yields to the whisky bottle. He drinks at breakneck speed, which inevitably leads to him lurching around the house ranting. I feel like I'm perpetually living in one of those moments when you're faced with something horrific and have to choose to fight or take flight. But I do neither. I stay on, caught in indecision, waiting for Sadie to say she'll leave with me. Too scared to go and leave her alone with him but unable to get her to talk to me. She dodges my conversational openers with practised grace and avoids being alone with me.

Anthony loiters, staring at me and Sacha, like he's looking into a void. He's only happy when he has Sadie to himself. Which he does frustratingly often. He's slotted himself into my space. If I go to see Sadie late at night when Sacha's still pacing around downstairs, Anthony is there in her bedroom. I hear the soft murmur of their voices. I can never make out the words, even with my ear almost against the wood panels of the door.

Sacha isn't especially cruel to me. He just treats me like a particularly ugly piece of furniture. On the fight days with Sadie he glares at me if I cross his line of vision, like I offend his eyes by existing. On the more placid days he smiles and looks at me like I'm a bemusing curiosity behind glass.

I catch Sadie on a night when Anthony is working an opposite shift and we walk to the hospital together. Her mouth is a pursed line of lipstick today, like a sutured wound, her face anaemic beneath her make-up.

'Sadie, can we talk about what's happening at home? I still think that we should just—' She cuts me off before I can say that I think we should leave Laurel House now.

'Later. I've got a lot on my mind.' This has become her stock answer. 'Don't look so worried. I have everything in hand.'

She turns to me and sees that there are tears of frustration in my eyes.

'We're not leaving that house, Laura. That's the end of it. It's now my house, whatever he thinks or says. It always will be. It'd be like losing a limb if I ever left.'

'But legally—'

'I don't give a fuck about the law. I'm not going. I need it and it needs me.' I see that. The house is like the henna she uses, the lipstick she applies or the heels she always wears. It's part of her persona.

She leaves me at the door of the ward and trots away down the dimly lit corridor. My mission failed, again.

The night shift is frantic. My fingers fumble for thready pulses under crepey skin. I coax cracked lips to take water and hold the hands of the frightened. The word 'nurse' is yelled so often that I start to hear it in my imagination. The work continues unabated like it always does. A confused patient absconds and I'm allocated the job of finding him. Sent on a fruitless trawl around the empty neighbouring corridors before I return half an hour later to have the auxiliary nurse casually tell me that he'd been lying on the bags of used linen in the sluice room, fast asleep. The phone rings all night and a delirious woman who was once a doctors' receptionist keeps answering it. Throughout all this the buzzers sound their usual chorus, the people in pain groan, scream or do neither.

I miss my break and my carefully rehearsed speech in which I try again to talk to Sadie about a sensible plan to leave remains unspoken. My rest time is spent alone in the ward sisters' office, sitting under a corkboard of yellowing notices with my eyes closed, too tired to even eat.

* * *

Anthony is slouching at the kitchen table when I get in. He looks as drunk with tiredness as I feel. The kitchen door opens and Sacha walks in. Anthony jumps up and leaves the room without speaking.

'Something that I said?' Sacha looks as if nothing happened to him, now he's recovered from the MDMA overdose. He's back to being the puffy-faced drunk that I first met. He's showered today, his hair damp and slicked back and there's a strong smell of Calvin Klein aftershave. His skin has progressed through saffron, to the colour of a faded bruise to the ruddy flush of the drinker. The area beneath his eyes looks puckered and purpled, as if he's not sleeping again. I ignore him and heft the annoyingly slow kettle onto the stovetop, beginning the interminable wait for it to start whistling.

'Unexpected drama while you were all at the hospital overnight.' He pauses, like he's waiting for me to ask what. I don't. 'Look.'

Sacha walks towards the utility room at the back of the kitchen. I have no choice but to follow. The window over the washing machine is smashed and there's glass all over the quarry tiled floor.

'Who did—'

'Stupid question, Laura. How the fuck would I know? There was another one of those pathetic notes, though. Wrapped around the brick like something from an old film.'

'Notes? Have you had more notes?' I've not had a single new note since whoever did this sent Sadie my journals. It had started to feel like a surreal memory or a hallucination until this.

'They don't frighten me. If someone wants to fuck with me then they'll need to try harder than this.' The tremor in his hand suggests the opposite. It's clear that if there is a campaign starting against him then it's begun to unnerve him. Last week someone threw a pot of crimson paint over the front door. It was one of Sacha and Sadie's non-fighting days and he was in that state of drunkenness where he might be considered fun to be around, if that kind of thing amuses you. They spent an afternoon scrubbing it away, laughing together as they worked, blaming it on local children.

'Have you told Sadie?' It crosses my mind that Sadie or Anthony might have thrown the brick. One of them could have sneaked back here on their break and done this as part of some twisted plan to get him out. I still have moments where I wonder if all the stuff with me was done by one of them but they're fleeting thoughts.

'Of course I'll tell Sadie. I need her to sort a glazier.' He points at the panel in the kitchen door. The door where there was a dent in the stained glass, the lead buckling where Sacha had rammed Sadie's former friend Portia's head against it and knocked her unconscious. 'At least it'll be cheaper than fixing that one would have been and I won't end up in the shit this time.'

'Don't you even feel guilty about that?' There's no accusation with my question. It's born of genuine curiosity.

'Don't ask questions about things you know nothing about.'

The kettle shrieks on the stovetop. I turn my back on Sacha and pour boiling water onto the coffee granules. For a second an image of me turning and throwing scalding water over him flashes into my mind. A vision of him screaming in agony, flesh bubbling up and eroding. My hatred for him is still strong, burning and gnawing at me. His effect on Sadie and the house rips into me.

'So when do you finish your course?' His tone is casual to start with before the arch tones come in. 'You'll be leaving us soon, I imagine.'

Sadie enters the room, dressed in a silk dressing gown with flounces round the neck and cleavage. Coco trotting along behind her. She looks like she's from a vintage postcard and is about to make a saucy comment to the milkman. 'Laura's not going anywhere, so don't start, Sacha.'

She makes herself a coffee, ladling in sugar, before turning to address him again. 'Are you going anywhere today?'

'Why? Thinking of moving out while I'm not here? It's not like I need you anymore is it.' The tone for their day is set.

The nearest thing to Sadie's hand is a glass. Fortunately her aim is off and it sails past Sacha's head, smashing against the wall. Coco begins to bark incessantly, almost drowning out the shouting. Her tail shoots between her legs and she moves herself against the back door, scratching at the panel to get out.

Sadie sails past and out of the room and I scoop the dog up.

'It's OK, little one.' I plant a kiss on her head. 'We'll be gone soon.'

I leave Sacha staring at the wall, his face motionless. I knock on Sadie's door as I head to my room.

'I'm fine, Laura. Go and get some rest.' It's only as I'm walking away that I realise that she isn't alone. I can hear the soft muttering of a male voice. Anthony again, sprawled on Sadie's bed where I should be. Another person listening to her, another voice comforting her. I press my ear against the door. This time their animated voices leach through the wood.

'Of course she fucking did it. Who else?' It doesn't take much to work out who or what Anthony is talking about. I steady myself on the doorframe.

'I'm not so sure. I can't see Laura restarting those pathetic notes. She certainly wouldn't smash my window. She loves this place as much as I do.'

'Leopards and spots, Sadie. That's all I'm saying.'

I can't listen to this. My heart pounds as I walk away.

I don't sleep much before the next night shift.

Chapter Forty

THEN

December 1993

I see Sadie briefly before we leave for work. She's in a long-sleeved dress. When she reaches down to pick up Coco the sleeve pulls back and there are finger-shaped bruises near to her wrists. She's tried to cover it with porcelain foundation but patches have rubbed away onto her clothes. She sees me looking.

We're working nights still and I'm back with Army Sue and truculent Michelle. Sue is intense tonight, barking out more military orders. Reminding me that although I might only have a few more weeks, I'm still 'getting bloody paid'. She's right. My performance is off. I drop an iron blood pressure machine that I've been trying to balance on my knee as I crouch by a bedside, reigniting a chorus of wails and shouts from a confused woman which no reassurance will stop. I miss doing a set of observations on a patient who's having a blood transfusion, forget to put sugar in the third black coffee that I make for Sue and accidentally tread on the toe of Michelle's court shoe as I step back behind the desk.

When it's time for my break I trek down to the smoking room. A departing group of first-year students hold the door for me as they exit, leaving Sadie sitting alone. She doesn't turn as I walk in. She's holding a lilac cigarette in her left hand, plumes of foul-smelling smoke dancing up towards the yellowed ceiling. There's a tower of ash and she seems to have forgotten she's holding the cigarette but snaps back to life when she hears me. We exchange the standard comments about how busy we are.

'Sadie, I'm worried about you.'

'Me? Why would you worry about me?' Her hand reaches across to her left wrist. I can see that she's applied more make-up onto the bruises and they're almost unnoticeable.

'All the fighting with Sacha. You've got bruises on your wrists.'

'Oh, well-spotted.' She stubs out the unsmoked cigarette and lights another.

'He might really hurt you. I mean, his history of violence and—'

'Take a breath, Laura. It's all fine.' Sadie moves over and sits next to me. 'I have a plan but it's complicated. I just need you to try and keep out of the way and not interfere. Maybe you should go and stay somewhere else. You could stay in that hotel again if you're worried.'

'No!' This isn't even a choice.

'Well, sit tight and it'll be fine. Sacha won't be here for long, I promise.'

She looks at the clock and stands to leave. As she stands she knocks her handbag off the seat. A mess of powder compacts and lipsticks rolls across the floor. I bend down to pick them up and there's a syringe that's fallen out of the bag. It's full of clear liquid, capped with a small plastic bung. I crouch there, frozen, not knowing what to do or say. I glance around for someone coming in but fortunately there's no one.

'Pass that to me.' Sadie's hand extends to me and I place the syringe into her palm, like a child surrendering something that I shouldn't have picked up.

'What . . .'

'Sit back down for a second.' Her voice is authoritarian. I do as I'm told, sitting staring at Sadie, dreading what she might say next.

'This is just my little insurance policy. I probably won't need to use it but I feel so much better having it here. I've been collecting morphine for a few weeks. There's more hidden away at home.' Her expression is bordering on gleeful.

'Why would you use morphine on him? It'd show up on a post-mortem.'

'He's hardly an example of clean living, is he? He's used most drugs known to man. I'd knock him out with some sedatives then inject the morphine. I'd have to be creative and make a little tableau. Put the empty pill packet in his pocket and leave an empty syringe with his fingerprints on perhaps.'

A ridiculous concern comes to mind. Sadie is talking about murdering her husband but what comes into my head first is that she might get into trouble at work. Morphine is monitored, locked away in double cupboards and logged in a ledger. 'How did you steal the morphine? If they find out you've been taking it then they'll go to the police and you won't be able to finish your training.'

'I'm not a fool, darling. There's a man on the ward with abdominal pain and we're giving him half an ampoule of morphine at a time because he weighs next to nothing. Whenever he has a dose, I pretend to throw the wasted half of an ampoule in the sharps bin. I pocket it and then decant it later.'

'That will take forever to collect enough to cause any harm to Sacha.' She shrugs and puts her cigarettes and lighter into her bag. 'More to the point, you can't do this. It's a crime. Why not just leave?'

'Leave my house? I'm doing this so *we* have a home.' She pats her bag with her hand. 'And this . . . It's insurance. I'm probably not going to do anything, am I? Now, come on or we'll be late and I know how you hate that.'

* * *

The shift is strangely quiet and the ward sister sends me home two hours early, an inadequate nod to the many hours I've stayed late. I walk home alone, the streets of our neighbourhood still alive at five in the morning. Thoughts about Sadie ricochet around my head. I don't spot the front doorstep straight away. As I go to put my key in the door I'm jolted by a flash of crimson on the stone. I look closer and there's a neat splash of fresh blood, pooling, reflecting the streetlight. Drips of red have oozed down and spotted the path below. I step over it and push the door. It's unlocked and Coco tries to nose her way out as I open it, her head diving towards the blood, tongue flicking at it. I ease her back inside and almost slip on a heap of flyers that has been posted through the door.

There's a crash of glass from the sitting room. Sacha is

sitting on the sofa, his face puffy and florid. I breathe in vodka fumes. The sharp scent of spirits is barely masked by his heavy aftershave. He's wearing a black jacket and he winces as he sits forward, trying to reach the bottle.

There's only me and him in the house. It would be anathema to me not to help. I begin by handing him the vodka bottle and telling him not to move. When I come back in with kitchen towels for the spill he's removed his jacket. His white shirt is stained with blood, smears of scarlet pattern the right-hand side of it, like the daubs of a child's painting. There's a tear in the fabric near his shoulder. The blood there is more concentrated, forming thick crusts and clots, fabric sticking to his skin.

'What happened? Have you been to—'

'Help me to get changed. I couldn't make it up the stairs.' A car door slams in the street outside and he jolts around, his dark eyes widening. 'Please.'

I do as he asks. I almost trip over a powder-blue suitcase with a satin lining that's in the middle of the bedroom floor. It's half open and Sadie's clothes and toiletries spill out, as if she's thrown them in there in a hurry. I snatch a shirt from the wardrobe and go back down.

'Here. This one's clean and it won't show any leaks.' I lay the navy shirt down on the sofa and help ease the torn one from his torso. He must have been to the hospital. There's a neat dressing over his shoulder with nothing seeping through. On the left side of his face there's a half-formed bruise, as if he's been punched recently.

The minute the shirt is on, he swigs some more vodka, not bothering with a glass.

'I was stabbed by some arsehole.' He doesn't look at me as he says this. As if being attacked is a source of shame. 'I went to the shop. For food, not drink. I hadn't been drinking till this happened.'

This isn't true.

'Someone ran at me. I was just putting my key in the door and I felt this pain. Then I noticed the blood.'

I ignore my instinct to run to the door and check it's locked. 'Who was it?'

'I don't know. If I'd have seen him I'd have had time to fight back.'

'How do you know it was a man? And did they punch you, as well? Your face is bruised.'

He doesn't answer, instead curls up and rolls onto his side with his back to me.

'Sacha! How do you know it wasn't a woman?'

'I've had enough questions from the police and the hospital. I don't need you. You can go.'

When I walk into the hall I see something I didn't spot on my way in. There's a pile of leaflets that I'd pushed to one side with my foot but on top of them is a white piece of paper. The familiar red letters.

I'LL FINISH THE JOB NEXT TIME.

Chapter Forty-One

NOW

Saturday, 17 April 2010

Even after all this time, I recognise Anthony's footsteps. He walks across the landing and up to the attic. The music stops and Elsie's voice shouts out, telling him to get out of her room. He doesn't. The door clicks behind him and I hear their voices raised in argument.

The stairs feel like gallows steps before me. The last time I came up here was when Anthony yelled for us and we ran and found him hunched over Amy's body. I close my eyes and force myself to concentrate, centring myself. My hand is slick with sweat as I grip the banister.

The door is now painted a blush pink and labelled with stickers. Residual mementoes of childhood with Elsie's name in lurid glitter. It's nothing like the scene that day that stays seared in my psyche. I lift my hand to the door knob but stop myself, instead pushing my ear towards the door. Old habits die hard.

'I don't know why you've bothered to come back.' Elsie's voice sounds strident and teenage.

'Don't speak to me like that, Elsie. I was working and then I was trapped in Denmark.' Anthony's voice sounds strained, like he's struggling to keep his temper under control.

'Seriously? You expect me to believe that?'

'Believe what you like but—'

'Just get out. This is my room in my mum's house and we don't need you here.' Elsie's voice is lower now, one of those deceptively calm tones that are hiding anger. Each word carefully measured and thrown.

'I'm your father and this is my house, too.' I stand back, ready to run back down if he moves towards the door.

'But it's not, is it? This is Sadie's house.'

'Elsie, enough.' Anthony's voice rarely ever used to go above his sardonic drawl. Now it's a bark. 'Don't speak to me like that. I'm. Your. Father.'

'I think the word you're looking for is donor. It's different.'

I'm just in time descending the stairs before he flies down after me. Ducking back into my room I hear him walk to the kitchen. My breathing is erratic as I recover.

I surprise myself when I start to laugh.

* * *

I stay hidden in the bedroom for a while. The laughter dies and my thoughts are ugly, rage gripping me hard. Anthony's mocking face lodges behind my retinas but it's not just him who I'm angry with. I'm furious with myself for my stupid pride. In not wanting to let him see me cede ground, I've missed a chance to find out what he knows that I don't.

I hear him walking around the house, humming to himself. A blithe presence as if this is a normal household and not one where someone is dying. I listen for the sound of him entering Sadie's room, like any spouse, partner or even friend would. There's nothing.

I hear the sound of two people talking outside on the street, their voices drunken, loud. The noises etch away at my jagged nerves and I want to scream. The landing is empty when I step out and I walk towards the room where Anthony's been sleeping. I know exactly what I need. Drink has never been a habit for me. I saw enough bad examples and I still worry that a sickness might lurk somewhere in me. I don't care tonight. My nerves are jangling and I need something to take the edge off this place and lull me into sleep.

He's not in his room. I snatch the bottle of whisky that I found when I searched in here earlier in the week, feeling like I'm committing a crime. I take it with me downstairs and stand at the sink, slopping some into a glass, trying not to gag as I knock half of it back.

'Drinking on duty, Laura? I would say that I'm surprised at you but you lost the ability to shock me with your actions long ago.' His voice sounds like he's suppressing a laugh. 'And of course, you had that sister . . .'

'*Have* a sister. And funnily enough, I'm not on duty and never should have been. She's all yours now, like you always wanted her to be.' I turn around and face him.

'You're welcome to drink some of my whisky that you've stolen, by the way.'

'I know I am.'

There's a pompous smile on his face and his lined cheeks crease upwards. He has the skin of a habitual sunbed user.

When I sit down at the table he follows and sits across from me. His presence infects the room like a virus. I set down the drink. It seems absurd now that I was even thinking about drinking alcohol in this house, of all places. I push the glass away. The anxiety I felt lying in that room feels so stupid now that it's just me and this pathetic man sitting here.

'I know you want to draw this out and torture me but tell me what happened on that last day.'

He takes a breath and begins to speak.

Chapter Forty-Two

THEN

December 1993

I must have fallen asleep on my bed. I'm woken by shouting. Anthony and Sadie must be back. I think of the bruises on Sadie's wrists and brace myself to run down to protect her. Anthony's voice rises up. The words are unintelligible but the fact that he's there reassures me. Sacha won't attack Sadie while he's there. I roll onto my side and wedge my hands over my ears. The daylight taunts me and I can't sleep so I get up, dress and go down.

'Where's Sadie?' I stand in the kitchen doorway, ensuring that I have an exit if needed. Sacha seems less drunk at the moment but the smell of spirits is overpowering.

'I told her and that arrogant little shit of hers to go upstairs out of the way.'

He points at the chair across from him at the kitchen table. 'I need to talk to *you* about something.'

I sit and he doesn't speak straight away. He leans back, swinging the chair.

'Sacha, I don't think it's a good idea to drink. Your liver cells are still recovering from the damage that they had after the incident. Do you think you could try to stop? Maybe eat something and drink some water. Try to sleep.'

I wait for an enraged response but there's none. He flashes a disarming smile at me.

'Always the nurse. Even caring about people who you hate. You can't help it, can you?'

'Shall we walk you upstairs so you can try to sleep it off and—'

'My drinking is my business. The house is what I need to talk to you about. I know you like it here and I'm willing to let you carry on living here. For free. If you do something for me.' He spots the stricken look that spreads across my face. 'Nothing like that. It's not sexual. I don't fancy you, obviously.'

I let the intended barb of the word 'obviously' pass. This feels like a chess game. Like he's waiting for me to make the next move. Our eyes meet.

'And what's the favour?' I half guess what's coming next.

'I need you to get me some stuff from the hospital. Nothing too excessive. Just the odd box of diazepam or two. I wouldn't need much. It's just that I'm having a bad time. This thing with the attack and those notes . . .'

'Absolutely not. I don't need to stay here, anyway. I'm not planning on living in London. I've arranged a job in Derbyshire and my mum has found me a cottage in the village. But thanks for the offer.' The lie about the job and the housing comes easily from my lips. My plan is to stay here and Sadie and I will find a flat to live in, once I convince her to leave. I've accepted the job on the oncology ward.

'Oh, Laura. If only it was that simple for you.' He stands and walks over to the door, leaning his hip against the frame.

'Could you move, please. I'd like to go to my room.'

'I think I can do what I want, don't you. It is *my* house after all.'

'I've got a couple more shifts, Sacha. Then I'll be gone.'

I reach for the door knob but he grasps my wrist. My attempt to move is no match for his thick fingers.

'You don't get away that easily. You see, silly Sadie is a bit of a careless friend. She left this lying around.'

He lets go of my wrist and pulls out the empty bottle of chlordiazepoxide with the hospital label on it from his pocket.

'Sadie says that you took these and I imagine that's what she'd say if I took the bottle to the college tutors and said that I found them in your room. Her loyalty won't stretch enough for her to take the blame. Imagine the fallout when they start asking why a student nurse had hospital drugs in her possession.'

'Look, can we just get this over with.' I try and fail to hide the tremor in my voice.

'Seeing as you *are* finally leaving, then how about a farewell gift to thank me for my hospitality? Just a few boxes. Any benzos will do. I'm not picky.'

'No.'

He stands back enough now that I can get out of the door.

'Don't make any snap decisions. Sleep on it and then let me know what you choose. But think about this. Even up in sleepy Derbyshire, I'm not sure that any job is going to take anyone who gets struck off before she even finishes her training.' He flashes a smile at me. His teeth sharp against the red of his lips. He wedges the empty pill bottle back in his pocket. 'I'll keep this safe. Speak later. Oh and sleep well.'

* * *

I knock at Sadie's door to tell her what Sacha has said and explain how he's tried to pit us against each other by lying. I don't believe that she told him that I stole the drugs. I know she wouldn't have done that. There's the muffled sound of her voice. When I walk in, Anthony is lolling on the bed while Sadie paces the floor of the room. Suitcases lie open on the floor with a jumble of clothes spilling out. I instinctively bend down and start to fold them.

'I'm beaten, Laura.' Sadie isn't wearing her usual make-up or vintage clothes. She's found an old *Frankie Says Relax* T-shirt that skims her thighs and has paired it with faded leggings. If she passed me in the street I wouldn't look twice at her. 'He's finally throwing me out of my own house.'

'Where are you going?' Sadie doesn't answer. Anthony slides off the bed like a snake and kneels beside me, refolding some of the clothes that I've already laid in the case.

'What's wrong with your arm?' There are red welts along Anthony's forearm.

'What do you think? Sacha was lashing out.'

'We're all going to have to leave today. It's not safe here.' Sadie's voice is a monotone.

She sits on the edge of the bed, near Anthony's feet and beckons me to sit with her. She takes my hand and lifts it to her chest. The motion of her arm as she speaks raising both of our hands up. The sound of a delivery van outside sends Coco jumping at the door, banging her paws against the wood.

'It's not fair that you have to go.' I take my hand back from hers. 'What will you do?'

Sadie steps over to the window, scooping Coco up on the way and whispering into her soft fur. When she turns I don't recognise her expression. Her cheeks are stained with tears, blotchy and ugly. I've never seen her cry before.

'There might be something that we can do. Don't you have any legal rights?'

She ignores the question and stares at the floor, her body still. I know the signs of her imminent rage. The flare of her nostrils, the raising of her brows, the change in inflection. Sinister omens like the persistent cough or burgeoning lump heralding a coming cancer.

'We'll be fine, Sadie.' I move to her side. Coco reaches up and licks tears from her face. 'We'll be paid more now we're about to qualify. We could rent somewhere together and make it exactly like this place.'

Sadie bends down and sets the dog on the floor. 'Do you have any idea how money and property work? How much it costs to live in this city? I might get a payout from a divorce but I'm not counting on it. He might even try to have it annulled. But whatever happens I won't have this place. That's all I want.' Her voice sounds petulant and whiny, like a child demanding a pony from her rich father.

She turns her back on me and walks over to the wardrobe.

'It's a shame that bastard didn't die in hospital. I'm going to have to come up with a new plan.'

'What do you mean a new plan?'

'It was all so silly, wasn't it? I was collecting morphine to kill Sacha by palming that patient's unused half ampoules but my supply ran out because the patient got better and went home.' I want to laugh at the petulant look on her face. At the absurdity of all this.

'I can't talk about it but I have something in mind.' Anthony glances across at her but doesn't say anything. She ignores my pleas to tell me what she's thinking, holding up her hand as I try to speak.

Whatever she's planning it won't be good for any of us.

Chapter Forty-Three

THEN

December 1993

The rap of knuckles on the bedroom door wakes me from a half sleep and I fumble for my watch. Four o'clock in the afternoon. I've only slept for a couple of hours. I've been thinking. Torturous and dangerous thoughts and plans that have led me to a conclusion.

I know how to save Sadie and restore order for us both.

'Are you ready, Laura?' I jump up and open the door. Sadie and Anthony are on the landing. Across the hall her bedroom door is open and there's a neat pile of cases waiting. 'Sacha's asleep. We've booked a taxi.'

'A taxi to where?'

'A hotel for now.' Her tone suggests she's saying something repellent, like 'gangrene'.

I look back at the room before turning to her. 'I'm not leaving.'

'No. Absolutely not, Laura. You can't stay here. You've seen how he is when he drinks.'

'It's two shifts, Sadie. That's all I have left to do. I have a lock on the door and I'll be careful.' Anthony rolls his eyes behind her back. 'I'm fine, honestly.'

I smile, hoping that it doesn't look like a grimace.

'I'm not going to allow it. You can't stay here.' Sadie moves to push herself into the room but I don't step back, continuing to block the doorway.

'I said I'm fine.' I close the door and listen to them arguing, Anthony saying to let me put myself in danger because he doesn't 'give a shit'. Eventually I hear them carrying the suitcases down the stairs. I'm sitting on my bed, making notes, when there's another knock half an hour later. She's sent Anthony this time.

'Here.' He hands Coco to me like he's passing a bag of soiled sheets. 'We can't find a hotel that'll take a dog but Sadie's working on it. She'll be back to collect her tomorrow morning.'

'But . . . I won't be here overnight. I have to go to work.'

'Look, it's taken me half an hour to get Sadie to agree to leave her here. Just take her. She'll be fine overnight. She's been left on her own often enough when we're all on shift. She'll just sleep.'

* * *

The shower neither wakes me up nor makes me feel cleaner.

'You stayed!' He sounds genuinely pleased, as if he's afraid to be left alone. Sacha's glass is filled with a dark brown liquid that looks like brandy this time. I have no idea how he's staggered to the shop to buy more alcohol. His words are now slurring into one long chain. His skin looks pink and scrubbed. His battered liver seems to be coping with a return to its usual state of being assaulted by strong liquor.

'I'll take that as a no for coffee?' I pour a cup for myself and sit down opposite him.

'Cheers.' He raises the drink, slopping an inkblot of fluid that looks like a Rorschach test onto the table.

'Cheers.' I sip the coffee and it scorches my lip. Coco appears and jumps onto my lap.

'Coco! Little Coco.' The dog looks at him with a startled expression as he extends his hand to stroke her but he misses by inches as she weaves her head to one side.

'Stay with me tonight, Laura.'

'I have to go to work.'

'I'm not . . . I don't want to be alone.'

'Lock the doors. I'll let Coco out before I go and then leave her upstairs. She'll be fine on my bed.'

'Will you get the drugs?' His lips are struggling to form the words. He takes a deep breath and sighs. 'I need to stop. I want Sadie back again. Vitamins and Librium. I can stop again. It's just been a few days. It won't be as bad.'

* * *

The ward is oddly quiet, a state that has a strange effect on nurses. They become superstitious. Scared that this unprecedented calm is just a portent or a trick of the light that will be momentary. Try saying the word 'quiet' to a group of nurses and they'll castigate you for cursing them, convinced that you've now brought down some sort of unholy wrath that'll result in chaos and carnage.

Michelle and I finish settling the patients down and I

record the observations while Sue parades the drug trolley up and down the ward, batting away any interruptions.

We have to perform last offices for a young woman of my age who had cancer. She'd died during the late shift but her mother has only just left the side room. I averted my eyes out of respect as Sue slowly guided her to the entrance of the ward. We're silent while we do what we have to do. When she's been eased into the mortuary trolley we return to the nurses' station. The quiet of the ward is oppressive.

'I don't trust this.' Michelle lines up four puzzle books with dated pictures of women with too much hair on the front. She pushes her bag under the desk, knocking my ankle. 'Are you all right?'

'I'm fine. Just tired.'

Michelle's expression has changed. She looks younger and uncharacteristically vulnerable.

'I had a sister who died who was the same age as that girl.' There's a steely edge to her words.

'Oh, I'm sorry.'

'Don't be. The bastard she married is the one who should be sorry. He's the one got her onto drugs and put her through all that suffering.'

Michelle starts rooting in her bag again, signalling an end to the conversation. I don't share about Suzie. Instead I think about how Michelle mentioned her sister's suffering. I've always concentrated my concern onto my mum and finding ways of helping her to cope, often seeing Suzie as a menace to us. Always trying not to think about the childhood memories of before Suzie got sick. The days out, the walks in the park and the evenings we spent snuggled on the sofa when Mum was working. All that ended and

Suzie became joyless. No, worse than joyless, she was pained. Thinking about my mum stopped me thinking of my poor, sick sister and the layers of hell that she was going through.

I can't be still so I get up and circuit the ward again, checking on the patients before I return to the desk.

The stagnant hours make me edgy. I look down at my hands, surprised that they aren't shaking.

'I don't think Mr Austin will last much longer, do you?' I hope Michelle's right, for the sake of his daughter. She's a bird-like woman who looks like she's on the brink of a nervous collapse, fluttering up and down around his bedside, never seeming to settle. Night after night.

Sue walks back round. 'The pump's alarming in room three.'

I jump up at my cue.

The ampoules of diamorphine resist me, the breaking point of the glass elusive. I snap the head off them one by one, drawing them up with the needle and tapping away the bubbles. I flash the vials in front of Sue to check the dose and expiry date and we sign the medicines book.

'He's on a fair old whack, poor chap.' Sue passes me the tray to put the syringe on and I miss. It bounces across the floor, knocking against the bin. 'For God's sake, Laura. There's no cap on the end of that so you've just made it unsterile. We'll have to start again. What's wrong with you tonight?'

'I . . . I'm sorry.' I scoop down and grab the full syringe, moving towards the sharps bin in the opposite counter.

'Use this one. It's nearer. Come on.'

I drop a syringe into the sharps bin.

It's not the one I just filled. It's a spare syringe full of water that I'd put in my pocket earlier. It makes a noise as it hits the soiled steel and glass inside the yellow bin. I could have just switched the syringes but then Mr Austin would have been without his medication and that would be entirely wrong. He shouldn't suffer.

The syringe full of diamorphine, or heroin to give it its street name, fits easily into my pocket, ready to go into my bag later.

Chapter Forty-Four

THEN

December 1993

If you could choose your final meal before you died then I suspect that you'd select something comforting. Maybe a dish from childhood or one that harked back to a memorable holiday. Perhaps something you associated with the great love of your life or a habitual staple that you cooked and ate with the TV blasting out as white noise.

Sacha's final meal is a limp ham sandwich and a glass of whisky laced with crushed diazepam.

'Thank you.' He snatches the glass that I put on the kitchen table and takes a gulp, discarding the sandwich that he's left erratic tooth marks in. He's more lucid again, his voice no longer slurred.

'I'm sorry about the pills. These are all there were but there'll be more tomorrow after the pharmacy delivery.' I've given him a strip with only six little blue 5mg pills. The half-empty strip in his pocket will be more than good enough as an explanation for the benzodiazepines in his blood stream.

Maybe dying in hope is the best way. Sacha will fade away gently with the notion that he's getting exactly what he wants. Palliation via a steady supply of his favourite medications. A state of calm optimism via the drugs supplied by me, a temporary quietening of the world he isn't capable of living comfortably in. This world that he also makes impossible for Sadie.

I smile across at him. 'I think I might join you.'

He raises an eyebrow in mock disapproval. 'Have I turned you to drink?'

'It'll help me sleep.'

'Good girl. I'm sick of drinking alone. Everyone here is such a fucking bore.' Liar. He doesn't care who's there, what time it is, where he is. Alcohol always wins and maybe always would have done for Sacha, were he not about to die. He takes another mouthful, his morning hands shaking and a drop spilling onto the table. I jump up and grab a cloth, wiping the drug laced fluid from the Formica.

'This is working. You're actually starting to look almost fuckable.'

I swallow my disgust. 'Well, sadly, you aren't. But cheers.'

I take only a tiny tip of the vile-smelling drink.

His head is bent slightly forward and, despite what I said, he's almost appealing for a second. That earthy masculinity offset by his doleful brown eyes, like he's a romantic hero from one of the old films. Such a waste of good genes. Because he's not the hero in this. He's the villain. A malignant force whose arrival brought chaos, violence and destruction to this house. Who rendered the atmosphere here to something caustic and filled with disdain, turning my safe haven into a war zone.

I can do this. It's just another necessary job to be done.

My thoughts are clinical and sterile.
The whisky tastes better the more that I drink.
We sit and both empty our glasses.

* * *

When he's compliant enough from the medication, I lead him through to the sitting room and lay him down on the sofa, arms by his side, like a corpse awaiting the porters to take him to the mortuary. His eyes close.

I focus, drowning out the voices that are screaming from inside of my head, shouting at me to stop. Reminding myself that this is for the greater good. That he has to go. I look down at these hands that are steady and efficient as I draw up the diamorphine.

My brain lists the steps of the procedure that I've observed so often and I pretend that I'm performing a mundane job at work. This task that's so counter to everything I once believed about the sanctity of life. I still have the same beliefs, just not about his life.

Sacha mumbles to himself and smiles, eyes still closed, as I attach the tourniquet. His veins are prominent and inviting. He opens one eye and says 'Hey!' as the needle pierces his vein. I push the plunger of the syringe and it gives easily, infusing his body with the fluid.

It's quick. The drugs swirl in his blood stream and hit his respiratory sensors.

It's not the first time that I've watched someone die. Death is a subject that I know too much about. Even if I were to stop being a nurse tomorrow there's a roll call of disquieting things that I can't unlearn. The dying process would stay imprinted on my mind.

It plays out like it usually does. His breathing slows and becomes uneven, his skin becomes sweaty and clammy, increasingly pallid. I wait, listening to each rattle and gasp, gauging the labour of his changing respirations.

Sacha's death is different, of course. This isn't my usual routine. It's like nothing I've ever seen. The terrain is all wrong, to start with. The creaking of Laurel House instead of the moans and screams of a hospital and a cloying smell of potpourri instead of disinfectant. Soft light from the fringed lamp by the sofa rather than overhead strip lighting blanching my skin to a sickly hue.

Unlike in the hospital, I have no official role at this scene. No uniform to wear, no lists of urgent tasks or rules to obey. I don't do any of the things I'd normally do at this point. There won't be any gentle moistening of dry mouths with damp sponges, no comforting of the soon to be bereaved. Not even any soothing physical contact from me.

Instead, I wait for the consequences of my actions to take effect.

Sacha's death is entirely different because I've caused it.

* * *

When it's done I remove the original diamorphine syringe and leave behind the kind of fine insulin syringe that he might have used were this self-inflicted. My fingers feel for his absent carotid pulse, and I wipe away a drop of the blood that is congealing in the crook of his cooling inner arm.

I know what this scene should look like. I've spent long enough cleaning up after my sister. I wipe the insulin syringe and press Sacha's fingers around the barrel, then place it on the floor as if it has fallen from his hand as it relaxed into the early stages of death. It now lies next to some kitchen foil that I've scorched using one of Sadie's lighters from her Sobranie drawer. The kitchen is cold as I scrub the glass that held the drugged drink, swilling it in scalding water and Fairy Liquid. My hands smart under the heat of the tap water.

Coco trots through, standing on her back legs and snagging my skin with her paws. She wolfs down the tin of salmon that I put down for her. I sit in the kitchen and wait for Sadie to come. I've learned on the wards that there's power in routine, so I ape my usual morning tasks. Bitter coffee on the table before me, toast on a plate, the kitchen tidied and the washer turned on.

The food and drink sits untouched, the idea of eating and drinking now revolting. The room is silent. I'm juvenile and senseless, waiting for Sadie like a child waiting for her mother to come home so she can show her what's she's created in her absence.

I put my head on my hands and sleep drags me down.

* * *

I wake from gaudy dreams, disconcerted, and it's as if a fever has broken. I'm unsure why I'm alone, what the time or the day is. The clock tells me that I've been asleep for fifteen minutes.

The killing comes back to me, tangible and fresh, bringing with it a fresh perspective and a sense of panic. It's like the delirium has lifted and I'm renewed and sensible again. A moment of hope flashes through me. I guide Coco back into the kitchen, sending a ball skittering across the floor for her to chase. I run through to check if this madness is reality or a nightmare, my feet tapping out a rhythm as I walk to the sitting room. He's cool to the touch, skin waxy and yellowing. The tableau I've set up is a perfect dramatic scene of a man dead because of his own sad and desperate actions. Bile rises into my mouth as my eyes skim the familiar sight of a recently dead person, my gaze lingering over his still chest and sallow skin. No longer Sacha but now a cadaver, collapsed onto the sofa, with half-opened eyes and a hand trailing towards the floor.

I've done what had to be done. My mantra is the list of the reasons why he deserved to die. The chaos. The violence. Sadie. She needs safety and calm. She needs this house and to be here with me.

My brain runs through the list of the right things to do now. Like phone an ambulance, maybe even see those same paramedics again. I picture myself rotating the dial on the ridiculous Bakelite phone.

The reality is that I do nothing. I'm inert. A second dead thing in this morgue that I've created. I close the sitting room door and go through to Coco kissing her on the head. 'I'll be back soon. I just have to go out for a while.'

I should wait until Sadie comes back to collect Coco but I can't be still. My trembling legs take me away from this house, pushed by shockwaves of adrenaline that course through me. I have to find breathable air that isn't contaminated by my guilt. Somewhere I don't feel this sense of dread.

The park is frost-rimed and bitter but I barely notice the ice of the bench under my thighs or the fact that I'm shivering. I ignore the glances of the occasional dog walker, the old Polish woman who's throwing bread to the water birds on the lake that bobs with empty lager cans. My watch isn't there when I look but I know I've been here in this trance for hours.

I look down and I'm in a coat that's not mine, a funky-smelling flannel thing that I'd grabbed as I ran, laden with the smell of cigarettes and a hint of musky sweat. I realise with a jolt that it's Sacha's coat. The path feels unreliable under my feet as I push my numb soles back towards the house, my arms wrapped around myself as I shiver back across the high street to find Sadie.

When I reach the end of the street I see her. Sadie is slumped on the front doorstep of Laurel House. Her dress rucked up, her knees at an odd angle and her head facing towards the looming laurel bushes. Her body is convulsed in sobs. I move forward but as I near her a figure appears in the doorway. Anthony helps her up. I want to go to them but my legs mutiny. I stand and stare.

As Sadie turns to go inside I see the blood. Blood all down the front of her dress. Her head turns and she spots me. She steadies herself on the doorframe, leaving a crimson handprint. I stare at the blood for a second. It shouldn't be here. There was no blood. Sacha died quietly and bloodlessly from the medical grade heroin. I look away, then look back, thinking it's an illusion born of my madness. Lady Macbeth visions. I look once more and it's still there.

'Sadie, what happened? Why is there blood?'

Cold eyes lock with mine before she turns her head away and steps inside, closing the door on me. Red fingerprints are left behind on the doorframe.

I wait a few minutes and let myself in quietly with trembling hands. The sitting room is silent behind a sealed door. Voices spill out from behind the closed kitchen door.

The sound of Anthony speaking and Sadie crying, words that I can't make out coming from behind the door.

I move closer and I hear the piercing noise of Sadie. A keening funeral wail.

'It's OK. It'll be OK.' Anthony is at his most honeyed and insincere.

'I can't believe it. I can't . . . I've got nothing now. There's nothing. I'll never get over this. It's impossible.'

'You will. You will.'

'I'll never forgive her. Laura is dead to me now. I should have known that something like this would happen because of one of you. I've given so much to you all and what do I get back?' Sadie's words sound like they're being spat out with force.

I flop sideways against the wall, my legs barely able to support me. Iced fingers knead at my stomach and I want to vomit. I pinch my arm hard enough that it makes my eyes water, reawakening my inert body. The only option is to run. I dash up the stairs and grab my bag.

* * *

The dwindling rush hour chaos on the tube almost distracts me from my whirring thoughts. Trying to breathe and to stay upright, wedged between the hot bodies and coffee breath of the morning commuters, is a distraction. The feeling of needing to be as far as possible from that house not diminishing in spite of the distance the train is shunting me away. The deafening screech of the train as it scrapes along the tracks feels like a punishment. Something that only I can hear.

My eyes unfocused, my mind thinking of only one image.

Sadie with the mysterious bloodstain down her dress. The look on her face that left no room for doubt. A look of pure hatred that told me to back off.

I've left a note for her: *Call me. We need to talk.*

A page from one of my ridiculous notebooks with the words and the phone number for my mum's flat. Somehow I manage to use a phone box to ring in sick for my last night, which won't matter, I'll still graduate.

It's in the café near St Pancras station that I'm almost sick. Two women with hollow eyes and track marks on their arms, the only other customers, glance over at me as I start to heave. They carry on talking regardless, lighting new cigarettes each time one ends. The café owner shoots across to usher me out, doubtless thinking I'm another of the drunk or drugged people who frequent the area.

'I . . . I'm sorry.' She rests her hand on my shoulder and says something but it doesn't register. The door knocks my shoulder as I dash out and wait in the grimy shed of the station with my hastily packed bags.

The woman's words come to me: 'Whatever this is, love, it'll pass.'

I don't think she's right.

* * *

'You don't look well.'

'I've been worried all along that being a nurse would be too much for you.'

'I didn't like the idea of you being alone in London. I said that didn't I, Suzie?'

My mum's voice rattles on and it feels more like recrimination than compassion. I sink down onto the sofa.

'I'm fine. I just need time to rest. Then I'll go back.'

There's a loud tut and then some unintelligible muttering before she leaves to go to work.

'Suzie, I'm expecting a call.' I look at her properly for the first time and she looks well. Her skin glowing, hair freshly dyed and make-up carefully applied. 'Will you wake me when my friend calls?'

She nods and places her warm hand on my shoulder.

I curl up on the sofa and fall into a dreamless sleep.

* * *

The community psychiatrist came to see me at home this morning. I think the GP sent him or maybe it was the nurse who came out yesterday. I've lost track of everything. I told the doctor very little and resisted when he suggested changing my medication. This isn't depression. It's a reaction to Laurel House. I'm sad, guilty and scared, which is different. My voice is here and unlike after what happened with Jessica I can speak, although I have nothing to say.

The call hasn't come. Days have turned into weeks and the phone sits silently by the sofa in reproach. There's been no call from the police and nothing from Sadie. I long to take the receiver and dial Laurel House but the image of Sadie's face returns and I don't.

I know she'll call me, in time.

I understand Sadie.

And she understands me. She must know why I did what I did.

I did it for her. It was all for her.

I had to protect her from doing anything stupid.

I gave her the house she needs.

So she'll be grateful once the shock recedes, desperate to have me back and we'll resume our life.

I've written her a letter and I keep it in my pocket. My hand reaches for it when I pass the post box on my daily walks but I can never quite make the move to let it leave my hand.

The oncology ward sister was understanding when I told her about my fictitious grandmother's illness and why I would need to delay my start by a few weeks. She was less understanding when I rang again, telling her that I wouldn't be taking the job at all as I wasn't returning to London.

I sit here, day after day. Suzie sits with me when she's home.

It's the blood that haunts me most. The jagged splash of it down Sadie's dress in the shape of a small country. The handprint on the door. A reel of Sadie that day runs on a loop in my head.

I don't know why she hasn't called.

But she will one day soon.

Chapter Forty-Five

NOW

Saturday, 17 April 2010

The kitchen is cooler and a watery light illuminates cobwebs and dust. I wrap my arms across my chest and lean across the table towards Anthony.

'So, tell me. I think I'm owed an explanation.'

'And exactly why would I owe you anything?' He leans back in the chair with his hands resting on his thinning scalp.

'You and Sadie having all this is due to me, isn't it?'

There's a pause while he shifts his posture. He closes his eyes for a second. My hands itch to grab him by the shoulders and shake him.

'I think I might join you in a drink.' Our eyes lock. 'You're a mess, aren't you? Do you think you should have come back here? It doesn't seem like it's doing you much good.'

I understand how this will play out. He has exactly what he wants now. He sees my weak spots and he knows how to feed off them.

'Ask me anything. I'm an open book,' he says.

The smell of the whisky now repulses me. I push it away.

'The blood. I don't understand why there was blood on the door.'

'Well, think about it. It wasn't Sacha's, was it? You saw how he died, obviously.' I let his patronising tone wash over me. 'And it wasn't Sadie's blood. You saw her and she wasn't injured.'

'Your blood? Why?'

'Cold. Very cold. You're nowhere near yet. Who else was there?' He drains the rest of the whisky, the ice cubes knocking against his teeth. I push down my urge to scream and force myself to sit upright, like I'm back in the refectory at boarding school.

'I was never very good at riddles. They bore me. You win.'

'Coco. You killed Coco.'

'I didn't kill a dog. That's absurd.' I feel like drips of cold water are running down my back.

'But you did. In your panicked rush to get out of here after you did what you did to Sacha you left the front door open and didn't latch the gate. Coco must have followed you.' I can't look at his face because I have a feeling that he'll be smirking and that will be too much to bear. 'Sadie and I came back and she was injured on the road.'

'Oh, God.' A physical pain hits me in my lower abdomen.

'Sadie was holding this poor, broken thing, howling like a banshee. She was inconsolable. You could do a lot of things to Sadie and she'd forgive you but harming her dog . . .'

I understand now. The image of Sadie that day covered in blood. She must have picked up Coco and dripped the blood onto her dress, smearing it on the door when she rested her hand there. Now the words I overheard from behind the kitchen door make sense.

I sit back on the chair, winded. There's a rush of footsteps on the stairs.

Elsie doesn't move towards him and he doesn't bother to stand.

'Hey, honey. I was just chatting with Laura. We were reminiscing about Sadie's old dog. I've been telling her how much we appreciate her being here but sadly she has to leave later. We'll be fine now I'm here.'

'No!' Elsie's reply is violent. 'I don't want you to go. I need you.' I link eyes with Elsie and give her a half-smile.

'But we're—'

'You haven't even been in to Sadie yet, have you? Because you don't give a shit. Not one single shit. Where have you really been, anyway?' Her voice is shaking. She turns on her heel and walks out of the room. I hear Sophia trotting after her on the stairs.

I don't move. It's like I'm hypnotised, reeling from his revelation about Coco. My first instinct is to run up the stairs and confront Sadie about the reason for my exile. I feel sickened about Coco, but it feels so unjust that this horrible accident stopped Sadie from contacting me for all this time.

I blink hard and pull myself back to the present.

'Anthony, Elsie's right. You should go in and see her.'

I get up and walk towards the door.

'I'd better say this now then if there's not much time.' His voice is quieter and I turn back to face him to catch his words. 'Thank you for doing what you did. The murder I mean. It was above and beyond. We've had the most marvellous life here.'

My chest constricts like there's no air in the room.

I have no memory of walking up the stairs. I lie on top of the bed, listening for Sadie calling me, expecting to hear Anthony walking up the stairs and going into her bedroom. There's no sound at all, other than the low thump of music from someone's car outside.

Chapter Forty-Six

NOW

Sunday, 18 April 2010

It's midnight when Anthony finally comes upstairs. I'm charting her medications and Sadie has just fallen asleep. He stands in the doorway, his eyes fixed on her. She's lying on the bed like the perfect patient, arms by her side over the blanket, hair neat on the pillows that are supporting her head. Her shallow breaths soft and hypnotic in the room.

'Well done. You were right, Laura. She's dying.'

I spin round but he's already gone. The door to the smallest bedroom closes and there's silence.

* * *

'There was Sacha . . . last night . . . or a dream? Alex. He's called Alex now, isn't he?'

'No, Sadie. It was Anthony. Your second husband.'

She looks at me with a dazed expression. Her brain is foggy today, words coming out in half-formed sentences.

Her chains of thought aren't easy to follow. She's too weak today to take even sips of water. I try to wet her mouth with a sponge but she resists, tightening her lips and clenching her jaw.

It's Sunday. That void of a day when health professionals are harder to access. I think she's close to death. Her food and fluid intake has tailed off to almost nothing and she's sleepier. It won't be long.

'Anthony told me about Coco.' She smiles at the mention of the name. 'I'm so sorry. I was . . . distressed and I must not have closed the gate.'

She doesn't speak but her face lifts up and her hand reaches out for my hand on the bed. She squeezes twice before letting go. Her arm flops back onto the bed.

'Coco!' Her voice is weaker now. Her face becomes flaccid and shuts down again. I think she's asleep and I turn away. I barely hear the next words. I feel something brush my leg and it's Sophia. I lift her up onto the bed and she curls up at Sadie's side.

'He's bad for Elsie.' Her eyes fix on mine. Her pupils are small, the whites of her eyes now the colour of spoiled butter. Her hand reaches down and rests by the dog's back.

'I think they'll be fine, Sadie.' I say this with bravado. I'm not at all sure that they will be. Elsie's left the house, becoming mute when I asked her where she was going and what time she'll be back. I have her mobile number if I need her to come back quickly, which is a strong possibility.

'Do it again.' Sadie's eyes are wild as words spill out in a hiss.

'Do what, Sadie? I don't understand.'

The bedroom door opens and Anthony walks back in. He looks freshly showered. His thinning hair is slicked back over his scalp with something greasy and there's a strong smell of Paco Rabanne. He's wearing jeans and a white shirt, looking like a blurred photograph of his former self. I look away.

'You've still got it, Laura, haven't you? That singular ability to look down on everyone and everything.'

'I wasn't—'

'You really haven't changed at all. A bit wider round the hips but otherwise the same. Now, how's my wife?'

'You can see for yourself. You're a nurse too, aren't you?'

He takes in a breath through his nostrils and lifts his head up. 'Actually, I'm not. I relinquished all that after you left.'

Three years of training for nothing. I loathe acknowledging this but he was good at it. 'What do you do?'

'I'm a sales rep for a pharmaceutical company.' A perfect job for him, using all that artifice and charm that he can turn on and off to woo young doctors. I imagine him flirting with both men and the women, bestowing free gifts and incentives to coax people to buy whatever drugs he's peddling.

Sadie stirs and opens her eyes. He walks to her side and takes her hand. I watch her carefully to see what her reaction is. Her hand recoils from his and her fist clenches as she clamps her arm to her side.

'I'm back now. I'm sorry you're having such a tough time. Laura's been telling me all about it. I would have been here but I was stuck in Denmark.'

'Not.' The word is spat out with surprising force.

Sadie closes her eyes tightly but I can tell from her breathing that she's not asleep.

I'm almost at the door when Anthony speaks again.

'Ignore what my daughter says. You need to go home now, Laura.'

I jump when Sadie shouts 'No!'

He pushes past me and walks out of the room.

Sadie keeps her eyes closed and doesn't speak. Once I'm convinced she's asleep I go down and make myself a drink with shaking hands, granules of coffee spilling from the spoon and scattering onto the worktop. There's a battered packet of Sadie's lurid cigarettes in the drawer. I wish I smoked. That quiet moment devoted to the habit when I could pause and try to untangle my thoughts.

* * *

'So, what time are you leaving?' He pulls out the kitchen chair and sits across from me, his hand resting on the table. His voice is honeyed and soft. I imagine this is his salesman tone that he uses to charm doctors' receptionists.

'I'm not.' I lift my head up.

'Not what?' His eyes narrow.

'I'm not leaving.'

'This sticking around where you're not needed is thematic, isn't it?' His accent has changed slightly. There's something more refined about his vowels. The endings of words are crisper.

'I'm going to stay to look after Sadie. It's what she wants and what Elsie wants, which is what matters.' I'm using my professional tone, masking my hatred of him like I would on the wards with a difficult relative who had pushed me to the edge.

'All this time and you still don't see it. It's pitiful, really.

Sadie's a grifter, Laura. She's always been a chancer and a liar. What part of that aren't you getting?'

'Yet you're the one who chose to stay here and leach off her for all these years.'

'It was a convenient base and she amused me.' He gets up and peers into the hall, checking to see if Elsie is around, before closing the door and sitting again. 'I've enjoyed being part of her fantasy. I was good at it and it was a fun role to play.'

I'm not sure Elsie and Sadie would agree.

'She's not even called Sadie.' He laughs when he sees my blank expression. 'You didn't even work that one out, did you? Sadie Browne with her glamorous history is really just plain old Sarah Brown from an estate just off the Old Kent Road. You should see where she grew up. It's an absolute shit tip.'

'I . . . I didn't know that. But it doesn't matter if she—'

'The lies about who owned this house, about her name, her family. About whose fault it was that Amy took that dodgy E. Don't you see the pattern? She's a twisted self-invention. Everything about her is a delusion. Even her clothes are elaborate copies. There'd hardly have been that many vintage clothes around in the right size for someone like Sadie. I realised early on that she lived in her own invented world.'

'If you think she's so twisted then how did you tolerate her?'

'Because I didn't care. I enjoyed it. I was happy to play along with her nonsense. Like you sometimes were.'

He's right. Part of me did play along. I dressed up and lived the lifestyle. I fed her delusions. I see now that it was likely that she realised that Amy was already taking drugs at the raves she went to. It was convenient for her to blame Sacha, though. And her role as prospective murderer was never convincing.

Anthony sighs and carries on speaking. 'I did love her once. Not in the conventional way but I loved her regardless. Giving Sadie my little donation for a daughter and going along with the sham wedding felt like small gifts.' He pauses and for a moment he seems almost benign.

The familiar sneer crosses his face again and I brace myself for the next barb. 'Sadie vacillates between states of belief. You must see that. Like now, she'll never accept that she's dying. She chooses not to. She's capable of convincing herself of anything.'

'Lots of people do that when they're dying. It's a protective mechanism. You'd have learned that if you'd have stuck around long enough in nursing.'

His face has changed. The sardonic look has gone and he's studying my face. It's like he pities me. 'The difference is that Sadie has spent her adult life playing parts that she believes are true.'

He pauses but my brain is whirring too much to think of anything to say. 'I'll give you an example. Not long before he died Sacha told me about what really happened with Sadie's friend Portia. She walked in on him telling me the truth and she lost it. She launched herself at him. Sacha had to hold her arms back to stop her punching him. That's how it always goes when you try to confront her with the truth or do anything to break her delusions. She loses it and lashes out. Remember the scratches on my arms that I passed off as being from Sacha?'

I think back to the time she smashed up the kitchen, the pull of my hair, the bruises on Sacha's face. If Sacha had been protecting himself from Sadie and holding her fists back then that explains why she had marks on her wrists.

'Sadie decided that Sacha was cheating on her, so she slipped into this elaborate fantasy of being the wronged woman. Then when that went to shit she flipped back and decided that he was this great love, who was being kept from her because he was in prison. She became determined to get him back again.'

I don't entirely believe him. Sadie behaved like any woman might do, if she was in love. I know enough about life to understand that. People sometimes love people who damage them.

'Then when things with Sacha went the way that they always had done she convinced herself that she could kill him and keep this house as the pathetic backdrop to her fantasies. She used poor Amy as an excuse for her anger at him. We all knew that Amy wasn't exactly angelic. She took more Es than anyone I knew.'

'Go on.' My words are icy.

'One minute Sadie believed she loved Sacha, the next she wanted to kill him. It's all about her fragile ego. She has to have this constructed world where everything is about Sadie. All the dressing up and this house as her scenery, living in her dream world that attracts drama. But other people fuck around with that by actually being real and not slotting in.'

'But it was Sacha who ruined things for them with his drinking and by smashing her best friend's head through the kitchen door.' Whatever truths Anthony thinks he knows about Sadie he can't deny this.

'Oh, Laura. You're not paying attention, are you? What part of Sadie being a compulsive fraud aren't you getting here? Everything is a lie. Sacha showed her poor friend Portia a shred of attention, so Sadie's fantasy became that she was the wronged woman. I imagine she even dressed the part, don't you? She'd have loved it. Drab Fifties clothes and tear-smudged mascara. She lost her temper, like she always did, because they refused to play along with her beliefs. Portia and Sacha denied it, because they hadn't done anything.'

'But Sacha went to prison for attacking her.' I want to shout but I moderate my voice, not wanting to bring Elsie into the room.

'Because he was stupid enough to love Sadie and he wanted to protect her. Portia didn't remember anything when she recovered and Sadie told her that it was Sacha who'd knocked her unconscious. Then Sadie did what she always did and decided to believe her own lies. He took the blame and ruined his life for her and she was the victim.'

'But she was going to kill him. She injected his drip with insulin and she collected the morphine to—'

'Lies and fantasy. She could hardly inject his drips on ITU. He had his own nurse. He just had an actual hypo because of his liver damage, so she decided she'd done it. She sees chances to make herself become something more exciting and she takes them. Like the ridiculous lie that she put benzos in Louise's bag. Louise was self-medicating for some issues with her abusive boyfriend. She'd already been warned once because she was seen by a staff nurse trying to slip a strip of pills into her pocket.'

'It doesn't make sense. Why would Sacha come back to her after the thing with Portia?' There's a creak on the stairs and we're both silent for a second as we listen. It's nothing human. Just Laurel House complaining and groaning, like old houses do.

'He came back because this was his house. He came out of prison with a plan to come here and throw her out but he stopped off to see one of his old drinking friends on the way and his addiction caught up with him again. So he hid away from everyone and nearly destroyed himself in a haze of faux hedonism. And when that became unsustainable, he returned here to get her out.'

'But then he married her.'

'Sadie's very persuasive, isn't she? And he was weak. Maybe he actually loved her. Because despite what Sadie said, he wasn't such a terrible person, just someone who was sick. Like your sister.'

The doorbell sounds. The shrill tone makes me jump. I ease myself up and walk towards the door.

Anthony stands up too. 'What a rude interruption. We were getting to the good part.'

He has a tired theatricality about him. There's a reason Anthony and Sadie have managed to coexist all these years. I see it now. Their shared sense of drama.

'There was a thing that Sadie wanted more than Sacha. More than either of us. More than she even ever wanted Elsie. That's the bit that's most amusing.'

He follows me as I walk out into the hall. His words sound like he's hissing them directly into my ear. 'People aren't what matters to her. She wanted Laurel House. She played on his weaknesses and used her coercive skills to bully him into marrying her. He didn't realise that she was doing it solely because she believed her own pathetic fantasy that she was capable of murder and would inherit the house that way.'

The doorbell rings again. The piercing noise rousing Sadie and causing her to shout out from upstairs.

'But you were too bewitched to spot what a crazed fantasist Sadie is. You were so beguiled by her that you didn't see that she was never actually going to commit a crime. That's the best bit of the entire story. The finale where a stupid little girl did it all for her and gave her exactly what she always wanted.'

Chapter Forty-Seven

NOW

Sunday, 18 April 2010

It's the palliative care nurse at the door. Tom must be able to see my shakiness, the pallor in my face. He puts a hand on my arm but I shrug it off. He won't think anything is amiss because he's used to seeing distressed relatives and friends. He's as practical and kind as always, sitting with Sadie for a short time. Watching her face, her breathing, gauging her semi-conscious form for signs of pain or distress. She rouses from time to time, mouthing random words. Her lips move but there's no sound. I can make out the occasional one. The last word I make out is 'stairs'. She whispers it three times.

People don't generally come out with bon mots or words of wisdom during the act of dying. It's a myth that's reserved for cheap novels. The reality of dying is prosaic and quotidian.

Her breathing is more laboured than it was earlier, each respiration effortful. I inject her with midazolam, not enough to make her sleep but enough to make her feel more placid. It works and the wild-eyed look is gone, her brow smoothens.

Anthony doesn't emerge to speak to Tom and I let him see himself out. I stay with Sadie, sitting in silence, thoughts darting around my skull like parasites.

'Still here?' I guess that Anthony means me, although it could equally apply to Sadie. 'I thought that the truth might have finally sent you scurrying back to whatever provincial hole you came from.'

'I'm staying. It's what Sadie and Elsie want, so back off.' I don't comment that he should be where I am. That the bedside companion of a dying woman would usually be her partner or family, not a woman who she hasn't seen for over a decade.

'Ah, she finally finds her backbone. The reality is that you're pathetic, Laura. A feeble little bitch who's so naïve that she accidentally destroys other people's lives. Like poor Jessica. No wonder Nathan wanted to hurt you for what you did to his sister.'

'What . . . how did you know about that?' I feel like he's slapped me.

'You discounted me and saw me as just some camp oddity but I saw things.'

'Saw what? What did you see, Anthony?' I feel an urge to laugh in his face. One of those stupid, inappropriate giggles caused by anxiety, like when you're at a funeral or in the middle of a dull lecture.

'I saw Nathan do it. He walked up to your coat and put an envelope in your pocket. He was quick and discreet, I'll give him that, but he wasn't quick enough for me. You were weeping on Sadie's shoulder about the note later on so I joined the dots.'

'How did you know that Nathan was anything to do with Jessica?'

'Easy. I was curious after we read your silly little Dear Diary thing. I went to the library and looked up the news reports about your schoolgirl incident on a microfiche and it mentioned a brother called Nathan in an obituary.' My urge to laugh is now replaced by different feelings. By nails, claws and teeth.

'Hang on. You were so interested in knowing about my past that you went to that level of trouble. But even when I was going through all of that you chose not to intervene and stop it? He could have harmed me.'

'I know! Maybe you should have been more careful before accusing me of being the culprit. Besides that, it amused me.'

My whole body feels tense. Muscles tighten, fists clench and my jaw locks.

'It was handy later, too, to have a way to try to fuck with Sacha. I picked up lovely Nathan's baton and ran with it. The notes were pretty easy to copy.' He stares at my face, as if gleefully waiting for a reaction. I turn away.

'You stabbed him on the doorstep. What the hell is wrong with you?'

'Oh, that wasn't me. I wanted to mess with things and get him drinking again. I was aiming to get him to finally throw us out so that I had Sadie to myself but I wouldn't have gone so far as to stab him. Harming him was more your thing, wasn't it?' He throws his head back and laughs. 'Sacha had a lot of enemies. He owed money. I expect it was one of them.'

He sidles over to the dressing table and idly flicks through my charts before walking out of the room.

* * *

I know what Sadie's fantasies are this time. Her dreams for the future and her wishes for Elsie. Her plans involve me. She's mapped them out with her solicitor.

My wishes are congruent. My urges are rational and sane.

I'm behind Anthony as his foot touches the top step.

'You could have stopped this from the beginning.' He turns his head slightly to hear me. I see his mouth begin to move. 'I went through all that for nothing.'

My hands fit perfectly in the small of his back. The perfect spot to upset his balance. My palms are a conduit that lets years of rage connect between me and his pathetic form.

He stumbles for a second, a weak shout of 'No!' coming from his mouth as he tries to grab at the banister. He's no match for my quick movement.

His body sails forward, not stopping. Not even a bang of his shoulder or hand on the wall to slow his descent. The crunch of his bones as he hits the floor tiles should be sickening but it's not. It's satisfying.

I scan down. His arms are splayed either side of his body and his neck is at an angle. There's a pool of blood forming by his temple.

I'm about to run down to check his pulse and ensure that this is done but there's a noise from Sadie's room.

The living require more attention than the dead. I go to Sadie and she's passed brackish urine onto the pad. She's trying to shift her body away from the moisture, so I gently roll her, replacing the pad. When I walk down the stairs the pool of blood has clotted into strings on the cold tiles. His eyes are glassy and lifeless. I don't need to check his carotid pulse but I do anyway.

The telephone operator sounds Spanish when I ring for an ambulance. I explain that I came down and found him already dead. They won't hurry.

I hope it isn't the same ambulance crew who came for Amy and Sacha all those years ago. That would be too much.

I sit in the kitchen and wait.

Chapter Forty-Eight

NOW

Monday, 7 September 2015

It's one of those mild September afternoons. The type where you wear a jacket into central London and then regret it when you're sweating on the tube. I'm reading on the sofa when there's the sound of a key in the front door.

'Hey.' Elsie's voice sounds even more like Sadie's now. Higher pitched and slightly breathy.

'So how did it go?'

'Good, I suppose. The other students are seriously odd, though. And not in a good way.'

I laugh, remembering what it felt like for me before Sadie befriended me. 'There'll be someone who you like.'

'There's a few men and one of them definitely likes me. He keeps staring at my tits.'

'Well, he's in for a disappointment.' Elsie has a partner, Sam. A bookish young woman who spends most of her time hanging out here. She's bewitched by Elsie and by Laurel House. She spends her time trailing after her, watching her with wide eyes, wandering around and touching Sadie's vintage ornaments. I caught her photographing things in the house and asked her not to. She looked blankly, telling me it's for her Instagram feed, as if it's normal to randomly broadcast other people's houses online.

'Let's eat and you can tell me all about your first day.' I've become adept at vegetarian cooking over the years.

'Sure.'

Elsie lifts a forkful of the lasagne I've made and swallows it down. 'Sam's been texting a lot. She's angling to move in. She's not keen on living in halls.'

Sam is in the first year of a journalism degree. Her parents have a vast house overlooking Richmond Park, so I suspect that they could afford to spring her out of halls and install her in a flat somewhere if she asked them.

'And what do you think?' It's Elsie's decision who lives here. Sadie left Laurel House in trust for Elsie till her eighteenth birthday. The paperwork was sturdy. The house was left in its entirety to Elsie with nothing for Anthony. Had he lived, though, he would have been in control of her until she was eighteen and would no doubt have remained a hopeless parent. I imagine he'd have tried to sell this house somehow.

The trustee if anything happened to Anthony was me.

I don't mind that I was the embodiment of Sadie's fantasy again. Another of her delusions come true but this time with a decent and worthy end result. She asked me to do it again and whispered the word 'stairs' and I behaved like the puppet I always was. Sadie was right this time. Elsie is safer with me here.

'She can wait till I ask, I'm not letting her beg her way in.'

'That sounds sensible. More?' Elsie's plate is clear. I get up and smooth the skirt down on my dress. It's something that Sadie would approve of. It's an original 1950s one that I picked up in a shop in Camden. They know me well there now and they give me a call if anything comes in that's my style and size.

A strand of my hair falls forward and I push it back. My hair is longer now, pinned up on top but still fair. I haven't dyed it red. I'm not Sadie nor do I want to be. I don't dress like her *all* the time, either. I certainly don't smoke those appalling-coloured cigarettes. But when I do dress up it suits the house.

I have to admit that I enjoy the attention on the streets. I see what Sadie gained from this, now. Clothing as reinvention. I get pleasant comments from other women. Elsie is the true aficionado out of the two of us, though. If we both dress in retro clothes, then people often mistake us for mother and daughter. We rarely correct them.

The kitchen is the same. We've replaced odd items here and there and there are now no pictures on the stairs. We repainted the hall but we kept the flooring. It's Edwardian, after all. I managed to scrub Anthony's blood from the tiles but we had it regrouted. Those stains would never have lifted from grouting.

'So, you're a student nurse now! This calls for a celebration.' I pull the bottle of champagne out from where it's been cooling in the fridge and pop the cork.

This is something to rejoice. Nursing is a difficult job, and things haven't become any easier with the political and economic climate, but I didn't discourage Elsie; she'll be a superb nurse. Her forthright manner and compassion are exactly what's needed. She will be a kind and thoughtful nurse.

She pulls a face and lifts the glass of champagne, taking a tiny sip. Neither of us are big drinkers. I doubt we'll finish the bottle.

'The uniform, though.' Her outfit is a smart tunic in a pale blue with a subtle piping and the name of the hospital embroidered on the chest which is nowhere near as ugly as what we wore. Elsie didn't like the cut of the trousers and came down wearing navy capri pants. I suggested she found a more suitable pair. It's important to obey the rules.

I suppose that my opinion doesn't actually matter now that I'm no longer a nurse. I've given it all up. That glorious job that I believed was everything turned out to be dispensable. I thought that if you'd cut me in half I'd be like a stick of Blackpool rock with the word 'nurse' written through me. I was wrong. I'm happier now, working part-time in a shop that sells nothing of much use. It's run by a strident woman called Joolz. She stocks it with an array of candles, cards and notebooks for the local middle-class women to buy. The area has become more gentrified so there's a demand. I keep the shelves immaculately tidy and always indulge Joolz by listening to her long stories about her florid love life. The rest of the time I look after this house and tend to Elsie.

I don't go back to Derbyshire often. I'm needed more here for Elsie. My mum and Suzie are happy. Their debts are paid off, thanks to my contributions over the years but also thanks to Suzie. She's found a job working as a carer in the local nursing home and they're keeping afloat. Suzie's on a methadone programme and she's doing well. I'm happy that she's no longer suffering. She deserves to be out of pain.

Laurel House is a happy place. There are so many memories. It's sometimes like Sadie is in the next room and we're young again. I could have had a different life. Tom called round a few times after Sadie's death. Ostensibly it was to check how me and Elsie were doing but I could see how he looked at me. I didn't want that. It's not like I'd ever be able to be honest with him and honesty matters in a close relationship.

We shouldn't pretend to be things that we're not.

'What shall we do this evening?' It turns out that Sam isn't coming over tonight, so it's just us.

We end up playing Yahtzee. We don't speak much. We often don't need to.

'Can I choose the music?' Elsie opens a drawer and pulls out a CD. 'I thought I'd get in quick before you put one of your awful records on.'

It wouldn't have been Peggy Lee or Dinah Washington. I might dress like Sadie sometimes and keep her house the same but I ditched the vintage women singers. I would have been more likely to put on some Kate Bush or Tori Amos.

The CD starts and the sound of Wolf Alice fills the room. I don't mind it.

'I don't say this enough.' I'm still not a person who effuses sentiment. 'But I'm so proud of you. Everything you've been through with your parents' deaths. You've been exceptional.'

The inquest for Anthony was traumatic for her but she retained dignity. She accepted the verdict of accidental death without any qualms. Sadie died of the effects of the cancer soon afterwards. I did nothing to speed that up. Whatever I was thinking at the time, I couldn't have harmed my patient. She died peacefully, with me and Elsie by her side, Nina Simone playing in the background and Sophia curled up at her feet.

A look crosses Elsie's face as if she's about to say something but she swallows whatever it is back.

'Yahtzee!' Elsie has rolled all sixes. She usually wins this.

I smile at her. We're happy here, even though I'm still not entirely well. I'm not cured from the PTSD. It isn't something that you automatically grow out of or leave behind. I have to work to keep myself well. I still write things down and take medication. I have ups and downs, like I always have had.

I think about Jessica often and Sacha less. They'll always be with me, as will Sadie. I never think about Anthony.

I did regret losing my temper like that. But it had been a long time coming.

And the end result has been correct.

Epilogue

THEN

Sunday, 18 April 2010

Elsie

I hear my dad on the landing when I come back in. Or 'The Donor' as me and Sadie refer to him. I sneak through the door and hide in the front room. I'll go upstairs once he's in the kitchen. My mum liked him once, or believed that she did, but she's blind to people's faults when she chooses to be. His flakiness, his disappearances, his relationship with me. All invisible to Sadie in her dream world.

Mum has ideas for my future. She's come up with a plan to take him out of the equation as the person in charge of me. Mad, right? It's one of her silly games that I play along with. She's had all these weird ideas about crushing pills in his drink. Stuff about pushes and shoves on the stairs. To be honest, she's always enjoyed these games more than I have. I'm growing out of them now but I still play along to keep her happy. She's supposed to be the adult but I've always had to act a lot older than my age. Anyone would around Sadie.

My mum would never have actually done it, anyway, would she? It's too late now. I don't think it's going to happen at all. He's not even going to die, so I'll be stuck with him. Not that he's been here much for the past few years. He has people who entertain him in ways that we can't, if you know what I mean. Sometimes he disappears because of 'his job', other times he doesn't even bother to lie.

He's been lying again now. I've known that all along. He left me here to cope with Sadie, which is standard for him. The ash cloud was a good excuse but not a solid one. Not when his passport was still there in his bedroom drawer.

There's a noise like a piece of furniture falling over. I'm confused for a moment. I peep through the crack of the door and my dad lands in front of me with a loud crack as his head hits the tiles. His eyes are closed and his neck is at a strange angle. I stand and watch as the bleeding kicks in. It's a trickle at first then a steady flow, turning the brown and blue tiles red. I haven't seen this much blood before. It's interesting. I didn't think it would be quite so bright.

I hear my mum shout out and then footsteps and a closing door as Laura runs to tend to her. Like the good little nurse that she is. She's an unusual woman but I don't hate her.

My dad's eyes are wide open and he's moving his legs, like he's trying to ride a bike while he's drunk. The blood is still flowing but it's less now. He stares at me.

'Laura pushed . . . My neck . . .' His voice is weak and pathetic. I stand over him, deciding what to do next. I look at the phone, wondering whether to call someone, then look back at him.

'Fuck you, you waste of space.' Mum's never minded me swearing but he does. He's wincing but it's not at my language. He struggles to lift his hand to his neck. He tries to speak again but his voice is thin.

I lean closer. The smell of stale whisky is coming off him. He liked that same wanky drink that Mum's first husband did. She knows how to pick a prick.

'Call 999.'

I think about apologising before I do it but I decide against it.

His head is hot in my hands as I twist it to one side with a sharp jerk.

He dies too quickly. He should have suffered more.

He wasn't a good person.

I check my hands and there's no blood on them.

My mother is a woman of ideas but I guess I'm more like Laura.

A woman of actions.

I slip back out of the house.

I think Laura and I will be just fine here together.

Author Note

If you have been affected by any of the issues raised in this story then the following organisations have further information:

PTSD/C-PTSD

PTSD UK are a charity supporting people with PTSD and their families/carers.

https://www.ptsduk.org/

The NHS and Mind websites have further information about PTSD and Complex PTSD.

https://www.nhs.uk/mental-health/conditions/post-traumatic-stress-disorder-ptsd/overview/
https://www.mind.org.uk/information-support/types-of-mental-health-problems/post-traumatic-stress-disorder-ptsd-and-complex-ptsd/about-ptsd/

Suicide

For anyone experiencing thoughts of suicide, the Samaritans provide a free and confidential listening service either via phone, email, letter or online chat.

https://www.samaritans.org/how-we-can-help/contact-samaritan/

Call on: 116 123 (free phone) or via calling NHS 111

https://spuk.org.uk/national-suicide-prevention-helpline/
https://www.thecalmzone.net/

End of life care

Marie Curie, NHS England and Macmillan have information about end of life care and links to sources of support.

https://www.mariecurie.org.uk/information
https://www.nhs.uk/tests-and-treatments/end-of-life-care/
https://www.macmillan.org.uk/cancer-information-and-support/treatment/if-you-have-an-advanced-cancer/end-of-life

Acknowledgements

As an inveterate people pleaser, I'm terrible at mass thankyous. I become frozen with anxiety that I'll omit someone vital and cause offence. So, in that spirit I'll offer a series of vague group thanks.

I've had overwhelming support with my debut novel and I'm eternally grateful to my partner and his family and to my amazing friendship circles. I've also been bowled over by all the bloggers, Bookstagrammers, booksellers, Netgalley reviewers, interviewers, podcasters and readers (many of whom have commented or sent heartfelt and kind messages). I'm indebted to the writing community, too. The support, advice and the willingness to offer blurb quotes for an unknown author has been staggering. There are way too many people to name here.

The team at Avon and Becky Hunter PR have all been exceptional and faultless. I feel privileged to have had such a smooth publishing journey (apart from the fact that I moved house/town on publication date for my debut. I don't advise doing this).

Special thanks go to my agent, Hannah Schofield and my editors Rachel Hart and Anna Nightingale.

Finally, thanks to all my former colleagues. There's been a lot of you over my thirty years as a hospital-based nurse. None of you are the basis for these characters. They're all plucked from my dark imagination.

A word on nursing as I suspect some readers may wonder how much I based this book on my own career or view of the profession. I know that I'd be pondering this.

Like Laura, I was an improbable and accidental nurse. Following a period of uneven mental health, coupled with teenage rebellion and a troubled family life, I flunked my A-levels and lost my university place to study English. I abandoned my lofty ambitions of being a journalist with the intention of one day writing novels and becoming a crime writer.

I worked in a toy shop for a couple of years where I coveted Sylvanian Families and tripped over children whilst wondering what direction my life would take. A friend suggested I'd be a good nurse, which bemused me but after minimal thought I applied on a whim and was offered a dropout place to start in four weeks' time. If I'd had more time to think, then I might have run as far and as fast as I could. I'm glad that I didn't.

Nursing suited me and I loved the job. I liked the speed and complexity of it and the human stories. Most of all, I enjoyed looking after people and quickly found that there's something about being empathetic that also helps the empathiser. I'm not saying that I was a perfect nurse who glided around being endlessly kind. I had moments of irritation and frustration and have human frailties and flaws as all people do.

Nursing can also be a difficult, overlooked and sometimes thankless job. I have a generally positive view of my career but it'd be a misrepresentation to pretend that my spine and mental health came away entirely unscathed.

In conclusion, whilst I might have vague parallels with Laura and her colleagues, I'm way more approachable and not at all murderous. I don't share her work/life ethics and her views on nursing aren't mine.

This is my torturous way of saying a huge but inadequate thank you to all the doctors, nurses, care assistants and allied health care professionals who I've had the privilege to know and befriend in my career. I'd also like to thank every patient and their significant others for what you've given back to me.

Finally, none of you are the basis for these characters. They're all plucked from my dark imagination and don't represent anyone who I know or have met.

Don't miss this twisty and twisted psychological thriller novel from Chris Bridges, perfect for fans of Shari Lapena, Lisa Jewell and JP Delaney.

Meet Emma. Emma is sick.
She can't work because of a neurological condition, so is stuck in her family's tiny council house.

Emma is sick of being told to 'get over it'.
Her stepfather, her doctors, strangers – everyone has an opinion.

Emma is sick of being the other woman.
Her boyfriend Adam is perfect: he's got a great job and an amazing home. His wife Celeste is the problem.

Emma is sick of being underestimated.
All she needed was a target. And now she has Celeste . . .